HER SINFUL SAINTS

HER SINFUL SAINTS

THE SEVEN SINNERS OF HELL'S KINGDOM. BOOK FOUR

by

GINNA MORAN

Cover design by Silver Starlight Designs
Cover images copyright Depositphotos

For Inquiries Contact:

Sunny Palms Press
9663 Santa Monica Blvd Suite 1158
Beverly Hills, CA 90210, USA
www.sunnypalmspress.com
www.GinnaMoran.com

This book is dedicated to Kase's tail and its majestic ability to multi-task. Because of this, I must declare it as another harem member. Thank you, Kase's tail, for helping ensure there is fun for everyone.

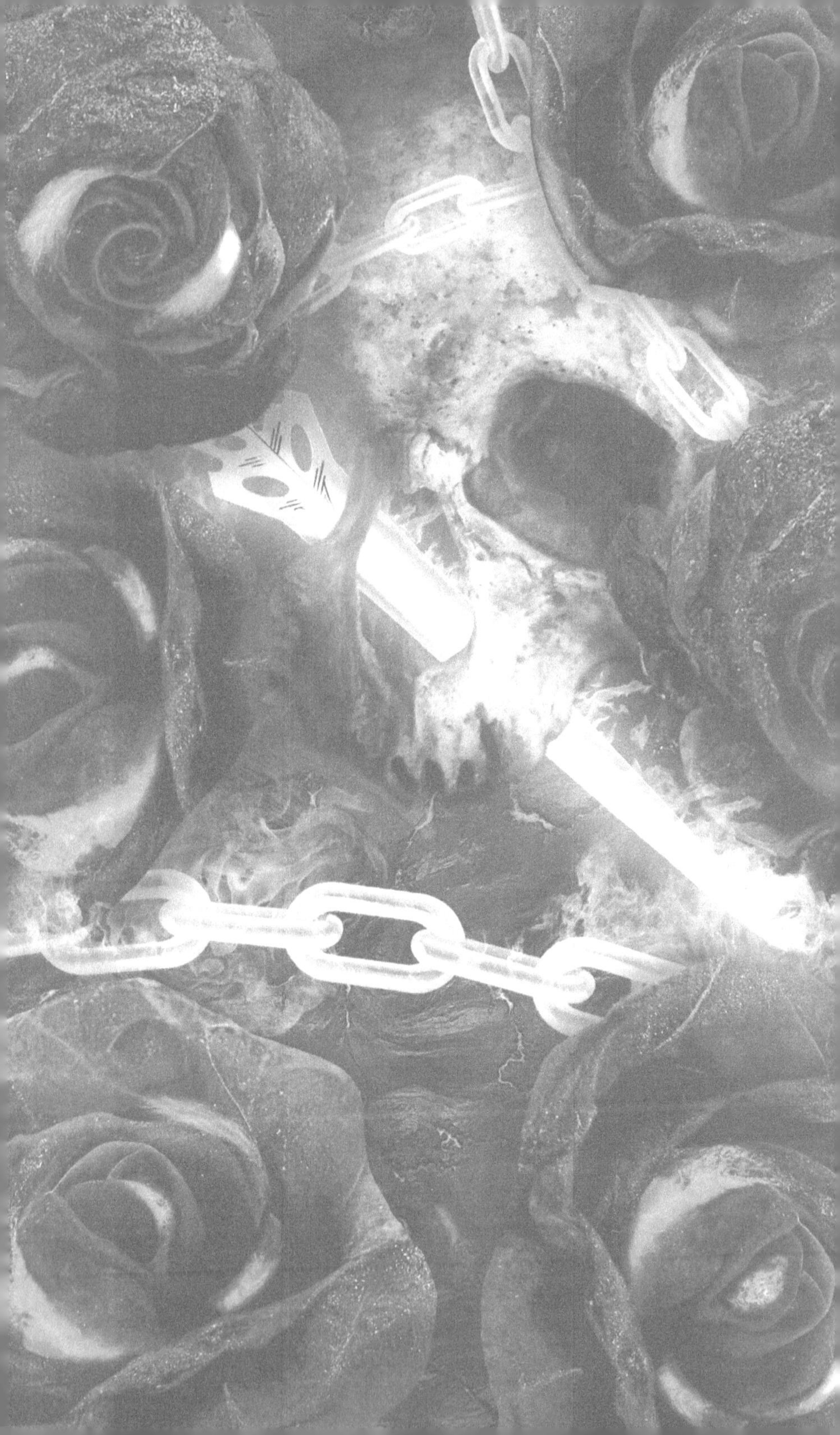

Soul Cycles

RAVEN

"I CAN TAKE you home if you'd like. I know you'd rather be scouring the mortal plane for your soul-mate." Micah rubs his warm hand between my shoulder blades, trying to ease my stiff posture.

I bounce on my feet, staring at my target. I should feel bad about torturing a soul in Hell, but this guy lived a twisted life eating people...and not in the good way. "It's easier to let the others handle it. I can't see souls like they can. Plus—"

I position my body, holding the ax with both hands. Flinging my arms forward, I release the ax. It sinks into the soul's chest. He can't scream, though. Micah shoved a rat in his mouth and gagged him with something that looks suspiciously like a hairy ball sack.

"Plus," I repeat, turning to Micah. "It's our time together. I've missed you."

"Yeah?" he asks and guides me to spin toward him. A smile lights his handsome face as he searches my eyes like he can't believe how lucky he is that I'm here. I love the feeling of his sweet adoration, the purity of it reminding me of right before he jumped from grace.

Standing on my tiptoes, I stretch up and brush my lips to his. "Do I need to tell you a million times to convince you? I'm not scared of your kingdom anymore. I'm having fun."

Chuckling, he summons a fiery blade in his hand. "Want to hunt some other evil bastards? We don't have to stay in my kingdom."

I offer a smile and bob my head. "Whatever takes my mind off things. I'm feeling a bit stabby. Can you use your power to make one look like Cass-hole?"

Using Elias's nickname for the infuriating prideful angel fills me with a mixture of emotions. I shouldn't be as upset as I am about Elias sacrificing himself to free my soul and going through another soul cycle, but a part of me fears what happens next. I want Hell to rise. I want to take the throne of Purgatory, and Elias made it possible...but I want him as I knew him in this life. I want my soulmate in the body I love now. Is that selfish? Maybe. I should be grateful he's not in Hell as a mortal soul, but—

"You have every right to grieve, Raven." Micah grasps my hand, pulling my attention to him and out of my thoughts. We've always had a mental connection, and he can listen to my thoughts, especially with the tether chaining him to Hell and all its power. "Elias was taken from you in the worst way."

"He was taken from you too, you know," I murmur, tightening my mouth to keep my lips from trembling. "How are you holding up? I know you only took the tether early to help him."

Micah's face softens with my words, and he scoops me into his arms and gets me to wrap my legs around his waist. I rest my forehead to his for a moment, savoring his closeness as neither of us gets out of control. We just be together and enjoy the other's company. I know Micah is more cautious with me now because of the circumstances and won't push me. I hate it and love it at the same time. I don't want him to be careful with me, but I also appreciate it.

"My beautiful heathen. You do not have to ask or worry about me. This isn't my first experience dealing with Elias's absence. I just wish you never had to." He nuzzles his nose to mine. "As for the tether? I chose to take it for more than just getting Elias through. I felt it was necessary. I had done what I needed in the Mortal Realm. Kase and Dante have been working hard in the Mortal Realm for so long, I couldn't ask either one of them to control Hell, and you need Andre. Lucian will serve us better there too, dealing with Cassius. I'm neither lonely nor bitter. I promise."

"I bet Heaven regrets everything they've done to you," I say, searching his fiery eyes. "You're my perfect devil. A fair and just ruler...and way too creative with what you've done here." Waving my hand, I motion to the onyx walls of the palace.

"You haven't seen anything yet." Flipping me onto his back, Micah stretches forward, transforming into his massive devil form.

I cling on to his hairy body, squeezing his sides with my thighs to hold on the best I can. Two long tusks jut from his boxy boar-like head, and the cute bastard swats me with his tail. Fire smolders the palace floor before us, setting the onyx ground aglow.

"What the fuck are you doing?" I ask, my shoulders shaking with laughter as he steps forward, rattling the world around us. "I'm going to fall or some shit."

"Just hold on tight. It's easier to show you what I want to this way." Micah stomps forward on all fours, forcing me to bend over and lie flush against his muscular, broad back. "My hound is a bit intimidating since you've never encountered one before."

My brows scrunch together. "A hound? Like a hellhound? I

thought Kase and Dante were kidding."

"Mine is a lot more special than the free-roamers. You'll see." Micah jets out of the palace and skids across the smoldering ground.

Souls move and wriggle, some in pieces and others far too big in the belly to stand. It looks as if someone forced a hundred gallons of liquid down their throats and it settled in their middles, dragging their stomachs to the ground and forcing the rest of their limbs with it.

I grip onto Micah's hair, stabilizing myself. Peering around the hazy land, I take in the view of Micah's kingdom and the demonic legion that obeys him. No one looks at us or tries to fuck with me, and it feels as if I watch things from a bubble.

"We're shielded," Micah mumbles, his gruff voice humming over the screams and shouts from the souls living their worst life after deaths.

"What's the fun in that? I kind of like it when the assholes grovel." I scrub my fingers into his hulking body, just exploring him in his devil form. He looks wicked as hell, and it makes me feel powerful how he carries me above the masses. "Like the fucking cannibal. He tried so hard to convince us that he was a decent guy who only had a problem. It's not like food was scarce."

"Would that justify his actions to you?" Micah asks, slowing down.

Uh-oh. Here he goes with his interrogation about my morals and what I find redeemable or not. It comes with the whole Purgatory level. If we manage to get Hell in order, souls who find themselves in Hell will ultimately be able to earn their way back into a soul cycle. They will no longer be trapped and tortured for eternity, especially the souls that should've found good grace but made a mistake—like me. But at this point, I can't see why anyone would want to chill with the bird-brains and their righteous attitudes.

Micah teases me by trotting, bouncing me up and down on his back. His movements pull me from my thoughts as he follows the outside of the onyx walled palace. I don't think I will ever understand how Hell power works. It boggles my mind because Micah can create basically anything out of nothing. His kingdom seemingly goes on forever, but I know all he has to do is think about another kingdom and we will end up there.

"Where exactly do you keep your hellhound?" I ask, shielding my eyes from the suddenly bright flames that light the sky above me.

Micah moves a bit faster, and he doesn't respond to my question until we reach a vast arched doorway with thick flaming bars caging something inside.

Wicked, animalistic growls rumble from within the cage. The hairs on my arms rise. My heartbeat picks up pace, and I clutch onto Micah tighter. "Whoa."

"Don't be frightened." He sits back on his haunches, forcing me to slide off his back and onto my feet.

I cautiously shuffle around him, keeping close to his body. "Says the beast-man overlord of Gluttony. I'm a snack for most here."

Chuckling, Micah flicks his tail at me again. "They wouldn't dare. You're mine to feast on in pleasure and ecstasy."

Damn, do I like the sound of that.

I gather my gall and make my way to the front of him. He transforms back into his human façade. Strolling forward, he leads the way and stops in front of the flaming gate. My whole body tenses the second a massive form appears. I wasn't sure what I was expecting a hellhound to look like, but now that I see it, I realize it was exactly like this. Well, except for the three heads. I always thought that type of monster was just a myth. Okay, I guess I thought all of Hell and Heaven and angels and demons were just make-believe as well. But now, I think I'd even believe in aliens. But I've never asked. It's already so much for me to take in.

"Raven, this is Hound," Micah says, touching his fingers to the flaming bars and using power to open them. "You don't have to be intimidated or frightened. It knows that you are mine."

"Wait a minute. You call this thing Hound? Isn't that a littl e...basic?" Mustering the strength to keep my nerve, I strut my way closer to stand beside Micah. I instinctively tuck myself under his arm, and I slide my hand around his back, hugging him close. "Technically, you should have three names for it."

"I'm not very creative. Why don't you name the guys?" Micah reaches his hand out and scratches the flames under the middle head's chin. "I'm sure they would love that."

I love how Micah has gone from referring to the hellhound as it and instead calls the three-headed beast them. Because clearly, each of the hellhound's heads looks to have distinct personalities. And despite them being on fire, with bright red eyes, frothy jowls, and coats that look as if they are covered in black goo, these beasts are kind of cute.

"Well," I say, pointing my finger at the head on the right. The beast stretches his neck forward and bows slightly. I reach out and gently graze my fingers just above the flames on the top of his head between his ears. "I think you should call this one Chaos."

Micah tilts his head and studies the beast for a moment. "That is actually very fitting."

"Is that so?" I ask.

"He is a bit hard to handle sometimes. He tends to interrupt the others and causes chaos when he is let loose among the rotten souls around here." Micah grins with his words like he remembers an incident that happened with the hellhounds.

I move on to the head on the left and let the beast sniff my hand. He puffs out a breath of hot smoke and then licks his sizzling tongue across my fingers. "I think you should name this one Spike." I reach up and touch the pointed ears on his head. It's not just two ears either. It looks like the beast has four. Or maybe the two extras are horns? I can't be certain. "What do you think?"

"I think that is perfect. Isn't that the name of one of the guys on that show you and Elias sometimes watched?" Micah scratches his fingers under Spike's chin.

"It's one of them. Which means that I think I want to name the middle hound Dean." I grin, thinking how Elias would appreciate the fact that I'm naming Micah's hellhounds after some characters in our favorite shows.

Micah turns to me and touches my cheek. "He would."

Silence falls between the two of us as we stare at the three-headed hellhound and just continue to pet it as if it's a cute fluffy poodle. Screams echo in the distance, and I shift on my feet and look behind me. I'm desperate for Micah to distract me more. I need to move. I need to cut a dick or punch a boob. I just need to get my mind off Elias again before tears prickle in my eyes.

"What do you think about having Dean, Spike, and Chaos, help us pick out the next bastard you practice on?" Micah pushes me back and whistles softly, getting the hellhounds to come out of the kennel.

"That would be incredibly awesome," I say, swiveling on my feet. "Can I just give them an idea of the type of evil soul I'm looking for, and they'll help us?"

Micah wiggles his eyebrows with his beaming smile. He obviously loves entertaining me any way he can, which I appreciate. I'm lucky to have him as my teacher of punishment and justice. It helps me feel better, knowing that I'm still his purpose in this eternity, and he enjoys standing with the devils. "That's exactly what you can do. It's a lot of fun. The beasts will lead the way, and we can sneak up and scare them from behind. Or maybe you can have them beg for some mercy first."

"Had I not known you used to be an angel, I think that you would actually be known as Satan instead of Lucian claiming the title of the most notorious devil. Because you are one sexy evil, just devil." I kiss Micah on the cheek and lace my fingers through his.

"I try my best to fill the position." Micah swings our hands and lets out another whistle, sending the hellhounds running.

"You do a damn good job," I say, twisting my body to plant a kiss to his shoulder. "Now, what kind of evil soul should I practice on next. I kind of have a thing for the fire chain that Lucian uses."

Micah doesn't get a chance to respond because the hellhounds swing their body around and release a harsh, throaty snarl. I tense and close the space to Micah. Something about the hellhounds' reaction scares me. I automatically think that something giant, disgusting, and evil is about to start a fight with the king of Gluttony.

"I knew that you liked my fire chain." Lucian's deep voice sounds from behind me. "Don't you think that it should be me teaching you how to use it?"

I don't know whether I should be annoyed or happy to see Lucian. I still have all sorts of mixed emotions about him. I know he's trying his best, but I do hold a long-ass grudge. I can't help it. But I also can't help the fact that my body goes crazy at just his presence alone, Especially in Hell. It's like my soul craves his darkness.

"I think Micah has it handled," I say, gliding my hands up Micah's chest and to his neck, reaching them around. I hop up and wait for Micah to catch me in his arms. "Isn't that right? You can teach me how to use any weapon."

"Maybe if his time hasn't started seeping into mine." Lucian narrows his eyes and strolls closer, ignoring the growls sounding from the hellhounds. "It's time to go, Raven."

I groan and hide my face in the crook of Micah's shoulder. Time passes much more quickly in Hell than it does in the Mortal Realm. At least that's what it feels like to me. I thought I'd get a couple more hours at least.

"Well, Micah and I were in the middle of something. Why don't you go check on all your dirty, vile souls in your level of Hell, and I will meet you there when I'm ready?" I ease away from Micah's throat and turn and peek at Lucian for his reaction.

"Not happening." Lucian's hot hands clasp my waist, and he pulls me away from Micah. The hellhounds growl louder, but they remain in place. "I have something to show you, and I prefer to do it now."

"What is it?" I ask, narrowing my eyes suspiciously.

"It's a surprise." Lucian spins me toward him and grasps my chin, looking deep into my eyes. "Please, I've been waiting all week for my day with you. Just give me a couple of hours."

I sigh and turn to Micah. "I don't want to leave you, Micah, but..." my voice trails off.

"I understand, Raven," Micah says, strolling to close the distance to me. "I like having all of my time with you as well. Plus, I think this will be good for you."

I look between the two devils. "Do you know what the surprise is, Micah?"

"Don't you dare fucking say anything," Lucian says, holding up his hand.

"You *do*," I say. I don't know where Lucian got that I like surprises from, but I actually hate them. I like knowing what I'm getting myself into. With Lucian, I never know. "You have to tell me, Micah. The last surprise that Lucian gave me was sticking his dick on my palm."

Lucian tips his head back and barks a raspy laugh. Damn it. I could listen to his sexy voice all day when he's not yelling and being a dick. "You know you loved it. It left quite the impression."

"I can name a million things that I love more than a surprise dick slap, you perv." I raise my palms to Lucian, keeping a foot of space between us. "Now tell me what the surprise is, or I'm not going with you."

Fire lights in Lucian's dark eyes. A smirk curls across his lips, and he flicks his gaze from Micah and to me. I can already sense what goes on in his mind, and I brace myself. The fucker is not going to give me a choice. Micah won't stop him either.

I tense and tighten my fingers in a fist, preparing to sucker punch him if I have to. "Don't you even think about it, Satan."

"Too late, you bratty little soul." Lunging forward, Lucian encircles me with his arms and lifts me off my feet. I smack him across the face and try to knee him in the gut, but all it does is make him laugh harder. He loves when I fight. He's a masochist. He loves all sorts of pain and doesn't even react when I reach down and sock him in the balls.

"Damn it, Lucian. Put me down." I thrash, trying to break free.

"No. I'm going to carry your infuriating, stubborn ass all

the way to my kingdom. If you don't start behaving, I will spank you the entire way there. But that's what you want, don't you?" Lucian proves that he isn't lying by flipping me onto his shoulder and slapping his big palm to my ass.

The sting of his smack radiates through my entire body, and I squeeze my legs together. This fucker. He knows exactly how to get to me.

"I am right, aren't I?" Lucian releases a gruff noise from his throat.

"Shut up and just take me already." I wiggle until he adjusts me in his arms, forcing me to wrap my legs around his waist.

The cocky bastard drops me a few inches until I feel his boner. "Careful what you say and how you say it, Raven. That kind of sounds like an invitation."

Ugh. My stupid body loves the sound of that. Apart from punishing bad souls to distract me, I love a good fucking session, and I haven't given in to Lucian yet. But we both know it's coming.

"Whatever. Not today, Satan. Just take me to your kingdom, so we can go home," I say and rest my head on his taut shoulder. "Hell might be getting to me, but not enough yet."

He hums in my ear. "We'll see."

I'm sure we will.

2

Devilish Surprises

RAVEN

I THOUGHT ALL of the other kingdoms were freaky, but Lucian's domain is incomparable. He has had a long fucking time to create the perfect kingdom for torture and punishment. But damn. This is insane.

"Is that...?" I shudder at the sight before me.

A vast lake of lava expands into the distance. Within it, I spot thousands, no, maybe millions of souls hanging from some sort of burning lines like the demons plan to use them as skin suits.

"This is so fucked up," I whisper, peering around from Lucian's arms. "How did you come up with this?"

Lucian strokes his hand down my spine and back up until he locks his fingers to the back of my neck. Leaning close, he meets my eyes. "I just took the actions of the bad souls and mimicked them to create my kingdom. I will not take credit for this fuckery."

I open and close my mouth, unsure of how to respond. Because he makes it sound like it's basically all of the mortals in this kingdom's doing. But I guess it could be. Lucian's Hell contains bad souls from every sin. He punishes the worst of the worst. In Lucian's Hell, there probably won't be any souls ever able to move through the levels to land in Purgatory.

"You're shitting me," I say, staring at the souls flying in the wind but unable to go anywhere because they are pinned by huge hooks to this weird-ass tether. Almost like how butchers hang meat in freezers.

Lucian chuckles and shrugs his shoulders. "This is where all of the nastiest murderers, rapists, molesters, and souls that you won't even grasp how incredibly evil they have been in life end up. The hanging lines come from one of the very first souls to enter my kingdom."

I furrow my brows. It's hard for me to process any of this. It's even stranger that Lucian recollects the first souls to arrive in Hell. "Oh." It's all that I can think to say. I'm not exactly sure I want to know more about the evils born into the world through humanity.

"Don't worry your pretty little head over it, Raven," Lucian says.

He loosens his grip on me and tries to set me on my feet. My body ignores my brain's request to be chill and not panic, and I squeeze onto him tighter. Like fucking fuck is he going to put me down out here. The hot breeze picks up, whipping the souls on the tether. With my luck, I'd stumble into them. No thanks.

Instead of making a snarky comment like I expect, Lucian drops his hands away from me, forcing me to hang on if I want him to carry me. This dick. We both know what he's doing, but my poor mortal soul, now unbound to Hell, doesn't like being so close to things I can't truly comprehend.

Lucian hums under his breath as he carries me down the long, winding path leading around the lava pit. Instead of hiding my face, I peer over his shoulder and drink in the sight of the demons moseying around. They don't sink into the lava lake like I expect them to. They manage to float just above it, probably because of the Hell power.

"I hope the tour of your kingdom isn't the surprise," I say, clutching onto his neck. "I'm not really into this kind of thing."

"You're lying, Raven. I saw how excited you were to punish souls in Micah's kingdom. You're a natural. If I didn't want you to run Purgatory, I would try to convince you again to be my perfect, wicked queen." Lucian flexes his muscles, and his body starts to morph into his devil form. This is one of the few times that I've seen him in Hell not in his beastly body. I've never asked him about it, but I've wondered if it has to do with keeping up with his satanic appearance as the big baddie of Hell.

"Lucian," I say, sighing.

"I get it, Raven. I know what you want out of this eternity, but it's still hard for me to think that the soul I had wanted will never be mine completely." Lucian's voice softens with his words. I don't think I've ever heard him so honest about something like this. He's usually an asshole. The only other time he has really opened up to me was when I beat him with his own fire chain.

"That's where you are wrong. Don't think of me as being separated between all the kingdoms. Think of me as the soul that tethers you all together. And if you keep up this honesty, I might consider rubbing your horns." I playfully lace my fingers around the two horns jutting from his head. Stroking my fingers from the base to the tip, I fake a moan, stretching up enough to put my boobs in his face.

He growls and plants his hot palm between my shoulder blades, pulling me close. I laugh and squirm as he buries his face into my cleavage. Excitement floods through me, and I continue to explore the length of his horns and work my way back down to his head.

"Don't start something you might not want to finish," Lucian says, kissing my clavicle.

"Is that a threat?" I lean back and grin at him. "Because if it is—"

"It's more than a threat. Just keep it up and find out what I mean." Lucian growls again, his voice vibrating over my chest.

My laughter fades into a breathless pant, and I imagine what he could possibly mean. Do I want him? Do I want to risk starting something when I'm not sure about our relationship and where we stand? I wish I knew. At this moment, I feel myself letting my guard down. My mind and body want me to use Lucian to forget about everything else. Is my coping mechanism fucked up? Maybe. I don't really care, though.

"That's what I thought." Lucian lifts an eyebrow and slides his hand lower until he squeezes my ass. "You're thinking about it."

Warmth travels up my chest into my cheeks. "Maybe." I will never give him the satisfaction of being right. He can think he's right, but I will never say it.

"What do I need to do to make you admit it," Lucian asks, a smirk crossing his handsome face.

"There is nothing that you can do." I grin and keep my eyes locked on his. "You were an asshole for far too long. You can't honestly think that you will ever get your way that easily."

Lucian laughs, his throaty voice echoing over the crackling flames of his kingdom. "You know how much I love a challenge, don't you?"

"Yeah—"

A high-pitched scream blazes through the air, stealing my attention away from Lucian's. Goosebumps prickle across my arms, and I suck in a sharp breath. It can't be. It really fucking can't be. I don't believe it, even though the familiar guardian screams in front of me.

Lucian tenses at my reaction. Without having to say anything, I know he didn't expect me to see the angel. The guardian must have escaped from whatever pit Lucian was holding him hostage in. Because once an angel enters Hell, there is no way Lucian will ever let them go. Before they fucked up my life, I'd have compassion and sympathy for them. That was the old me. The new me wants nothing more than to steal Lucian's fire whip and show this angel exactly the kind of pain he put me through by fighting against us.

"One of my minions must've screwed up," Lucian growls under his breath. "This bastard shouldn't be anywhere near you right now. I will disembowel the demon who released him."

"That's not good enough," I say, wiggling in his arms until he has no choice but to put me on my feet. "More needs to be done. He has to know something about Elias."

"If he did, I'd have found out already, Raven." Lucian remains expressionless, though his eyes light with fire.

Smoke puffs from his nose and his veins light up as if the lava around us travels through them. Even in his devil form, he looks handsome to me now. And dangerous. It's the only reason why I summon my courage and break away from him.

I dodge past Lucian and run in the direction of the screaming angel. Dark shadows move and swirl around me, the heat of the strange entities sizzling across my skin. Lucian calls my name, but he doesn't try to stop me with power. His heavy footsteps quake the ground with jolting tremors. My fear instincts go crazy as he chases me. I only use my fear to push me faster, to make me run harder, and to give me the power I need to face this bastard angel.

Something sparks in front of me, and fire explodes from the red stone ground. I nearly eat shit as something wraps around my leg. I screech and manage to rip my ankle free before the monster grabs hold of me.

"Raven, catch." Lucian's voice booms through the air, drawing my attention.

I spin and brace myself as a fiery chain slashes through the space between us. I don't know how I do it, but I manage to snatch the end of Lucian's chain. I try to rip it from his hands, but he doesn't release it and yanks me back. The world blurs around me in vibrant colors of red, orange, and yellow, and I smack right into Lucian's hard chest as he catches me.

I heave a breath, trying to find my bearings. Lucian stomps forward with me in his arms and jogs toward the figure emerging from the ground. My eyes widen at the sight of the angel breaking free. The fucker sure has some fight left in him, because he unsheathes a sword that should light up with heavenly light but doesn't.

"Lucifer! You can't keep me here for eternity. I will not bow to you. I will not see you destroy everything the Higher Power has done for the sake of humanity and the rest of the universe." The angel straightens his back. He tries to expand his wings, but they are severely damaged and burned. They almost look as if they are about to disintegrate and fall off his back at any second and the only reason they remain in place is that he refuses to give in to his fate.

His words set me off, and I shove from Lucian's arms and stumble across the fiery ground. Lucian growls, but he doesn't try to snatch me up again. Instead, he lets me grab his chain and yank it away from him. The edges of my vision turn red with my fury, and I spin around, swinging the fiery chain.

"Where is he?" I ask, swinging the chain at the angel, snapping at his feet. "Where is Elias?"

The angel ignores me, not reacting to my threat or my question. He keeps his gaze trained on Lucian as he looms behind me. But this will be his biggest mistake. He's concerned about

Lucian, but he should be concerned about me. No one can mess with my devils or my soulmate.

Taking advantage of the angel's focus on Lucian, I lash the chain again, striking the asshole in the chest. He jerks his attention to me. His expression morphs from rage to confusion before he composes himself.

Again, he flicks his focus back to Lucian. "Lucifer, call your little abomination back."

Is he fucking kidding me? He's in Hell for fuck's sake, and I'm the abomination?

Lucian snarls from behind me, but I remain in front of him. I know he purposely lets me stay ahead, and I'm nearly certain he wants me to put this bastard angel in his place. And I'm happy to. I want nothing more than to beat this guy into submission and make him bow to Lucian. I want him to bow to me.

Flinging my arm, I whip the fire chain, lashing the angel in his side. He hollers in pain, finally reacting. He attempts to touch the chain, but his hands sizzle. The fire will continue to hurt him until he falls and accepts the fact that he is never returning to Heaven.

I crash into the angel and knock him off his feet. Punching him in the nose, I yell out my frustration. He grinds his teeth together and tries to block me, but Lucian stomps forward, grabs the angel's hands, and pins them above his head. Smashing his hooves into the angel's palms, Lucian stretches upright and sends fire cascading around us in a protective circle. Jabbing my hand to the angel's neck, I get in his face and scream. I can't help it. All I can think about is hurting him.

"This is the final time I ask you. Where is my soulmate? Tell me where Elias is, and I will free you."

The angel laughs, his voice hoarse. "The traitor is gone. You will never have him. Heaven will not fall."

"You're wrong," I snap. I swing my arm and sucker punch him in the face again. "I will find him. Hell will rise and you will be here suffering. Even if you bow to the devils, you will not find anything but an eternity of torture because of this. I will guarantee it." Tipping my head back, I meet Lucian's gaze. "Show me how powerful a devil you are."

Snatching me up, Lucian tosses me over his shoulder and onto his back. I cling to him and watch with my hazy vision. Excitement rushes through me. I'm so twisted, and I don't even care.

"Anything you want, Raven," Lucian says, summoning another fire chain while leaving the one I abandoned scorching the angel's chest, keeping him down.

"Make him hurt as much as Heaven hurt me." I glower at the angel.

The righteous bastard only closes his eyes and murmurs a prayer. The words sting my ears, and I dig my fingers into

Lucian's shoulders.

"The Higher Power can't hear you," Lucian says, his deep voice vibrating across my palms through his skin. "You're in my domain now."

Gathering Hell power in his hand, Lucian thrusts the energy at the angel. The man screams, the shrillness of his voice hurting me. I tighten my legs around Lucian and cover my ears. I can't look away. I don't want to. Relief floods through me as Lucian pummels the angel over and over again, burning him and beating him until he falls silent.

Tears burn my eyes, and my body trembles. What felt incredible a second ago now feels as if it turns against me. New emotions surge through my very being, and the sensation of ice diminishes the heat coursing through me. Lucian's darkness swells around me, consuming me. My soul screams, and I hide my face in the crook of his shoulder. Hell got to me. Heaven got to me too. It feels as if I'm being ripped in half. Oh fuck. This is what it feels like to be trapped in the middle. I might be intended to rule Purgatory, but not without a price on my being. On my soul. And it hurts so bad that I feel as if I might die here in Lucian's kingdom.

The world turns black as I lose consciousness. Voices hum in my ears. I can't move or open my eyes, and all I can do is listen to the cacophonous noise around me. Cool fingers caress my hands and travel up my arms until ice blossoms in my chest.

A pinprick of light penetrates the darkness, and I focus on the glowing orb, feeling the peculiar familiarity of it. I try to summon the image of a face, or even a name, but all I can think about is the light and how it breaks through the darkness.

"Raven," Lucian says, his voice prodding at me. "Listen to my voice. Focus on me."

I try to concentrate on his words, but the glowing light distracts me too much. I don't want to wake up and find myself in Hell again. I don't want to remember the evil that I allowed to happen. All I want to do is lose myself to the brilliant light that tries to consume me.

"Raven," Lucian repeats. "Return to me. Come on. Don't be a stubborn little brat. I know you're stronger than this."

I can't help but think that he's wrong. I don't feel strong in this moment. I feel disconnected and weak and without the strength I usually summon from my connection to Hell through my devils. And the light? It won't leave me alone. It's like it can't get to me completely, but it also can't give me answers. Answers to what? I have no fucking idea.

"Don't make me punish that sweet ass of yours to get you to open your eyes. I know that all it will take is one blow from my power to get you to return to me. Is that what you want?" A hot burst of energy jolts through me with Lucian's words.

Like the light is afraid of Lucian, it suddenly vanishes and releases me from its hypnotic glow. I snap my eyes open and gasp for breath. My skin buzzes as energy courses through me. Through my blurry vision, I stare up at a monstrous figure towering over me. Fire glows in the world above, haloing Lucian in its vivid light. His body flexes and morphs, and Lucian returns to his human façade. He reaches down and caresses his knuckles across my cheek. He stares at me in silence, waiting for me to move or to speak, to do something other than stare up at him. But I'm so confused and disoriented. What the fuck happened?

"Fucking finally," Lucian says, his voice hard but his face soft with his expression. "I thought you were going to stay unconscious for the rest of my time."

"You say that like I wanted to," I rasp, my throat burning.

A smile creeps across his face. "I never know with you. I thought perhaps that you regretted your decision to ask me to punish a righteous bastard."

I scrub my hands into my cheeks and try to remember everything that happened. The angel's image flashes through my mind but quickly vanishes with the memory of the bright light.

I shake my head, my hair whipping around me. "No. That guy deserved it. It was something else. I can't explain it. I was fine one second, and in the next, it was like my soul split in half and was battling itself. It felt like Heaven somehow got into Hell and it was fucking with me."

Lucian takes my hands and helps me up, righting me on my feet and steadying me to make sure I don't fall over. His big hands rest on my shoulders, and he tilts his head, staring into my eyes. He looks more angelic than devilish as he drinks me in. I shift on my feet, squirming under his scrutiny, but I don't look away. The way he looks at me sets my body ablaze in a good way, and I don't want him to stop. It makes me feel better. It makes me feel stronger and more in control.

"It's possible. Your soul is no longer indebted to me. Heaven could very well try to influence you to make you feel as if you don't belong here. And being close to an angel that refuses to bow didn't help. I'm sorry. I should've realized the effect that it would have on your soul." Lucian licks his full lips, drawing my attention to his mouth.

"You're apologizing?" My tone rises with my comment. "Satan himself is apologizing for something out of his control? Maybe Heaven didn't only get to me." I tilt my head and reach out my hand, pretending to stroke my fingers over invisible feathers of wings long gone from his back. "Oh fuck. Are those wings?"

Lucian knits his brows together, unamused by my teasing. "Careful. Tease me too much and I will punish you for trying to make me think that you question my darkness as a devil."

I widen my eyes, refusing to stop. I want to push him. I want to test the boundary I set up between us, knowing that it weakens with every day that passes. I can't help it. I now know a side of Lucian that I didn't know before. And it takes a lot of prodding, punching, teasing, and poking at him to get him to show himself as he doesn't want people to see him.

"Do you feel those?" Again, I pretend to stroke my fingers over imaginary wings. "They just sprouted from your back. Wow. Lucian, I didn't know that it was even possible."

He remains even in his expression. "Last chance to be a good girl. Keep it up and find out what happens. This is your one warning, Raven. I mean it."

"Keep what up?" I ask, biting my bottom lip between my teeth. "I don't know why you find it so hard to believe that maybe it wasn't Heaven that got to me. Summon a mirror or something. I'll prove it."

His jaw twitches, and he flares his nostrils. He is starting to believe me. I can see it in his eyes. He's worried. He hates the idea of wings returning to his back, especially after it was he who removed them himself like the crazy bastard he is. This is too good. I can't just give into him and tell him I'm fucking around.

I gasp and reach my other hand up and pretend to caress his invisible wings. "I have never seen such a color before. No wonder they called you the Morning Star. They are beautiful, Lucian."

He huffs a breath. "Stop fucking with me, Raven."

"Fucking with you? I'm not. Seriously, summon the mirror and look for yourself. They are amazing. Like Cassius's, but far more gorgeous." I lean closer and pretend to inspect his fake wings. "He would be so jealous."

Lucian transforms into his devil façade, and his huge horns jut from his head. Fire lights his eyes and he releases me, dropping me to my feet. I nearly lose my balance and have to catch myself by grabbing onto his waist. Lucian gathers fire between his palms and summons the mirror I told him to.

He brings the mirror up to look at himself, and I spin around on my feet, dashing away. The ground shakes as he releases a play-growl and chases after me, threatening me that I better hurry my ass up because if he catches me, he is going to spank me until the sting radiates through me for the rest of eternity.

I laugh and beg my legs to hustle, despite my body being thrilled by the idea. Stupid vagina. Stupid ass. It thinks it wants this, but Lucian is all about the punishment and no mercy. The last thing I want is to walk funny forever. The other devils will never let me hear the end of it.

"If you stop, turn around, and get on your knees, I might allow you to beg for forgiveness for fucking with me, Raven," Lucian shouts, whipping his chain next to me. "And maybe if you be a good little soul and give in to that dark desire lingering inside you, I might even return the favor and show you exactly what it's like to be on the good side of me instead of being a bratty soul."

"In your fucking fantasies," I call, searching my surroundings. I realize we are inside a palace with blood-red walls, a huge glittering ceiling, and fire burning across every surface, but it isn't hot. It's beautiful. "It'll take a lot more than a threat to ever get me on my knees for you. You know how much I want you to work for it."

"You stubborn fucking soul. Here I come." Lucian whips his chain beside me again, lashing the air, and I startle and twist on my feet, holding up my palms to him.

His eyes flash with his blazing fire and he hooks his arm around my waist and pulls his knee up, draping me across it. And holy shit. My whole body slackens as he manages to balance on one leg and smack my ass as I lie on his knee.

The sting of his spank radiates through me, and I groan and tense.

"See what happens when you fuck with me, Raven?" Lucian locks his fingers into my hair and stretches my neck back, forcing me to look at him.

I stick out my tongue. "Is that all you got? Because if it is then—"

He spanks me again in the same spot harder and hotter, leaving me breathless. I remain placid on his knee, dangling my arms toward the floor. And fuck. My body wants him to do it again. I almost open my mouth to get him to. If a strange whimpering sound didn't echo through the palace, I would have. But the sound of a tormented soul, all alone, digs under my skin. I recognize the feminine voice. It zaps pain right into my heart.

"Raven, get ready—"

"Lucian, stop," I say, my voice trembling with my nerves. "Put me down. Please."

I expect him to argue or to spank me again to silence me, but he listens to my pleas and sets me on my feet. My eyes dart around the palace, and I search everywhere in sight, trying to find where the strange whimpering voice comes from.

"Tamia?" I ask, pulling out of Lucian's hold. "Tamia? Is that you?"

Lucian steps in front of me, blocking my path. I try to dodge around him, but he locks his fingers to my wrist.

I try to rip myself away from him. "Lucian, what are you hiding? I know I'm not hearing things. Where is my cousin?"

He closes his eyes for a second and scratches his hand to the back of his neck. "Raven, don't freak out. This was my surprise. I found Tamia and I brought her here for you."

A mixture of emotions swells through me, and I clutch on to Lucian, using him to support my weakening knees. I thought about my cousin a hundred times since I pushed her through a Hell portal. I've cried over her. I was so upset and hurt that she allowed an angel to possess her. I was furious at the angel for doing so in the first place. If the angel hadn't, Elias would have never protected me and got himself shot. He would be ruling Hell now. We would be one step closer to having our kingdom rise.

"I don't understand," I say, my words coming out a whisper. "Why would you do that?"

"Because even though you were angry at her and you feel betrayed, I know you never wanted her here. While I can't do anything about the way her soul swayed, I can control her place in Hell. But first, I wanted your permission." Lucian searches my eyes as if he'll find the answers in my soul.

"My permission to do what?" I ask.

"To turn her into a demon to serve our cause." Lucian touches my cheek. "What do you think?"

I lick my lips. "I don't know."

I really fucking don't know.

3

Demon

RAVEN

TEARS BURN MY eyes as I stare at Tamia lying within a burning circle in a massive, vaulted room within Lucian's palace. She doesn't stir or sit up. Her soul remains in an ethereal state that I can barely comprehend. Darkness twines around her, restraining her limbs.

"It's okay to get close but don't enter the circle. Her soul is damaged, and I'm mending it the best I can. Heaven did a number on her." Lucian drapes his arm over my shoulders and pulls me in close.

"If you change her into a demon, what will she be like?" I twist my fingers together, keeping my gaze trained on my cousin. "Will she be enslaved to you?"

"She will be bound to me but not a slave. As for your other question, I don't have that kind of answer for you. It all depends on Tamia." Lucian guides me forward and closer to the circle of hellfire. "Every demon is different depending on the soul."

I sigh. How am I supposed to decide if I don't know how she'll act? I've seen a ton of demons. Some are okay, like Gia. But then there are other demons like Vincent. If Tamia turns out to be like the demon that managed to bind Elias's soul to Hell, I don't know if I could deal with that. Tamia was always good. Well, mostly. But now? I don't know how much Hell will affect her. I have so many questions to ask her. She should be the one to have the final decision because it's her soul and her eternity.

"Would you like to talk to her?" Lucian asks, leaning forward to get a better look into my eyes. "I can enter the circle and speak for her."

I automatically nod my head. "I need to know why. Why would she allow an angel to possess her? Why would she do any of this in the first place?"

Lucian lifts and drops his shoulders. "Are you sure you want those answers?"

"I need some sort of answer. Anything is better than nothing." I pull myself from his arms, putting space between us.

I motion toward my cousin. "It won't hurt her any, right? I mean, any more than being in Hell does?"

"Promise," Lucian says.

"Then do it. Connect with her." I hold my arms over my chest and watch in silence as Lucian transforms into his devil façade again. He towers over Tamia as he steps into the circle of hellfire and looks down upon her.

The floor quivers with his movements, and I find myself crossing my legs at my knees and lowering myself to sit. I'm afraid if I remain standing, my legs will give out on me. It's unsettling to see Tamia here and have Lucian kneeling beside her and touching his palm to her forehead, setting her whole body aglow. But it's not her body. It's her soul.

Lucian whispers under his breath, too low for me to hear. I stare at the two of them and wait in silence until Lucian whips his head up and looks at me.

"Ray? Oh, my God, Ray, what's going on? Where am I? Did it work? Are we in Heaven?" Lucian's mouth moves, but eerily enough, it's not his voice that comes out. It's Tamia's.

I don't respond to her question right away. How am I supposed to tell my cousin that she's in Hell?

"You don't remember?" This sucks balls. It would be easier if she knew what was happening.

"Remember what?" Tamia asks, using Lucian to speak to me.

I kind of wish that I could speak with Lucian at the same time, too. I'm a coward. I would rather him tell her what happened instead of me. But I know I have to do this. It's better to find out from someone that cares about her. I need to be brave.

"Tamia, you're in Hell," I say, my throat tightening with the words as my eyes water. "You let an angel possess you and tried to kill me. Your actions stole my soulmate from me." Grief slices my being into pieces as I confront her instead of gently telling her. I can't help it, though. Talking about Heaven brings out the worst in me.

"I—" Lucian snaps his mouth shut, his expression reminiscent of my cousin despite them looking nothing alike. His features morph from shock, and his face hardens with angry lines, setting his eyes aglow. "I'm in Hell? I don't understand. How am I in Hell? I did everything that the angel asked of me. She promised that my sacrifice would save us both."

Lucian shakes his head, whipping it back and forth. He straightens his shoulders and removes his palm from Tamia's head. Without having to ask him, I know that he disconnected from Tamia's soul. He scrubs his hands over his face and rises to his feet, stepping out of the flaming circle.

"I'm sorry, Raven," Lucian says, strolling toward me. He gets to his knees to be more at my level. "She wanted time to think things over."

"Think things over? How can she think things over if she doesn't remember?" Resentment and annoyance rush through me, and I scramble to my feet and try to run toward the flaming circle.

Lucian scoops me up and turns me around, restraining me to his chest. His muscles flex, and he doesn't budge no matter how hard I fight and thrash to break free. I want to confront my cousin. I want to know what she was thinking. I have been without answers for weeks. I thought she was lost. Damn it.

"Bring her back. Get back into her mind and make her talk to me." I wiggle in Lucian's arms, trying to find out if I can escape if I fight hard enough. "I deserve answers."

"Raven, this is not how you're going to get them. Her soul is in a fragile state, and she's not resilient like you. Until you decide whether or not you want her to rise as a powerful demon of my level, I'm not sure she will ever be strong enough to give you what you want." Lucian's eyes flick over mine as if he can break into my mind and listen to my thoughts. "I'm sorry for bringing you here. I thought I was doing the right thing. Obviously, that's difficult for me to do."

I inhale a ragged breath, trying to get my emotions under control. Hell is getting to me. Everything is getting to me. I wish that I didn't feel like I was on the verge of exploding, and I wish that I could just forget everything involving what happened but I can't.

"Actually, I'm not even sure if it's possible." Lucian purses his lips. "I should just take you back to the Mortal Realm."

His comment digs into me, and I realize that he feels terrible. It's not something that I expect from him, and I feel my soul drawing to his.

Leaning closer, I surprise him by crashing my mouth to his, kissing him in a way that I have never done before. It isn't out of desperation or anger. It isn't to get something I want or because he manipulated me into doing so. I kiss him for the sole reason that I want to.

And fuck, does he react.

Lucian tangles his fingers through my hair and doesn't let me ease away, guaranteeing that he steals my breath. It's not that I want to stop him anyway. All I want to do is explore his mouth, taste his tongue, and really find out what it's like to be with the most notorious devil.

I rub my fingers over his head, feeling his short hair until his devil form starts to break free, riled up by the passion between us. I gasp at the points of his horns pricking my palms, but he keeps them in check. He doesn't turn into his beastly form like I expect. He remains as human as I am, even in Hell. Even in his kingdom where he is most powerful as a devil. But this isn't about power. This is about something more. It's about his darkness twisting with my light and what it does to us.

He breaks away from my mouth and kisses my jaw, working

his way down my neck as his hand moves between my legs. Fuck. I know that he will push me to my limit, and I won't stop either. I'll let him do as he pleases.

"I've thought about this for a century," Lucian says, his breath heavy with his desire. "I thought about it even more the last month. I want all of you. Give me what I want, Raven."

Damn it. I want to. I want to submit to his desire to fuck my brains out. I want him to bend me over and fuck the Hell into me like he has promised over and over again since I've met him. I think I'm ready to cross that line with him, because I know that the other devils will keep him in place. And if they don't, I will. I'm no longer afraid to face him or any of the other demons in Hell, for that matter. They will bow to me, just as Lucian has.

"I won't give you anything," I say, bowing to nip his shoulder with my teeth, rolling my hips to feel his hand rub against the fabric of my pants. "But I give you permission to take it. Show me that you aren't all talk. Fuck me and make me scream your name."

Lucian releases a guttural noise from his throat, and the sexy sound vibrates over my clavicle as he lifts me higher and kisses the top of my boobs peeking out from my low-cut shirt.

"You fucking beautiful, infuriating, absolutely devastatingly pure soul." Lucian leans back to meet my eyes. "You're going to feel my darkness for the rest of eternity. Every time you look at me, you'll get wet with excitement. You will crave me bending you over to fuck you over and over again. That I promise you."

"We'll see about that," I say, laughing with my words.

Lucian narrows his eyes, flips me around, and pins me to the scorching wall with my hands above my head. His body presses flush against mine, and he uses his knee to lift me off my feet until I can feel the hardness of his cock against my ass. I moan as his hand slides around my side and down my stomach, and he slips his fingers into the waistband of my pants. My heart crashes against my rib cage, and I squirm, wanting nothing more than for him to hurry up. He purposely tortures me with the slow caress of his hand as it works its way down my pelvis.

With his free hand, he combs my hair off the back of my neck and licks my skin, sucking it in between his teeth and leaving a mark. It doesn't hurt, but it does send a zap of power through my body.

"I'm going to enjoy you for as long as I want," Lucian says, drawing his tongue up my throat until he sucks my earlobe. "This is for all of the times you rejected me."

This bastard and his need to punish me in the best way possible.

"You can try to torture me all you want, but you're only punishing yourself." I moan again, wiggling and trying to shift my body to force him to touch me between my legs. "I like when you tease me like this. I know you'll give in soon enough.

You wanted me for far too long not to take what I offer imme-diately." He can't be the only cocky one, now, can he? I know how much he likes his games, and I'm willing to play them.

"You're wrong." Lucian tightens his hand through my hair. "I am a patient devil."

This is going to turn into a battle of wills, and I am com-pletely prepared to go down with this fight. I can't help it.

"You're only patient until someone else takes what you want," I tease. I grin as he growls. "Have you forgotten that you're not the only devil who wants me?"

"You bratty fucking soul." Lucian flips me around, locks his fingers to my throat, and squeezes without cutting off my airway. I'm not even sure that he could if he wanted to. I'm in Hell, after all.

A smile lights my face, and I laugh, loving how annoyed he is that I don't just obey him. He knew that I would never be an obedient little soul. I don't comply without a fight. It'll take a lot more than a growl to push me into submission.

Neither of us gets to find out because a screech rips through the air, stealing the warmth for my blood. A hulking figure flies into the room and crashes into the lava-like wall a couple of feet away. I startle at the sight of the disgusting demon. He's the worst one I've seen yet, with swollen, bulbous blisters covering his body. Lucian sets me on my feet, summoning his fire chain, and lashes it at the demon, sending pus splashing across the floor.

The demon howls in agony.

Abandoning me, Lucian stomps toward the gross demon-ic man and roars, transforming into his Hell form to tower over the monstrous beast. I stare in shock with my body still buzzing and watch as Lucian swings his clawed hand, slashing it across the demon's chest, cutting through more disgusting blisters.

I realize now that the blisters aren't natural. The liquid in-side them sizzles across the floor as if his skin has been infused with holy water. He's been hit with heavenly light.

"You better have a damn good reason for interrupting me with my queen," Lucian says, shaking the demon hard enough to smack the monster's head into the wall. "I was about to fuck her brains out."

I palm my forehead at his nonchalance at his declaration of us about to get it on.

"I'm sorry, my liege. It's urgent. You're being summoned to the Mortal Realm." The demon flicks his attention to me.

Punching the demon in the face, Lucian smashes the de-mon's cheek into the glowing wall. He leans in and roars into his ear. "Look at her again, and you will no longer have eyes to see. I don't give a fuck if I'm being summoned. I'm busy. Tell Kase to fuck off and wait his turn. Raven is mine."

Ah, fuck.

Lucian has a case of possessiveness. He knew that the devils were trying to contact him, but he ignored them to be with me. I can't blame him. I might have done the same. But now that I know they were trying to reach him, I feel as if I must say something.

Gathering my nerves, I risk facing the wrath of Lucian. The demon still tries to break free as if it's even possible to be a devil. I gently touch my hand to Lucian's lower back and rub a soft circle.

"Lucian, it might be something important. We should at least check, okay?" I keep my voice low and brace myself for Lucian to spin around and growl at me.

The heat of his anger radiates from his very being, stealing away his ability to think about anything other than lashing out at the demon and anyone else who dares interrupt us.

"We can finish what we started later. Promise. This isn't going to be the only time you'll ever get to show me what it's like to be with you." I continue to stroke my fingers against the skin of his lower back, feeling his muscles ripple as he settles down.

Dropping the demon to the floor, Lucian kicks him, sending him rolling. The demon scrambles away without another word, trying to escape Lucian's need to punish him for being a messenger.

"If I was someone else, you would continue and ignore every

distraction," Lucian says, his voice laced with his annoyance.

I press my lips together. "Don't even fucking start by comparing the relationship I have with others with what I'm trying to build with you. I mean it. You will not make me feel bad that I worry about what is happening in the Mortal Realm. You damn well know that Kase wouldn't call you if he didn't actually need you."

"I'm not trying to make you feel bad, Raven," Lucian snaps. He turns to me with fire in his eyes. "All I'm saying is—"

I cut him off with a kiss, knowing that if this conversation continues, we might get into a fight that leads us right back to passion, and the devils need us. I know what Lucian's doing. He thinks he can manipulate me, but I'm mostly immune to his dickish behavior.

Lucian reacts by moaning under his breath and picking me back up. I ease away and lock his attention to me with my eyes, watching as the fire diminishes, leaving me drowning in the dark depths of his gaze.

"You are really going to make me take you back?" Lucian asks, sucking my bottom lip into his mouth again. "You know it could be another week until we get the chance."

"I can fuck you whenever I want." Reaching down, I brush my fingers to his cock, pressing against the material of his pants. "I don't need to follow any schedule. You know the rules."

"Fucking fine, Ray. I'll give you what you want now, but next time we are doing things my way. I will make sure those assholes know that they need to figure out how to deal with their own shit when I'm not around." Lucian summons hellfire and throws it across the floor, opening a portal to the Mortal Realm.

"As long as it works the other way around, Satan. I want things to be fair." I grin at his glowering reaction.

But he doesn't argue. Instead, he exhales a smoking breath and jumps with me into the portal. The world blurs, and I screech at the sensation of falling. I will never get used to traveling between Hell and the Mortal Realm. It's disorienting.

The ground rumbles, and vivid light blinds me. My heart sinks into my stomach as we land in the middle of a ring of fire in the center of a bar.

"Lucian, watch out!" Dante yells, his voice echoing around me. "Incoming. Bastard guardian."

Neither of us gets a chance to react as the angel flies toward us.

We fall back into Hell.

Battle Plan

DANTE

“IF YOU WOULD have come when we summoned you, Raven wouldn't be knocked the fuck out, you asshole.” I wring my hands together, staring at my pretty soul as she lies on her stomach in the middle of my king bed.

“She was going to let me fuck her. You damn well know you would've ignored me too.” Lucian clenches his fingers into fists.

I fucking hate that he's right. I do ignore him all the time. But it's different for me. At least, that's what I keep telling myself. I don't give a damn.

“You need to get over yourself, you asshole,” I say, meeting

Lucian's eyes with a glare. "We have more important things than you getting your dick wet. We need to find out what the fuck is going on. The angels should be leaving us alone."

"Have you considered that they are just trying to get all of us to return to Hell and to leave the Mortal Realm for good?" Lucian asks, his smug-ass tone digging under my skin.

Of fucking course I thought of that. I thought of a lot of things. But something inside me screams that it's more than the little bird bitches wanting us to go back to our kingdoms. No, they definitely have something plucking their feathers.

"Don't you think he thought of that? You are stupid as hell if you think he didn't." Kase stands in the doorway of my room and whips his tail at Lucian. "We aren't dumbasses, you fuckhead."

I grin at Kase and flick my tongue out at him, showing him my appreciation for standing up for me.

"Well, I thought you two were smart enough to handle shit while I went and got Raven. How was I supposed to know that you two were missing a couple of brain cells from fucking each other senseless?" Lucian tries to step forward and closer to Raven, but Kase wraps his tail around Lucian's ankle and pulls his feet out from under him.

If Raven didn't release the most pathetic, cute whimper I have ever heard, I'd kick Lucian in the nuts. We all freeze and turn our attention to our pretty soul. She groans and arches her back, stretching her arms over her head. And damn, does she look sexy as her smooth stomach peeks out from her shirt.

I saunter across the room and plop down on the bed beside her, pulling her into my arms and hugging her. She blinks a couple of times as she tries to process what the fuck is going on. The quick relocation from Hell to the Mortal Realm and back to Hell fucked with her soul.

"Hey, pretty soul. How are you feeling? What can I do for you? Do you need water? Something to eat? I could just cuddle you for a bit until your body realigns, if you like." I stroke my fingers over her cheek and smile, waiting for her to realize that she's in my arms.

She doesn't respond right away, but she doesn't break her stare from mine either. Kase joins us on the bed and kneels behind her, rubbing his hot hand up and down the length of her back.

"What the hell happened?" she asks, inhaling a soft breath. "Are you okay? Are any of you hurt? Where is Lucian?"

Fucking hell. The cocky son-of-a-bastard loves the fact that Raven asks about him. Jealousy sneaks up on me, and I flare my nostrils, trying to keep it in check. I thought I was over Raven showing others affection and attention. But damn. I'm not used to this. I knew that I'd be sharing Raven, and I knew Lucian would get a part of her too, but I feel as if he still needs to do a lot more to earn her concern.

"I'm right here, Ray." Lucian steps closer, a smile widening on his face. "I'm okay."

Scrunching her nose, she snatches the pillow from the bed and swings it, clocking Lucian in the face with it. It catches him off guard, and he tears it in half to get it away. Feathers fly everywhere, drifting through the air. Flapping my wings, I send a gust of them toward Lucian. His skin burns as they pelt him, the angelic feathers a souvenir from one of the assholes who fought against us. I had been using that particular pillow as a form of pleasurable punishment for my pretty soul. The fabric gave just enough protection to prevent her ass from blistering, but it gave quite the sting to really get her adrenaline going.

"What the actual—" Lucian growls as Raven chucks another pillow at him, cutting him off.

"That's for ignoring a summons, Satan," Raven says, shaking her fist. It's as threatening as a newborn hellhound, and I can't help chuckling.

Lucian tries to snatch her by the ankle, but I hiss. "You don't think having to wait two days for you to wake up wasn't punishment enough? We could've been banging already."

I must admit that he's good.

He knows exactly what he's doing. The game he plays, taking the blame and making him sound remorseful will get our soul to give him what he wants.

But not now.

"Maybe if you pick up all of my feathers and put them back where they belong, I will give you what you want." Raven rubs my thigh as she talks to Lucian biting her lip like the seductress she is.

I knew it. I want to call him out on it, but I also want to see how far the two of them will take it. Twisted? Maybe. I enjoy a good boundary-pushing, and Lucian knows how to push every damn one of them. I can't help it if I find the devil attractive. Raven is sweet enough to invite me to join. But as much as I want a little fun, we have shit to do. I don't have the time nor energy to fight my envy against Lucian. He is just as bad as I am, except for maybe now.

I bend forward and scoop a couple of the angel feathers off the duvet cover and gather them in my hand, not even flinching as they burn my fingers. "You don't even have to bribe me to get me to do it, pretty soul. You know how much I like taking care of you."

Her smile widens, and she flicks her gaze from Lucian to me. "This is why I love you, Dante. You always know exactly what I need." She shoos Lucian back. "Why don't you help Kase clean up whatever mess he needs help with? Me and Dante can figure some shit out. Maybe we can find Zade. I'm sure he's lurking around somewhere."

"Fuck, I love you too, my pretty soul." I look over at Lucian and flick my tongue at him again. "I've missed Raven too much, and it's my day. You're going to have to wait to seduce her. I can't stand the thought of letting you have your way with her without me involved. So, unless you want to share her right now with both me and Kase, you're going to have to chill. We have things to do."

"Fine, but I get her first." Lucian play-growls and manages to grab Raven by her foot. She screeches as he drags her across the bed and to the edge. Lifting her legs up, he positions her in a way that all he'd have to do is burn right through her pants, and he could take her right now.

The fucking bastard. My balls scrunch with excitement. I guess I'm all in. Lucian wins this round.

Raven kicks her foot, knocking Lucian's head to the side. "You guys can't plan this kind of adventure without consulting me first. I mean, you don't look like you will wait your turn and will just start going at me. The last thing I need is for you guys to fight over which hole you put your fucking cocks into. Because with Kase, that means we are one short with his damn tail unless it goes into one of your two's assholes."

Kase releases a loud laugh, tipping his head back. "No fucking way. I'm only in the mood to double up on you. Just imagine."

Raven clenches her ass and manages to cross her legs and kick Lucian back hard enough to put some space between them.

She whips her head back and forth, sending her hair sweeping around her. "One of you is already a tight squeeze."

"Oh, come on, angel-girl. You handle Andre just fine." Kase flicks his tail at her, wraps it around her wrist, and hoists her into the air, dangling her in front of him. Leaning in, he kisses her, taking his time to show off the fact that if he does it long enough, she might agree.

Blush curls up her neck and into her cheeks. "Then maybe I need to go warm up with him. Like Dante said, you guys have stuff to do."

Fuck. Denied.

"None of that is important. I'm sure these two dickwads are just being overprotective. We are good. Heaven can't do shit, even if they do send us all to Hell. They can't keep us there." Lucian wags his brows at me.

Raven wiggles from Kase's hold until he sets her on her feet. "I don't know..."

Lucian tightens his jaw. "But I do."

"Enough," I say, getting to my feet. I drape my arms over Raven's shoulders and snuggle her from behind. "It's obviously something Raven wants us to look into. Hell, something doesn't feel right to me either. I don't think it's as simple as what you suggest. I think your cock is just too damn swollen and horny for you to think straight."

Lucian doesn't care as much as we do about taking care of

our little heavenly problem. I know deep in my gut that there is more to it than just these bastards wanting to fuck with us. And there's only one way we can find out.

"Agreed," Kase says, patting me on the head with his tail. Even if he didn't truly agree, he'd still take my side.

"But we can look into it, just to be safe, Lucian." Raven reaches out and touches his cheek. "You and Kase can see if you can corner Cass-hole or something. Dante and I will try to get Zade to come out."

"That sounds perfect. Right, Lucian?" I flick my fingers at him, keeping him from sandwiching Raven between us. "It doesn't bother me any having to wait a couple of hours. Raven is always worth it to me."

Fuck yeah. I can see it written all over Raven's face that she agrees with me and wants to figure this shit out before doing anything. It might be the only way she can relax and have fun, anyway. And I'll do anything to see to it. My pretty soul has been through enough over the last few weeks.

Lucian groans and scrubs his cheeks with his hands. "You owe me that wet ass pussy of yours later, Ray. I mean it."

She wags her finger at him. "Like I said, maybe you can take what you want."

Fucking damn. I can't stand the thought, so I scoop Raven up and flap my wings, propelling us toward the door. I don't wait for anybody to respond and race out of the apartment, launching into the sky the second I get a clear path out of the trees from our new home. We keep moving around to prevent the angels from keeping tabs on us.

Raven shifts in my arms and tightens her thighs around my waist, leaning in and kissing me with tongue. I hum under my breath and savor the taste of her mouth. She knows how to get to me in a way that leaves my whole body aching for her. She's lucky that I don't try to fuck her while flying. If I didn't have to be on high alert, I would. I'd fuck her so hard that she would think that the stars were falling from the sky.

It takes everything in me to let her ease away from my mouth. She combs her fingers through my hair and rests them on the back of my head, cradling me with her palms. "Your envy is showing," she teases, nuzzling her nose to mine and kissing me again.

"I can't help it that you drive me wild. It's been days, and I can still smell Lucian on you." I adjust her in my arms, pulling her in closer to keep her warm from the icy air blowing around us. "This wasn't the welcome back from Hell I had planned to give you."

"I don't care about having a special welcome home. All I care about is spending time with you, figuring out where Elias is, and now fucking breaking every damn angel we come across." Her beautiful blue-green eyes dim with her thoughts.

"At least this now confirms that Elias isn't in Heaven. For a second, we were a little bit worried." I regret my words immediately. From the look Raven gives me, I realize that she didn't even consider the possibility that instead of reincarnating as a human again, that he could've ended up elsewhere.

It's something that the other devils and I have discussed on multiple occasions, especially when we realized Elias wasn't in Hell.

"What?" Raven asks, her voice rising in pitch. "You have to be shitting me. That wouldn't have happened, right?"

"Like I said, we don't have to worry about it now. It would've been a longshot." I turn my attention away from Raven and to the world around us. "That's why we need to find an angel and see if we can either seduce it or beat it out of him. If we find Zade, I know which one to expect. He's going to jump from grace any fucking day now."

Why and how he hasn't done so already? I have no fucking idea. He is sloth. He doesn't do shit, except stalk us and look at us with desire but without the bravery to actually make a move.

Huffing a breath through her nose, Raven says, "I'm starting to think I'll have better luck with getting Cassius to jump before Zade. And I kind of hate the thought. All I want to do is dick chop that stupid prideful angel."

"Hey, at least you can still have some fun with it. I could have it dipped in gold or glass or some shit." I grin with my words.

Raven giggles and shakes her head. "You are so fucking kinky and freaky. I love it."

"We still have a lot to—" A flash of heavenly light steals my attention as a blasted angel materializes from a portal and into the Mortal Realm.

Fuck. Raven is my lucky charm. This bastard doesn't even see me until it's too late. Moving Raven to my hip, I unsheathe a throwing knife from my jacket and chuck it at the angel, sinking it into his wing.

The angel hollers and thrusts heavenly power in our direction, but I spin and fold my wings around Raven protectively, keeping her safe.

I freefall beside the angel and throw another knife, sinking it into his other wing. Raven squeaks with a sudden drop but manages to keep herself from screaming by sinking her teeth into my shoulder.

I touch down on the street first, landing in a crouch. The angel plummets into the branches of a tree and crashes to the ground. He smacks his back on the concrete, yelling out. Before he can get up, I rush him and summon a circle of hellfire around him, trapping him.

"Release me before all of Heaven's army comes to destroy you and this abomination of a soul." The angel presses his palms to the ground and pushes himself up.

Fury explodes through me, and I spit venom at the fucker,

searing his chest through his shirt. I set Raven on her feet and link my hand with hers, keeping her close but also ensuring that we can both fight. I don't know if more guardians will soon follow this dickhole.

"The only place I will release you is into one of the pits in the bowels of Hell." I flash my fangs, unleashing my monster appearance.

The guardian widens his eyes like he's never seen a devil before. And maybe he hasn't. I don't know who the fuck this guy is. And if I don't know who he is, it just means he's one of Heaven's good little soldiers and completely expendable. He's probably one of the souls that actually made it into Heaven his first lifecycle before shit got real in the Mortal Realm.

"You won't be able to keep me there. Things are changing, and it'll be you who begs for the Higher Power's mercy." This fuckhead. He's a cocky, self-assured son-of-a-bastard, isn't he?

"Changing? How so?" I ask, raising an eyebrow.

"I will not betray Heaven." The angel ruffles his feathers and continues to glower.

"Dante, make him tell us. He will give in. Or let me," Raven says, squeezing my hand tighter. She straightens her shoulders and doesn't back down, even though the angel tries to threaten her with his heavenly light.

I could never deny her, so I march forward through the barrier and grab the angel by the front of his shirt and lift him off his feet. I growl in his face, baring my fangs at him. He tries to act like a tough son-of-a-bastard and doesn't close his eyes. Big mistake for him. I spit a stream of venom into his face, purposefully missing his eyes.

He howls in agony, whipping his body back and forth, but unable to break free from my death grip.

"Tell us how you think things are changing, or I will take your eyes next time." I hiss under my breath, and Raven shifts behind me.

She's anxious and torn over my threat. I know she dislikes seeing others get hurt, even if it is one of our enemies. It's just part of her beautiful, light nature.

"Never," the angel growls, now choosing to close his eyes.

I hiss again, extending my fangs. The angel braces for pain and agony, and I would gladly do it on Raven's behalf for the fact that this is about her. No one will ever fuck with my girl if I have something to do about it. I will destroy everyone who even thinks about it.

Raven rests her hand on my shoulder.

Okay, maybe not. But only because Raven won't let me.

"Dante, wait." Raven slides up next to me within the circle and nestles into my side. "I've changed my mind. I don't think this is the right way to go about things."

I see what she's doing. She wants to play the good soul and have me be the badass she loves.

"How the fuck do you want to go about it then? He obviously isn't going to give us answers easily." I fake-glare at her and wait for her to gather her thoughts.

"I think he might give us the answers if maybe I show him that it will be worth it for him." Raven licks her lips, and her eyes flash with fire. She's tapping into my power through the bond without even realizing it. I don't have to have a contract with her to be close to her soul. She automatically allows me in.

"Are you insinuating what I think you are, pretty soul? You would really put that pretty pouty mouth of yours around this fucker's cock?" I ask in amusement.

She shrugs. "Maybe. There are other ways to get angels to comply. Remember Andre? It all started with a simple caressing of my tongue."

Damn. I harden at just the thought of her getting on her knees.

"You abomination! Stay away from me!" the angel shouts, gathering heavenly light in his palms again.

Raven grabs the front of her shirt and flashes the guy her tits. The angel freezes, his eyes widening, and I realize that her gesture got him right in the cock.

"You concubine! Cover your body and show respect for yourself." The angel shields his eyes, sounding like a fucking mortal from the past. "I will not stand here and let you seduce me. You will not entangle your tainted body and soul with mine. I would rather burn than risk letting you get to me. I don't care if you have light inside you. Do you understand?"

I clench my fingers into fists. "Are you denying my girl?"

"It's okay, Dante. I don't actually want to do anything with him anyway." Raven draws her finger in a circle as if she's highlighting the angel's boner through his pants. "He is unworthy of me."

"As you are unworthy to carry such a magnificent light," the angel snaps. "It is such a shame that we can't send you to Hell at this moment. But we can send your masters."

His words prod at something inside me. What does he mean about not being able to send Raven to Hell in this moment? She's not absolutely pure. We do taint her with our darkness. She allies with Hell.

Fury rushes through me, and I charge the angel knocking him from the fire circle and onto his back. "Tell me what you mean," I demand. "Tell me now or you will go to Hell."

The angel doesn't respond.

I summon a dagger and stab him in the chest. "Tell me!" My hellish nature consumes me. All I see are flames.

Intervention

ZADE

M Y ENTIRE BEING darkens at the sight of Raven and Dante trying to break the guardian. It becomes more of a struggle every day not to stand up and ask the guardians to step back and let me do my job acting as Raven's moral compass. I feel that it is my purpose to try and guide her on the path of good grace.

I know she is lost. I know that she feels as if she never had a choice in any of this, and maybe she hasn't. But now? With a little push in the right direction, she still might be able to save her soul. It is what happened with Elias. He managed to sway his soul from Hell and back to an even ground. If only it didn't make things worse for Raven. I know he did what he did to save her from Lucian. And now Heaven's army is out to ensure the devils can't repeat everything over again.

Heaven believes that if Raven dies, it could trigger her soul to cycle again and find Elias. If the devils know this, they might push her into starting over. At least, that's what the others think. I, on the other hand, know that they wouldn't do such a thing. They love her too much as she is. Starting over could mean a number of things. It could mean that they never see her again. No one knows the Divine's true purpose.

Not the guardians. Not the devils. Not me.

If only I could turn back time and convince Andre that Raven needed him more as an angel instead of the devil he has become. I think about him more and more these days, especially when he seeks me out. I know what his intentions are, and he's trying to use our companionship against me. I just can't give in to what he wants. I truly believe that Raven will do far more good if she doesn't fall to Hell. Unfortunately, Heaven's army doesn't agree.

It hurts me on a soul-deep level. I feel lost, yet I still feel as if I'm doing the right thing. If only others would agree with me. It would make things easier, and Azrael wouldn't be in this position. He thinks he's strong, but he has no idea. The guardians manage their power by staying together and acting as one. I am not a guardian. I am a Savior, which is different. I work on the bigger picture things, while the guardians follow orders. The only thing I follow is the light and right now, Raven's shines incredibly bright. More so than I have ever seen her shine. I want to lose myself in her light.

Azrael screams, his pain and agony crashing into me as if it was my own. I whip my attention from the ground and watch as Dante cuts off Azrael's wings. Raven surprises me by kicking the angel hard in his back, sending him into the portal to Hell.

"Oh, Raven," I say, my voice barely coming out a whisper. "What have you done?"

I realize too late that I said the words too loudly and both Raven and Dante hear me. Raven covers her mouth with her hand, and her face morphs into a frown. It's like realization sets in, and she understands what she has done. Her eyes glass over with her tears, and my heart fissures at the sight of her sadness. It's not her fault that she has found herself in this position. I wish I could rush to her and comfort her, but I know if I make even a move, I might find myself getting launched into Hell.

Dante's eyes flash with green light, and he spreads his wings wide. I don't have a chance to brace myself as he flies at me. Shoving his hands into my chest, he knocks me into a tree trunk and pins me in place.

"You will not make her feel bad for standing up for herself and our cause. I will cut your wings off if you even try." Dante growls deep in his throat, and the sound reverberates through me.

"Dante, you can let him go. Zade has every right to be shocked and scared by seeing one of his brethren going to Hell." Raven's voice draws my attention away from Dante and to her as she comes up and slides between us.

I gasp at the zing coursing through me. Her body presses against mine, and I can feel her heart beating against my chest. I automatically suck in a breath of her sweet fragrance and place my hand on her hip. I had no idea how much I missed her until now. It's been a hard few weeks keeping away as best as I could...or at least, staying hidden.

After Andre convinced me to taste Raven in a way I never imagined I would, I knew that my fate was in jeopardy if I continued to cross the line. She knows that I never wander far, but I can't handle that influence. My feelings for her run rampant in a way I can't explain. I love her. I love her with my entire being as much as I love Andre. I can't help it. It is in my nature to love fully, irrevocably, and unconditionally. Whether or not it's the same kind of love the devils claim to feel is something I don't know. Their emotions are dark and toxic. They eat away at Raven's light and feed on her. But they never hurt her. Well, at least not in a way she doesn't like. It's all so confusing.

"Zade," Raven says, touching her warm fingers to my cheek. "I'm glad you were here. It's been a while since you've shown yourself to me. I thought maybe you had abandoned me with all of the craziness going on."

I don't respond right away. The softness of her voice squeezes my heart, and I wish that I were brave enough not to run back to hide in the shadows. I never wanted her to believe that I had abandoned her. It hurts me deeply that she ever felt that way.

"I'm sorry. I'm so sorry." I bow forward a bit, getting into her breathing space. I want nothing more than to kiss her and show her how much I have truly missed her. But I'm afraid. Dante glowers at me from behind her. I don't know what he will do, but he's not as encouraging as Kase and Andre. His envy makes him dangerous. I know it takes everything in him to control it in regards to Raven.

"You don't have to apologize. Just kiss me." Raven stretches the rest of the way to me and presses her lips to mine as if she could read my thoughts. I tense at the hot sensation of her mouth. She tastes of fire and something sweeter that I can't put my finger on. It takes all my restraint not to kiss her more deeply, more fervently, and show her that even if I was shielding myself, I was never truly away.

"Careful, pretty soul," Dante says, sliding his hand between mine and Raven's stomachs. "I might want to join, and I don't think this asshole is ready to climb aboard the Kink Express with us. I know from Andre that Zade ran away after he tasted the gloriousness of your pussy."

I scrunch my nose. "I did not run away. Raven was upset over discovering that Elias was not in any of your kingdoms." Oh no. I shouldn't have said that.

Dante reaches over Raven, hooks both his hands around my neck, and flips me over her and his head. He drops me behind him, and if I hadn't opened my wings to protect myself from the fall, I would have crashed into the ground.

Dante jumps onto me and shoves his hands to my chest. I don't move or fight back as he restrains me, his anger escaping him with sprinkles of his venom. They pepper across my face, stinging my skin. Still, I don't move. I worry that his rage will get the best of him, and Raven will get between us and get hurt in the crossfire.

"You told the guardians, didn't you? I thought you were better than that, you prick." Dante fists his hand, preparing to punch me in the face.

Raven scrambles closer and laces both her hands around his. "I don't think he would do that. Right, Zade? If you said something, they'd have ensured you'd never come around me again. They'd have known that they hadn't won."

Dante doesn't respond to her and instead shoves his hand harder into my chest. "You know why the guardians started attacking again, don't you? You need to fucking tell us. I've had it with giving you the benefit of the doubt. I know you're too chicken shit to finally see the truth, and you're just too scared to do anything about it, but this is Raven's life and our kingdoms that you're fucking with. So, tell us, Zade. Why are they attacking now? How do they know that Elias isn't in Hell?"

My whole body screams and argues with my mind, my mouth refusing to move as I think about what to say. I haven't known that the guardians knew for long.

"Don't make me rip it from you in front of Raven. She likes you, and I don't want her to be pissed off at me. But it is important." Dante's eyes flash green, and his two long fangs protrude from beneath his lip.

Raven kneels beside me and caresses her fingers to my face. "Please, Zade."

I squeeze my eyes shut, concentrating on the world around us. Saying a silent prayer, I ask for guidance. I need to know what to do. I'm tired of having to make these decisions for myself. Mortals are the ones who should have complete free will. Things would be much simpler if I didn't. Because that's what this is. It's a test to see what I decide. And I'm going to fail. I know it. I want to. I want to show Raven that she can ask me anything, and I will answer to the best of my ability. I want her to know that even though we are on opposite sides of a war in the universe, I am here for her. I am here for Andre as well. I can't deny that I want what's best for them, even if they don't realize it or know what's truly best.

"Last chance," Dante threatens, hissing with his words.

"I swear I didn't tell them. I've been staying away from everyone. The test given to me by the Higher Power is far harder than I expected, and I can't face Cassius or the guardians until I find my way and know exactly what path I'm following." I flex my muscles and try to get Dante to loosen his grip on my shirt. He tightens the collar so much so that it's hard to speak.

Dante bows closer, getting into my face. "That didn't answer our question."

"The guardians know that Elias isn't in Hell because he's not in Heaven like he was supposed to be." I sigh with my words and tip my head back, staring up at the spattering of stars above us. "His soul had swayed toward Heaven. Even though his life was taken so suddenly, it was already over to begin with. He should have never been put in a new cycle. It's freaking everyone out. They think that you will do something crazy to Raven, trying to speed up the reunion between her and her soulmate."

"What is that supposed to mean?" Raven asks, tugging at Dante's shoulders until he releases me.

"It means they think we're going to fucking kill you or something. It takes basically the same amount of time as it does with a pregnancy for a soul to get cycled back into the Mortal Realm. The fastest way to bring yours and Elias's souls together again would be to trigger another cycle with you." Dante reaches out and snatches Raven by the wrist and pulls her hand to his chest. "Which is something we never considered and would never consider doing. This cycle your soul is in is the one we want eternity with."

I was right. The reason why I knew it was because I agree with him. I don't want Raven to go through another cycle and take on another life and another mortal form all over again. I didn't know her before like Elias had, but I know her now. I love her now.

"Oh." Raven is stunned silent. It's obvious by the look on her face, her eyes shining over with tears. I don't think she thought about the possibility. I'm not even sure that's the reason why she reacts as she does. Maybe she's thinking about Elias.

"Don't worry, pretty soul. We're going to take care of the guardians and find your soulmate, even if we have to send all of Heaven's army to Hell in the process."

Dante shifts off of me and gathers Raven in his arms. I take the opportunity to roll out of the way and get to my feet. As much as I want to stay here and be by Raven, I can't. I need to go. I need to find Cassius and figure out what is going on. He would know what the guardians are planning. I want to be able to help Raven the best I can. I may not be able to tell her, but at least if I know what to expect, I can prepare myself better.

Expanding my wings, I bend my knees and launch into the air. I expect Dante to holler and chase after me, but he lets me go. I glance below and catch sight of Raven tipping her head back to stare up at me. She waves her fingers with a pout, and I steel myself and flap my wings harder until the world brightens from night to day and the familiarity of home envelops me.

It's been at least two weeks since I've been to my sanctuary. My whole being buzzes with light and love, helping me believe things are going to be okay. I should've come here sooner. I don't know why I haven't. Raven has been occupied and hasn't been left alone this whole time. I just can't seem to keep away.

I stroll along the glittering path and enter into the pristine building made of heavenly power and the pure goodness of the Higher Power's grace. I freeze in the doorway, spotting Cassius sitting in front of my arched window with a view of a heavenly portal.

He doesn't look at me, keeping his head bowed. I wonder if I should turn around and head back to the Mortal Realm. I thought I could face him, but if he asked me where I have been, I know I can't lie. I don't have it in me.

"Zade," Cassius says without looking at me. "How are the devils? I see you still have your wings."

I release a breath and stroll forward, keeping my gaze trained at the brilliant light Cassius stares at. My heartbeat slows, settling down because of the peace I find here.

"Of course, I have my wings." Annoyance washes through me at his accusation. "I thought you knew me better than to think I would stray from my path. You know that I know my purpose. I am not involved with the devils or Raven. I have only been watching over them. Had you had come to me, you would have known. Where have you been?"

"I'm sorry, Zade. I didn't mean that. It has just been so difficult lately. With everything that we have discovered with Elias, I worry about the state of the universe." Cassius reaches out and pats the spot beside him on the bench. "Come, Zade. I think we have some catching up to do, don't we?"

I join him on the bench and rest my elbows on my knees. "That we do, Cass. The devils know that we know Elias has gone through another lifecycle to start over. With the way the guardians just started attacking, we now face a far worse threat from Hell. I have come here to see if you agree with them. Because I fear the consequences. They aren't as strong as we are. I just watched Azrael get sent to Hell after he was unable to withstand being interrogated by Dante."

Cassius whispers something under his breath. "I feared that would happen. They are all brute force without the strategy they need. I need you to join me and stand by my side to hopefully guide them in the right direction. Can you do that for me, Zade?"

"Are you sure they will listen with me around? I had assumed they thought I've lost my way." I couldn't resist saying it. It still bothers me that he mentioned that he expected me to have lost my wings.

"I assure you they will. Because like you told me, you are keeping watch. You will prove to them that you are following your rightful path." Cassius sits on the bench and stares at me until I look at him. "Right? You will give them the answers they seek?"

All I do is nod my head. I don't know what kind of answers they would need or if I'm really willing to give them to them.

Heaven help me.

"Good. I've missed you being around. It's just so hard these days." Patting my knee, Cassius tries to comfort me in silence, but I'm pretty sure he is the one who needs comforting. Unlike me, who still sees our fallen brethren, Cassius keeps away.

"I understand. But you must have faith that it will get better." I keep my gaze on the window of light. "The Higher Power knows what It is doing." I just wish I knew what It was doing, and what It truly wanted from us.

Cassius gets to his feet and holds his hand out to me, helping me up. He doesn't comment and just shrugs his shoulders. "And we will continue to serve Its will."

A soft knock sounds from the archway behind us, and I stiffen at the presence of Mikail. I don't have to look to know it is the guardian. He has probably been lingering by this entire time. Privacy isn't a thing, even in my own sanctuary. We are all separate entities, but we still can come as one on a spiritual plane, especially in the place that is connected to Heaven and the Mortal Realm.

"Welcome home, Zade. My heart fills with joy and light that you have decided to re-join us." Mikail offers me a smile as he darts his gaze from mine to Cassius's. "I am assuming you have an update on the situation? The guardians are gathering now with more news. They don't want to wait long before they go after the devils again and it's pertinent you know our plan of attack. We need you."

Cassius thins his lips into a line. "Zade won't let Heaven down."

"I will not fail my purpose or fall from my path," I say, clenching my fingers at my side. It feels as if everyone has been waiting for me, and some expected me not to return. It's like they didn't want me to even have a chance to prepare for any of this. But what can I do now?

Mikail leads the way from my sanctuary. Strolling beside me, Cassius stares at the side of my face as if he tries to read my mind. I keep my gaze focused on the pathway ahead of us. The world glows with heavenly light, and I spot dozens of figures gathering nearby. They are near the portal to the Mortal Realm.

"It is with utmost importance that we move quickly." Meri,

Mikail's companion, unfurls her wings. "We need to strike hard and fast before the devils become aware of the situation at hand."

"Zade has agreed to help us with the initial attack. The mortal will trust him, and he will be able to persuade her to come with him. And when we have her, we can assure Hell never gets what it wants. She will be sensible. She has to be." Mikail clasps his hands together and bows his head. "Is everything clear?"

I scrunch my brows in confusion. Nothing is clear. It's as if I've missed everything. And maybe, that's the way that they intended it to be.

"No," I say, peering around the brilliant light radiating from the angelic army. "I need a better explanation. Raven might trust me, but it's not enough. Why would she come with me? I need something to tell her."

Mikail tips his head to the side. "Zade, it is not in our best interest to share all the answers you seek."

Anger burns through me, but Cassius rests his hand on my shoulder and turns me toward him. "Zade will do what it takes. We are the saviors, or have you forgotten our power and strength? It is important that he knows why we are after Raven now. The complete truth."

"What are you talking about, Cassius?" I ask, my heart picking up pace.

"We found Elias's soul." Cassius holds my stare. "The situation is far worse than we could have ever imagined."

My eyes widen with his words. "You found him? Where?"

Unfurling his wings, Cassius shifts on his feet. He turns to the angelic army and says, "Come with me, and I'll show you myself. It's better if you see, so you can prepare."

Prepare for what? I have no idea, and I have a feeling no one will tell me.

"We're counting on you, Zade," Mikail says, squeezing my other shoulder. "All of humanity is."

If only it didn't feel as if they were counting on me to fail and fall. If only it didn't feel as if the path they try to push me on was the wrong one.

Please, Your Grace. Give me your light to find my way.

The world shifts around us as Cassius pulls me into the Mortal Realm and on humanity's plane.

And then I see it.

The brightest, most devastatingly beautiful light. It's not the Higher Power's light I've needed all along. It's Raven's.

Things become clear.

Touching Grace

KASE

RAVEN SITS ON Dante's lap beside me. There are too many devils in such a small room that our soul sparkles with sweat from our heat. It doesn't help that Micah sits within a summoning circle, letting in the rank stench of his kingdom. Raven insisted that we all meet together, and I know that she feels awful for Micah because he took the tether to Hell, so she tries extra hard to include everyone even though it's not necessary. No one will tell her otherwise. Not now, at least.

"I think it's time to relocate Raven again. I don't trust Zade not to give away our location." Dante bounces his feet, giving

Raven a little ride on his lap. The fucker unintentionally turns me on. It's like Raven knows his intent, because she snatches my tail and squeezes like it's a damn thing to brace on.

I grunt and twist my tail around her wrist, dragging her from Dante and onto my lap instead. She wiggles her ass, teasing me even more. If everyone weren't watching us, I'd get up and start banging her right here, right now. Fuck it, I still might.

"I don't think he will," Andre says as he shifts on the edge of the coffee table like he needs to be close to Raven. The horny bastard flares his nostrils, and I'm sure he catches the scent of Raven's desire. So he's probably drooling over mine too. Hmm, maybe I should give him what he wants. Everyone could use a good show to calm their balls down.

"Oh, he so fucking will." Lucian crosses his arms, leaning against the far wall of the apartment like he needs to keep space between himself and Raven. I bet it drives his cock nuts seeing her with me now. I know his ass still plans to fuck her the second he gets, but I'm not going to make it easy. She's my soul next. He's just going to have to wait and learn his lesson for his bullshit. I love punishing the bastard, especially after all the shit he's pulled over the centuries.

Raven tries to slide off my lap, but I don't let her. She gives in and leans back against my chest instead of fighting me. She knows better. Fuck, I know she likes it when I'm in control of her. "Where will we go?" Raven asks, peering at the rest of the devils and then to Dante. "I don't want to hide from Zade. I still need to make him jump. It's more important than ever. Don't you think?"

"What's important is that you stay safe until we find Elias." Micah speaks up from the crackling circle of fire. "We still have plenty of time to work on Zade. Maybe keeping your distance will drive him crazy enough that he will realize how much he wants to be around you."

"I think Micah is right. Look out the window. Zade is close." Andre twirls his finger toward the glowing light, radiating in between the cracks in the curtain. "It's been a while since he showed himself to me."

"Maybe he comes with more answers for us," Raven says, turning to look at me. "I think we should invite him in."

"Only if you go to my room, get your sexy ass undressed, and prepare to corrupt him." I get to my feet with Raven and smack her ass, making her jump. "Use your seductive little mouth on him. Don't let him get away with denying you. I'll hold him down if I have to."

Raven lifts an eyebrow at me. "You are so dirty and psycho, you horny bastard. I love it. Meet me there in five."

Dante play-growls. "You better run, pretty soul. Because I am taking you first."

Squealing, Raven yanks from the hold on my tail and dashes down the hallway. Dante wags his eyebrows at me and winks, following behind her. I hope he's prepared for what he's about to get into. There's no way that if Zade makes it into my room, that he's getting out without having a good time, and I don't need Dante getting jealous.

"Fucking damn it." Lucian glowers from his spot, his envy already getting the best of him. I can tell it's taking all of his will power not to chase after both of them.

If a soft tap didn't sound on the window, I think we all might get into a wrestling match. I know Raven isn't quite ready to take on all of us at once. She has it set in her mind that she needs to fuck each devil individually first before she starts bringing us all together for one hell of an awesome time. It's whatever for me. I could not give a fuck if the others get to claim her for the first time in front of me. I'll help them out. I'm good like that.

"Looks like it won't take much getting him to come in," Andre says, standing up from his spot sitting on the edge of the coffee table. No one says anything as he crosses the room to the glowing light at the window.

Why Zade doesn't use the door and ask to talk to us like a normal fucking person is beyond me. Angels just love their stalkerish behavior. He's lucky Raven is an exhibitionist and loves being watched. It's kind of her thing now.

I straighten my back and crack my knuckles. "Just fucking send him to my window. He can be a perv there and have

Raven invite him in," I say, strolling a couple of feet towards the hallway, hearing Raven and Dante laugh. I wouldn't put it past him to start fucking her without us, and I don't want to miss out on a second of it.

Andre nods his head at the same time as he cracks the curtain open to see Zade at the window. "Go to—"

"Cass is nearby and waiting for me. Someone needs to go after him. Please. It's important," Zade says, cutting Andre off. "The angelic army is waiting for his call."

Lucian growls and summons his fire chain. I guess this solves the issue of inviting him to join us. Andre twists and looks at me, his eyes glowing with his Hell power.

"The two of you go. We need someone in the air." I stride forward and open the front door. Lashing my tail at Zade, I restrain him by the neck and drag him into the apartment. "You're coming with me. Raven wants to talk to you."

Zade locks his hands around my tail. "But—"

I swing my attention to the other devils. "Lucian and Andre, go now. They want a war, so give it to them." I turn to Micah. "Be ready. I want you to round up every damn angel the second they enter Hell. We are going to show them exactly how powerful we truly are."

Lucian, Andre, and Micah all follow my order without question. I lock the wards, ensuring that no other angels can get in. Zade gives up fighting and lets me drag him toward the hallway. But I don't take him directly to Raven. Instead, I smash his back to the wall.

"You better tell me exactly what you're doing here." Red power sizzles across my palms, burning the front of his shirt.

"I've come because I'm being forced into it by Heaven's army. I don't have a choice if I want to stay in good grace." Zade's chest rises and falls with his deep breathing. "Please, let me talk to Raven just for a minute. It's important."

"I don't think she wants to talk right now," I say, smirking as I stare down the hall. "You see, we were about to bang our soul. Me and Dante."

"Oh." Zade flexes his muscles.

I flick my gaze down. "You like the sound of that, don't you? Do you want to watch? You can talk to her while I make her cum. I can't promise she'll talk back."

Zade slowly nods his head. He makes it far too easy. He obviously underestimates his restraint when it comes to Raven, or maybe it's just an excuse to get in because he knows she is his weakness.

"Good," I say, letting go of the front of Zade's shirt. "You might as well just get undressed. You know you're going to end up wanting to participate anyway."

"I can't stay that long." Zade turns his attention toward the living room like he can see angels sneaking up outside. No one's there. None of the heavenly variety is getting through our wards.

I pat his back and push him in the direction of my room, getting him to walk with me. "Sure you can, asshole. Andre and Lucian will give you enough time to at least catch the beginning of the show."

Zade licks his lips, his lust obvious by the bulge growing in his pants. "I don't know. What I have to tell her might..." His words trail off as he catches sight of Raven on my bed, completely naked, with her hands bound above her head.

Fuck. Dante went all out, and I forgot everything that was swirling through my mind.

Zade inhales a soft breath and freezes. "Oh, Heaven."

"Look what the cat dragged in," Dante says, grinning from his spot standing at the side of the bed next to Raven. Opening a chest, Dante reaches inside and pulls out a vibrator. He clicks it on, and the soft sound hums through the air.

"I told this fucker that he could talk to Raven as long as he's cool if we are screwing the Hell into her." I wag my eyebrows at Raven and stick my tongue out at her flicking it quickly. "Is that okay, angel-girl?"

"Kase, come on. What kind of—" Raven releases a loud moan and arches her back as Dante touches the vibrator to her clit.

Her eyes roll back with her pleasure, and I adjust my pants, giving myself some room to pull down the zipper. Because damn. I'm about to bury my face between her thighs.

I kick my pants off and punch Zade in the arm. "Go on and tell her what you have to say. Hurry up." I slide my tail around his back and point with it.

Zade watches Raven in silence, shifting on his feet. He ignores me completely.

I chuckle. "Or you could taste her for a bit. I know she liked it when you did it last time. She told me all about it. It makes us all question if you were actually a pure little bastard."

Raven moans again as Dante teases her with the vibrator. Calling out my name, Raven beckons me with a plea, striking me right in the nuts the way I like. While I like being in control, I also love giving her what she craves. Her pleasure is the most important.

I saunter to the bed and slither my tail up her leg, making her squirm in anticipation. "You want me to fuck you with my tail, don't you, angel-girl?"

She hums in agreement.

"What do you want from Dante?" I prod, teasing her with only the tip of my tail. "You want him to fuck your ass? You know how much he wants to."

"I'll take good care of your sweet ass," Dante teases, grabbing one of her ankles and stretching it up. Using his cock, he gives her a little swat to her ass cheek. "Or do you want to fuck me again? I'm up for a switch, pretty soul." Straightening up,

Dante grabs a strap from the harness he helped me secure to my ceiling. It's technically my room, but most of his collection scatters through the whole apartment, making sure we're fully prepared for anything Raven wants. And lately, it's been trying something new to keep her busy.

"Neither," Raven says, playfully trying to break her leg free from Dante. "I want—"

Arching her back, Raven moans as Zade surprises the fuck out of me by touching Raven's exposed clit with the vibrator Dante left on the bed. I was far too caught up with finding out what she wants from us that I ignored him enough to miss the bastard angel joining us.

"Hell yeah, Zade," Dante says, snatching Raven's other leg. Using the ceiling harness, he secures her above the bed with her legs spread with a support band across her lower back to ease the pressure of her bindings.

Her pussy clenches my tail as Zade uses the vibrator in silence to make her orgasm. Raven's body grips me hard as fuck, and I groan with pleasure, the tightness leaving me panting.

"You want a taste of Heaven, angel-girl?" I ask, stroking my cock with one hand as I slide my tail in and out of her. "Why don't you let Zade discover what helped convince Andre that you were the most incredible woman in the world?"

Dante shakes Zade's shoulder. "You ready for that, asshole? Do you think you can handle this kind of adventure? Because

I'm not sure you can."

Zade swallows, the noise audible over Raven's moans. "If that is something that interests Raven." He's a fucking goner. Whatever he had planned to say is now lost to him as Raven steals his complete attention. Once she gets her sexy hand or mouth around your cock, there is nothing else important.

"Show him how I like it," Raven says, her voice breathless.

Zade follows Dante's silent command and moves toward the head of the bed, leaving me to have my way with Raven's pussy and ass. I use her slick wetness to slip my tail into her ass at the same time I thrust into her, keeping her in place. She gasps, and Dante twists her hair in his fingers and stretches her neck back enough that he can squat just right to glide his cock into her mouth.

I rub my finger over her clit, grinning as she moans, the muffled sound surely vibrating over Dante's cock. Zade unbuttons his pants and pulls his dick out, finally giving in completely instead of watching. Dante wags his eyebrows at me as he pulls his cock from Raven's mouth, and Zade slowly rocks his hips forward like he's nervous about hurting her.

"Give her the whole thing. Our soul doesn't have a gag reflex." Dante smacks Zade on the ass, getting him to thrust deeper and faster, finally giving in and fucking Raven's face how he craves.

Raven continues to moan her pleasure, completely relaxed

and complacent as she submits to us, trusting us to care for her in every way she enjoys. Ecstasy zings through me, and I watch Dante and Zade take turns until Zade's eyes widen and he tenses. Before he can pull back, Dante restrains him to get him to cum in Raven's mouth.

And holy shit.

Her soul beams, the light of her essence so bright that I shield my eyes. Electricity zaps me in the cock, and I grunt with my orgasm, set off by whatever the fuck just happened. Zade didn't open a portal to Heaven, but it sure felt like it was close. My skin stings just a bit and I can't stop my devil form from peeking through. Dante hisses and clicks the quick releases on Raven's restraints. I catch her before she falls to the bed.

"What the fuck was that?" Dante asks, nudging Zade away to give him room to untangle Raven.

"That was way fucking stronger than the time Andre fucked Heaven into her mouth," I say, flopping onto the bed beside Raven. I shift her on her side and pinch her chin, getting her to look at me. "You okay, angel-girl?" I ask, inspecting her rolling eyes as she blinks, trying to orient herself.

"Yeah, I-I think," she says, her words stuttering. "That was weird. It was like...I can't describe it. I felt...like I was out of my body but I wasn't alone. I felt—fuck. I felt complete. I felt like the piece that felt missing suddenly returned to me. It—I think I felt Elias. What the fuck?"

"Heaven help me," Zade whispers, wringing his hands together. "What have I done? Please tell me what to do now. I was so lost in her light that I lost sight."

"What the fuck are you going on about, dickhole? Prayer doesn't work here," Dante snaps, shoving Zade hard enough to get him to show his wings.

Zade's mouth quivers. I swear to fucking-fuck if he cries those angelic tears, I'm going to have to relocate him. Raven has a weakness for seeing the softer sides of dudes, and she'll be a puddle, hugging him and all that shit if he starts.

Ignoring Dante, Zade fixes his pants and grabs Raven's hand. This is a shitshow for after sex, and it pisses me off. My power flickers across my palms. It takes everything in me to chill the fuck out.

"Raven, please. I need you to listen to me. I'm sorry I got caught up in all this. It was never my intent to...partake in sexual acts. I couldn't help myself." Grabbing the sheet, he tries to wrap it around her. All Raven does is clutch the fabric to her chest with wide eyes.

"Dante, grab him," I say, my chest heaving in rage. He's fucking everything up. "Get him out of here now."

Raven presses her palm to Dante's chest. "No, wait. Let him speak."

Zade flaps his wings and flexes his muscles. "Raven, I need you to come with me. It's important. I—"

Snarling, I transform into my devil façade and lunge at Zade. Raven yells and tries to grab me by the tail, but Dante pulls her into his arms protectively. I swipe my claws at Zade, forcing him to scramble away. He unsheathes his heavenly sword, his body glowing with power. The fucking nerve he has to threaten me in my own room.

I whip my tail around his wrist despite burning myself. "You are not taking Raven anywhere. Now tell me why or I will throw you into the pit of Hell."

"Kase," Raven says softly.

I ignore her. "Spit it out now. Last chance."

Zade clenches his jaw, flaring his nostrils. "I need to take her to keep her safe. The guardians found Elias. They—"

"Oh, fuck. What? They found him." Raven whacks Dante's chest, getting him to set her on her feet. "Where? You have to tell us. Please, Zade. Please."

Raven shoves me off of Zade and grabs him, trying to help him to his feet, but he remains frozen, looking at me. I growl in warning, my Hell power buzzing in shocking waves across my skin.

Dante looms over them. "Answer her."

"He's here," Zade finally says. Reaching up, he presses his hand to Raven's stomach. "His soul is here."

What. The. Actual. Fuck.

This can't be.

What he's insinuating...unholy Hell.

Raven gasps and yanks away from him, rushing to Dante's arms. "You're lying! You're a fucking liar! Why would you say something like that?"

Except Zade wouldn't lie.

My mind whirls with a thousand thoughts, and I transform into my human façade and snatch Raven up. Turning to Dante, I say, "Get him out of here. We can't trust him. Go find the others and meet us in my kingdom, okay? Don't tell anyone yet. We need to be sure."

Dante nods once and hauls Zade from the floor. Without waiting for him to leave, I break open a portal to Hell, cracking the apartment's foundation. I should've used the summoning circle, but I'm afraid for once in my damn life.

I need to get Raven out of here.

We have to go into hiding.

Raven can't say anything as I adjust her in my arms and jump into Hell.

7

Soulmate

RAVEN

THIS CAN'T BE happening.

This can't be fucking happening.

My mind whirls as I think the words over and over again. Zade told me I'm pregnant. He said that Elias's soul was inside me. What the actual fuck? It's impossible. What kind of twisted fate is this? I wanted to find Elias. I did not want to have him fucking inside me like this. It ruins everything. I could never be with him like we had before ever again.

I thought I was grieving before, but it's nothing compared to what I'm feeling right now.

"Here, Raven, piss on this." Dante slaps a box down on the

counter beside me.

"No. Zade is lying. Heaven is doing this to fuck with my head. There's no way I could be pregnant and have Elias choosing to be my fucking son. I'm on birth control. You know that. There was no way I was letting Joel knock me up, and it lasts several more months." I cover my face with my hands.

I ended up getting the Depo shot because I knew Joel would've said something if he found the pills. He would have accused me of sleeping around while I was living under his roof while he was taking care of me even though I called off our engagement. It just wasn't worth it.

"Don't make me tickle you until you piss yourself, angel-girl," Kase says, standing in the doorway to our temporary new place in the penthouse room of a condominium tower outside of Angel Canyon. "We need answers. Now. I thought your soul was only shining brighter because of all of our darkness surrounding you constantly. If what Zade says is true, we have to do everything to keep you safe."

My mouth quivers, and my eyes water. I can't even think about this. It hurts me on a soul-deep level. "I'm fucking scared, okay? If I don't take it, I can still believe that Elias is out there somewhere."

Dante kneels on the bathroom floor beside me and wraps his arms around my shoulders. "I know this is hard, Raven. But please. It's important that we know for sure, so we can prepare and handle it."

I don't look at either of them and just stare at my stomach as if I can see Elias's light inside me. But I can't. I also can't help thinking about the weird out-of-body experience I had when I was giving Zade a blow job. It felt as if Elias was near me again, but I just can't believe it was because his soul decided to cycle again through me. I'm sure he will kick the shit out of himself if he ever remembers.

"Raven," Kase says, joining Dante and me. He wraps his fingers around my wrist and pulls my hands from my face. "It's going to be okay no matter what. It doesn't matter in the grand scheme of things how Elias reunites with us. As long as he takes his throne in Hell, things will be as they should. You will not see him as your child any longer. You will see him as your soulmate and a king of Hell." Touching my stomach, he rests his hand on my body for a moment. "This is just a flesh bag."

I scowl at him. I know he's trying to make me feel better, but he has no idea what the hell he's talking about. Whatever human being I make, then push the fuck out of me, will be my child forever. It doesn't matter in this life here or in the next. It will change. The man I knew and loved is gone. He's really, truly gone.

"You are wrong. If I'm having a baby, even if it was once Elias's soul, it will not be him any longer. It'll be my child.

There is no turning back from that. This is not just the fucking body. It is so much more." Tears burn my eyes, and I untangle myself from in between Kase and Dante. "Now, give me some privacy to do this. I don't want you guys hanging around me while I piss on a stick. Please, just wait outside the door."

Dante opens his mouth to argue, but Kase slaps his hand over his lips and hauls him to his feet. I shift on my feet nervously and watch as the two of them enter the suite and shut the door. I can hear them mumbling to each other just outside, but I ignore their quiet discussion.

"I can do this," I say to myself, tearing open the box and pulling out the plastic stick. "This isn't your first pregnancy scare. Remember the last one? You thought Joel knocked you up. At least this isn't that situation."

Thinking about that fucked up time so long ago helps me with my nerves, and I manage to get everything set up to take the test. I know I shouldn't, but I can't help thinking a silent prayer. Not to God. Not to the universe. But to Elias. I don't know who else I can pray to in this moment. Maybe there was a mistake, and the angels were wrong. Please, please, please let them be wrong.

My eyes blur with burning tears, and I can't see anything apart from my sadness clouding my vision. It only takes a minute, and I set the stick down on the counter and wash my hands. Turning on my feet, I stride to the bathroom door and pull it open. Dante and Kase wait anxiously outside. I can't gather my nerve to look at them, so I slide between their two hulking bodies and rush right to the bed and flop onto it. I roll over, cocooning myself in the blankets, and listen as the two of them go into the bathroom.

I hold my breath, listening for any sort of reaction they give. I expect Kase to swear and shatter the mirror or something. I expect Dante to hiss. But silence greets me, and I can't tell if it's good or bad. Whatever that means.

The bed rumbles, and the familiar scent of Hell permeates the air as someone opens a portal in the suite. I keep my head covered, squeezing my eyes shut tightly. I'm even more nervous now, because I haven't seen the other devils since Zade's arrival hours ago.

"Where is she?" Lucian asks, his deep, gruff voice echoing through the suite. "I need to take a good fucking look at her."

I don't move, remaining silent as I lie on the bed. I'm too shocked and confused to face them. I am chicken shit and don't want to face anyone. I just need a moment to think, but I know I can't get one. And I kind of hate myself for feeling as if I need it because I know my devils love me, and they want to be here for me. I just...I don't know. I can't explain it.

"You don't have to explain anything, heathen," Micah says, whispering into my mind. "I will ensure you get some space even if we are all in this room, okay?"

I exhale a long breath. "Can you tell me what the test says? I was too afraid to look, and Kase and Dante haven't given anything away."

Before Micah can respond to me, a hiss sounds through the air. Something crashes, and a thud breaks the heavy silence. I yank the comforter away from my face to watch Micah standing between me and everyone. The cute bastard is taking his job literally. They communicate in the form of monstrous noises and growls, and I can't help wondering if Micah told them telepathically that I requested space. Dante and Kase are known not to give me any. Ever since the one and only time they did when I first met Micah, they refuse to unless I'm with another devil. Right now, I'm a mopey, frightened coward who wants the world just to stop.

I sit upright but keep the blanket around me. "Micah, it's okay. I don't want you guys fighting."

"But you asked for breathing room, and they want to smother you," Micah argues, gathering his power in his palms, managing to expand the makeshift summoning circle even more.

"I want to do more than smother her. I want to fucking get a reading on her soul." Lucian whips his fire chain at Micah, using Micah's slight distraction of talking to me against him. "I think those bastards are lying."

"The test is positive, asshole." Kase growls with his words.

I jerk my attention to him and clutch my stomach. "What?"

Like my voice drenches the heat of the devils in ice water, they cool off and turn away from each other to stare at me.

"So, it's true. I *am* pregnant." Fuck me.

Holy fuck.

Holy shit.

I don't know what to think or how to feel about any of this. I knew I wasn't prepared before. I also had a small amount of hope that it wasn't true. But now? Oh, God. What do I do now? I don't know how to be a mom. I don't think raising a kid in Hell is something that I should do. Like, how the heck am I going to raise this baby with my devils? How do I tell it when it grows up that his biological father is actually him? This is twisted. Like why? Why me? I was fully set on just living my life, having a good time, and breaking some angels, and then helping the universe.

This changes everything. It's not just my soul I truly have to worry about.

"I can't do this." The words hurt me to say out loud, but there has to be another way. Can I restart a soul cycle? This really stabs me in my morals. I had never thought about any of this.

Shuffling forward, Andre comes to me first. He sits beside me and takes my hand. "Yes, you can, little hellion. You are the strongest soul I know. You tame devils and break angels. You give light to darkness. This will be amazing. I'm so happy to stand by your side through all of this and raise your spawn."

His words startle a laugh out of me, and I gasp. My laughter quickly turns into a sobbing fit. This is crazy. This is beyond crazy. Andre did not just tell me that he wanted to raise my spawn with me. Spawn. I guess it's better than if one of the devils actually knocked me up. I couldn't imagine what kind of outcome that would have.

"He's right, angel-girl. You're going to fucking be an amazing mother to this dumbass. He's lucky since he just had to go and mess everything up all over again. I'm sure you won't let me remind him." Kase sits on my other side and pokes the side of my stomach with his finger. Leaning closer, he lifts up my shirt and presses his hot lips to my skin. "Do you hear that, Jizz Master? I get to be your daddy now."

Jesus. I don't even know how to respond to that.

"You better fucking hope you don't turn out to be a girl," Dante says, kneeling in front of me and spreading my legs so he can get close as well. "If you are—"

"You don't have to do this, Raven," Lucian says, speaking up. He strides closer and narrows his eyes at me. "There are ways to start another cycle. I'm sure you were aware of them. The problem is that it's not a guarantee. The Higher Power's made things uncertain."

I furrow my brows and twist to look at Kase and then Andre.

I think I understand what Lucian is insinuating, but it sounds like the other devils don't consider it.

"The risk might not be worth it. With Elias's soul here, we know exactly where it is. Starting a new cycle could lead to us losing him. It could mean we never get him. I don't think we should take the chance," Micah says, his voice soft as if he's afraid to say the words.

"We could always kidnap Zade and have him relocate him into a new host." Dante's jaw twitches with his words.

"Or we can just restart them together. We already know that Raven struggles with the situation and having Elias reborn while she remains the same." Lucian rubs his hand over his head and tips his face up towards the ceiling to stare. I know he can't look at me when he says the words. Why? I don't really know. But what he says? That might be a viable option.

"No fucking way," Dante and Kase say in unison.

"Why? Are you afraid that all of this was a mistake, and her next cycle could lead her to be in my arms only?" Fire lights Lucian's eyes, and he clenches and unclenches his fingers.

Shit. Everyone's getting worked up, and all I want to do is curl in a ball and take a nap now. I want to wake up and find out that this was all just a fucked-up dream.

"It might be the best way." Andre drapes his muscular arm over my shoulders, pulling me into a side.

Kase growls. "My answer is still fucking no."

"A fucking savior or guardian could swoop in and take them both from us. It's not worth it. I'm not losing Raven." Dante reaches out and snatches me from between Kase and Andre. Lifting me up, he holds his wings around me protectively. "I will take her from all of you to ensure it. Don't fuck with me. You will regret it."

"Dante," I say, brushing my lips to the crook of his neck. "Please don't do this. I know that you love me, and you want to do what you feel is right, but in the end, the decision is mine and mine alone to make."

My chest clenches with my words. I'm not saying that my devils' opinions don't matter, because they absolutely do, but I need to be the one to really think this through. It's my soul. Elias is one of the loves of my life. Everything I have counts on the relationships I want with the devils.

"You infuriating pretty soul," Dante mutters, adjusting me in his arms. "You know it's more than love. I am fucking obsessed with you. I will die without you. My cock will be a limp, unused piece of man meat if you choose to leave me."

"I'm sure you and Kase can keep each other busy if I do decide to try this shit again," I tease, patting his cheek. I shudder at my words. Starting over? How will I ever do it? I already don't remember my past life. They wouldn't be the only ones losing me. I would be losing myself.

"No one has to make any decisions right now." Andre expands his wings and blows a gust of hot air in our direction. "We have time. You never know what will happen and if a soul will take to her as a host or if another soul will overpower it. You know how it goes."

What? This is all so fucking complicated. I want to ask more about what he means, but I'm exhausted trying to sort through this bomb of information.

"That's absolutely true," Micah says, twirling his fingers and making the fire ring around him grow and retreat with his movements. "Especially if this was not in the plan of the Higher Power."

This is too much. My brain shuts down, and I just rest my cheek to Dante's shoulder and close my eyes.

"I think this is enough talk about souls," Dante says as he adjusts to cradle me like a blushing bride. "Raven has been through a lot, and I was unable to give her the proper aftercare she needed from me earlier."

"Yeah, her mental health is fragile right now with everything. So, get out. Go do something productive. We'll call you if Raven needs anything." Kase flicks his fingers, motioning toward the other devils to leave.

Before anyone can argue, I hold up my hands. "Wait. I don't want anyone to go yet. I just want you all to sit around me. Maybe tolerate one of my favorite shows. I just don't want to talk about you know what." I wiggle in Dante's arms until he sets me down. "Can you all do that for me? Just be here while I process everything and think things through?"

"I don't know, Ray," Lucian says, sharpening his features. "Will you let me bang you first? I have the sudden need to find out if I can push that soul out with my darkness or maybe just add to it. Everybody always feared the idea of the anti-Christ."

I grimace. "You did not just suggest that you want to knock me up. I don't exactly see you as dad material."

"Then let me just pretend to be your daddy. You know I love to make bad girls cum. You need to be punished for all the teasing you do. I'll take care of you how you need." This fucking bastard. He loves pushing boundaries and being absolutely inappropriate. Why do I like it?

"There's no fucking way I'm being your Little unless you call me princess, and instead of punishing me, you reward me for behaving." I grin with my words, a new lightness easing the weight seemingly crushing me.

"Like you could ever be good." Lucian summons hellfire in his palm. "I mean, you can't resist being bad."

I stroll closer to him and grab the front of his shirt. "You know what? I'll consider it if you can behave for once and keep your mouth shut unless it's to say something either really sexy or really sweet. If you say something like the asshole you are, then no. What do you say? Is it a deal?"

Lucian flares his nostrils at the mention of a deal. I know he can't resist. "It's a deal as long as you sit on my lap. I can't be the only one to be tortured."

I shrug my shoulders with a smile. "Oh, so you think that you will be torturing me like that? Ha. It's a deal." I turn to the others. "Whoever moves the couch close enough for us to be next to Micah can sit next to me."

Kase, Dante, and Andre all race and lift up the couch, throwing it in Micah's direction. I laugh and cheer at the competition, letting them fill me up with love and adoration.

Maybe things won't be as bad as I think they will be. Maybe I will get through this. It's all I can hope for. Because this is the life I want. I want to be with my devils. I want the life I choose.

It's in this moment that I realize that this is going to happen. I can't go through another cycle.

I will fight for everything I have now.

I will always be Raven Rose.

8

Familial Support

RAVEN

"I HAVE A surprise for you," Lucian says, holding my hand as we stroll together toward the bar.

I peek around in nervousness. I didn't expect to leave the hotel suite, but the devils all swore that this area was protected. There are only two angels that can get in and out, and they are both my mark. I don't know if Zade or Cassius will ever show their faces, but I can't just sit around in hiding. It's more important than ever to break them.

"I hate surprises." Grabbing his hand, I make Lucian touch my stomach. It doesn't feel any different, and according to Dante, I'm probably only a couple of weeks along, but I can't help thinking about Elias's soul inside me. "And this unexpected craziness solidifies my hatred."

Lucian raises an eyebrow. "Fucking fine. I'll tell you. We came here because Tamia is ready to return to the Mortal Realm."

Oh, fuck. I don't know if I want to deal with this right now. To me, it could be a completely different person. Actually, she is different. She's no longer human. She's a demon and now part of Hell's army.

"Am I supposed to be happy?" I don't mean to sound ungrateful because Lucian saved my cousin from eternal torment. I just—I'm confused. I don't know how to feel or how to deal with any of this anymore. I wasn't kidding when I said that it was becoming too much. It was one thing to make an angel fall for me so I could seduce them. It's a whole other thing to have to face a war I never wanted to be a part of or have my family be a part of it too.

"No, you're supposed to be a brat and smack me or some shit." Lucian's eyes light with fire, and he grabs his cock and gives it a shake through his pants. "Right here. Hit me as hard as you can. Show me how fucking pissed off you are that I dragged your cousin into this. That way we can fucking move past it and keep going. I know you're upset right now, but in the long run, I bet you're going to get on your knees and thank me in the best way you can. Having Tamia on Hell's team means that you will never lose her to Heaven."

Why does he make sense? I shouldn't want my cousin, who also used to be my best friend before Joel ruined it, to have gone to Hell. But it makes me feel a bit better that we kind of are going together. Something I've never really thought about.

I sidestep and cut Lucian off, placing my hands on his taut chest. He nearly plows me over, not expecting me to try to block his path before we enter the bar. I yelp and clutch on to him. He sneaks his arms around my waist and pulls me flush against him until our bodies rub against each other.

"You're right. But I swear you better not tell anyone that I said as much," I say, narrowing my eyes. "And thank you. I'm not sure if I have done that yet, but I do appreciate what you've done and what you're trying to do."

Lucian's face softens, and he offers me a handsome smile. "I love the sound of that. It's not often someone thanks me. Say it again. Why don't you show me how thankful you are?"

This bastard. I swear he just loves making me regret every-thing in our budding relationship.

I press my lips into a line, trying not to react to his comment. Instead, I raise my hands to his cheeks, cup his face, and drag him closer to kiss him. But I don't do it for long. I only do it to make him crave me more, and then I pull away and punch him in the stomach. He growls and tries to grab me by the hair, and I slap him right on his hard-on and spin on my feet, dashing away. Andre opens his arms for me as he stands in the doorway to the bar like he expected me to do something like this.

I laugh and jump up, letting him engulf me in his wings. "I was going to totally suck your dick for being sweet and then you had to go ruin it," I say, peeking out from Andre's wings at Lucian as he shows me a glimpse of his devil façade. "Now I'm just going to have to take Andre into the bathroom or something. Or maybe under the table. I have to see how dirty it is. I never know with these demon hangouts. Some of the fuckers are disgusting."

Lucian rushes us, and Andre throws a knife at him getting him in the shoulder. Play-fighting for them always leaves blood somewhere, but at least I know Lucian won't try to hurt Andre with me in his arms. As for Andre stabbing Lucian like that, I'm sure he deserved it for something or another. Plus, I know he likes that kind of bullshit.

"You better hustle, Andre. Lucian's horny and getting impatient. I gave him permission to take what he wants if he can manage it. So don't let him catch me right here." I kiss the skin below his ear. "And who knows, maybe I'm not just playing around about rewarding you for being my hero."

Andre groans with a moan of desire and hauls ass inside. He doesn't go to one of the booths like I expect and instead carries me through the crowded bar and toward the back.

"If I catch you, you're going to be on your fucking knees,

Andre. Don't think that you're going to use your lust against me. I have the same lust power as you. In more ways than you realize, except I can control mine." Lucian's voice echoes through the air from behind us.

"You better not be saying what I think you're saying," I call out. Because damn. It's already a marathon sleeping with Andre because he just can't help himself, and his cock engorges itself and doesn't let me go until he's had his fill of my desire.

"You're going to find out very fucking soon, Raven." A burst of fire sparkles against the wall next to the door leading to the kitchen. Lucian laughs from behind us, and my whole body buzzes with sudden lust.

Ah, Hell. Lucian is setting Andre off. I bet he's doing it on purpose. Once Andre gets started, it's difficult for him to stop, and he is willing to switch into a more submissive position just to participate and get his hunger for lust and desire in control.

"Keep it together, Andre. Your fucking pheromones are starting to turn me on. If they turn me on, you know that the whole place will be affected. Do you really want to start an orgy here? I mean, look around. It's like Hell. It's not a good show." I wiggle and pat his chest. "Just let me down and go splash some cold water or something on your face."

Andre listens to me and sets me down, rubbing himself through his pants. "I'm sorry, little hellion. I'm just…"

"You don't have to explain anything. Just go into the bathroom for a second. I'll meet you in there." I give him a soft kiss and turn around, bracing myself for Lucian to lunge at me. But he stands twenty feet away and just stares at me and Andre. He's not stupid. I bet he realizes what he's done. For the first time ever, he doesn't push the boundaries. He only likes to do it with me and not with the other devils. Maybe it's an unsaid rule or something, but I appreciate it.

"Andre, your boyfriend is here. Can you sense him? I think he's out back." Lucian's words snap me out of my thoughts. I guess I was wrong as to why he stopped chasing us. Maybe he wasn't certain if Andre would try to take me out back or something.

"Take Raven to one of the booths. I'll go scare him away," Andre says, nudging me toward Lucian.

I shake my head. "No, just leave him out there. It drives him crazy if we don't pay him any attention. You know this."

Glass shatters, drawing my attention away from Andre, and I spot Gia at the bar, smashing another glass over a man's head. "Get out of my bar before you end up in pieces, you fucking bastard. I can see you holding this human hostage from a mile away. You don't belong in this realm anymore. Leave. That guy's soul is mine."

My chest tightens at her words. The guy is not a demon. But he's not an angel either. I can't see what she's talking about, but it's not the first time I've encountered a ghost possessing someone. A fucking ghost possessed me. I can't help feeling uneasy just seeing how he sits there cupping a glass between his hands.

"You heard the boss," Tamia says, popping her head up from behind the bar. "Don't make me escort you out. You won't have a body to hold onto. Exorcisms are my specialty."

"Oh, God," I whisper, regretting my words immediately.

I swear every demon in the bar looks at me as if I just tried to summon the angelic army even though I was just shocked at seeing Tamia in this realm again. The man at the bar takes the opportunity to leave without fighting, and I watch him go.

He hovers in the doorway for just a second, his eyes meeting mine, and a wave of hurt crashes over me.

"Ray? Oh shit. You're here." Tamia swipes the shards of glass left on the counter from Gia and collects them into a bar towel. She drops them in the trash and rushes out from behind the bar and toward me. "Lucian, you didn't tell me you were bringing her by."

I raise my hands, getting her to stop. "Please give me space. Don't touch me."

Tamia's face falls as if my rejection hurts her on a deep level. I wish I could pretend that she didn't shoot Elias, but I can't. And I grow emotional by the second. I want to yell at her. I want to scream. The last thing I want to do is to step into her arms for a hug.

Lucian steps between us and blocks my view of Tamia. I flick in between his shoulder blades because he intercepted me and stopped me from getting riled up. It's like he knew I was going to start shit.

"Give Raven a moment," Lucian says, reaching behind him to try to snatch my fingers to stop me from flicking him again. "It's been a rough morning for us. She found out that Elias impregnated her. So, you can understand why she's upset, all things considered."

This time, I whack him with my open palm upside the head. I can't believe he just told her that. No one should know unless I tell them. The last thing I need is for word to spread among the demons too.

Tamia gasps and leans over to peer at me from in front of Lucian. "What? Are you serious? I don't understand."

My anger gets the best of me and I shove Lucian in the side to confront my cousin. Heat burns over my skin with my fury.

"How can you not fucking understand? Elias and I had unprotected sex, and my birth control failed." I huff a breath, clenching my fingers, stabbing my nails into my palms. "What's worse is that you fucking killed him. You let an angel possess you and ruined everything. He would be on his throne and a king in Hell if it weren't for you. You had no right to do what you did. Why did you even do it?"

Tamia doesn't respond to me and instead looks to Lucian

like she expects him to answer for her. It only pisses me off even more.

"Tell me. Give me a reason why I shouldn't demand that Lucian throw you back down into Hell to suffer in the pits for what you've done. Because what I see is him doing me a favor, and one I didn't ask for." My vision darkens as a hostile, intoxicating feeling courses through me. It's the same feeling that I had punishing souls in Micah's kingdom.

Tamia takes a couple of steps back, and her human figure starts to morph. And unholy fucking Hell. The once beautiful woman that I knew turns into a demon before my eyes. It solidifies the fact that she is no longer my relative. She is in fact a servant of Hell.

I refuse to turn my eyes away from her and study her new features. A dainty crown of horns protrudes from her forehead. The sharp points look as if they are dipped in blood. Glowing veins twine around her neck and travel down her arms and wrap around her wrist. Two-inch-long claws cut through her fingertips, and I notice an unsettling tint to her skin as if she might glow in the dark. It's greenish yet neon.

Parting her lips with her grimace, Tamia flashes a double set of fangs. I try not to react to her change in appearance, but I can't help it. A part of me fears her now. An even bigger part regrets my actions. She didn't choose this. She's in this position because of me. The angels would have never gone after her if she wasn't my cousin. But still, I need to know why.

"I'm sorry. I didn't mean what I just said. I'm overwhelmed and scared out of my mind," I whisper, wringing my hands together. "I'm so sorry you're like this now. I wish you weren't in this position."

Tamia surprises me by opening her arms and engulfing me in a hug. Lucian growls and tries to snatch me back, but I stomp on his foot and hold my cousin tighter. She smells of burnt roses and something spicy like pepper, but it's not bad. Lucian obviously gave her more power than other demons because of me. She didn't have to earn her place to come to the Mortal Realm.

"I'm sorry too. I swear, Ray. I was tricked into letting the angel possess me. They showed me horrible things and convinced me that you were in trouble. They told me that Elias was purposely going to damn you and that you would be a slave for all eternity in Hell. They told me if I allowed them to take my body and sacrifice myself, we would both go to Heaven." Tamia's voice cracks, the new softness reminding me of her growing up.

"Except they didn't realize that I would push you into Hell," I say, the memory flooding me with wild, dark emotions.

"I don't blame you for doing that. I would've done it myself if I had control. I deserved it." Tamia eases away and meets my gaze, her demon façade now hidden again. "I want to make things up to you. I want to try to rebuild what we had. I miss you. I can't imagine spending eternity without you, and I will do anything I can to see to it that you get what you want."

I had no idea how much I want that until she says it out loud. I have missed her too. I wish I could go back and change things, but all I can do now is try to manage how things are in our future. Now that I have a new awareness of what's going on, I can prepare and help Tamia prepare.

I slowly bob my head as my thoughts click together. I wonder if she can help me in Purgatory. Maybe she can be my right hand. I would love it and love knowing that she didn't go to Hell just because of my anger. Maybe this was in the plan all along.

"You have nothing to make up for," I say, peering around the bar. "And I want to start over. I want to have you in my life. I could use your support right now." I touch my hand to my stomach. "I'm so fucking freaked out."

Tamia hugs me again. "I'm here for you. Anything you need, I will see to it that it gets done. I will fuck up the entire angelic army if they even try to touch you."

I laugh in exasperation and shake my head. "I don't want you going anywhere near those bastards. I don't trust them."

"You are not going to start treating me as if we're kids again, are you? Do I need to flash my freaky-ass horns again? Because I'm pretty sure that you're the one who needs to stay away from those assholes." Tamia shivers as she shows me her crown of horns once again. "Like that bastard outside. He's such a creep."

I cock my head and stare over my shoulder at the glowing light coming in through the kitchen window. "That's not Zade," I say, looking at Lucian. "That's your fucking brother."

Growling, Lucian says, "Go to Andre. I'll be right back."

Lucian storms away, but I race after him, grabbing onto the back of his shirt to keep up. He tries to spin to get me to stop, but I hold on tighter and force him to slow down.

"I said go to Andre," Lucian says, scowling at me.

"No, I'm going with you. I know you'll protect me." I say what I do to get under his skin. It makes him more confident in his power. And I'm right. I know he'll protect me. He's fucking Satan, after all. "I want to see him. I want to confront him, and I know you will help me get answers. I've been waiting for this moment. You were not going to leave me out."

"You know I'm never going to fucking call you princess with this kind of behavior, Ray," Lucian mutters. He grabs my hand and squeezes my fingers far more tightly than necessary. But I don't react.

Instead, I wiggle my free hand. "Well, I don't give a fuck about that. Give me a damn fire chain. Now. I'm going to whip Cass-hole until he breaks."

"So aggressive. I love it." Lucian summons a fire chain and

holds it out to me. "I want you to go out front, and I'll go around back and grab him. Then you can do whatever the hell makes you feel better. Who knows? Maybe he will break. He is afraid enough."

"Wait, do you want me to go out alone? Are you fucking kidding me? What if he tries to fly away with me?" I hate how my tough-ass attitude suddenly dwindles, and I slow my pace. Even with the fire whip, I don't feel as if I can protect myself from someone like Cassius. All he can see is what he thinks is supposed to happen and nothing else. He probably is losing his shit, knowing that I'm pregnant.

"What happened to my tough little princess?" Lucian grabs my chin and leans in, staring deep into my eyes. "Don't let an angelic bastard intimidate you. He will not grab you. I bet he will only try to convince you to do the right thing." Making a face, Lucian tries to sound like Cassius and makes fun of him. "Which we all know you're too stubborn to listen to anybody, but especially someone who's trying to boss you around. So, toughen up, get that whip ready, and distract him. If you don't, it'll be me who breaks the bastard. And I know you'll be disappointed that you don't get to participate in the fun."

It's like he knows me on a deep level that I don't want to admit is there. Lucian is right. I don't want him to do anything to Cassius. I want to be the one that gets him to jump from grace. If he falls from Heaven, it'll be because either I pushed him or because he jumped. He will swallow his damn pride and realize that I will take Purgatory, and he will be a fucking king of Hell even if it's the last thing I do as a mortal.

Inhaling a deep breath, I straighten my shoulders and stride forward toward the door. Lucian smacks my ass, and I startle at the sting, jerking around and lashing the fire chain at him. He hops out of my way with a laugh and rushes toward the back of the bar. I meet Andre's gaze as he stands next to my cousin. He's been quiet this whole time, that it was easy to lose focus on him. But now that I see him, I feel a lot better. He's watching me, and he will fight for me if Cassius tries anything.

I curl and uncurl my fingers at him. "Will you come stand by the door? Don't tell Lucian. But I am a little nervous."

Andre nods and offers me a smile. "I was going to already. I know you can handle yourself, but I will always be your backup in case."

"I'll be here too," Tamia says, following behind Andre.

I use their presence to fill me with strength and turn toward the door, where I can still see Cassius and his heavenly glow. I do hope I wasn't wrong and that it is him. Because if it's a guardian...

I spot the familiar bastard, and my nerves turn into a wave of rage. It's like my feet take on a mind of their own and rush me outside. I don't look around for other angels. All I do is glower at Cassius as he stands out in the open at the end of the parking lot.

He uses his heavenly power and turns the world around me into shadows as he shifts me into an alternative realm between somewhere. I don't really know. It's not the first time he's done this, but I know he does it to try to keep the devils away long enough for a moment of my time.

"I know Lucifer is coming around back. I can also sense Andre right inside. So, I'll make this quick, Raven. I know you rejected Zade and refused to go with him, so I'm going to give you a chance to come with me. If you do that, I promise you that you will be safe. No one will hurt you, and no one else has to be hurt because of you." Cassius unfurls his wings and spreads them out wide, the bright white of his feathers sparkling even without any light around set them aglow.

I clutch the fire whip tighter. "People did not get hurt because of me. They got hurt because of you and because of your fucking army. Don't you dare try to shift the blame to me."

Cassius scrunches his nose. "Had you just—"

Snapping his mouth shut, Cassius jerks around to see Lucian rounding the corner. I use his distraction against him and rush forward, lashing the fire chain at the same time as I close the distance. He doesn't even get the chance to block me. The fire chain slashes across one of his wings, and he hollers in pain.

Lucian doesn't even have to close the space to restrain him.

Jumping on his back, I knock Cassius to the pavement and shove my hands between his shoulders, pinning him down. My hands sting as they touch his feathers, and he automatically uses his heavenly power to make them disappear.

He freezes. "Raven, get off me. I don't want to hurt you."

Darkness rises through me, and it feels as if I lose complete control of my body.

There's no way I will let Cassius hurt me. I don't even give him the chance to try because I take the chain and wind it once around his neck, making him holler again.

"I'm done waiting for you to see reason, you fucker," I say, tightening the chain even more. "It's time for you to claim your throne."

A bright flash of heavenly light bursts through the air, and Lucian roars. My whole body lights up, starting from my belly and working its way outward until it breaks the strange shadows of the realm, sending us back to the mortal plane.

I fall away from Cassius, only to be dragged back by Lucian. Hopping to his feet, Cassius catches his neck and jerks around, looking from my face and down to my stomach.

"Oh, Heaven. I have been blessed." Cassius steps forward a foot as if he's entranced by the bright glow. "Elias, you have done the Higher Power's good work helping me. You will get what you've always desired. I promise."

Shock leaves me speechless as he speaks to my stomach as if

Elias can hear him. I don't even get a chance to react before Lucian lifts me up, his skin burning from touching me, but he doesn't let go.

Cassius smiles, the gesture creepier than I expect it to be. And then he disappears.

So does my light.

I allow Lucian's darkness to consume me.

Angel Baby

RAVEN

"YOU'RE LUCKY I can't get to your annoying ass, Elias. Because all I want to do is remind you of your fucking place. You can't be pulling that angelic shit. You are on team Hell." Lucian points at my stomach, glaring as if he can see Elias.

It weirds me out, so I swing my hand and smack him upside the head. Lucian snatches my wrist and pulls me closer, touching his palm to my stomach. This time, the otherworldly light doesn't burst free. He doesn't get burned like he did before.

"That's better, dipshit," he mutters, tightening his jaw. "Though I did enjoy how you gave Cassius hope. I can't wait to fucking steal it away from him. We can use this."

I comb my fingers through my hair and pull it out of my face. I don't know how much longer I can take having Lucian have a conversation with my stomach as if Elias can respond.

"That's enough. Can you talk to me and not my stomach? I want you to tell me what the hell happened and what Cassius thinks." I shuffle back and get him to remove his hand from my middle.

"He obviously thinks the fact you were radiating heavenly light might change things." Lucian rubs his hand over his head.

"Yeah, it could be a bit inconvenient if we suddenly can't touch you comfortably." Dante's voice comes from the doorway of the hotel suite.

Opening his arms, Dante silently asks me to go to him. I rush from Lucian and close the space to Dante and let him engulf me in his arms.

"You took forever."

"Well, since we can't use you as bait, it takes a bit of time to set the angel traps. But they're done now." Dante pulls me up higher until our lips meet. Kissing me softly, he savors my mouth for a moment. "Plus, we had to also find you an obstetrician. Kase is getting things set up now."

"Why do you guys have to go and make shit so real?" I ask, scrunching my nose. "Like, are you bringing someone in? Do I get to pick? Is it one of your contracted souls?" A million questions run through my mind. I don't know how I would feel if it was one of their contracted souls. A lot of them are really fucking awful, and I kind of don't want someone like that near my vagina. I mean, sure, they are the devils, but they are not anywhere near as horrible as some of the mortal souls. They just are here for balance and punishment for others' wrongdoings.

"Fuck no. We are getting you the best of the best. No deals involved." Dante sets me on my feet, but he doesn't let me go. "And you're not just getting one doctor. You're going to have a team. You can fire anyone if you are uncomfortable with them."

I release a breath in relief. I didn't realize how worried I was, thinking that I was going to get stuck with someone I disliked. I should've known better than that. My devils love me too much to torture me in a bad way.

I open my mouth to thank him, but the balcony door flies open, and Zade tumbles in, rolling across the floor until he smacks into the bed. Andre stands tall in the doorway, filling the frame. His eyes light with fire, and he heaves a couple of deep breaths.

What the actual fuck? What is he doing bringing Zade here? I thought we decided to keep a bit of distance from him and definitely not let him know where we are at now.

"Andre? What is this about?" I shuffle forward, and Dante

remains right on my heels, his chest touching my back. "Why is Zade here?"

"I thought I would be good with letting him make up his mind and finally join us, but I am not. I can't risk him doing something regrettable. I don't trust that he won't try to break our wards to come for you. So I brought him here. He's yours now. No more waiting for him to make the choice to take his throne." Andre folds his wings and closes the balcony door. "He will be your prisoner."

"My prisoner? Oh, no. He's *your* prisoner. I can't just keep him locked up here. It doesn't feel right to me. He'll hate me." I shuffle closer to Zade and kneel beside him as he remains on the floor.

It's now that I realize he's been bound. His wings are damaged, and it looks like he and Andre got into a fight.

It took everything in me to keep my anger in check. This is not like Andre to do something so rash without consulting me. I wonder what has gotten into him.

"There's no way he could ever hate you," Andre says, towering over me.

I ignore him and touch my fingers to the back of Zade's head, combing my finger softly through his blond hair. "Zade, are you okay? How badly are you hurt?"

"He's fine." Andre growls with his words. "I only roughed him up enough to bring him here. He was making it difficult."

"Of course, he was making it difficult!" I snap, whipping my head up to look at him. "He's being forced off the path that he thinks is where he should be. You shouldn't have done this. I want you to let him go."

"No." Andre flexes his muscles, steeling himself.

I grimace in annoyance. "Andre—"

"Raven, I think Andre was right in his decision to bring Zade here." Lucian moves closer and stands next to Andre. Is he really doing this?

"I'm afraid I have to agree, pretty soul. You are in a fragile state, and I know that you want us to treat you as if you're made of steel, but the fact is, you are made of flesh and bone. It's not your fault. We don't think you're any less tough, but you need to think things through. It is possible that Elias might be connected to Heaven right now. There's no other explanation as to why you were glowing like a damn angel."

I can't believe they are all teaming up. They are totally doing the whole majority rules thing. The only way they will let Zade go is if maybe I can convince Kase and Micah to side with me. Unfortunately, I don't see that happening. I don't know if it's worth the argument or fight.

"Are you sure about that?" I ask, continuing to comb my fingers into Zade's soft hair as if it will give me the strength to keep my cool. "Do you think they're right, Zade?"

He doesn't respond to me, keeping his cheek pressed against

the floor. Seeing him like this hurts me on a deep-seated level. I want to stand up for him, not against my devils. I don't know who I want to face in regards to Zade, but everything just seems so unfair. Why does it have to be like this? Things would've been fine if the guardians would've just left me the hell alone. I almost pray in silence for an answer, but the thought vanishes.

I inhale and exhale a long breath and turn to my devils. "I need you guys to give me some time alone with Zade. I know you're all riled up and shit, but he's not going to talk to me with you here. And I really want to talk to him."

Andre looks ready to argue, and so does Lucian, for that matter, but Dante grabs them both by the back of their shirts and yanks them away.

"We will be next door. All you have to do is holler," Dante says. "But don't take too long. Kase should be coming any minute, and we desperately want you to have an exam with the obstetrician."

I only nod instead of responding to him. I remain with Zade on the floor until the three devils leave the suite and head to the one joined with ours with only a door separating it. I wait for a moment, seeing if Zade will turn over or look at me, but he doesn't. I gather my nerves and nudge him until he finally rolls over. I manage to get the Hell bindings off of him without burning myself, and they vanish before they hit the floor. I hover over Zade and touch his split lip with my fingers, watching him wince in pain.

"I'm so sorry." I don't know what else to say.

He looks so defeated with his blue eyes shining with unshed tears. Blinking a few times, he clears his vision. The second our eyes meet, something changes in his expression. His features soften, and he slowly reaches up and caresses his knuckles to my cheek.

"You're so beautiful," Zade says, his words just a whisper of a breath. "Andre was right. I should be here. I need to be here with you. It's the only way I can guarantee you're safe."

Stretching up, Zade surprises me with a sweet kiss, his lips tasting tangy with blood, but I don't pull back. I practically attack his mouth with my own, deepening our kiss and sliding my tongue in his mouth. He reacts with surprising passion and pulls me flush against him, grabbing my ass in the process.

If I didn't know any better, I'd think he had already jumped from Heaven.

But he hasn't. His wings keep flickering in and out of existence as he grinds me against him, letting me feel the hardness of his cock.

"I want you," I whisper, keeping my voice low as if I'm afraid he will automatically reject me for saying such a thing.

"You do?" Zade asks. He sucks in a few breaths and searches my eyes like he will find the answers he seeks within my gaze.

I nod my head and lick my lips. "So much. I don't know

what it is about us in this moment, but I feel as if I need you. I crave you. It hurts me to even think about you rejecting me. I know I shouldn't push you, but I want to so badly."

Zade groans, the husky rasp of his voice vibrating through me. "Push me. Break me. I'm tired of resisting. I'm tired of straddling the line that my whole being has already crossed, even if I haven't on this physical plane. So push me. Show me what you want from me."

My heart races at the thought of yanking his shirt over his head and brushing my lips to his taut chest, working my way down to suck his cock into my mouth like I had done before. My mouth waters at just the thought, because the last time he came in my mouth, it was if I was having an out-of-body experience. And he tasted so incredible. Even better than he smells. It's strange and exciting.

"Are you sure? This could be it for you. Do you think it's worth it?" I hate asking because I don't want to know the answer. I don't want to know whether he thinks I'm worth it or not. But I have to put the words out there. It needs to be said.

"You're the only thing worth anything to me right now." Zade flips me over and bends down, drawing his tongue over my neck until he reaches my ear and sucks my lobe into his mouth. "I love you, Raven. You have given me a gift that I never knew I wanted. You've always been so caring. You even let me see Andre when you didn't have to. You are the most perfect, pure, balanced soul in the entire universe."

I smile at his words, letting them fill me up with warmth and excitement. His light entangles with mine in a world that seems to fade away until it's only me and Zade. His wings press the ground beside me, and I can't help running my fingers over the glittering feathers. I expect my hands to burn, but they don't. I thought that maybe I still couldn't touch something so heavenly because I burned myself on Cassius, but I think that was different. He might have done that on purpose to keep me from hurting him. But Zade? I've never felt anything like his wings before. They're soft and light as if I caress a cool mist, but my fingers remain dry. It's unbelievable. Miraculous even.

"How is this possible?" I ask, unable to resist voicing the questions running through my mind. "Your wings still glow with heavenly light, but I can touch them as I touch Dante's. Do you think you've abandoned grace?"

He shakes his head, easing away to look into my eyes. I search his face, my stare drinking in Lucian's mark still branded on his cheek from when I slapped him weeks ago. It glows, but it looks the same. He looks the same. There's no Hell in him yet. But I know it's going to change. I can feel it.

"I don't have to abandon grace just to be with you, Raven. I don't know when it'll happen. It's not as easy as just deciding. But I don't want you to worry about that. I want you to be with me. I want to feel what it is like to claim your body. Will you let me?" Zade slowly draws his hand from my cheek and down my chest until he cups my boob, strumming his thumb over my hard nipple through my shirt.

"Yes," I say, knowing he needs to hear the words for sure. "Show me what it's like to be with an angel."

I wonder if it will be gentle. I wonder if it will be more like making love than having sex. I also can't help but wonder if I should be the one in control to teach him what I like.

I don't get the chance, because Zade uses his wings to launch us from the floor and to the bed. The lamp crashes from the nightstand, knocked over from Zade's outstretched wings. I grin and kiss him, locking my fingers to the back of his neck, exploring his tongue with mine. Reaching between us, Zade grabs the hem of my shirt and tugs it up and over my head. He shifts his body until he nestles between my legs and kneels, undressing me faster than I thought him capable of.

My body quivers in anticipation, and goosebumps prickle over my skin. He licks his lips and stares at me as I lie naked and exposed before him. Taking his shirt off, he starts to undress for me, going much slower without taking his gaze from my body. His wings flap, sending a cool breeze over me. I shift and squirm in anticipation, the intensity of his gaze as hot as any of the devils' Hell power.

I half expect one of the devils to come charging in from the other suite, but they don't. They won't unless I call for them because I asked them to give me a moment alone with Zade. What I choose to do with it is up to me. I'm sure Lucian will complain, but he'll get over it. Maybe.

Zade's muscular body ripples with his movements, and I drink in every inch of him, from his bright eyes down his abs and to his thick, massive cock. It's comparable to Dante's, but his body is more natural where Dante manscapes. It doesn't bother me any. I honestly don't care either way.

Zade breaks our staring contest first, and he lowers himself between my legs and kisses my thigh. I squirm at his torturously slow pace as if he's nervous but also wants to savor every inch of my skin. His eyes dart up to mine, and he smiles. It's unlike any smile I have ever seen cross his face. He's usually broody, completely conflicted about everything. But now? It's as if he finally feels free.

Curling my fingers through the soft strands of his hair, I guide him toward the apex of my legs. He kisses me gently at first, just gliding his tongue over the seam of my body until he uses his fingers to spread me wider and sucks my clit into his mouth. I moan at the sensation, my back arching. Pleasure courses through me, and Zade licks his tongue over and over again like Andre told him to do, working me over in just the right spot to get me to come in a matter of minutes. I tighten my legs around his head, my whole body tensing with my orgasm.

Zade grabs my hands and links our fingers together and just holds onto me through the wave of ecstasy until I release my breath. My chest rises and falls, and he makes his way up my body, licking along my torso until he reaches my nipples and kisses each of them until he finally gets to my mouth.

His body rests between mine, his hard-on pulsing between my legs in anticipation. I know he wants to fuck me already, but he's holding back just a bit. He's not one to take initiative. So I know it's got to be me. He wants me to claim him. To show him what it's like to be with me.

I reach between us and lace my fingers around his cock, stroking him. His wings flap again, and his whole body lights up with his angelic power. I close the space and kiss him, slipping my tongue over his at the same time that I align his body to mine. He moans, just testing me, teasing me with his tip, and I nip him, stretching his pouty lip with my teeth.

The gesture sets him off, and he thrust into me, the pressure feeling so incredible as my body adjusts to his girth. I shift my leg and stretch it up, opening my body wider for him, and he rests his hands on each side of my head, looking into my eyes as he makes love to me. There's no other way I can explain it. Zade isn't like the devils. But he isn't exactly tame either. His desperation and desire envelop me, and it makes it easy to lose myself with him. My vision lights up as he glows brighter and the purest emotions spill from him to me.

"I want you to treat me as you would one of the devils," Zade murmurs, his blue eyes sparkling with his angelic glow. "I want to know what it's like to be with you as they do."

Damn. It's as if instead of loving my light, he craves my darkness. It's completely opposite of what the devils like when it comes to my soul. It almost feels as if Zade loves me at my darkest and not my brightest.

Something comes over me, and I shove him off and climb on top of him, watching his face sharpen with his lust. I realize that he wants me to control him. He wants me to treat him as if he's not a pure, virginal angel. And I love it. I want to push his boundaries. I want to know what gets his light to dim and his being as dark as mine in this moment.

"Are you sure that's what you want?" I ask, grabbing his hands and pulling them over his head. "Do you want me to show you how rough I like it? Or how I want to restrain you like all the times I've been restrained to have my way with you?"

I hadn't realized how thrilling it would be to take this kind of power. I don't know how I manage it, but fire erupts in my palms, and I summon a chain similar to Lucian's but smaller and just long enough to restrain Zade.

"I told you that I want you to push me. Make me feel as if Heaven abandoned me." Zade stretches up and grabs me by the hair, bending my neck to the side. He sucks my throat hard enough to leave a mark and set me off.

I use my strength to push him back, and I grab my small fire chain and wind it up around his wrists. He grinds his teeth at the pain, but instead of fighting against it or begging me to take it off, he manages to shift his body, getting me to slide down more until I feel his hard-on smack my ass cheek.

"Tell me how much you want to fuck me," I say, adjusting my body until I sit on his cock and slide up and down, letting him feel my wetness. "Beg me."

"Please, Raven. Fuck me. Treat me as you would one of the devils. Fuck me hard. Make me cum." Zade's voice deepens with his demands, and something shifts in his features. I catch sight of a blip of fire in his eyes, but it doesn't belong to him. It belongs to me.

"You want me to sit on your fucking cock, don't you? You're tired of being an obedient little angel, yet you're too afraid to just take what you want." I purposely push him, wanting to see how long it takes before he finally does something and steals the power back from me.

"I want to give you what you want," he says, rotating his hips, trying to feel more of me.

"Because that's all you ever do. You always do what others want. You are too afraid to do things for yourself." I rock up and down his shaft but don't let him slip inside me. "Always such a good angel, even when they question you and treat you as if you are less than. I bet Cassius isn't even looking for you. All he cares about is his own pride. But you wouldn't do anything about it, would you? You're the embodiment of sloth. Never do shit."

"You're wrong," Zade says, flinging his bound arms up and over my head. He sits up with my legs around his hips, and even bound, he manages to lift my ass up and sinks into me. "I'm not good. I don't help the guardians. All I do is think about how not to do what they ask of me. And now all I think about is you."

I gasp as he bounces me on him with the chain trapping me in place. Catching on to him, I let him guide my body and just hold on to his shoulders as he takes what he wants from me. Zade sucks my neck and works his way up to my mouth. He steals my moans with his kiss, and I lose myself to everything he is. His light blends with the tendrils of darkness seeping from me, but it doesn't last for long. Because suddenly, my whole body sets aglow, and Zade inhales a sharp breath. His wings wrap around me, cocooning us from the world. Our beings blend together as one, and I feel the absolute most perfect parts of him.

Our utter closeness sets me off, and I orgasm, my body clenching his so tightly that he tenses and grunts as he cums. The most shocking and incredible thing happens. Zade and I explode with light, turning the world into a room of white.

I feel his heavenly spirit, and it shatters the darkness winding around me. Tranquility and pure joy crash through us, our beings merging into one. It's the strangest, most exhilarating thing. But it doesn't last forever.

A loud crash snaps us from the ethereal plane, bringing us back to the Mortal Realm. Voices bounce around the room, but it takes me a moment to orient myself. My mind, body, and soul must come together first.

"Whoa, what the fuck happened?" Andre asks, his voice neither upset nor angry.

"Lucian, Andre. I don't know what is going on, but the ward has broken. You guys need to go now. The angels could come at any second." Dante's shadow looms over me, and his warm hands touch my shoulders. "Raven, hey. I know you're kind of busy fucking Zade, but he just fucked enough Heaven into you to damage the shields keeping the angels out."

I blink my eyes, but my brain can't comprehend what he's saying. My body slackens, and I rest against Zade, just feeling his heartbeat against mine. My eyes still shine with the light.

"Shit, I can't touch her properly. Zade, you better fucking cooperate, or I will cut your wings off this instant. Bring Raven and come with me." Dante's sharp voice stabs at me.

Removing the chains from Zade's wrists, Dante wraps a blanket around me from behind. Zade slides out of me and adjusts me in his arms, stroking his palm up and down my spine.

No matter how hard I try to focus, I can't. The only thing I can concentrate on is the scent of Zade's skin. It helps calm my racing heart. If Dante wasn't nearby, and if Zade wasn't still holding me, I might be a little afraid. I can't get my limbs to move. Everything is still so bright. At least instead of feeling terrible, I feel amazing.

"Kase, have the doctor set up and ready. We're going to be there in a minute. Something happened with Raven." Dante's voice trickles to my ears, barely sounding above the thumping of Zade's heart.

I can't hear Kase's response, and I'm certain that Dante is talking to him on the phone.

"Raven," Zade whispers, his voice so low that I don't think Dante can hear him talking to me. "I think I was wrong. All of Heaven was wrong."

I open and close my mouth, wanting to ask him what he means by being wrong. If Dante didn't growl, and if Kase didn't suddenly appear next to us and touch my chin, getting me to look at him, I would try harder. But my voice doesn't want to come. All I want to do is just let Zade cuddle me. I feel as if I'll start bawling my eyes out if he stops. I don't want this feeling to end.

"I knew he wouldn't be able to resist her," Kase says to Dante. "Do you think he gave her some of his light? Isn't that what happened with Elias? I don't know how any of that bullshit works. I've been a devil for too long."

"No, that light is not mine. It's new. I've never felt it before. Take a closer look." Zade's voice rumbles with his words as he answers Kase, speaking for himself instead of allowing Dante to do so.

"Oh shit. It's different. What did you do to her? A little angelic cum should not have changed the soul." Kase's comment strikes me in my heart. What does he mean by that? I can't help thinking about what the devils were talking about when they were speaking about Elias and how souls sometimes don't take.

My mouth just doesn't work to ask. Everything turns fuzzy, and I think I black out for a moment. One second, I am in Zade's arms, and in the next, I'm lying on a bed with a sheet around me. An unfamiliar woman hovers at the side of the bed and sets up what looks like an ultrasound machine.

"I'm just going to take a quick peek before I draw blood to run some tests to make sure everything looks good," the woman says. "I want you gentlemen to step outside."

"Like fucking hell we are," Kase snaps, the red of his power illuminating in the edge of my vision. "That's our soul and baby. I don't trust you yet."

Sighing, the woman grabs a bottle of clear jelly and puts it on a wand. "Is that okay, Ms. Rose? I will make them leave if that's what you prefer."

I slowly manage to get my head to nod and reach out to grab for any one of their hands. Kase links fingers through mine and touches my cheek.

"I'll go ahead and get started then. This will be a bit uncomfortable, but if you're not far along, it's best to see if we can get a visual internally." The doctor's voice remains even as she adjusts the sheets and helps reposition my legs.

"That's nothing compared to what she has taken before." Dante chuckles with his words, the softness of his joke helping to relax my bunched nerves. The bastard. He's lucky that my body doesn't cooperate, or else I would smack him.

Taking my other hand, Dante draws smooth circles over my palm. Zade stands nearby with his back to the wall instead of up close with my devils. I half-expect for Lucian, Andre, and Micah to come rushing in, but they don't. I kind of wish they would though. I need all of them around. I never realized how much their support gives me strength.

Silence falls over the room as the doctor brings up an image on the ultrasound machine. I can't really make out anything on the gray, black, and white image, so I wait for her to say something.

Kase becomes impatient and says, "Well? Are you going to tell us what the fuck you see, or are we supposed to be able to tell what's going on in that uterus of hers?"

The woman clears her throat and reaches out, hitting a

button on the machine to zoom. I squint my eyes as if it'll help with my blurry vision, but all I can see is nothing really. Tapping her finger on another button, the doctor creates a staticky noise before the sound of my heartbeat pounds from the speaker. And then I hear the most beautiful thing. Another heartbeat. And then something else. One more.

"I almost didn't see the second one," the doctor says, her voice remaining even. "It's strange. See this dark shadow here? I'm not sure what it is, but it was blocking the view of baby B. Baby B also looks to be a bit bigger. It's hard to determine how far along you are."

"What are you saying, doctor?" Dante asks. "I already told you when her last menstruation cycle was. She should be, I don't know, five weeks."

"I am not going to say anything until I run some test. But right now, it looks as if baby B is about three weeks ahead of baby A. The best we can do is wait and see. I've never dealt with…something like this." It's obvious that the doctor knows what's going on. I'm surprised she even helps. I wonder what she gets in return. But I don't ask. Instead, I just stare at the screen, letting her words swirl around my head. Baby A and baby B. I'm having twins.

"One of those fetuses is not mortal. The other one also doesn't have Raven's light. It's not Elias. It is born from Heaven though, and it must be his. As for the other, those shadows are chains of Hell." Zade steps away from the wall and expands his wings. "I must leave. I need to seek answers."

Kase growls and grabs Zade. "Fuck no. You're staying here. No one can know until we know what we're dealing with."

"I know what we are dealing with," Zade snaps. "Raven is carrying the spawn of a devil. And also one blessed with angelic light. New light."

What? That can't be right. It can't even be possible.

But then I look at the screen again.

Oh, fuck.

Someone help me.

If Elias isn't here, then where is he?

How can my heart handle this?

My soul feels as if it shatters.

Lost

ELIAS

I NEED TO get into that hotel, but the security measures are too tight. I can't even get a block within the place. It hurts too much. I can feel the darkness of Hell surrounding Raven's location, keeping her away.

"Come on, Elias. It's just a little pain. Remember, it's in your head. This mortal can handle it. He can walk through wards without a problem. It's in your head. Think about the ward filled with Hell. Once you got past that first shield, the pain went away." The strange gruffness of my voice doesn't grow on me. Neither does this mortal's body. But he was the only one who agreed to allow me to possess him. I didn't know what else to do. I still don't know what else to do. If the angelic army discovers that I am here, they will drag me away to Heaven.

I don't give a flying fuck if I now have wings again. I don't want to go back. I don't want to leave Raven. So here I am, an angel, possessing a mortal man with his permission. At least I can't hear the fucker. Actually, he's been dead for a while. He was too gravely injured from the fight, and I just happened to die at the same time he was going to let go of it all. He's damn lucky that I remembered how to send his soul off to Heaven, because otherwise, he'd be in Hell for his actions.

I was in a good mood despite getting shot and dying. Because I knew Raven would be okay. I expected to be in Hell and have all the devils pissed off at me. What I didn't expect was to have my self-sacrifice send me to Heaven only to drop me right back down as a savior. I was too good for another cycle. And I was too far gone with my mortal life that I don't think it would've mattered anyway.

Oh well. There's nothing I can do now except stay out of view until I can figure out what to do next. Raven means everything to me. She is my sole purpose in eternity. I felt it before when she was Grace, and I still feel it more than ever now. But I don't think I can fall from grace again. I tried. I cussed out the Higher Power. I tried to act like a devil. But nothing works. And I haven't been able to get close to Raven to talk to her.

Well, that is, until she strolled into the Demon's Den with Andre and Lucian. I would've been fine had the demons not kicked me out. I would've waited for Raven to leave, but then fucking Cass-hole showed up.

At least I know where the devils are keeping her now, considering they've abandoned the mansion.

"Go. Go. Go. You can do this. You felt worse pain." I chant the words like a mantra and push harder against the shield.

The world around me quakes, and pain sizzles across my skin. I holler and keep pushing forward. And then the strangest thing happens. The shield suddenly snaps and blinding light blasts through the air.

I feel as if the force of the heavenly light will knock me straight out of this mortal man's body, but I manage to brace myself until the shaking world subsides and I get my shit together.

I tip my head back and stare at the sky above, expecting the guardians to come circling around like a bunch of annoying seagulls.

The sky remains clear, and I jog forward, the Hell barrier no longer keeping me away from the hotel. I rush toward the trees to take cover and straight along the shaded sidewalk. My heart pounds, and my angelic being hums the closer and closer I get to being within reach of my soulmate.

My mind races. This is it. This is what I've been desperately awaiting for weeks now. If the devils hadn't made it so hard, I could've told Raven what had happened to me. I could've asked for help from the devils. But instead, they either think I'm in a new cycle or lost in Hell. It hurts me on another level to even think of the agony and grief Raven has been through these last couple of weeks. It's so unfair that the Higher Power put her through this, and that the angelic army just can't see reason. I fully believe that Raven is the universe's destiny in bringing ultimate balance. With her, souls won't have to suffer forever, especially those who don't necessarily deserve Hell. And it pisses me off that the saviors and the guardians can't see that. They are just far too concerned with keeping their power over humanity and over Hell and basically over the entire universe.

It also doesn't help that they are the reasons why Raven and I are in this position in the first place. They pushed me and her. They ensured that we could never have a life together in the past. Grace was intended to be mine. I gave her my light. We were going to have an eternity together, but then the saviors came. They tried to take her from me, and it left us no choice but to end our own lives and go into another soul cycle.

Cars zoom across the street, and I sprint through a red light, nearly getting hit by some asshole. Yeah, sure. I might be the asshole, but I should get a pass. I'm on a damn mission to reunite with my soulmate. I need to be there. Because the longer Raven and I are apart, the more power Heaven will get. If I can't get to her, and they find me, it might be over. I don't know what will happen after that.

"Make sure you stop any fucking angel, mortal, anyone. I don't give a fuck. No one enters the hotel." Lucian's deep voice reverberates through the air, and I watch him open a portal to Hell.

The ground quakes again, the Hell portal fighting with the Mortal Plane because it's not supposed to be here, and remnants of angelic light fill the air. How? I have no fucking clue.

I spot Andre taking flight, and I slow down. Lucian isn't exactly the one I want to approach. He will probably murder this body before I even have a chance to open my mouth.

So, I wait. I wait until Lucian expands the Hell portal, sending fire around the entire hotel. I've never seen a devil go to such lengths to protect something, and I wish I were on the other side of this now flaming wall. Because I want what he wants. I want what all the devils want. I just want to be with Raven and protect her.

Lucian circles the building, disappearing around the parking garage. I take advantage and manage to cross the street. I stop and toe the flaming circle with my boots. I wonder how much it would hurt to push this body through. I wonder if I could even make it without burning it alive.

Fuck me. Fuck this life. Fuck this body. Fuck everything in

this damn world for keeping me from Raven. Neither of us deserves this. I don't think a celestial being has ever felt like I have felt. How I feel. It takes everything in me not to shed this flesh bag and expand my wings to fly over the flames. The one thing about the hellfire is that it will stop all of the other angels from crossing, but not me. Raven and I share angelic light. Her soul is mine, and my soul is hers. It's funny because angels don't have souls. But I do because of a twist of fate.

A loud whistle cuts through the air, and I peer up and catch sight of a couple of massive, winged shadows flying through the air. I should've known that the angels would be here the second I felt the wards break. And there are a ton of them coming. I have to get through this fire. They're going to need my help.

Hellfire bursts above me as Andre shoots a stream of it at one of the guardians. I duck back under a low branched tree and hide like a coward. I just can't trust the angelic army to give up on Raven and to come after me. If they get me, it's over. At least if they go after Raven, I know she's safe. The devils won't let anything happen to her. It's funny how much I trust them now, even Lucian.

"Come fucking face me, bastards!" Lucian shouts, striding from around the building. "Are you guys scared little assholes?" His muscles twitch and flex as he transforms into his massive devil form.

Like the nearest guardians can't resist fighting the most no-torious devil, they fly toward him, summoning angelic light in their palms. Lucian fights back with a basketball-sized orb of hellfire, knocking one asshole off course.

Another one attacks the fire with heavenly light, trying to break the Hell barrier protecting the building. I watch the flames dancing and moving, lowering just enough in a certain area that I think I can jump over it.

The angel flies back up into the air, dodging out of the way of Lucian's wrath only to find himself face-to-face with Andre. In his devil form, Andre whips his long tail over his head and stabs the angel right through one of the wings. The angel freefalls in Lucian's direction, and the big beast bastard stomps his hoof and cracks the floor open. The angel doesn't even get the chance to fight before Lucian lashes his fire chain around the angel and tosses him into the portal to Hell.

A dozen more angels attack from the sky, all concentrating on sending Lucian into the portal. Andre tries to fight them back, and he manages to damage a few of the angels' wings, but it's not enough to stop them. Lucian's skin burns, and red lines of power course around his body. He continues to fight, throwing punches, whipping his fire chain, and even impaling a bastard with his horns, but it's not enough. One angel finally manages to get the Hell barrier down in a section, using his heavenly light to keep it from burning him. He crosses over and charges Lucian, stabbing him in the back with his heavenly sword.

I take advantage of the situation and rush forward, jumping over the diminishing Hell barrier. Lucian and the angels are too caught up in fighting each other that no one sees me. Pushing my legs to move as fast as I can, I sprint toward the entrance of the hotel.

Cool air engulfs me as I step through the automatic doors and into the lobby. It's as if the devils have cleared out the entire building completely. Actually, I know they have. I wouldn't put it past them to have cleared the entire area of anyone that could be a threat.

Now, if only I could know exactly where to go to find Raven. There are over a couple of hundred rooms in this building. I don't have time to knock on each one of them. The noise of the battle outside grows louder, and I spot an angel using his sword to stab at a second shield keeping him out.

Fuck. I can't let him get through.

Running toward a sitting area, I grab a chair and hide off to the side of the automatic door. I wait a couple of seconds to see if the angel will give up, but he persists with his war on the protective shield. So, I swing my arms and release the chair, surprising the hell out of him. The angel falls back and lands on his wings, only to propel himself up again.

I could use heavenly light to push him back again, but I'm

afraid to give myself away. I hate how much of a coward I am. I should just reveal myself and fuck this asshole up, but it has been too long since I've been an angel. It was hard enough to possess this body. I don't know how to easily summon my power. I haven't tried much, because I know that the guardians and the saviors will be able to sense me.

Once again, I grab a chair and throw it out the automatic doors. The angel growls and ducks this time. I move out of the way and hide, so he can't see me.

The elevator door dings from behind me, and I freeze, my nerves getting the best of me. A woman steps from the elevator at the same time that a ring of fire erupts in the middle of the lobby. Micah materializes in his devil form, his hulking body standing tall and threatening with his huge tusks protruding from his face. The woman halts in her tracks and screeches at the sight of him. She stumbles back and trips, smacking her head on the tile floor.

Micah ignores her, and he reaches down and grabs onto a scary-ass demon, hauling the creature from the pits of Hell. The snake-like man hisses and slithers across the floor. His arms tuck into his sides as he doesn't use them, and I'm nearly certain the smoking trail of liquid he leaves behind will devour anything that touches it. It's moving toward the woman as if the liquid comes alive. And who knows. Maybe it is.

The brightness of the woman's soul draws my attention as I

try to tell if she is bound to Hell. She's not. I don't know what she's doing here, but if I don't do something, she's going to die in the most painful way I can imagine. I'm sure that liquid is like acid.

Micah reaches down again and pulls out another demon. He continues to grab these monsters from Hell until he has a small army. With a roar, he commands them to join the fight outside. Kase and Dante must be with Raven, protecting her. And the devils are no longer playing games. This is an all-out war. I don't understand why the angelic army is going after Raven so hard right now. They should believe that I have started another cycle. I know that they had assumed I had one, so something has changed. I need to find out. Fuck, I just need to get to Raven.

But the damn woman. I can't just leave her. It's like a part of my nature won't allow me to.

"You! What the fuck are you doing here?" The familiar feminine voice snatches my attention from the woman. "Micah, that bastard is possessed."

Oh shit. It's Raven's cousin Tamia. Just the sight of her gets me on a level that makes me think that Hell is about to claim me. She shot me. She's the one who ended my life before I could claim a throne in Hell. And my rage gets the best of me.

Slapping my hands together, I summon angelic light for the first time since taking this body. Tamia's eyes widen, and she takes an automatic step back in fear. A deep, guttural snarl rips through the air. Micah sets his attention on me, summoning orange power between his palms.

"Wait!" I yell, hoping that Micah doesn't attack and gives me a chance to speak.

I should've realized that it's not him I should be worried about, because I barely have time to move out of the way as a burst of ruby power explodes in front of me. Tamia uses Hell power to drag my attention from Micah. I have no choice but to chuck my heavenly light at her, getting her to back up.

"Fuck! Dante! The doctor!" Raven's familiar voice echoes through the lobby. My whole body screams with an intense need unlike anything I've ever experienced.

As if my soul takes control over my mind, I rush forward and toward Raven without thinking. I don't make it far before an orb of red power crashes into my chest, stealing my breath away.

"You're going to fucking burn in the pits, you asshole!" Kase yells, launching toward me in his devil form. "How did you even get through the shield? No human or angel should've been able to pass."

I open my mouth to tell him that it's because I'm fucking Elias, but I don't get the chance. A blinding light steals my vision, the whole room lighting aglow with heavenly power. I shield my eyes, trying to see where it comes from.

My heart pounds at the sight of Raven in a halo of breathtaking light.

All of the devils and demons yell and shout, but they can't do anything as the ground cracks open, and they fall into their kingdoms.

Raven screams, her eyes wide in fear.

I don't rush to her. I'm afraid of scaring her.

"Raven, it's time. The Higher Power has fated it to be this way," a familiar voice says as the world dims. Cassius stands at the entrance of the lobby. "Don't make this hard. We will not hurt you. But you and Elias need to come with me."

He doesn't look at me as he says the words. I don't think he sees me at all. I must be shielding myself in a way that I didn't know was possible.

"Heaven was mistaken. I am not carrying Elias's soul. So stay the fuck back. I'm not going with you," Raven says, her body trembling.

"What do you mean? I've seen it for myself." Cassius flaps his wings, sauntering forward while Raven steps back.

He's going to grab her. He's not going to give her a choice.

I do the only thing I can think of. I launch from my place and jump on his back.

But Cassius doesn't hit the floor.

He propels the two of us forward, flinging his arms around Raven. We all fall into another plane.

Reason

RAVEN

"I'LL RIP YOUR wings off!" I scream, my voice ringing through the air. Fear and anger collide through me as the Mortal Realm melts away, leaving me in a strange place of light.

I hit my back on the ground, the icy sensation burning my skin even though it's not hot. Cassius slams his palms on each side of my face, holding his weight up so as not to squish me. Another man, one I've never seen before, clings to his back. Swinging his fist, the strange man whacks Cassius in the side of his head.

"Let her go, or I will send you to fucking Hell," the man yells, punching Cassius again. "She's mine! You can't take her!"

What the fuck is he talking about? I have never seen this guy in my life. But a part of me doesn't fear him. He's helping me. I don't understand.

Cassius jerks his head back, smacking the guy in the face. Blood sprays across me, and I manage to break my hand free from between Cassius and me. Clawing my fingers, I scratch Cassius across the cheek. It's enough of a distraction that the guy manages to put Cassius in a chokehold, and the two of them flip off me.

I scramble to my feet, my heart clattering around my rib cage. It's hard for me to breathe. The terror rushing through me at watching my own body turn against my devils to send them to Hell still lingers with me.

I can't believe that happened. Why did it happen?

What is this little angelic spawn doing?

I can barely even process what I know about the other one. My little devil baby. Kase and Dante both claim that it belongs to them, because of course, they can knock me up. I'm their soul.

I don't even know what to think. All I need to do right now is to get out of this weird in-between world. I need to escape Cassius and the strange guy who is fighting on my behalf.

"Who are you, and what is your rank?" Cassius growls with his question, and he manages to pull out his heavenly sword.

Flipping the guy onto his back, Cassius aims his weapon. "You cannot claim her. She has been blessed with a child belonging to Heaven. She needs to go somewhere safe."

The man's eyes widen, and he freezes. "Raven's pregnant? Holy fuck."

Tipping his head back, the guy glances at me. Cassius clenches his jaw and looks ready to stab the guy through the chest with his sword.

"Cassius, don't!" Zade's voice booms through the air, and a burst of heavenly light crashes into Cassius, knocking him off the guy.

The two angels standoff, both looking as if they will try to send each other to Hell. Panic tightens my chest. I can see the turmoil crossing Zade's face. Actually, it matches Cassius's. They don't want to fight each other. Yet, neither of them wants the other to take me.

"Don't do this, Zade. You know the importance of our path. You promised me that you wouldn't leave me. You promised that you would be by my side and help Heaven. What you're doing is dangerous. You've crossed a line." Cassius puffs out a breath, peering around the room.

"I can't let you take her. The angelic army will see her as an abomination. They will hurt her. They will try to take her children, and it's unfair. I can't stand by and let them do it in the name of Heaven." Zade tenses his shoulders, keeping his focus on Cassius.

I'm so enthralled with the conversation that I don't see the stranger move until he touches my hand. A strange sensation envelops my fingers. The light of the man crawls up my hand and to my arm, slithering its way to my chest. I gulp a breath, turning my attention to the stranger.

"Raven, it's me. Come on. We have to go, darlin'," the man says, his raspy voice humming with a familiar melody.

My heart nearly explodes at the nickname. "Oh fuck. Don't mess with me. If this is some sort of joke, I will send your ass to Hell." Because only Elias calls me darlin'. But how could he be here in this man? He died. His soul left. He was supposed to cycle again. There's no way he could be this age.

"Please, I'll explain everything. We just have to go. The angels are swarming, and I need to get you somewhere safe until the devils can resurrect. Trust me, Raven. It is me. It's Elias." The man tightens his jaw as if he's not going to give me a choice whether or not I go with him. "I'm not as strong as Cass-hole. And the rest of the angelic army doesn't know I'm here. Please."

Tears burn my eyes, and I throw my arms around Elias, the strange difference of this new body making it hard for my mind to grasp that it's really him.

Elias adjusts me in his arms and lifts me off my feet. Without waiting to see what unfolds behind us between Zade and

Cassius, he heads toward the back of the hotel lobby, heading toward another exit.

"I don't even know how to think or feel," I whisper into Elias's ear. "How? How long have you been in this body? Why didn't you find me sooner?"

A million thoughts swirl through my head. Elias strokes his hand along my spine and shoves his shoulder against the back exit. He hesitates and peers around. A few angels soar above us, and Elias makes a run toward a tree-lined path.

"Just give me a second, darlin'," Elias says, jogging until we are about half a block from the hotel. "It's better if we get far away first."

I snuggle my face into the crook of his neck and kiss his skin. It should be weirder than it is since he is no longer in the body I am used to, but he still feels the same. His soul still calls to me. I feel complete in his arms.

"Fucking A. I've missed you," Elias murmurs, his muscles rippling around me as he tightens his hold. "You have no idea how awful and torturous it has been these last few weeks without you. It was nearly impossible to find you until now. The devils really know how to keep you safe. I am thankful for that, but it was fucking infuriating."

"So you've been around for weeks? I've been grieving. I've been so scared that you went through another cycle, and I wasn't going to see you for a long fucking time." The words tumble out of my mouth, and my body shakes with a silent sob as I recall how horrible it felt thinking that. "It was even worse when the angels thought that you were cycled into me."

Elias inhales a sharp breath. "What the fuck? So it's true? You're pregnant?"

I nod my head and lean back, peering into his unfamiliar face. It's as if some of his features remain the same, like his beautiful eyes, but he is definitely someone else in this body. He might be younger, and he's definitely taller than he was, yet the way he purses his lips reminds me of him before.

"I can't believe it. I'm going to be a father. You have no idea how happy that makes me. I never thought it was even possible. I'm so fucking sorry that I couldn't get to you sooner, darlin'. This must've been so hard." Elias's eyes flick back-and-forth as he searches my face, as if he's trying to read my thoughts. "I swear that I will protect you. I will not let Heaven get you."

I lick my lips and nod again, my mouth trembling. It's hard for me to form words. I don't know what I was expecting out of his reaction, but a wave of relief washes over me.

I open my mouth to tell him more, to share with him what the devils and I found out during the ultrasound, but Elias surprises me by unfurling the most beautiful wings I have ever seen. They're a mixture of iridescent pearl and platinum but not solid like all of the other angels' wings I've seen. They look as if they're made of pure light.

"I need my hands free, just in case, so hold on as tightly as you can." Elias gathers a dazzling glowing orb in one of his hands.

"You're an angel," I breathe, my voice barely even sounding from my mouth. I can't believe it. Silently repeating the words doesn't help either.

Elias offers me a smirk. "Looks to be that way, but things are different this time around. I don't feel as I had before I became mortal."

I want to ask him more, but he picks up his pace and launches the two of us in the air. I clench my jaw to stop from screaming at the sudden ascension, far faster than Dante or Andre has ever flown with me. My eyes blur with the icy air, Elias's new body cooler and not doing much to keep me warm as we propel higher and higher until the mist of the clouds above shields us.

Elias flies me in silence, keeping his guard up, ensuring that we don't come across any angels. "Darlin'? Where should I take you? I don't want the devils getting pissed off that we've disappeared."

I keep my eyes shut to stop them from watering. "I don't know. We were at the hotel because the angels were tracking us. I just need to be able to summon Micah. He can get the devils to us."

"I wish I were still capable of opening a summoning circle.

But my heavenly light doesn't allow me." Elias's voice softens with his words. "Do you remember how to do it? I know it can take a lot out of you."

"Yeah, if you could just get us somewhere safe long enough to do it. What about your old house?" I ask. I know what the answer is already, but I'm not even sure where to go. "Or maybe the Demon's Den? I can always ask Gia."

"The guardians will surely be surrounding all of the demonic hotspots. We just need to figure out somewhere they won't look." Elias flaps his wings, keeping us level in the air.

"What about somewhere sacred? Somewhere heavenly?" I manage to rest my head to peer around the misty world. "Somewhere that the devils wouldn't go."

"Neither of those would work. Demons always look around places that they think they can corrupt souls. But I have an idea." Elias suddenly closes his wings, nosediving from the clouds.

He flies so quickly that I can't even make a noise, my whole body tensing with fear. I'm not afraid of falling. I'm afraid of getting caught and maybe a little afraid of getting sick. I know that he just wants to get to the ground as quickly as possible, but I could've used a little warning.

The world slows as Elias touches his boots to the ground with a thump and runs a couple of feet until we can take cover under another tree. I gasp, my heartbeat rapping furiously against my ribcage.

I swallow and try to settle my wild nerves. And then my stomach twists, and I dry heave, my empty stomach not allowing anything to expel from it.

"Shit. I'm sorry, Raven. I just wanted to get out of sight as quickly as possible. Take a slow breath," Elias says, stroking his fingers across my lower back without putting me down even though I could throw up on him.

I hug him tighter, just getting used to his new body.

I can feel a rush of something familiar crash over me. Without looking, I can feel his gaze boring at the side of my face. So, I tilt my head to look at him, and I drink in his features. Long dark lashes that match his hair, a couple of shades darker than his other body, rim his round eyes. I reach up and caress my fingers along his jawline, memorizing the curve that leads to a less prominent chin than what he had before. His face shadows with stubble, and he lets me touch his slender nose and thin lips. In places he had muscles before, Elias's new body is a bit softer and sinewy.

And he's handsome. I don't know if it's because his very being calls to me, but I feel as if I know him already. I love him. I don't care what form he's in. That won't ever change. He is Elias, regardless.

"I wish I didn't have to take on this new form. I know it's different. The only way I could have a body that you were familiar with is if I listen to the calls that try to get me to go to Heaven. I just can't do it. I could never leave you." Elias takes a couple of steps from the tree with his words, keeping his gaze on mine and managing to navigate the lawn of what looks like the courtyard of an...elementary school? Fuck. It is. Children play on the playground as a supervisor blows the whistle. I don't think anyone can see us, but it is weird as fuck to be here.

"Your appearance doesn't matter to me," I say, sitting up straighter now that my stomach doesn't threaten to make me sick. "I can feel your soul as if it's my own. I'm just so incredibly relieved that you are here. I missed you so fucking much. It has been torture thinking that I lost you."

"I know, darlin'. The whole situation is fucked up. I don't even really know what's going on with myself. I don't remember the moments between dying and waking up in this body except that the man who owned it gave me permission to take it. He hung out for a little bit, but then he moved on and left me with it." Elias strolls closer to the buildings nestled together with outdoor corridors. "But honestly, I don't care. Right now, all I care about is you. And what happens next. Fuck. I still can't believe you're pregnant."

I can't help the smile crossing my lips at his words. The softness of his voice wraps around me, and I can feel his love. I can feel his heavenly light. It makes me feel as if the shitshow will actually turn out fine in the end.

"You can't believe it? I can't believe it. But here I am. I saw it myself, and I have something more that I need to tell you. I'm having more than just a baby born with your light. I'm having twins, and one seems to be a little...devilish." I brace myself for his reaction, because I was a little bit freaked out hearing the news and seeing the shadowy form next to the pure light on the ultrasound machine.

Elias's brows pinch together, and he gapes at me in confusion. "What? How? I mean, I know fucking how. But damn."

I laugh in exasperation, my voice echoing through the air. "You read my mind. All I know is that it is what it is, and Heaven is going to try to keep me from them. They're trying to stake a claim—"

"Over my dead body. My angelic soul. Over my fucking power and psycho ass as an angel will I allow that to happen. The devils will help. We just have to summon them." Elias finally sets me on my feet. I nearly ask him to pick me up again because I don't want to be even a foot away from him, but I know he wants to have a better view of the world around us in case he has to do something to protect me.

"You're shitting me. You want to summon a Hell portal at an elementary school?" I shake my head, whipping my black hair around. "Why here? Couldn't you find a church or something?"

"The angelic army would look at all of the churches and

cemeteries around. They look at the demon-run bars and basically everywhere else except an elementary school. Demons and devils do not mess with the innocent. They'd rather corrupt a damn nun or something. The angelic army will never look here." Elias expands his translucent wings, the brilliant light making me squint my eyes. "Now, if we can just find what we need."

I don't even know where to start. The supply room? The teacher's lounge? Maybe even the parking lot. All I know is that we need some salt, fire, and a candle.

I wish it wasn't so hard. I wish I could just call upon my devils and have them come bursting through the ground.

The ground shakes at my thought, startling me. A couple of the kids' screams rip through the air, and a supervisor blows a whistle. I spread my arms wide, trying to keep my balance through the earthquake. He swears under his breath and reaches for me. The ground cracks open, and the scent of Hell wafts through the air.

Fire bursts from my hands, and Elias jumps back, holding up his palms with heavenly light. But it does nothing as fire engulfs the world around me, and the portal to Hell opens up with me in the middle.

I fall into the fiery pits.

Elias shouts my name.

Screeching, I flail my body, expecting to crash into a burning lake of lava. And if I don't, I'll probably end up in some disgusting demon's belly.

The drop from the mortal plane only lasts a couple of seconds, and my world comes to a halt as muscular arms wrap around me, catching me before I hit the liquid fire of Hell.

"Heathen, what happened? I don't understand. I know that the devils were sent here without you. I was trying to locate you, but the hotel was surrounded. And then you just summoned me, but instead of pulling me through a portal, you fell through. Where were you? How did you get away?" Micah asks so many questions, but my brain can't catch up as I think about Elias on the other side of the portal. Just the thought of falling away from him freaks me out. What if I can't find him again?

"You have to take me back. I was just trying to call for you guys, not come here. Please, Elias is up there." My voice rises with my panic. "If they find him, they'll take him to Heaven."

Micah frowns, his beautiful brown eyes glowing orange with his power. "I'm not sure I'm following—"

"Take me back! Now!" I hook my fingers to his shoulders as if I can hoist myself up and somehow get back through the shimmering portal above.

Growling under his breath, Micah shoots hellfire around us and the world shimmers, and I find myself within a giant ring of hellfire. Blinding light rips in my vision and steals some of my senses away. I throw myself from Micah's arms. I can't help it. I know that Elias can't go into the Hell circle, and I need to find him. What if he's already gone? He moves a lot slower in the Mortal Realm.

"Raven, fuck!" Elias calls, his cool hands grabbing me by the wrist and yanking me toward him.

"Don't touch her," Micah snaps, and his snarl reverberates through my bones. "I'll drag your ass to Hell. Release her now."

My body suddenly goes from hot to cold and then to hot again, and fire and heavenly light blaze over each of my arms, the unexpected power radiating from deep in my soul. I can't do anything except shake my hands and send it spilling across the grass. But then Elias pulls me even closer and envelops me in his arms.

"This was a mistake. Something feels off. I don't think you should be near him," Elias says, tightening his arms around me.

"What?" I ask, my whole body tightening with anxiety. I don't understand. What does he mean by he doesn't think I should be near Micah?

Elias doesn't get a chance to respond, because Micah throws a dagger, sinking it into Elias's stomach.

I scream as Elias hits his knees.

All I can think about is how his temporary mortal body could die.

I might lose him all over again. What will happen now?

I'm afraid that Heaven can steal him from me. If that happens, all will be lost.

Heaven will have won.

12

Drag Him to Hell

MICAH

"NO! OH, FUCK! Elias, hold on." Raven kneels next to the bastard angel, pressing her fingers around the sharp edges of the blade I chucked at him.

Did she just call him Elias? I don't understand.

"Micah, what do I do? He can't die. He possesses this body. If he loses it…I don't fucking know. Help me. What do I do?" Raven sobs with her words, trying to stop the bleeding and light from seeping from the man's wounds. Not just a man. Elias. Elias possessing a mortal in his angelic form. Now that I can focus, I don't want to murder the bastard for trying to steal Raven from me. I can see the truth in her words. It is Elias. He did not go through another cycle. He's here, and he found her. But he's an angel. He's a heavenly being, yet I can see a chain of darkness sneaking from Raven and tethering to him.

"Can you bring him here?" I ask, curling and uncurling my fingers.

I keep my gaze locked on Elias, focusing on his essence. It's strange because he looks like he had as a mortal. He kept his soul, yet he carries Heaven's light. I can even see good grace coursing from his back and sprawling out on the grass with his invisible wings.

"Raven, don't. Please. He's going to try to drag me to Hell. Being so close to the portal already hurts me so deeply." Elias groans and rests his hands on top of Raven's.

"Elias, your body could die. Micah could help you. Maybe this is how it was supposed to be. What if you can take your throne now?" Raven bites her bottom lip between her teeth, her expression tight and pinched together with her fear and pain. It's not physical pain, but I know she can feel the agony Elias experiences in this moment.

"I can't. Please, I don't want a throne in Hell. I just want you and me. I want to be how it was supposed to before the saviors forced our hands. We were supposed to be together like this always. I can see more clearly now." Elias's chest rises and falls with his panting breath. "If I die in this body, it won't be forever. I will—"

"No. I watched you die once. I'm not doing that again." Raven thrashes her head, whipping her black hair back and forth. "I'm taking you to Hell. I'm not letting that pure angelic light fuck with our future. You're mine, and the rest of the devils are mine, and this is going to be our eternity. Don't fight me."

I didn't know that I could love her even more than I do at this moment. She will not stand down and let Elias's halo blind him.

"Darlin', please," Elias begs, removing the blade from his stomach. "You have to trust me."

"I do trust you. But you're going to fucking trust me right now. Now brace yourself. This might hurt." Raven uses her Hell strength and drags Elias toward me by his wrists.

Screaming, Elias thrashes and flaps his wings, but Raven's determination doesn't allow him to break free. She's so sexy and strong as hell, and I kind of wish she would manhandle me like that sometime. I had no idea I'd want her to, but seeing her with Elias like that? I miss them both. It feels like it's been years, even though I know it's only been a day since I've seen my beautiful soul.

"Stop fighting. You're making me feel bad, but this has to be done. It's going to be okay, Elias. Trust me." Raven manages to get him closer to the circle despite his fighting. "You can go to Hell just fine. Zade has done it a bunch of times. Use my soul.

Please. I can't watch you die. I can't."

"Listen to your soulmate, Elias," I snap, my voice deep and growly. Frustration courses through me that he doesn't make it easy for our soul. "You are acting like a little bastard. Devil up and let us do what we need to. I will kick your ass if you bleed out before you get to Hell. And you don't want that. I will use my devil form. You won't be able to sit for eternity."

Raven jerks her attention to me, her face a mixture of awe and shock at my words. It stops Elias from resisting just long enough for her to pull him into the summoning circle.

He hollers as I wrap my fingers around him, and Raven jumps on me, clinging to my side. I drop from the Mortal Realm and land in the middle of my palace near my throne. The ground rumbles and shakes at the force. My devil form breaks through, sending fire over my skin. Raven falls off me and lands on her ass, her eyes wide with shock. Agony licks across my skin, and I squeeze my eyes shut because of Elias's blinding light. I don't know if he's doing it on purpose, but he somehow manages to tap into Heaven even here in Hell.

"Elias! Elias, stop!" Raven yells, scrambling to her feet. It's in my very nature to get between her and Elias as she tries to plow into him to get him to stop. Raven dodges around me and crawls through my legs. The feisty heathen launches from the ground and crashes into Elias, knocking him on his back. His light engulfs her, and I surround myself with Hell power, easing the sting of Heaven sneaking into my level of Hell.

"Elias! Control yourself. Stop it! You're going to end up hurting him. We're just trying to help you. Stop acting like a bastard angel. It's not you. This isn't you." Raven shakes Elias's shoulders, straddling his waist.

His light finally dims, leaving shadows in my vision. Raven clenches the fabric of his shirt in her fingers and pins him to the ground, making sure he doesn't fight or try to get back up.

"See? It's okay. You're okay." Raven releases him only to cup his face between her palms. Going forward, she presses her lips to his, kissing him softly yet desperately. My mind and body go to war at the sight of her kissing an angel that I'm not used to. While I recognize Elias's being, it still bothers me because he doesn't look as he had before. I'm not sure I can get used to him possessing this body.

But I might not have a choice. The only way he will return to the form that he desires is if he takes a throne. Right now? He's not going to do it. His heavenly light is far too strong and powerful.

Elias groans and massages his fingers into Raven's back, working his hands up to her neck until he combs them into her hair and brings her even closer as if he's not going to let her go. Jealousy sneaks through me, and I can't stop from stepping forward. My close presence is enough to get Elias to break the kiss. Raven clutches him tighter, practically smothering him with her breasts to stop him from trying to get up to fight me.

"We have to go back, Raven. We don't belong here. It's taking everything in me not to blow this place apart with my heavenly light. It feels deep-seated and instinctual. I know that you don't want it to happen. I know you love Micah. It's just so hard for me to focus on anything else except for the need to escape." Elias manages to sit up but keeps Raven on his lap. "I don't know what's wrong with me. It's like my rationale is fucked up. Why don't you just have Micah send me back? You can stay here. I'm not sure I'm so good for you right now."

"Like fucking hell am I letting you abandon me. We are going to work through this and figure it out. Do you understand?" Fire lights from Raven's palms, and she shrieks and jerks her hands back in fear.

Elias freezes, the skin on his cheek blistering from her burns. I've never seen her do that before. She manages to tap into my Hell power. I'm listening to her thoughts, desperate to know what's going through her head. Her mind races, and I can't even make out anything. It's too much. She's scared. All she wants to do is kiss Elias and make him chill out.

I want that too.

Striding the rest of the way to him, I grab Elias, hoist him up, and toss him toward my throne. Dozens of souls creep from the onyx walls and lace around his angelic body, securing him in place for me. They can't resist being near an angel. I'm sure they're whispering for salvation. They're begging him for mercy. It's enough to get him to just stop and focus on them. He will hear them out. It's in his nature as an angel.

Raven swivels her torso and turns to me. "What's going on? Does this mean he's claiming a throne in Hell?"

I shake my head, hearing the sorrow flitting through her mind as my gesture sinks in. "No, but we will have a couple of minutes to think things through. The souls will keep him busy. He can't help it. As an angel, he will want to save them even if he can't."

"I don't know what happened. He was fine when he took me from the hotel. It was his idea to summon you. We even went somewhere that the angels wouldn't look for a devil to do so. But something changed, and now he's acting like a fucking asshole. I'm scared that I'm going to lose him. What if he does try to go to Heaven? What then?" Raven moves closer until she tucks herself under my arm, silently begging for a hug.

I pull her in closer and kiss her temple. My human façade finally takes hold and suppresses my devil form. We stand in silence together, watching Elias as his light begins to grow brighter and brighter. It won't be long until he manages to bless the souls away and reject them.

"I can keep him here. That way, we can make sure he doesn't go. But I think it's best if you leave. I think your presence makes him fight harder, and he can't think clearly, especially feeling his soulmate in Hell. It probably hurts him at his very being." It's the only thing that makes sense. Raven said he changed so suddenly, and I bet it's because his angelic being recognized that Raven was swaying toward Hell. He will want to do everything he can to ensure she doesn't end up here, even if he knows that's what she wants. It's strange. I remember what it was like until I finally realized that she deserves more than being rejected by Heaven in the first place. And now that they want her and can't have her, it'll be even harder on the angels.

"Maybe you're right. Maybe if he's here and I'm not, you can talk some sense into him. You can remind him of the plan and why it's important." Pain crosses Raven's face at the thought. I know she doesn't want to leave him, and I can't blame her. It's the same feeling I have thinking about her leaving me.

"I promise you that I will take good care of him. I won't hurt him, and I will remind him of our companionship. I'll remind him what you really need in this life is for him to be on the same page as the rest of us. I will also remind him that Hell isn't bad, and it's not going to destroy you. It'll only make you more powerful." I stroke my fingers across her cheek, pulling her dark hair from her face.

She licks her pouty lips and stretches up a bit until I close the space and kiss her softly, sweetly, reminding her that I love her and will always stand beside her.

"Thank you, Micah. You are so good to me. I don't know what I would ever do without you. I just wish that you weren't stuck here." Raven kisses me once more, gliding her tongue into my mouth and deepening our kiss, knowing it's what I crave.

If Elias didn't groan, I'd keep kissing her. I'd do more. I would help her forget everything that's happening and drown her in desire and love.

"I should get you out of here. I think Andre is closest and should be here any moment. Let's wait outside." I lace my fingers through hers, guiding her toward the arched hallway that will lead us from my palace.

Raven bobs her head and glances behind us at Elias once more. She takes the chance to drink in the sight of his glowing body, his groans turning into an impressive guttural, growling sound. He's resisting the souls and trying to get them back.

I pull her harder, practically dragging her. I know if I don't get her out of there now, she'll want to stay. If she stays, then Elias might not listen to me. I wish it didn't have to be this way, but his being plays on her soul. Their connection will be what pushes him to fight as hard as he can to take her.

And I can't allow it.

"Hurry. He's tapping into Heaven. I've never seen anything like it." Instead of dragging Raven, I scoop her up in my arms and rush away from the throne room and Elias. My heart hammers in my chest, the strange discomfort brought on from his light turning painful.

"Elias said he was different. He couldn't figure it out, but he said that he had a soul still." Raven's voice hums in my ear, and she clutches me tighter. "You don't think he can escape, do you?"

"I wish I had the answer to that. I don't know. All I know is that I need to get you out of here." The world trembles around us, and I charge forward and out of the palace.

A wave of darkness crashes over us. As if we have become magnetic to souls, thousands upon thousands of them flood around us. Raven screeches, her whole body tensing as dozens of voices scream and beg for help. She digs her nails into my shoulders and releases a soft sob. I growl and throw out one of my arms, blasting away the souls trying to sweep over her with my Hell power.

"What's happening? I feel sick. What are they doing?" Raven's voice cuts through the cacophonous noise surrounding us. "Make them stop."

I throw power again, sending souls scattering. It doesn't keep them away for long. It's as if I've lost control of my kingdom.

"I'm going to open a portal. I need you to go. Something about Elias and you are attracting all the souls here. I don't think Andre is going to make it before their darkness hurts you." Again, I throw my arm out and shoot hellfire through the souls.

Raven stifles her panicked sob. "Fuck. I'm scared. Why am I a coward? Fuck." She says the words to herself, and the only reason I can hear her whisper is because she thinks the words at the same time.

I wish I had time to console her, but the souls grow thicker and thicker around us. I need to get her out of here. And fast.

Clapping my hands together, I send a blast of hellfire around us, and the world shimmers as I shift us from my kingdom and to the Mortal Realm. The night sky glitters overhead, the world only lit by the stars and moon and hellfire. Raven clings onto me, and I know she doesn't want me to let her go.

"Andre will be as fast as he can. Stay in the circle." A wave of darkness explodes around us, chaining me so tightly that I can't fight.

Raven screams as the two of us are dragged back through the portal and into a lake of congregating souls. She gasps and hides her face in the crook of my neck, her thoughts racing, and she thinks about how disgusting and cold the souls feel. Not only can she sense they're evil, but I'm sure she can see it too. The souls are open and hover with their wrongdoings pinned to them for scrutiny.

"Raven, I'm coming!" Elias shouts, his voice booming over the discordant anguish humming from the damned. "I'll get us out of here. I promise."

"Micah, do something. Please." Raven grips me tighter, hugging me with her whole body. "I just want him to see where he belongs. I can't believe that Hell has messed with his head so much."

"Not Hell. Heaven," I say, shooting bright orange fire from my palms again, clearing a path in the souls. If I can get close enough to the edge of my kingdom, Andre can help me.

"Raven!" Elias shouts, and he summons angelic light, shooting it far and wide, dispersing it through the souls to clear the way.

Raven's body trembles and my skin begins to sting. She uncontrollably radiates with the same angelic light that Elias does. It's as if he triggers her and she can't do anything except allow the light to push away the darkness.

I grind my teeth, refusing to let her go. I will accept the pain of a thousand burns from Heaven before I drop her. Agony is nothing compared to what it will feel like if Elias manages to take her from me.

"Elias, stop! Please. If you can't see what we do because Heaven screws with your head, then you need to go. Go back to Heaven. I will not let you hurt Micah like this. I will not let you take me from the devils. My place is in Hell. I want your place to be too, but I understand if you just can't accept it right now." Raven's voice rises, though her voice cracks.

"You have to come. You are my soulmate. We belong together." Elias spreads his wings made of pure light, bringing a piece of Heaven into my kingdom.

The world around us shakes with the imbalance, because Heaven doesn't belong in Hell.

"Come any closer and I will hurt you," I say, struggling with my rage. I will not allow him to do this. He will break Raven's heart if he does.

"It must be done." Elias gathers more heavenly light and flaps his wings, charging in our direction. I flip Raven behind me protectively and summon all of the power from Hell.

I crash into Elias, jabbing my huge devil hoof into his face. I don't stop. I can't.

Raven screams from behind me, and I try to suppress the urge to let Elias go.

"Get away from me!" Raven screams.

"I'm sorry. We have to go. You belong to Heaven. This proves it." Cassius's voice trickles through the air to me, stealing my breath away.

Elias's eyes widen, his shock just as great as mine. I scramble up and spin on my heels, preparing to attack the savior. But all I see is a portal. Light consumes Raven.

It's not Elias who takes her from me but Cassius.

I can't believe I failed her.

I failed the universe.

Elias won't be the only one I drive to Hell now. Cassius is next. He will regret ever stealing my soul from me.

13

Satanic Spawn

CASSIUS

I WATCH RAVEN sleep on the pile of blankets in the middle of the barely furnished apartment. I must wait at least a day before relocating us somewhere Hell can't find. The devils will be hunting every single spot in all of the world for her. If I try to leave before more time passes, I'm sure one of them will find me. Right now, I have to focus all my energy on blocking the entire universe out.

I have to say, Raven's fight was quite impressive. I had no idea that she could summon divine light. It was enthralling, seeing her glow even brighter. It's such a gift to Heaven that she carries angelic light inside her on a greater level than being angel-kissed. She is truly blessed by the Higher Power.

I feel blessed for succeeding in getting her safely away from Hell.

This war can finally be over. I just know it.

The soul growing inside her is brand new and will change everything. It is born from the purest light and will serve Heaven accordingly. I am just so thankful to the Higher Power for giving me access to Hell through this light. And I will protect Raven and the new soul with everything in me. I will not let them down. It is one of the most brilliant miracles I've ever experienced, and I can't help falling to my knees and pressing my palms together in prayer.

"Your Almighty Grace, thank you for hearing my prayers and giving me the strength to fight the darkness and bring the light of Raven home." My soft voice swirls through the room, but I can't keep the words to myself. I need to say them out loud.

As if Raven hears my prayer, or maybe feels it, her body lights again with angelic power. A smile crosses my face, and I can't stop the wayward tear from splashing on my cheek. She is the most beautiful soul I have ever seen, and I can finally admit it now that I know she won't destroy everything we've fought for and everything we've worked hard to maintain in the name of Heaven.

Crawling on my knees, I close the space to Raven, basking in her glow. I bow my head more and clutch my fingers together.

"Your Grace, please give me the strength to see this through. Please help guide me down this treacherous path as I face the darkest entities in the universe. I put all of my faith in you. You have never let me down, and I vow to never let you down. I will not fail. Heaven will rise and keep Hell at bay. I promise you. Please, just help me show Raven everything she needs to see to agree with me." Another tear splashes on my cheek, and I close my eyes tighter, willing with everything in me to channel even an ounce of Heaven into this empty apartment.

"You fucking creep!" Raven swings her palm and smacks me across the face before I can even move or react to her words. "I will rip every single one of your fucking feathers off your back."

I try to move out of her way, but Raven grabs my shirt and yanks me to her. I catch myself on my palm, trying my best not to squish her under my weight, and the little abomination swings her leg up around my side and manages to flip me off her and get on top of me.

Jabbing her fist, she sucker punches me in the nose. Pain swells in my face, and I grind my teeth. She is as strong as a devil and just as feisty, and it takes me grabbing her wrist and squeezing hard to get her to stop trying to pummel me.

"You bastard! Fuck! Help!" Her scream rips through the room, the loud pitch enough to make me wince. No one can hear her through my protective shield, but it doesn't stop her from trying.

"Settle down, Raven. I'm not going to hurt you. You are safe. Here, let me help you. Look into my eyes and take a breath." I flare my nostrils and try to capture her with my gaze, hoping my heavenly light steals away her fear of me. I never intended for her to be afraid of me, but the devils have done a number on her. They have solidified it in her very soul to be frightened of Heaven as if we are the bad guys.

Fuck them. Fucking-fuck. If I could face Lucifer this instant, I would stab him through the damn throat. I can't believe that Raven trusts him over me. It takes me a moment to quiet the profanity roaring through my head.

"Go to Hell, Cass-hole," Raven says, breaking one of her hands free again. She reaches between us and snatches my groin, squeezing tight enough that I have to throw her off me. I'm not invincible on the mortal plane. The last thing I need is for her to incapacitate me by hurting the weakest part of this human-like, male form. I fucking hate having balls.

"You know I've already been there, and I would prefer not to go back. I don't know why you like that disgusting, dark place. You are far too light and pure to have such a twisted desire." I move away from her before she tries to launch herself at me again. Pushing my hands to the floor, I stand up and cross the room, ensuring a dozen feet of space between us. "Are you hungry? Do you have to go to the bathroom? Does anything hurt?" I decide to ask her questions about what she might need instead of focusing on what she wants. I hope it's enough to distract her. I think that if I could just change her focus and get her to listen, she might see reason.

Miracles do happen.

"Let me go. You can't keep me here. The devils will find me," Raven says, ignoring all of my questions.

I can play her game too. Shifting my eyes, I stare at the door for a second, trying to gather my thoughts. "I can make you a sandwich while you take care of your other mortal needs. The bathroom is through that door over there. It's been a while since you've relieved your bladder—"

Hellfire spews from Raven's palms, and I barely have time to fly out of the way as she scorches the spot I was standing. Holy Heaven. Not only can she summon angelic light, but she can also tap into Hell. What is going on? I don't understand.

Raven tries to hit me with hellfire again, not giving me a chance to ask for guidance.

"The only thing I want right now is to pluck every single one of your feathers from your wings. After that, I will cut off your balls and shove them down your throat." Raven bares her teeth with her anger, her usual vivid blue-green eyes now flashing with firelight.

I automatically hide my wings from her and cup my hands

over my groin protectively. As much as I want to abandon her in this room, I can't leave. I need to ensure that the shield stays in place. If it even cracks a millimeter, the devils could find her. If that happens, I will have to let them take her. I can't fight against them alone.

"What have my balls ever done to you? Or my wings? I don't understand why you have such anger and want to hurt my body." I stroll backward as Raven looks for an opening to attack me.

"I want to hurt your body because it would hurt you, you fucker. What you're doing to me is ruining my life. You fucking kidnapped me. You're trying to keep me from the father of one of my babies." Raven narrows her eyes at my groin, and the way she looks as if she will destroy it awakens something dark inside me.

What is wrong with me?

Her words snap my attention away from my erection, and I focus on her. Did she just say what I think she said? She said, babies. Multiples. How is that so? I've seen the soul she carries, and it's just one.

"Actually, you're keeping me from both of their fathers. They won't stop until they destroy all of Heaven if you don't return me to them. Just do yourself a favor and stop it with this bullshit. If you're so worried about Hell taking over, why don't you just take your damn throne already and make sure that things go smoothly? A throne in Hell is fitting for you, considering how awful you are." Raven lunges at me, her quick movements startling me enough to have me summon angelic light in my palms.

But she doesn't stop.

She's as afraid of my light as I am afraid of the sudden darkness eating away at the light she carries. Plowing into me, Raven shoves me into the wall hard enough to crack the plaster. I heave a breath, her forceful punch winding me. And then she knees me in the balls. I bow forward only to take her knee to my jaw. Raven grabs my hair and twists her fingers through it, yanking my head up. Her eyes glimmer with hellfire, and she growls at me like a demon.

Heaven help me. What have I gotten myself into?

"You have five seconds. Don't think I won't force you into Hell and turn you into my little bitch. And when you comply, I will give you to your brother to punish for the rest of eternity." Raven pushes me hard enough to send me sprawling on my back.

I should fight. I should keep her away. But something about her in this moment freezes me at my very core. Her light and darkness confuse me. I've never seen anything like it. It's not her, but it comes from her.

"The Higher Power will not allow such a thing. Now settle down. Your admission about having multiple babies growing inside you confuses me." I remain on the floor, and Raven towers over me. Shifting, I risk sitting up.

She uses her foot to shove me back to the floor again and pins me under her shoe. "Do you honestly think I'm going to give away the rest of my secrets? You're the enemy."

"Like fucking Hell, am I your enemy. I'm trying to help you." Anger burns through me. The devils twisted her mind so much so that she can't even see when she is being helped.

"How is this helping me? I know what the angelic army will do to me and my babies, and I won't let it happen. You cannot take them from me." Raven flares her nostrils as she sucks in a few deep breaths. "It's so fucked up that you even consider that to be helping me. You call me an abomination, after all. I'm pretty sure that you just want to end my life on the mortal plane and wash your hands of me."

"Raven, have you fucking heard a single word that I've said? I'm not going to kill you. I only want to protect you. I cannot allow Hell to have that beautiful blessing growing inside you." I lower my voice, speaking softly, hoping that it calms her down.

"A blessing? You say that now. But you won't think the same when you realize the truth. And you know what? I think I will tell you just to see your face. You've already let your guard down enough that you're showing me the real you and how alike you are to Lucian. Your high and mighty ass will fall, and you'll be shouting all your fucks all the way down." Raven glowers at me in silence, letting her words sink into me instead of clarifying.

I repeat what she has just told me over and over again, trying to figure out what she means. I am far from being like Lucifer.

"Just because I am capable of using profanity does not mean I am like Lucifer." I don't know why I defend myself instead of asking her about the supposed truth. I can't help it, though. It bothers me on a deep-seated level that she even considers me to be similar to the fucking bastard that continuously destroys the greatest work of the Higher Power.

"You just proved my point, Cass-hole. I mean, look what you're focusing on. You are far more concerned about how you appear to me than the more important thing. You are just like him. Prideful, selfish, dense as fuck sometimes. You're also lonely. You think that it is everyone else's fault that your brethren turned their backs on you. You're blaming everyone but yourself." Raven surprises me by putting some space between us. She gives up trying to attack me and returns to her spot on the couch.

Her words hurt me more deeply than I expect them to. It's like she can look inside my mind and see how sad I am over losing my closest companions. All I have left is Zade, and I'm afraid that he will abandon me soon. I know he will. I could see it in his eyes when he stood against me.

I stand in silence, staring at the strange light and darkness swirling around Raven's middle. I don't know how to defend myself, so I don't. We obviously will never be on the same page. She's far too involved with Hell to see just exactly what it has done to her and the rest of humanity.

Shifting on the couch, Raven lies back down. She presses her hands together and whispers something under her breath that I can't hear. I don't think she's praying to the Higher Power, because I would feel her trying to connect with Heaven. If she's not praying to Heaven, it means she's praying to Hell. Just the thought prods at me in the worst way. She will not get any answers or help from the place that the dark souls go to spend eternity.

"Raven, you're wasting your breath. Why don't you do as I have suggested and go to the bathroom, get yourself cleaned up, and I will make you something to eat. You might feel better after. I know how uncomfortable it is to not have your needs met. Think of your blessing. You have to stop thinking about only yourself and your dark desires." I straighten my shoulders, expecting her to spit fire or something at me.

She ignores me completely and turns on her side, facing her back to me. I can't force her into taking care of herself, so I do the only thing I can think of. I stroll the short distance to the kitchen and grab a loaf of bread from the counter, doing my best to put together a sandwich for her.

With the plate in one hand and a glass of water in the other, I cautiously make my way back to Raven. She doesn't look up at me despite my form shadowing over her. I feel a bit defeated that she doesn't even try to talk to me anymore. Her silence is deafening. I don't know how much I can take.

"This should be suitable until it's safe enough for us to relocate," I say, braving her fury to sit on the edge of the couch at her feet. "You must be hungry. Don't punish yourself for something out of your control. Please just accept my offering. You don't have to talk to me, but I would like to see you eat."

She releases a loud sigh, exaggerating her annoyance. Sitting up, she narrows her eyes at me again. I hold out the plate with the simple turkey and cheese sandwich, offering it to her with what I hope looks like a soft smile. I'm trying really hard not to scowl despite her infuriating behavior. I don't want to be her enemy any longer. It was never her I had a problem with. It is and always will be Hell.

"What, no pickles? Haven't you heard that's kind of a thing for pregnant ladies?" Raven lifts up the top piece of bread and drops it back onto the turkey. "You expect me to hang out with you fucking featherheads, and you can't even manage to give me something good? No way. I guarantee the devils would have everything already taken care of. They even found me an obstetrician. You, on the other hand, are too concerned with everything around you to realize that I am not yours to claim. Giving me a sandwich and saying I'm going to be safe is nothing. My devils have promised me a magnificent future. They promised to take care of these babies, no matter what. None of them care that one is graced with heavenly light, even though I accidentally have been burning them lately. All they care about is me and them and the world and universe we create together."

I gawk at her, listening to her describe what is ideal for her life right now. She wants pickles. Okay. I can manage that sometime. I will also ensure her children are safe. Unfortunately, I don't know exactly what she means by only one of them being blessed with heavenly light.

"They would also distract me with a good time, and they would make me feel incredibly loved and adored right now. They would also give me a million fucking orgasms. They know what to do to take my mind off of the shitshow revolving around our mission." Raven nudges me with her foot. "Are you going to offer me some of those? I don't even think you know how to please a woman. I bet you only ever stroked your own cock."

I try not to take her bait, because I know she uses lust and desire to her advantage. But fucking Hell. She is really testing my resolve to stay calm. I don't need to give her an orgasm to make her content.

She bites into her sandwich with a smile, purposely chewing

with her mouth open as if such a sight could ever bother me. I have seen the worst of the worst in humanity, and Raven is far from it. Her weakness lies with her need to accomplish the impossible. She thinks that building Purgatory will help in the end, but she is wrong. Most of the souls in Hell will never even make it to the level of complete balance.

"You love testing me, don't you? Your seduction won't work. I have nothing to prove. Plus, I do not have to be physical with you to make you feel as if you're touching Heaven." I purse my lips in satisfaction, her smile faltering.

"What do you mean by that?" Raven asks, her voice turning soft. "If you can somehow make me feel better right now, then do it."

I raise my eyebrows, surprise washing over me. This is the last thing I expected for her to ask. I thought she would just keep trying to get to my body.

"Are you sure? There are no orgasms involved." I need permission to touch her soul, because I refuse to get whacked in my groin or head or some shit. "It involves me touching your soul."

Raven rubs her lips together and sets her plate down. She adjusts her feet on the couch and crawls closer to me, kneeling by my side. I slowly turn to meet her gaze, her blue eyes vibrant as they practically devour me. My heart picks up pace, and the strangest thing happens, she reaches out and gently cups my face.

"Do it," she says, leaning in close enough for me to catch the scent of something tropical and fruity wafting from her skin. Maybe it's her hair. I don't know, but it smells spectacular.

I swallow my nerves, wondering if I am making a mistake by getting so close to her. But I need her to see that I am not the enemy. I need her to see that Heaven is not against her. But mostly, I need to know exactly what I'm dealing with. If I can just touch her soul, I can find answers.

Inhaling a deep breath, I say, "Open your soul and let me in."

Her brilliant light consumes me.

14

Pride

RAVEN

I FINALLY FIGURE out how to get to Cassius. Because I know sexual advances don't seem to work on his uptight ass, I must use the thing he wants most. To be recognized as my hero. If it takes him thinking that he is a worthy angel, saving me from the big bad devils, then I guess I'll give him just a teensy ego boost. I don't mind a little soul-touching anyways. It's strangely intimate on a level I can barely fathom but allowing Cassius in to get a good look at me might be what I need. I haven't had a chance to do it before because he has always been such an asshole and constantly just wanting to stab me with his heavenly sword. But something has shifted inside him. I don't know if it's because of my surprise pregnancy or because I struck a nerve by commenting on how he is alone, but I honestly don't give a fuck right now. All I care about is changing his perspective. If I can use my light to show him that he's not all sunshine and rainbows and that he is capable of the same amount of darkness as the devils, then maybe I can get out of this. Maybe I can drag him with me. I am in the mood for a good beating. I bet he likes it just as much as Lucian does. They are born from the same light, after all.

"It's difficult to connect to your soul, Raven," Cassius murmurs, leaning in close to where there's only an inch of space between our faces. "Are you allowing me in?"

"I think you're the one who is resisting. I am completely open to you." I shift my mouth a little bit closer, breathing in the same breath as him. His wings unfurl and expand, creating an even brighter light from behind him. I know exactly how to get him to loosen up and pull that stick out of his ass. All it will take is a simple kiss. I know that helps Lucian connect with me.

"I've never had this problem before. I'm failing. This is supposed to be what helps you see what I see." Cassius sighs and surprises me by resting his forehead to mine. "I'm sorry."

I wish he didn't sound so pathetic in this moment. I kind of have a thing for sad angels. Or confused little bastards that just need a little push in the right direction that isn't Heaven.

"May I try something?" I ask, letting him rest against me. "It involves our lips touching."

"A kiss?" Cassius pulls back another inch, clearing his eyes and my vision with the distance. "I suppose we could try that."

It takes everything in me not to smile and high-five my damn self. I had expected him to resist or to push me away and reject me, but the jerk angel is too enthralled with my closeness. I can tell. I will use it to my advantage.

"Whenever you're ready," I say, licking my lips and rubbing them together. "But it has to be you who kisses me. I'm not making the move. You're the one who wants to show me that you can make me feel better."

Cassius audibly swallows, and his jaw twitches at my words. He totally expected me to make the first move. And there's no fucking way. If he wants to do this, he can do this on his own. This is all on him. I'm going to stand here and smile, watching him squirm under my scrutiny. I want him to question his entire existence and what he's doing with me in this room, especially when he finally gets the nerve to bask in what he assumes is the heavenly gloriousness of my soul. What he isn't prepared for is to learn that within my light still lingers a shadow. I'm not an angel like him. I'm a mortal, after all.

"You don't have to use tongue if you are afraid that you might like it," I tease, trying to get my lips to stop from smiling. "I'm not interested in corrupting you, like you assume. I just like fucking with you. You are so...uncomfortable when it comes to me."

"I am not. I'll prove it." Cassius inhales a soft breath and closes the distance completely, brushing his lips to mine.

I stand frozen, not reacting to the sensation of his light kiss. I don't even hold my lips to his or try to kiss him back. If he wants me to do it, he's going to have to really convince me.

As if he can read my thoughts, he slides his hand around my neck and tilts his head a bit, moving his lips more, kissing me deeper until I do give in and kiss him back.

It should be weird kissing Cassius. I shouldn't enjoy it as much as I do, but something about this kiss is unlike anything I've ever experienced. I don't know if it's because he's a cocky, prideful bastard who is trying to prove to me that he's not afraid or what, but he kisses me in a way that weakens my knees. All I know is that I'm going to silently invite him to explore my mouth by parting my lips. He takes me up on my offer and glides his tongue over mine, deepening our kiss as a light grows around us until the apartment fades away into a realm of pure white.

I expect him to pull away and tell me that's enough, and I almost do it myself, except it's as if we are two magnets attracting each other. I can't stop myself from letting my body take control. If a kiss could break him, he'd be in a million pieces right now. But this kiss also makes me feel...strangely together.

Moaning, Cassius's hand releases my hair and rubs down the length of my back until he reaches the waist of my jeans. His fingers dig into my skin under my shirt, and he pulls our hips flush together.

And damn. He's so hard. I can feel his shaft against my pelvis. He really has no shame because he doesn't even try to hide it. Not like he could anyway.

"I told you that I am not uncomfortable with you, Raven," Cassius murmurs, only stopping for a second to whisper the words. He caresses his lips to mine again like he can't resist kissing me like this forever. It's obvious he's not only kissing me to touch my soul. He'd never admit it, though.

"This doesn't prove much. All it does is show me that you're not afraid of a little tongue." I flick my tongue across his lips and nip his bottom lip between my teeth, stretching it.

He moans deep in his throat, the sexy sound vibrating over me. "You really want that orgasm, don't you?" A smile crosses his lips, and he moves his hand lower until it cups my ass. He's growing more bold by the second.

"I don't think you even know how to accomplish that, so no. I'm not in the mood to teach you. Show me what you meant about making me feel content without physical intimacy. Right now, I think you're all talk. I think you just wanted to kiss me and touch my soul under the ruse that you'd be helping me. You like it, don't you? I bet if I'd let you, you'd soul fuck me." It's my turn to smile because I'm totally right, and we both know it. Angels have a different set of desires than humans. They love feeling pure souls as much as the devils.

I ease back even more and put about six inches of space between us. Cassius frowns as if the space hurts him, but he doesn't close it. He continues to look at me as if I'm all he's capable of seeing. And maybe I am in this pure white world just as he is all I can see. But I think it's different for him. I can see him as he is an angel. With the way heavenly light illuminates from him, I think he sees me as a soul without my physical form. We are not on the same plane as we were. This is the spiritual realm, and it feels like the same place that Lucian has brought me several times.

"Raven, it's more than about what I like and dislike about you. Of course, I enjoy being in the light of your soul. It is unlike anything I've ever experienced, especially now that you carry a new being created from the purest light in the universe." Cassius brushes his fingers along my cheek, pushing my black hair from my face. Drawing his fingers down my clavicle, he traces around the curve of my boob and to my torso until he plants his palm on my stomach.

As if his touch triggers me, a blinding light explodes through the air, quickly followed by absolute darkness. But the darkness doesn't devour the light. It twines and blends, creating a glittering shade of gray haze.

"Blasphemy," Cassius whispers, his wings spreading out wide. "This can't be. You cannot create something made of light and dark." I don't know if his words are intended for me or if he's thinking out loud, but either way, his comment pisses me off.

Anger bursts through me, and I slap his hand away from my stomach. The sudden change in his demeanor upon seeing the beautiful darkness created from my love for the devils causes me to build a steely guard around my soul to protect me from him. I cut him off but can't figure out how to pull myself from this spiritual realm.

"Why the fuck do you think that? Obviously, anything is possible. I'm intended for Purgatory, so of course I can create two beings that encompass such a beautiful balance together. This is why you're going to fail, Cassius. This is why it was pointless for you to bring me here. You think that I somehow carry a new light to serve Heaven, but you're wrong. We don't serve anyone but humanity. Now, release my soul. I don't want to be here with you anymore. I knew you would fail to do as you said and just take advantage of me." I shuffle a couple of steps back and fold my arms over my chest protectively. I try to will the world to return me back to the apartment, but nothing happens.

"You're wrong. You belong to Heaven. Purgatory is a devil's fantasy to sway power from where it belongs." Cassius summons divine light between his palms. "I'll show you. Enough light can help. Devils were once angels. Maybe this is why I was put in your path. Maybe—"

Pure, inky darkness swells around me, growing and moving as if the shadows come to life. Cassius's eyes widen. For the first time in a while, I know he fears me. Well, not me. He fears the darkness swirling around me, taking over the spiritual realm he has me in.

"No, this can't be happening." Cassius summons more heavenly light in his palms, trying to use it against the darkness. "You have to stop, Raven. Please, something is extremely wrong. Make it stop."

I narrow my eyes, wishing he'd stop. "Why? So you can continue to plot against us? So you can drag me to the guardians? So you can try to end this beautiful being born from love and justice? From balance?"

"I don't want to end it. I want to fix it. I want to help you, so the darkness doesn't consume your light. Look at everything around us, Raven. It needs to be controlled. Can't you see? What if it manages to consume all of Heaven's light? Then what?" Cassius tenses, his muscles rippling with his nerves. The more the darkness emanates from me, the dimmer his light shines.

It's enough to tighten my chest with fear. What if he's right? I don't want to destroy Heaven. I don't want the goodness of the world just to vanish. So what he says now? I can't believe it. Nothing about the strange darkness feels bad. It feels powerful and perfect. It feels like love.

"You need to have faith. Nothing about this feels wrong, Cassius. Let me show you. Do you know how you opened my soul? Let me touch your being." I summon the courage to step forward.

Cassius takes an automatic step back, his fear scrunching his features. "Raven, please."

"Cassius, you have to trust me. I don't want to destroy your light. I think my body is just reacting to your threat. So let me touch your being. You can cling on to the light of my soul if you want to." I take another couple of steps forward, expecting him to disappear or something. I expect him to cower in fear. Or maybe try to fight me.

Instead, Cassius straightens his back and sharpens his features. He holds out his hands to me, his demeanor guarded, but he reluctantly gives in to my pleas.

I fucking hope this works, because I need him. Hell needs him.

"Just don't resist. Don't try to fight back with your light either." I gently rest my hands in his and pull him close enough to wrap my arms around his neck. His eyes glow with heavenly light, and I catch my strange reflection. I'm a blur of light and dark and gray and everything in between. I'm only soul and spirit as whatever grows inside me overpowers my very essence.

"Raven," Cassius says.

But I cut him off by pressing my mouth to his, and I kiss him just like we kissed before, except this time, instead of letting him touch my light, I touch his. I bask in the glory of his pure angelic being until we merge as one.

The world turns dark.

Cool fingers caress my forehead, drawing me from the most peaceful place I've ever been. It's hard to explain what I had experienced with Cassius, but I know that he felt what I felt with the two vastly different beings growing inside me. My babies, however they come, will be incredible. Because even though they're so incredibly tiny, they already have an impact on everyone who comes across me.

"The army is ready. We can band together in this relocation. A proper home has been found off the coast, and it will be easier to shield an island. We not only can keep the devils away, but we can also make sure that only trusted mortals will be within reach of Raven." The unfamiliar voice triggers panic through me, and I jerk upright.

"Hey, Raven. Don't attack. You are safe." Cassius's voice

draws my attention away from the deep wrath of an angelic guardian. "We are just trying to work out the logistics. Mikail thinks it's better to relocate you and keep you isolated, but I know that would be far too stressful and difficult."

I can't tell if Cassius is doing it because he knows I will destroy every fucking bastard angel that tries to touch me, or maybe he knows the dangers of provoking the one soul the devils love, but regardless, I'm thankful he doesn't tell me to suck it up then to comply.

Something shifted inside both of us. I don't know what he's feeling now that I let him soak in the darkness growing inside me, but I do know that he isn't afraid like he was before. If anything, he now has a sense of relief. There's no way he wouldn't have tried to murder me on the spot with his heavenly sword if things were awful like he thought.

"As much as I want to cater to her feelings, the child inside her must be completely guarded. It is our duty to see that light survive. Heaven needs such a victory." Mikail tightens his jaw and narrows his eyes at me.

It takes everything in me not to attempt to summon the darkness to devour him with. Because I know what will happen if I do. He doesn't know what Cassius knows. I don't think Cassius is ready to share the information. If he had, I'm sure Mikail would've said something.

"This is a victory. Raven understands what we're trying to

do. You have to make the compromise. It is her life and her child, and she has free will to make decisions for herself. It is not our purpose to intervene." Cassius shifts closer to me, resting his hand on my stomach as if it's the most natural thing.

I swat at his hand, getting him to move it. All he does is place it on top of mine to squeeze my fingers.

"Divine intervention is a must, Cassius. This has gone on long enough. Do not question my path. The Higher Power put this before me because you couldn't handle it." Mikail flicks his gaze from me to Cassius.

Oh, fucking shit. I want Cassius to punch the bastard in his smug-ass face. For the first time ever, I consider standing up for Cassius. But I don't. I brace myself to make a run for it instead. I will figure out how to break the shield and get out of this crummy apartment.

"That is unfair to say," Cassius says, his voice remaining even.

How can he not smack the asshole upside the head? I can't believe he manages to keep his cool. He has lost his shit with the devils a dozen times. I don't get it.

"I'm saying it with pure love and devotion. Just because you couldn't handle it doesn't mean that you were any less powerful than you are. You just unfortunately have a bond to those who have lost their way and perished in the fires of evil, my brother. But you can amend things. Heaven needs you." Mikail pats Cassius on the shoulder. "Once you have your army once more, with me by your side, we will right the wrongs in the universe. I will make sure you don't fail again."

I grimace, twisting my lips to the side. "Who the fuck are you to talk to a savior like this? Weren't you once one of these human souls you're so afraid of Hell corrupting? You act as if you have power comparable to the devils. I can't wait to see the look on your face when they rip your damn wings off and send you to the pits with the rest of your fallen failure fuckheads."

I know I shouldn't instigate the angel. He could lash out at me, call me names like an abomination, or even do something crazy like threaten my life on Earth, but I'm not afraid of him. He is far from intimidating. And I know in this very moment, Cassius won't allow him to do anything to provoke the darkness brewing inside me, tangling with the bright light in what could be the most powerful connection the universe has ever seen.

Mikail ignores me, keeping his gaze on Cassius. And it pisses me off more than it should. I hate being ignored and treated as if I am not even here. I'm not used to it. With my devils, I'm usually their sole focus. It takes a lot to distract them, and even then, they still have some attention on me.

"I still think we should wait a bit longer," Cassius says, squeezing my fingers harder. "The second we leave this apartment, if the shields are even down for a moment, the devils will be able to pinpoint us. They are too focused right now."

"Maybe we can suggest a trade for Zade. Use him as a distraction. The devils will think they're getting Raven, but we'll attack. We can set a trap. I'll handle Raven and get her away safely." Mikail straightens his shoulders, his muscles bunching as he flexes his hands. "It will be best if you don't know her location, so they can't use you."

What? No. Fuck no. There's no way I'm letting Mikail take me.

"I don't think so, Mikail. Raven is more familiar with me." Cassius unfurls his wings. "I know you think you're doing the right thing, but her mental state is important during this time."

Mikail glowers and snatches my hand, surprising me. "Cassius—"

My body reacts, and I manage to summon hellfire, burning Mikail and getting him to release me. Cassius swears under his breath just loud enough for me to hear, but Mikail is too concerned about his own pain. I take advantage of his distraction and blast Cassius next. I spin on my heels and rush toward the apartment door. It hums and crackles at my closeness, and then something purely amazing happens. The fire in my palms turns into light, and the door swings open, allowing me out of this bare-bones apartment and into a lively complex.

I open my mouth to shout for help, but a woman lands in

front of me and expands her golden wings. I automatically attack, summoning a fire whip from the bowels of Hell. And holy shit. The wave of power coursing through me zings me to my very core. My connection to Hell startles the angel, and she jumps back. I expect her to try to hurt me or try to capture me, but all she does is launch back into the air.

"Raven! Please! Come back here," Cassius shouts, his voice bellowing behind me.

I don't respond to him.

I don't look back either. Instead, I thrust more hellfire over my head, keeping the angels back.

And then I run.

15

Abandoned

RAVEN

I RUN AS fast as I can, keeping my eyes on the world around me. I'm afraid I won't make it far before the angels swoop down and snatch me off my feet, stealing me away and not giving me a chance to fight.

I'm pretty damn sure that the angels are shielding this whole area, and I'll have to get far, far away before I can call my devils to save me. I wish I were more athletic. If I were, I wouldn't be so out of breath. I wouldn't be tempted to pray for the energy to keep going. Also, I'd probably stand a better chance. It seems a bit pointless to be running, but my devils would punish me if I didn't at least try to escape. I'm too stubborn to admit that

I face defeat because of my mortality.

"Raven, why bother fleeing? You know this is over for you. Heaven has won, and we will not stand by and watch this beautiful gift you carry be destroyed by Hell." Meri lands on the sidewalk in front of me, expanding her wings to block my path. This bitch. Can she read minds like Micah? I hate that she confirms my thoughts about not being powerful enough on my own. "Please, show some reason. We are not your enemy. We want what's best for you and that beautiful, angelic light of the soul you carry."

"Don't bother trying to convince her. Darkness grips her at her very core. It will devour anything heavenly if we allow it. This must be handled accordingly, even if it means we have to use everything that the Higher Power has given us to see to it and she doesn't fall back into the hands of Hell." Mikail's voice sets me off, and I spin to see him standing behind me. A dozen feet away, Cassius remains quiet like the coward he is with his arms crossed over his chest.

I should've never let him get close to me like he had when I allowed him to touch my soul. I don't know what I was expecting. Maybe, I wanted to change his mind about me. Maybe it was something else. But now? I can't stop the hurt coursing through me. I know he saw how beautiful both of my babies are because I allowed him in, yet he just stands idly by acting just like Zade. I'd confuse him for being Sloth if I didn't know any better.

"Come any closer, and I will open the Hell portal and kick your sorry ass into it. Just leave me alone and let me go. You have no idea what is right or wrong for me. It is solely my decision." I fist my hands, trying to keep my shit together even though I want to panic. If I panic, they will overpower me. I need to fight. I need to do something.

Come on, body. Give me some Hell to throw at them. Give me the strength to do something other than hope for the best.

"You no longer get a say, you abomination. You should have already lost your soul to Hell. How you still manage to have such a connection to Heaven is beyond me." Mikail's words send fury simmering through my soul.

What a fucking asshole. I thought Cassius was bad, but he is nothing compared to this douche.

I turn to Cassius, catching his gaze. "You are a worthless piece of shit. How can you let these two fuckers treat me like this? You said it yourself that it was not your purpose to intervene in my life. Shouldn't you stop them from doing it?"

Cassius straightens his shoulders, remaining expressionless towards my words.

"You will not talk to him. He does not have a say in this matter any longer." Mikail has the nerve to step closer to me and grab at my hand.

Like his touch detonates a bomb, bright divine energy explodes from me more powerful than before, and it knocks him and Meri away.

I dodge around Meri, heading toward what I hope is the front of the complex. All I need to do is get to the street. If I get to the road, I can find somebody that can let me use their phone. This isn't the first time I've had to rely on a stranger to get me out of this mess.

With that thought comes one of the most horrible moments of my life, when Andre was still an angel and his presence set off a good Samaritan and the guy ended up dead because of me.

A shadow crosses over my head, blocking the sun, and I try not to scream as an angel lands on the path in front of me.

I gasp, my panic turning into relief. I can't believe it. Zade stands before me in all of his angelic glory, his muscles rippling and his beautiful eyes shining with his heavenly grace. I should make sure he hasn't all of a sudden turned against me to stand beside the guardians, but I can't help myself. I rush forward and jump at him, forcing him to catch me in his muscular arms.

"Go. Go. Go. Hurry and get me out of here," I say, tightening my thighs around his waist as I hug him with my whole body. "The guardians want to take me to some island or some shit to keep me hidden. You can't let them."

"Zade, what a relief to see you. We thought the devils were

holding you captive." Mikail's rumbly voice calls through the air. Annoyance laces his words, and I'm nearly certain it's because he had planned to use it against my devils in the supposed trade he wanted to fake to create a distraction. "Please bring Raven back to me. It is our duty to protect her and Heaven's gift."

Zade adjusts me in his arms, keeping me close at the same time that he steps toward the angels. What the actual fuck? He's going in the wrong direction.

"You have no idea how special Raven truly is." Zade ruffles his feathers, shifting on his feet. I can feel his anxiety unlike anything I've felt radiate from him before. I can't tell if it's because of the angels or me. Maybe both.

"We are well aware," Meri says, her sharp voice snapping my attention, "even without you being forthcoming."

The way she talks to Zade as if he's stupid pisses me off.

The righteous angels get on my damn nerves. How dare somebody with less power act superior. If I were Zade, I would lash out at her. I would lash out at both of them. Even Cassius, the quiet asshole, needs a good beat down. I thought we had a moment together. The bastard. I should've known he'd disappoint me.

"Don't talk to Zade like that," I say, twisting my torso to glare at Meri. "I should blast your ass to Hell."

Meri ignores me, not even giving me any of her attention. I

hate being treated like this. I hate how they act as if I am just a soul to claim and not a mortal.

"Give her to us now, Zade," Mikail says. He takes a step closer, summoning a heavenly sword. I can't believe he threatens Zade like this. I'm pretty sure he would attack him if he put his guard down.

"Don't you think about it, Zade. You know what they're going to do to me. Please, get me away. If you can get me out of here and close enough to the devils, they can handle them." I remind him that I care about him by kissing his throat.

"You know I would never give them to you, Raven," Zade says, adjusting me in his arms. He flips me over onto his back and summons his glowing sword.

Zade struts forward, his whole body tense and rippling with his heavenly power as he faces his comrades. I hold on tight, so he doesn't have to worry about me. Meri and Mikail both stand straight and rigid, their expressions morphing into pure hatred. I can't even look at them without feeling as if they will smite me. Instead, I turn my attention to Cassius, meeting his gaze. His amethyst eyes sparkle with what could possibly be tears. What the hell? He cannot be upset about this. He knows that I will never comply and go with the guardians. I will never allow them to take me from the devils. They are mine, and I am theirs. I'm having one of their babies. I'm having Elias's baby. And I don't have time to deal with their righteous attitudes.

"Are you standing against us, Zade?" Mikail says, aiming his glowing sword at us. "If you do, that is an act against Heaven. We will take your wings."

My heart hammers in my chest, rattling against my ribcage at the thought. The moment when Micah lost his wings flits through my mind. It was one of the worst things I have ever seen. Watching an angel have his wings severed feels as if Hell crashes right into you. And for Micah, it did. I don't want Zade to go through the same thing. Losing his wings will not only hurt him on a spiritual level, but it will also prevent us from getting the hell out of here.

"If you so much as try, I will open a portal to Hell right now. I can use Raven to do so. This is your one chance to leave us in peace." Zade clenches his fists, preparing to do something I have never seen an angel do.

Meri raises her sword next. "We can't."

Zade flies forward without warning and strikes Mikail with his elbow, while spinning and slashing at the front of Meri's shirt. I've seen him fight before, but his moves now? Damn, he's good.

Spinning around, he jumps back and sets me on my feet. "Stay guarded. Call out if someone even dares come near you. I must teach them their places. I'm done with this madness." Zade's words strike me on a deep level, and I stretch up and kiss him.

The two angels close in on us, but he doesn't give them a chance to strike. He spin-kicks his leg, sweeping their feet out from under them. Meri calls out to Cassius for help. Just the sound of his name echoing through the air pisses me off. I know Cassius and I aren't exactly friends. But I swear to the universe, if he tries to stand against me, this will be my last effort at playing nice with him. He knows the truth. He's felt the darkness, and he knows it isn't bad. He knows how perfect the balance is.

"Cassius, you must fight him. He has made his choice." Mikail growls and gets back to his feet, lunging at Zade again.

"I can't," Cassius whispers, his voice barely sounding over the noise of the fight. "He still has his grace. He is not on Hell's side. He is just upset. Please, stop. Don't fight him. We can figure out a way to make things work with everyone."

"This is the only way," Mikail says, gathering heavenly light in his palm.

Surprising Zade, Mikail launches into the air and throws the power over his head, shooting it in my direction. I cover my face and scream, trying to protect myself. It won't hurt me, but it will knock me back or out or at least leave me vulnerable for a couple of seconds.

Zade hollers and jumps into the air, swinging his sword at Mikail. Meri uses the moment to rush toward me. I shout for Zade. I can't face this damn bitch. Mikail grabs onto Zade's feathers, stopping him from trying to get to me and stabs his sword through Zade's wing.

Darkness explodes through me, turning the world pitch black. It swallows Meri and her heavenly light, forcing her away from me before she can get within a foot. Her scream rips through the air, and I blink, trying to see through the haze. I no longer see Zade or Mikail. The only one who stands within my new darkness is Cassius.

He holds his hand out to me. "Raven, you have to stop this. I only have control over this plane for a second. You can't destroy them. They might not understand the whole situation, but they are doing what they feel is right until we can change their minds. If you send Meri to Hell, it'll be a war far worse than what it is now. The angels will consider you a bigger threat than even Hell."

His soft voice comes through the air, lacing around me and drawing me closer to him. Ice travels up my spine, cooling the heat radiating from my skin. I close the distance to Cassius, placing my hand in his. With our simple touch, light flashes through the air and devours the darkness.

I'm thrown back into the Mortal Realm in the middle of an angelic battle. Zade stabs Mikail through his wing, stopping him from flying into the air. I gasp at the sight of Zade in this moment. His light is gone. Blood drips from his wings, and he begins to shift right before my eyes. Most of the time, the devils don't show me their true appearance until they are comfortable with knowing that I won't hold it against them. And Zade? He knows that I accept him for who he is regardless.

Long hair sprouts from his head, and he bulks up in his height and muscles. Fire rolls over his skin, devouring his angel façade. He looks half-man and half-horse, his ears pointing and his face elongating. Hooves stomp the ground, shaking the world around us until a crack forms. Heavenly light crackles through the air, and whatever heavenly shield was put in place explodes and disappears.

I stand frozen in awe, drinking in the sight of Zade in his devil form. His sleek, muscular body changes with his new blond fur glossing over his skin, left behind by the fire but now travels to his hands. I can't help how distracted I am by the looks of him. He's far from scary to me, but I can tell that the two angels are utterly terrified. They back up and try to launch into the air. Zade thrusts his hands in their direction, sending a mesmerizing purple fire at them. It's as pretty as Kase's ruby power.

"Zade, no!" Cassius yells, thrusting his own angelic light at Zade. "Please, don't hurt them. You know that they follow what they feel is right."

"I'm sorry, Cass. I can't stand by any longer and do nothing. I've tried everything in my power to stay on my righteous path. I didn't want to abandon Heaven, but I don't know what else to do. I have to protect Raven and her babies. She is our future. She will help humanity far more than any of the angelic army can. I think they're afraid because they realize it. They were once mortal, too, you know. All they probably see is change, and change doesn't always settle well with some. Because what will they do if they no longer have to guard humanity? They will no longer have a path to follow." Zade's voice deepens with his words, his comment stabbing me in the soul. If what he says is true, it would explain so much. It would tell me exactly why the guardians are so determined to ruin me and my life. It proves why they want so badly to keep me from my devils. If I take Purgatory and my devils all have their thrones, we will change the balance. It won't be in Heaven's favor, but it also won't be in Hell's. It'll be in Purgatory's.

"That's not true. You know that they will always have their paths to follow. They just want to protect that precious light growing inside Raven. I know this because I want the same." Cassius wrings his hands together, jerking his attention to me. "I want to protect her more than that."

"Then you agree what must be done. You don't have to say it. I know you are far too cowardly to admit that you were wrong." Zade grows taller, his hooves bigger, and then suddenly horns jut from his shoulders, turning him more monstrous with his transformation. It's strange how I know I should be a bit unsettled by the sight of my sweet, angelic

Zade turning into this powerful, beastly devil, but I'm not. I feel relief. I feel closer to him. It's hard to explain, but it feels as if another piece of me has come together. It eases the stress and ache that has been tightening my whole body ever since I discovered that Elias isn't on another cycle without me.

"I will not admit such a thing because it's untrue." Cassius summons his heavenly sword, and light crackles over the blade. "This is your last chance to just stand down. Take Raven and go."

Mikail growls with his annoyance. "Cassius, you cannot allow that. I will not stand by and let you just give her to Hell. Must I go after your wings next?"

Cassius doesn't have a chance to answer, because Zade charges forward and blasts his mesmerizing purple light at Mikail. The angel twists, trying to avoid it, but the power smacks right into his chest and knocks him on his back. Meri expands her wings and glares. I tense as her focus shifts from Zade to me.

Cassius steps forward, trying to steal my attention, looking as if he will attack. His face sharpens with his need to stop the guardians but also to stop Zade.

"Grab him, Cassius. Grab him now, and I will get Raven," Meri snaps, flexing her muscles. Angelic light glows from her, and she dashes forward in my direction. Jumping into the air, she takes flight and circles around us.

I tip my head back and stare at her in the sky. The bitch summons heavenly power and tosses it at Zade. He tries to launch into the air, but his hurt wing doesn't allow him to do it. Another blast of heavenly light hits him, and I watch in anger as Mikail attacks from his fall on the ground.

"Cassius, now!" Mikail shouts, his voice booming through the air. His anger ramps up his angelic light, nearly blinding me. "You are a savior. This is your duty."

That fucker. I can't help feeling bad for Cassius. It's as if Mikail knows how to manipulate Cassius's pride. And who knows? Maybe he does.

Cassius scrunches his face and nods his head. I close the space to Zade and grab onto the back of his shirt. We are outnumbered. He can't fly us out of here. Meri also won't stop attacking from above, and if Cassius joins Mikail and his fight, I'm afraid of what will happen.

"Raven, get on my back and don't let go." Zade holds his hand out to me without looking in my direction.

I do as he instructs, and he pulls me closer until I can hop on his back. His wings vanish, though his devil features remain the same. It's freaky when he bows forward and plants his hands on the ground. Kicking his back legs, he manages to knock Meri away as she tries to grab me. The sound of bones crushing echoes in my ears, and the angelic woman screams in pain.

I grab onto Zade's blond mane and hold on for dear life as

he bucks like a damn bull. It reminds me of the one time that I tried to ride a mechanical bull at a bar and ended up getting thrown off in a matter of seconds. I am not cut out for this shit. If I didn't have Zade's mane to hold and a strong will to stay attached to him, I'm sure I'd be on my ass right now.

"Surrender Raven. We don't want to hurt her. Please, Zade. I will take her myself, and I will protect her. Just stop fighting." Cassius stays just out of reach, but the two other angels don't stop attacking.

"Never. Raven is mine. She belongs to Hell. So do you. Stop resisting, Cass. It's pointless." Zade snaps his huge teeth and manages to bite the tip of Mikail's sword and flings it away, leaving him with only his heavenly light. But it doesn't hurt Zade like it does the other devils. I think he's still too new.

"Raven, you have to talk some sense into him. He will send them to Hell. Please remember what I said about the war. Just trust me. I know that we have some darkness between us. I know that I have done nothing to earn your trust, but I've touched your soul now. I want what you want. I want to ensure that those precious gifts you carry survive and flourish. I will do anything to see to it. Right now, you are standing in the middle of a war. Let me get you away from all of that. Please." Cassius extends his hand to me, his amethyst eyes shining in the light. He sounds so earnest with his intentions that I believe him, but still, I don't want to go. I am not going to let anyone push me around or make decisions for me. The angelic army has been warned. They need to learn the consequences of trying to stop us. We can't be stopped. I will take a throne in Hell. I will nurture these tiny new beings with both light and dark and show the world how it should be. I'll teach them how important humanity is.

I shake my head. "I'm sorry. I can't. Zade will defend me. He is mine as much as he now belongs to Hell."

"Raven—" Cassius doesn't have a chance to finish his plea, because the ground between us opens up and fire licks the pavement before exploding toward the sky.

Zade spins and ducks his body again, using his big hooves to kick Mikail. The angel flails and flaps his wings, but he can't do anything as he crashes and rolls toward the Hell portal.

"Mikail!" Meri screams. She flies down and grabs hold of Mikail by his wings.

Cassius swears, flying at the two of them. He tackles the two angels and gets them out of the way before Zade can kick them into the fiery pits.

I expect for Zade to try again. I expect him to launch into the air in his devil form and grab onto the angels to take them to Hell, but he doesn't. He stops.

Actually, the whole world stops. Dark haze ripples through the air, morphing the Mortal Realm into the spiritual plane I had found myself in before. This time, it's not Cassius who stands in the darkness with me. It's Zade. He's no longer in his devil form.

Light sparkles from my hands and swirls through the air, wrapping around him, drawing him closer. He gasps, his beautiful blue eyes glittering in my light. It's so strange. I know that he jumped from grace, but in this moment, he still feels like an angel. The light dances over his skin, healing the wounds caused from the battle. He drinks me in, his mouth open with his surprise.

"Raven, I don't understand. How are you doing this?" Zade asks, reaching up to caress a finger along my cheek.

"What am I doing?" I tilt my head, pressing my cheek harder to his fingers to feel his touch as it teases my soul.

"You're manipulating my very being. You shouldn't be able to. Only angels and devils can access this world. And none of them can mess with each other's beings." Zade licks his lips, his eyes looking back and forth as he stares at me, trying to find the answers that I can't give him.

"It's hard to explain, but something set my body off. I think it's the babies. I don't know why they're so reactive suddenly, but it's like they figured out how to use me to do things like protecting myself and them. I think finding Elias and also touching Heaven again with you triggered the power of my baby created from the purest light in the universe. And with that light, I think the darkness of my devil baby rose to help balance it. But that's just a guess. I have no fucking clue. And I'm scared. I just want to go back home and see the other devils. We need to figure it out." My voice turns soft with my words. I wish I had better answers than this.

"You have to release us. If you do so, I will take you there." Zade continues to caress my cheek working his way to my neck and down my shoulder.

"But the angelic army," I say, shifting on my feet. "If we go back..." I don't want to think about it. I don't want to see those bastard angels at all. I don't want to see Cassius either. He's left me feeling so conflicted and rejected and completely out of my mind. I don't even know how to handle him or if I even should try.

"Let me try." Zade inhales a deep breath and closes his eyes. Placing both of his hands on my temples, he leans in and caresses his lips to mine.

I expect the world to shift. Expect the light to bloom from the two of us. What I don't expect is for the light glowing around us to vanish.

A wave of ice and heat, pain and relief, and new, unusual emotions pours over me with strange shadows.

"Oh no. Raven." Zade's words hum, the sound muffled to my ears.

There's nothing I can do as he disappears.

I vanish next.

16

Balance

RAVEN

"YOU HAVE TO make sure that stays on her at all times. If it comes off, she won't be grounded to the mortal plane." Lucian's voice trickles to my ears, pulling me from a weird state of calm.

I remember being scared as hell as Zade disappeared, and I found myself in a world of nothingness, but that's it. I don't know how long I was on another plane by myself, but it's long enough for me to lose my shit.

After basically crying myself into oblivion, my being kind of just shut off. Until now.

I want to know what the hell really happened and if I actually did get lost in a weird spiritual plane. If only I could gather enough strength to open my eyes. It feels like it's been years since I've seen any of my devils, and all I want to do is jump on them and smother them with my love. Maybe let them bury their faces between my boobs. I'm sure they'd prefer me to smother them with those instead.

"Maybe I should be the one to take Zade to his kingdom," Andre says, his husky voice remaining low as if he's afraid of speaking too loudly.

"You're really going to be a bitch ass about this? Kase and Dante thought it would be better if she woke up to you instead of me." Hot fingers touch my forehead and comb my hair away from my face. I can feel Lucian's presence hovering over me.

"They just worry that you won't treat her as delicately as they want her to be taken care of right now. You tend to be rough, Lucian. She has been through a lot." Andre touches my hand, the familiarity of his skin against mine sending my heart racing. "If you remember to be gentle, considerate, and not an asshole, I think everything will be okay. You're better at this sort of thing. I'm still learning. Zade would prefer me to help him anyways."

I wait for a second, trying to decide if I want to argue and beg Andre to stay with me or if I want to give in to his need to help Zade through his transition. He's a bit right about Lucian. But he's wrong that his roughness bothers me. Sure, it annoys me, but there are far worse things in this universe than dealing with a jerk. He's not so bad lately anyway.

"I guess we could just fucking ask her what she wants. I see you're awake, Ray. Don't think you can get away with eavesdropping on our conversation." Lucian pets my cheek, and my eyelids darken as he leans in close. "Do I need to kiss you to get your sleepy ass to pull yourself from your darkness to face me? I will gladly take some of it off you. It's as intoxicating as the light of your soul."

Andre growls. "Do not mess with her soul right now, Lucian. It is fragile. You know she struggles to stay present in the Mortal Realm."

I snap my eyes open, afraid that the two devils will start fighting. The room feels hot with their power already, not to mention that I can feel the wave of their wild emotions coursing through me. It's the strangest thing. I don't know if it's because they have both touched my soul or what, but it's unlike anything I felt with them except for during those times of soul fucking.

"Fuck. Did you feel that?" Lucian furrows his brows and whips his attention from me to Andre. "She totally just tried to fuck me on a spiritual level."

Heat warms my skin at his words. "What? I didn't do anything to you. I just opened my eyes."

Lucian sits beside me on the bed. "Yeah, keep telling yourself that. I know you felt what I felt."

I narrow my eyes at him, his cocky bastard smile making him incredibly handsome in this moment. I don't know what comes over me, probably just the fact that I am so fucking glad to be away from all the bastard angels, but I jerk upright and fling my arms around him. Lucian crashes to the bed with me on top of him, and he grins wider.

"All right, Andre. Go with Zade. This sexy woman chose me." Lucian grins and flips me onto my back. Resting his elbows on each side of my head, he holds his weight off of me. "Isn't that right, princess?"

"Not exactly...Daddy." I tip my head back and laugh like a maniac, not able to keep a straight face. I can't play this game with Lucian. I'll be his princess, but there is no way I could keep this up. He can be king or some shit. Fuck, he can just be Satan. "I couldn't help myself. I'm so happy to be home. You happened to be the first one I saw. Don't let it get to your big ass head."

"You mean this one?" Lucian growls with a wicked grin, reaches between him, and whips out his dick, smacking it to my leg. "Too late for that. Look what you've done to me." He thumps the tip of his cock to my skin another time, letting me feel it slap against my thigh.

And damn him. It takes everything in me not to wrap my fingers around it and give it a little jerk.

"Maybe it was Andre. You know how good he is at turning anyone on." I stick my tongue out at him and shift to smile at Andre. "You can stay and kick him out if you want. But if Zade wants you, you should go. I know it's been rough for him. Get him ready to be my king and my devil of Sloth."

Slowly nodding, Andre offers me a soft smile. "You can count on me. I know how important it is that he gets on the same page as us."

"Just remember, asshole. Don't go fucking him. You haven't discussed that with Raven. I'm sure she would prefer to have you both the way she takes on Kase and Dante." Lucian flicks his fingers, shooting a burst of fire at Andre, getting him to back up.

"That is an unnecessary reminder. Zade and I are not like that. He is my companion." Andre tightens his jaw and turns back to me. "I will see you soon, little hellion. And when I do, we're going to catch up. I am so starved for your attention."

Damn. I am really certain I am starving for his too. I wouldn't mind getting trapped in his arms for a while.

Lucian grabs my chin, forcing me to look at him. He digs his fingers into my cheeks and gets into my face. "Don't even think about it unless you want me to flip you over, pin you down, and smack that horny little ass of yours. I can see you wanting to get stuck to that massive dickhead. That's not happening. I'm staking my claim on you right now, Raven. Do you understand?"

"No." I grin with my word, shoving Lucian back and off of me. "You're not my boss, Satan."

I try to rush from the bed to jump at Andre, loving fucking with Lucian way too much, but he grabs me by the back of my neck, dragging me to him.

"Get the fuck out of here and take Zade to his kingdom. Micah is waiting." Lucian summons his fire chain and whips it in Andre's direction. "Hurry. I can tell you're getting turned on and don't want to leave, but Raven is mine right now. She needs a good fucking and to feel my power. I will care for her properly."

Damn. Why do I like the sound of that?

He sounds harsh but sweet, and I'm here for it. I can't believe that I'm already set on letting him have his way. I don't know if it is because I've been through fucking Heaven or what, but I just want someone to take care of me. I want to forget that the angelic army wants to destroy me and steal my unborn children.

Andre hovers for a moment longer, and I curl my fingers and get him to come closer once more for another kiss. Lucian doesn't say anything, but his gaze burns over my face as he watches Andre struggle to stay in control as I kiss him sweetly.

I don't even get a chance to prepare myself for what Lucian has in store. The second Andre closes the door, Lucian grabs my legs and lifts them up enough to hook his fingers to the back of my waistband. He drags my pants off, not giving me a chance to do anything. I want to resist just for fun. I bet he is hell-bent on taking advantage of our moment after being interrupted the last time we were together like this.

"Are you in a hurry, Satan?" I ask, quickly crossing my legs at my knees, preventing him from trying to rip my panties right off me. "With the way you're rushing, it kind of feels like you're about to wham, bam, thank you ma'am me in this moment. If that's the case, chill your balls. I'm not in the mood to just be used as your little sex toy."

Fire flickers in Lucian's eyes, and he raises an eyebrow. Instead of stopping, he leans forward and summons hellfire in his palms. Cupping my boobs, he smolders the front of my shirt until the fabric disintegrates. The shock of his gesture makes me laugh harder and try to press my hand to his chest to keep him back.

"Don't make me tie your hands up. I want to feel them all over me but if you keep this shit up, you will leave me no choice." Lucian stares at me, his darkness practically overpowering me inch by inch. "Drop them this second and let me have my way."

I hesitate for a second, the thought of him following through with his threat turning me on. A part of me wants to push him. The excitement and thrill I get out of screwing with Lucian satiates my desire. Another part of me is tired of constantly putting up a fight. I just want to be taken care of and appreciated. Can Lucian do that? I have no fucking idea. I'm sure I'll find out.

Licking my lips, I slowly nod my head and drop my hands away from my chest, exposing my boobs to him. Lucian offers me the most dazzling smile I have ever seen on him. His pride swells, his muscular chest puffing out because, for once, I actually obey him willingly. I can tell that he loves the fuck out of it.

"What a good little soul, Ray. I don't know whether I should still tie you up or not. It feels as if you are waiting to strike me like a damn snake. That's Dante's thing. I just want you to be my princess and let me show you what I'm capable of. I want to show you that you have underestimated me. I know you think I'm selfish, but the only thing I'm selfish about is wanting you to myself and everything I want to do to you. I want to show you what it's like to really experience my darkness. I want you to look forward to being my queen."

Lucian rests his big palms on my knees as his hot fingers slowly massage into my skin, getting me to relax and uncross my legs.

"I swear that you better not turn into a raging asshole. More than what you have been if I let you continue. You have to promise me." I shift, my nerves making me a bit anxious. I shouldn't be nervous. I know what it's like to give myself to a devil. To multiple devils at once. I just worry that it could change things. It took a lot of beating Hell into him to get him to realize that it's not about just him.

"The only reason I'll be a fucking asshole is if someone either hurts you or if an angelic bastard fucks this up again. I'm tired of waiting. You have no idea how badly I want you on this level after getting to fuck the Hell out of your soul all those times before." Lucian slowly spreads my legs, resting on his knees between them. "Now, tell me what is off-limits. I know you get fucking kinky with Dante and Kase, but I don't want to assume that you'll do that shit with me. I understand boundaries despite always wanting to cross them with you."

I rub my lips together in thought. "My ass is off-limits. Also, your horns are too fucking sharp, so don't even try using them."

Lucian cocks his head, tilting it to the side. "There's no way I'm picking your ass before I get a piece of that pussy of yours."

"Also, I think you should remain in your mortal form this time. I've been experiencing a little…angelic light, as you know. I don't want to accidentally blast you away." I can't help crinkling my nose with my words. "That would really suck, because with my luck, it'll be right before I orgasm or some shit. So keep your satanic self in check and save that for another time."

Lucian chuckles, his handsome face lighting up. "I get that you love all the other devils and don't care about which form they take, but I prefer this form. I will only transform into my glorious, sexy, powerful, devil self if you get on your knees and beg me."

I scoff and shake my head. "Well, that's never happening."

"We'll see. I have a feeling that you won't be able to resist, especially when I'm through with you. Now anything else? I'm tired of talking bullshit that Dante demanded I do before I fuck your brains out." Lucian glides his hands up my thighs and stops just short of my panties.

"And to think I thought you were caring." I wag my finger at him. "I almost got on my knees for you. But whatever. I like seeing you on yours."

"My knees? No. You are going to ride my fucking face until you beg me to let you off." Lucian surprises me by lifting up my hips and throwing himself back while still holding me.

My knees hit the mattress as I straddle his face, and he surprises me by using his teeth to tear the fabric of my panties.

I gasp as he uses his finger to pull at the back and get them off me completely, snapping the fabric hard enough to sting. The pain doesn't last long because he licks the ache away, dragging his tongue across my clit before kissing me between my legs. The way he eats me out shows me how starved for my body he truly is. Usually, my devils start slow and work me up, teasing me and testing me. Lucian sets my body ablaze with energy that curls my toes and tenses my muscles. He gets straight to getting me off, his mouth working so amazingly against my body that my vision shadows around the edges. I brace myself, bowing forward to press my palms to the mattress. I'm already going to cum. It's as if he wants to just start out with a fucking unforgettable bang. And he is.

I moan so incredibly loud and rock my hips, increasing the pressure. If he wants me to ride his face, I'm going to fucking ride his face until he begs me to get off him. If I could suffocate him with my thighs, I bet he would like that.

Lucian digs his fingers into my legs, his nails biting my skin, the sensation incredible. I'm not usually a masochist, but the way he does it now, turning me on and getting me off, gets my adrenaline pumping like crazy. I start to bounce on him, and he hums deep in his throat, guiding me to rock harder as he sucks and kisses every inch of me until I explode so intensely that my whole body quivers and I fall forward, unable to stay upright.

Lucian hooks his arms around me and flips me off him, kneeling between my legs again. His eyes glow with the fire, and he summons his fire chain and grabs my arms and legs and twines it around my limbs, keeping them up in the air.

"You're starting to shine with angelic light. This will help keep you in control. Is that okay?" Lucian asks, licking his bottom lip and sucking it into his mouth.

I pant with my excitement, feeling vulnerable yet safe in his presence. "Only if you take off your clothes too. I want to see more of you. I want to taste you."

"You love getting fucked in the mouth, don't you?" He adjusts my legs enough to get a view of my ass. Swinging his arm, he spanks me right on my ass cheek. "Tell me or I will spank you again. I know that you sometimes need a little encouragement to behave."

It takes everything in me not to smile. He is totally into dominating me, and I love it. I don't have to show him or tell him what I like or what to do. He's been very aware of everything surrounding me that he knows what gets me good. He's always been right about my loving it a bit rough. I like having my hair pulled, my ass spanked, and my body used as the thing the devils want most.

"I want to feel you in my throat," I say, gliding my tongue across the seam of my mouth. "Show me how you plan to fuck me."

Lucian grabs his belt and unfastens it, sliding it off. He folds it in half and snaps it, the sound echoing through the room. I automatically flinch, and he smiles, his handsome face loving my reaction. He truly is a devil. Punishment and pain get him off. It gets me off seeing how much he enjoys it more than I knew possible. My whole body zings with lust, the high of my orgasm wrapped with desire leaving me on the edge with him.

"You want me to spank you with this, don't you? You're a bad little soul who craves my punishment. You want to feel it for days, don't you?" Lucian glides his belt over the backs of my legs. The way he has me tied with his fire chain leaves me incapable of doing anything except lying here exposed. Dipping his finger inside me, he tests my body. "You're so wet for me. You're dripping. I want you to sit on my face again and drown in your fucking pussy juice."

"Whatever you want, but after you give me your fucking cock, Satan. I'm starting to think that you're nervous." I narrow my eyes with my words, wiggling and shifting, trying to stretch my limbs against his fire chain that has me tied up like an animal.

Lucian growls and uses his belt to whip me just hard enough to tense my whole body. I gasp and manage to flip myself onto my side. It gets him going even more that I purposely struggle. My strength increases with my desire and with being so close to Lucian's power that I manage to snap his fire chain and free myself.

Jerking his arm out, he tries to grab me by the neck, and I dodge out of the way. Throwing myself forward, I jump on him and rip at his shirt, using my strength to tear it at the hem. He grabs one of my wrists and tries to restrain me, but I smack him hard enough across the face and go for his pants next. I snap open the button and slide my hand into his waistband, lacing my fingers around his hard cock. I stroke my fingers along the length pulling it out of his pants. He once again grabs my wrist, stopping me. He likes that I fight him and try to do what I want. He loves the idea of being able to overpower me. My strength matches his, and it really is a war for control. I had no idea that I would like to try dominating him as well.

"You're going to have to try harder than that if you want me to be your good little princess," I say, managing to drag his pants down. I crawl back and squeeze his cock hard enough to make him hesitate.

"Are you sure you want to play this game, you naughty soul? If you start, I will finish. Do you think you can handle that?" Lucian reaches down and grabs a fist full of my hair, yanking my head back enough to look into my eyes.

"Careful what you threaten, Satan. I can handle seven devils. How about you? You are all talk." I jerk my head back, and he releases my hair only enough to give me room to go down on him. "Now stop trying to get me off. It's my turn."

Lucian releases a guttural noise, watching me with parted lips and heavy breathing as I bow forward and suck his dick into my mouth. I bob my head while rubbing my fingers over his balls, spitting and slobbering all over him, making him slick. He moans with pleasure, his hand tightening and yanking my hair as he takes over. I stretch my jaw wider and let him thrust, fucking me in the mouth just how he wants. I moan and watch him, our eyes locked in a staring contest. He pushes himself up, guiding my head with him until I'm on my knees, and he is standing with bent knees on the bed. I purposely scratch my nails into his ass cheeks, pinching him hard as he continues to thrust, treating me like I am only here for his pleasure. And right now, I am. I don't mind.

"You're fucking amazing, Raven. I can't get enough of you. Let me touch your soul." Lucian eases my head up just enough to get a clear view of my eyes as he rocks his hips, sliding his cock in and out of my mouth deep enough for me to feel it in my throat.

I nod my agreement and open my mind to him, feeling his darkness seep from his being as his eyes light aglow and hellfire licks over his skin, revealing his devil form for a split second. He won't transform, though. I know he won't because I told him not to. But it is hard for him. I can tell.

Lucian groans with his pleasure, ecstasy scrunching his face, and then his darkness spills into me. I inhale a sharp breath as his being merges with mine, and he grunts with his orgasm, cumming into my mouth. The spicy cinnamon flavor of his cum overwhelms my senses, and I see fire explode all around us as I touch his devil form in a way I have never done so before. Usually, when we touch souls, he is in his angel form. But now? I get to drown myself in the power that has the angelic army scrambling for control. Lucian's power is far more addicting than I realize, and it sets me off. The darkness growing inside me blooms like a thousand black roses, and something happens that I can barely explain. My whole body buzzes with static. I watch myself transform into what I can only describe as a demonic form. My skin reddens and blood-red nails sharpen on the tips of my fingers. If I had a mirror, I could see the dainty crown of horns protruding around my head. I automatically touch the spot heating with Hell and prick my finger on the sharp points.

As quickly as the image envelops me, it disappears. Bright light shines with Lucian's darkness, consuming the both of us, and I snap my eyes open to find myself laying on top of him, feeling his hard-on press between my legs.

"Whoa. Fuck. What was that?" I ask, planting my hands on his muscular chest.

"Our future," he says, fire dancing across his gaze. "And you are fucking gorgeous. The most beautiful woman I have ever seen in all of my existence. I'm so glad that you have accepted me as your king. You are mine, Raven. You're Hell's. Do you understand that?"

I nod my head, slowly inhaling and exhaling to steady my heartbeat. Lucian doesn't give me long to get myself together before he kisses me, setting my body off again. Our tongues glide and fight each other, and I scratch his shoulder blades in battle with him to stay on top. I shimmy down, rocking my hips and grinding on his hard cock, trying to position him just right to slide inside of me.

"Tell me how bad you want me to fuck you," he says, grabbing my thighs and returning my need to fight him until I get my way by scratching me back.

I adjust my body again and finally manage to align myself just right to sink onto him. I don't tease him. I don't test him first. Instead, I bounce hard and fast, feeling him stretch my body in a way that leaves me aching in the best way.

"I will not beg you for anything, Lucian. I plan to always take what I want when I want it. Because I'm not only yours. You're mine. You're my devil and my fucking pleasure beast." I reach down and grab the back of his head, leaning in and forcing him to arch up to kiss me again.

He moans with my movements and kisses me deeper, sliding his tongue into my mouth and stealing my breath away. His hands lock onto my hips, and he guides me, lifting and dropping my body harder and faster until my legs weaken. I have no choice but to give him control. Without pulling out, he flips me over and gets on top of me, using my legs to hold onto as he spreads my body wider and thrusts with the power of Hell, hazing my vision until all I can do is scream in ecstasy as I orgasm.

My body pulses around his, and Lucian smiles wickedly.

Sliding his hand between us, he strums his thumb over my clit as if he plans to make me orgasm again and again until I can't take it anymore. Until I beg him to stop.

It wouldn't be the first time a devil has done so.

My whole body trembles, and I lose myself to the passion, to the pain and pleasure, to the power consuming me as Lucian fucks me hard enough to make me forget that there is more outside of us.

He cums, his moan as loud as mine, and he finishes with a final thrust that I swear sends my soul out of my body for a second until he grabs me and anchors me back.

My heavy breathing fills the air, and Lucian falls beside me, sliding his hand beneath my body, and pulls me to him until I curl against his side with our legs tangled. The heat of his body keeps me warm, and I close my eyes and listen to the sound of his heart beating. Of our hearts beating together. It's the last thing I had ever expected to have with Lucian. But I wouldn't change it. He brought me into this world with a shitty deal, and as much as I hated him in the beginning, he's grown on me. He respects me and what I'm capable of, and he treats me more than just a soul to own.

"Fuck, you have no idea how much I want to bang you again. I want to fuck you for the rest of time." Lucian draws his hand over my boobs, caressing my nipples. "I swear on all of Hell that I will destroy the angelic army for you. I will protect you.

Fuck, maybe I'll even knock you up."

I laugh in exasperation and prop up on my elbow, meeting his gaze. I stroke my fingers over his cheek, just staring into his dark eyes. "Not fucking happening. The world doesn't need Satan, Junior."

A smile crosses his face, and he leans in and kisses me again. "Fine, if you don't want my spawn, then I will just create a magnificent kingdom for you. But first, it's time to get you nice and relaxed. Draw you a bubble bath. Maybe lick your clit some more. I haven't decided. All I know is that you aren't doing anything while you're in my care. You're my soul right now."

"I had no idea you could be romantic," I tease, tracing my finger around his abs and back down to his cock.

"Just wait, Ray. You have no idea what's in store for you." Lucian lifts me into his arms and carries me from the bed.

Bright light bursts through the air, stopping him in his tracks. He growls and spins around, setting me behind him. Summoning his fire whip, he transforms into his devil form and slashes at the bright light in front of us.

Cassius swears, his voice booming through the room. He materializes into view and catches the end of Lucian's chain, stopping it from whipping him.

Fear clenches my chest at the sight of Cassius.

Heavenly light glows in his eyes as he looks at me. "Raven,

we have to go. Now."

Lucian and I don't have a chance to react as Cassius launches at both of us. The world shifts, blending with light and darkness.

Cassius forces both of us away from the Mortal Realm.

Everything explodes into fire.

17

Brother's Pride

LUCIAN

I'M GOING TO rip his fucking balls off. His cock will be down his throat and out his ass the second I manipulate him to lower his guard. I have had it with Cassius and his righteous, divine intervention. He will not only be switched off course from his path, but I'll also break the damn road and make it unable to be traveled down at all. I will burn every damn bridge he tries to create to overcome the obstacles I put in his way. The treacherous fucker, who should've stayed by my side as Kase, Dante, and I jumped from Heaven, will pay for his actions.

If he hadn't been a coward and chickened out at the last

second, Andre, Zade, and Elias would have followed him. We would already have Hell in order.

And now? He's trying to steal her from me again. I will not allow him to take Raven from Hell. The devils have their claim on her, and if he wants a piece of her, he's going to need to lose those fucking wings and devil up.

"I don't want to fight, Luce," Cassius says, scrambling back and summoning his heavenly sword once more. But he can't summon the light he needs to fight me. He thought he could outsmart us and use a plane to shift us from the protection that I put in place to keep Raven safe, but he had no idea that I have tagged her with my mark that will not allow him to do so. She hasn't even noticed the new ring on her finger. She was just so damn horny and so happy to see me that I forgot to even mention what I had done.

"If you don't want to fight, then get on your knees and bow to me. I have grown tired of your games and your pride. You are too self-absorbed to see that no matter what you do, you will lose. You were destined to join me in Hell. And look around, Cass. You are here now." I twirl my fingers and gather hellfire chucking it in his direction.

Cassius jumps, but he's not fast enough to avoid the circle of flames I used to entrap him. The fire rises up and cages him within the circle. He scowls at me, flexing his wings, expanding them out despite not being able to fly. He's not going anywhere.

"Cassius, what the fuck?" Raven asks. She pulls her shit together, finally realizing that she is in my kingdom and not in some heavenly plane Cassius tried to take us to. "How are you even here? Why are you even here? You picked your fucking side and have no right to invade our lives."

"I will hold him if you want to fucking cut his dick off for interrupting our fuck session," I say, turning my attention to Raven.

"I don't know how we ended up here. Perhaps you should ask Lucifer. I was only trying to shift you from the Mortal Realm to the spiritual one." Cassius clenches his jaw, his purple eyes glowing brighter as he tries to break free of my circle.

He sounds so fucking broken that I can't stand it. I know that Raven has a soft spot for dejected angels, and right now, Cassius is the biggest one of them all.

Raven turns her attention to me, her eyebrows high on her forehead. For fucks sake. "What is he talking about?"

I say with a scowl and twirl my finger at her hand opposite of the one where she wears Micah's ring. "I have you bound to Hell. It is how we decided to handle the whole angelic spawn. We can't have you blasting us back to our kingdoms by accident like you did. Consider it my promise to keep your sexy ass safe."

Raven gawks at the ring in silence. I hope she likes the ruby stone. Unlike Micah, I didn't just steal it off some random bitch. I took a moment to actually look around for something that would look beautiful on her hand.

"I hope it's up to your standards," I add, feeling the silence that both Raven and Cassius leave in the air. You would think that they would expect stuff like this now.

"See. I told you it wasn't me. I would never bring you here." Snapping his attention to me, Cassius points his finger in my face. "And no, it's not up to her standards. A ring of Hell is far beneath her. Just as you are, my wayward brother."

Raven surprises the hell out of both of us by stomping up to Cassius and swinging her arms, smacking him across his smug face hard enough to leave a smoldering handprint behind. "Don't talk to him like that. He has done more for me than you have."

"Are you kidding me? I risked everything to break through the protective shield using your soul to warn you that the angelic army was coming hard and fast, deciding that they don't want to show mercy. It is not going to be a question of where you go and when and with who. You will be their prisoner if they catch you." Cassius rubs his hand over his cheek. I wish Raven would've left a mark on him like she had with Zade. Zade will never hear the end of it having my mark bitch slapped on his cheek for the rest of eternity...Cassius can claim the same since he wears a pentagram as well. At least, I think he does. I can't imagine he would rip it off his skin like I had my wings.

I stroll closer to Raven and drape my arm over her shoulders, pulling her into my side. I drag her back a couple of feet away from the circle that traps Cassius, and I shift her, staring down into her beautiful blue eyes.

"We won't let that happen, Ray. He is overdramatic even considering that the angelic army will get within arm's reach of you again. Like I said, I have bound you to Hell. Andre helped me. If you get shifted to another realm, it'll automatically bring you and whoever tries right here to my kingdom." I brush my fingers along her cheek, hoping that she believes me over Cassius. "You and those twins are safe. If anything, those bastard angels are in fucking trouble. It's tempting just to let them try to see them here in my kingdom."

"You don't know what Heaven is capable of, Luce. Things have changed since you've abandoned us." Cassius remains rigid and squares his shoulders. "If they are determined enough, they will get to her. They will figure out how to escape Hell. You know I am only standing in your cage out of respect. I don't want to fight. I only want to see to it that Raven gets the time she needs to grow on a spiritual and physical level. I have seen the darkness in her, and it is incomparable to anything I've ever come across, especially because of the new angelic light she carries."

"You're full of shit." I whip my attention back to Raven,

standing tall in my devil form to block her view of Cassius. "Cassius is capable of lying. He is incapable of doing unholy things because of our deep-seated connection. He instinctively swears. He thinks dirty-ass thoughts. And he's capable of coming into Hell whenever he pleases, even without tapping into your soul. He is my twin, after all."

I expect Cassius to bitch at me and try to convince her otherwise, but he remains silent, watching the two of us.

Closing her eyes, Raven tries to shut out the world around her. She bows forward and rests her head on my pec, just sucking in deep breaths. I stroke my hand up and down her naked back, wondering if I should summon her clothes. She can't be cold here, and I know she doesn't care if Cassius sees her sexy ass body, but she still clings on to her human rationale that probably feels uncomfortable standing so exposed.

Despite the idea of covering her body bringing great agony to my aching balls, I summon a T-shirt and shrug it over her head for her as she remains in her own headspace, trying to figure shit out.

"Come on, Ray. Let's let him sweat for a bit and see if we can find Micah and Elias. Maybe it will help you to see your soulmate." I kiss her on her forehead, hoping that she will come out of the darkness twining around her and acknowledge me.

"Elias is here? I don't understand." Cassius flares his nostrils, unable to remain silent at hearing my words. "Hell? He was not Hell-bound. He should have entered Heaven."

"He wouldn't leave me," Raven whispers, answering Cassius. She digs her fingers into my sides and continues to just breathe in my scent.

"He wouldn't have had a choice." Cassius attempts to break through the fire cage, sending flames shooting toward my palace ceiling. He growls and swipes his sword, trying to snap it open.

It's so fucking satisfying seeing him trapped after he just said that he was standing in the cage to prove that he wasn't here to fight. Like I said to Raven, he is a lying bastard.

Raven finally eases her head away from my bare chest. "He was mortal. He—"

I press my fingers to her mouth, cutting off her words. Tilting my head, I brush my lips to hers, ensuring that she doesn't say another word. She's already said too much. Fuck. Actually, it was me. I didn't really think much about it. I thought that Cassius was smart enough to figure it out by now. But I guess only one of us can have the brains and brawn.

"He's not on our side. Let's not give him something to use against us." I lace my fingers through hers and tug her until she shuffles by my side, quietly following me away from Cassius. "I just want you to take a breath and remember the fun fucking time we had together. I will handle this. I will also summon

Kase and Dante so they can come to you. I know how much you appreciate their ability to help you through spiritual turmoil. I'm not good at that kind of thing."

"Obviously," Cassius says, his sharp voice stabbing me enough to get me to spin around and snarl at him in my devil form. "There's a reason why you've been isolated for so long."

I know I shouldn't react. I should ignore him and take Raven out of here. My wrath gets the best of me, and I charge at Cassius, ramming my clawed hands into his chest, knocking him twenty feet away until he crashes into the wall. I jab my fist at his face, punching him in his jaw. He doesn't fight back and goes limp, crumpling to the floor as if my one swing incapacitated him.

"Lucian, please stop." Raven's whispery voice cools my boiling blood, smothering out the fire raging inside me. "Beating him up will accomplish nothing. I know you have the need to punish him, but why don't you prove to him that he's wrong instead. You have helped me on a spiritual level. You were the first devil to glimpse my soul. Cassius only says the bullshit that he does because it's the only way to make himself feel better. Your roles have reversed, and while he's losing everyone he has cared about, you're gaining what you've always wanted. His pride can't stand it."

Damn it. I had no idea that I could want to fuck her brains out more than I do in this moment, especially feeling the seething rage and annoyance flitting through Cassius. Raven struck a nerve, and if he could shoot fire, he would.

"Enough!" Cassius flaps his wings, launching past me and toward Raven. "I've had enough!"

Summoning my fire chain, I whip it toward Cassius, missing his wings by a foot as he flies at Raven. She raises her hands protectively, and I charge forward, hollering. I don't know what bullshit he plans, but he can't take Raven from Hell. I'm afraid he will hurt her in the process, his pride too much to allow him to see clearly, especially in the one place that thrives with the sin that will be his downfall. He's so close to planting his ass on a throne that I consider letting him try to capture Raven. If she didn't scream my name, I would.

The last thing I want to do is jeopardize the relationship she's finally accepted. She doesn't allow anyone to push her around, and if she decides I'm on her shit list, I'll have eternal blue balls.

Closing my eyes, I gather a wave of hellfire and release it at Cassius. It swells over him, burning the feathers on his wings and throwing him off course. He yowls in pain, but instead of slowing down, he propels off the ground and opens his arms wide. Pitch black shadows explode from Raven's hands, creating a wall of darkness. Cassius disappears into it, the shock of Raven creating another plane right in the middle of my palace utterly mesmerizing and shocking.

As quickly as Cassius disappears, so does Raven, and I rush

toward the spot that swallowed them and stole them from existence. This should've been fucking impossible. Raven wears the ring with a tether to Hell, not unlike the power source that Micah currently holds within him.

"Lucian!" Raven's scream rips through the air, and I spin on the balls of my feet, trying to glimpse even a flash of her soul.

The ground beneath me trembles and shakes, and I head toward the archway that leads to the rest of my kingdom. I can still hear and feel Raven despite not being able to see her. If I can just get within reach of her soul, I can reel her back to me.

"Get away from me!" The fear in Raven's voice tightens my chest.

Her screams strike me in my very being, flooding me with rage and fury. How could I have let this happen? I should've been faster. I should've tried harder to stop Cassius. Now, I'm afraid I have failed her. Raven deserves a man who can protect her, not some asshole like me.

"Raven!" I yell, stomping my hooved feet, shaking the ground. "Raven, look for my darkness. Grab onto me. Use your ring to find me. It is tethered to my power and kingdom."

I squeeze my eyes shut, gathering more of my Hell power in my hands. To her, it'll look like black shadows that entangle my being, keeping me bound to my kingdom. If she's in another plane, she should be able to at least get near enough for me to peer through all the planes.

"Lucifer, control your souls. They have followed us into a weird spiritual plane that seems to be intended for darkness. They are the worst of the worst. Irredeemable." Cassius's voice hums in my ears. "Call them back to you. Your anchor has backfired. They are surrounding her as if she is you."

Fuck. I can't believe that this has happened. If those souls get to Raven, they will destroy her light completely. I know it. She might be tough, but she is not invincible. She has her breaking point.

Rushing toward the fiery pits surrounding my palace, I stop at the edge of the lake full of souls trapped in agony and raise my hands out. "My souls, return to me. Bow to me and beg me for mercy, for I am your keeper."

Fire swells from my hands and crashes into the lava lake. Energy hums around me, and I can feel the souls beginning to gather to swarm in my direction. I continue to shoot my power at the lake, screaming at the top of my lungs for the souls to obey me. I demand their attention and turn myself into a vortex of pure power to suck them back.

"Lucian! Lucian, it's working! Thank fucking Hell!" Raven's voice booms in my ears, her new confidence giving me the strength to continue on even though I want to drop to my knees from the force of having to bring back the souls from my kingdom. "Lucian! Look for my light. I don't know how to get back to you. Please."

Shadows surround me and I spin slowly, narrowing my eyes to search the abyss of my kingdom. It takes me a moment, but I finally manage to spot a breath of light within the masses of damned souls. Focusing on Raven, I summon my fire whip and lash out. It cracks in the air and breaks through the shadows, whipping around her pure light. I yank it back and spot her flying through the air toward me.

Opening my arms, I brace myself to catch her. Her whole being crashes into me, flooding me with the purest light I have ever felt, even more so than when I have previously touched her soul. This is new. This doesn't belong to her but is still a part of her. And for the first time in what feels like all my eternity, I feel as if I touch Heaven. But Heaven isn't the same. This paradise that I carry in my very being at the moment is Raven. It's my perfect woman and soul.

Something inside me shifts, and I exhale a long breath as she materializes in my arms. Cassius falls to his knees behind us, ruining the moment. I roar and swing around, kicking him so hard that he flies back into the lava lake, unable to catch himself before the souls engulf him.

"This is your fault!" I holler, watching Cassius try to pull himself free. "Let this be a lesson. You cannot come into my kingdom and try to steal Raven. You cannot lie and manipulate her. I won't allow it."

"Brother, please. Don't abandon me. I have good intentions." Cassius struggles to pull himself up, but the souls drag him down. "Luce, I know you have it in you to see what I see. I know that for once, we can agree on things with Raven."

"No. You don't have a say in her life and soul. The only way that will ever happen is if you join me by my side how we had originally planned." I shift Raven in my arms, petting her hair, trying my best to show her that she's safe. All she does is cling on and squeeze her eyes shut, forcing the world away.

"I can't. Raven needs someone like me. She needs someone in good grace. Now help me. Prove to me that you have changed." Cassius stretches his arms up into the air as if some force will drag him from my fiery pit.

I slowly shake my head, turning my gaze from his. I have nothing to prove. His opinion of me doesn't matter. He doesn't matter. "I haven't changed. And you know what? I will abandon you again. You were supposed to follow me, and you didn't, so this is how things will be until you realize your true purpose. Goodbye, Cass."

Cassius hollers my name again, but I ignore him and summon hellfire, creating a wall between us. I use it to trap the souls, keeping them from trying to leave the pits of Hell.

Squaring my shoulders, I carry Raven with me and head in the direction of Micah's kingdom. In this moment, she needs us all together. She needs to know how to fight and keep the darkness of humanity's worst souls away. We will all teach her.

Together. And Cassius is wrong. Raven doesn't need him. If she needs Heaven's good grace, she has Elias right now.

Honestly though, the only thing she needs is Hell.

All she needs is her devils by her side and for the seven sinners to join me in creating the eternity humanity and Raven need.

I will do so. I will take down all of Heaven if I have to.

Hell will rise.

Kingdom Come

ANDRE

"**Y**OU CAN DO better than that. Boredom can be torturous, but it's nothing to freak out about. The souls need to learn a lesson. They cannot grow otherwise. Our goal is to see to it that when Purgatory rises, they have a chance to go there." I scratch my fingers across the back of my neck and watch as Zade tips his head back as if he is still trying to tap into Heaven for answers. It will take him time to get used to his new power, but he will get there. I know it. My companion has always been adaptable despite everything. It'll just take him some time getting used to having control over his path instead of following one put before him.

"I don't know exactly how I want things to be yet. Give me some time, Andre. All I can think about right now is Raven. I worry about her. The things that I've seen the guardians do need to be addressed more than coming up with ways to punish the wicked. I would much prefer to focus my punishment on those bastard angels. They ruined everything. I can't believe how disgraceful they have become. It makes me question everything." Zade plops down on the onyx ground and rests his head on his knees. His wings still heal from the attack of the heavenly blade of one of the guardians.

Strolling closer, I sit down beside him and touch my hands to his wings. I summon a bit of Hell power and manage to singe the blood still dripping over his now ruby feathers. He winces and turns his head to me, meeting my eyes. I wish there was more that I could do or say to comfort him, but all I want to do is celebrate that he finally made the right decision, and we are together as companions again.

"I think you should help me cut them off. I can't stand them. I don't need them anymore." Zade tightens his jaw with his words.

I raise my eyebrows. "They come in handy, Zade. You might regret it. Once they are gone, they are gone forever.

"That's what I want. If I need to fly somewhere, you can do it. Lucian and Kase manage just fine. I can still feel the sting of Heaven coursing over my back because of them." Zade unfurls his wings and expands them out, showing the clusters of missing feathers and revealing parts of black bone. "I don't think I can even heal from this anyways. Raven managed to mend my body but not my wings. I think the damage is permanent. They got me mid-descent as I took on a devil form."

I nudge him, getting him to shift on the ground so I can get a better look. I stroke my fingers along the ruby feathers and to the black bones, feeling the sting that he feels. He might be right. They might be useless after all.

A part of me aches for him, and I blink my eyes a dozen times, clearing my vision. I don't know what it's like to make such a decision because my wings are still here. They transformed with me.

"I think you just want me to carry your ass around all the time, you sloth fucker." I force myself to smile with my words. "I've seen how you've watched Dante flying with Kase and Raven. You just want to be in the middle of our sandwich, don't you?"

Zade's shoulders shake with his silent laughter, and he glances over his shoulder at me with a beaming smile. It's the first one I've seen on him in a long time. He's usually a broody bastard, and it's nice to see him like this again. I hadn't realized how much I had missed our friendship. It has been difficult without him around.

"You just want to try to grind against me when there's nothing I can do about it," he says, his smile widening even more. "I'm not sure about that."

I laugh, the deep sound of my voice bellowing through the air. "You might change your mind. Honestly, though, I don't care where the pleasure comes from as long as somebody gets it. It's exhilarating."

"I can't say I understand, but I'm not going to say never with Raven involved. I know she likes that kind of thing, and…I don't know." Zade averts his eyes and stares at his hands, his smile faltering as he loses himself in his thoughts. I can smell his lust building as he thinks about everything he wants to do with Raven, and maybe even me. I just want to feel the power that comes with my kingdom. It's hard to explain. I am content when everyone else is. What I want from our eternity is to always have our desires fulfilled.

"I think I'll talk to Raven about it when I get a chance. I don't even know if she wants me anymore. I nearly failed her." Zade releases a long sigh and shakes his head, pushing his thoughts away. "Right now, I just want you to help me with my wings. My decision is final. If you don't help me, I'll figure out how to do it myself. I would just really appreciate you doing it for me."

I rub my hand over my jaw. What if he resents me for agreeing? I really disliked our time on separate sides of humanity.

"Please, Andre. I won't ask you for anything again." Zade

grabs his shirt and tugs it over his head, giving me a clear view of his near completely healed wounds by Raven from his battle with the guardians. No one knows how she did it, but it's incredible.

I stare at them in silence, nearly feeling the same pain that he feels in this moment. It angers me more than I realized that the guardians turned against him and hurt him so much. They should pay for what they've done.

"It's going to hurt," I say, summoning a blade from the power of my kingdom.

"Just be fast. Leave nothing behind," Zade says, tensing his muscles and balling his fingers into fists. "I just want it over with."

I bob my head and clasp my hands to the base of his right wing and get him to stretch it out. He grinds his teeth loud enough for me to hear, and I position my blade against his back. For it to cut clean, I can't just chop it. This is far more torturous for me than I expected. I should be able to just do it. I don't want to hurt my friend and companion.

"Brace yourself, Zade." I raise my hand a few inches, and without waiting for him to say anything, I swing my blade down and cut into the base of his wing.

Zade hollers with his pain before covering his mouth with his hand to stifle his agony. I cut all the way through and let his wing fall to the ground with a thump. Grabbing his left wing,

I do the same thing over again, severing his wing from his body until all he has left is two large open wounds. Summoning hellfire, I swipe my hands down the length of his back where his wings were and staunch the bleeding.

Zade falls over on his side and curls his knees to his chest. I can't stop the ache from stabbing into me at the sight of him looking so broken. I know it's what he wanted, but it doesn't make this any better.

Positioning myself on the ground, I lie next to him and wrap my arms around his body, hugging him from behind. There's nothing sexual about this moment. All I want to do is to help him through the transition of power. He needs me as much as Raven needs him.

"Just take a few more breaths. The pain won't last forever." I squeeze him tighter and rest my chin on his shoulder. "I promise you that."

We lie together in the middle of his sparse kingdom, just breathing in unison and savoring each other's presences. I feel a shift in the air around us, and I open my eyes and catch sight of Raven in Lucian's arms. He frowns as he carries her limp body in our direction, but I can see her eyes are open.

It's enough to get me off the ground. Zade sucks in a deep breath, catching the same sight as I do, and he scrambles up. He flexes his arm muscles as if he tries to stretch his wings, taking a second to realize they're no longer there. I blast them with hellfire, preventing him from seeing them on the ground a moment longer.

Lucian glances from me to Zade and then to the ground where the wings burn. He tightens his jaw and flares his nostrils, but he doesn't comment on catching the two of us cuddling together in comfort. He knows better.

"We all need to meet in Micah's kingdom. Raven needs us right now. Come on." Lucian adjusts her in his arms and glances at Zade. "Your kingdom can wait."

"What happened to her?" I ask, rushing to close the space between us. Raven tips her head and meets my gaze, her eyes sheening with unshed tears. She looks as if she has been through something terrible, and just seeing her in shock like this enrages me. "You were supposed to take care of her."

"It's not his fault," Raven whispers, her voice barely trickling to my ears.

I open my arms and silently demand Lucian to give her to me. I feel as if I will destroy the universe if I don't have her in my arms this second to make sure that she's okay.

Lucian reluctantly hands her to me, but he remains close enough that my arm brushes his naked chest. The bastard just strolls around with his cock swinging like a damn elephant trunk as if this were his kingdom. As much as I admire his size and the handsomeness of his body, it's a major distraction.

I do the only thing I can think of. I swat my hand, slapping his cock on the side. "You need to summon clothes or transform into your devil self immediately. Your state tests my control."

Lucian rolls his eyes and claps his hands together, sending fire spewing across the ground as he uses his power to create a pair of shorts. "Better, you horny bastard?"

Zade comes closer and hovers in front of me, peering down at Raven. Reaching out, he strokes his fingers over her cheek and jerks his hand back as if touching her pains him. "Souls have been touching her. Why? How? I know you wouldn't have allowed them such access to Raven."

Growling deep in his throat, Lucian rubs his hand over his head. "You can thank Cass-hole for that. You can thank him for us being here at all. He tried to take her from the Mortal Realm."

I thin my lips in thought. I hadn't expected that Lucian would actually have to use the anchor. "Where is he? I will fucking destroy him for putting her through this turmoil."

"He's stuck in one of the pits. He will be there for a while. Leave him. I want him to suffer." Lucian glows with his hell-fire, and he cracks his neck. "Right now, Raven is our priority. I need you to get into her mind and help her clear out the darkness. You're the only one who can get to her on that level, Andre. Do you think you can handle it?" Lucian refers to my ability to dream walk and get to a level unlike any of the devils can.

I look down and study Raven for a silent moment. Nerves bunch my muscles, because a part of me is uneasy getting into her mind in this state. What if I make it worse? What if I go into her soul and realize there's nothing I can do? The way she looks so fragile in this moment leaves me a mess, and I don't want her to see me like this.

But I agree anyways. I nod my head and turn to Lucian. "Call the others together in my kingdom. I will do it there where I am closest to my power."

"Whatever it takes," Lucian says. "Our soul will no longer be weak. It's time that we all join together and give her the strength she needs."

I will give her everything. She will be the perfect queen.

"So, are we going to spirit fuck or what?" Raven teases, her face smirking, but her eyes aren't into it. Something bothers her on the deep-seated level, and she refuses to acknowledge it.

"We are spirit fucking already." I reach out and caress my fingers along her cheek, tracing her jaw and down her neck until I reach her shoulder. Pushing her hair to her back, I get a better view of her body in the spirit world. Being with her awakens a part of me that I keep caged and dormant when I'm not around her. But right now, I open myself up to her as much as she is open to me.

"I don't see the point in this, Andre. I know you're trying to help, but I'm okay. We can wake up and get to the good stuff. I know you want to satiate your hunger," Raven says, covering my hand with hers as she guides me lower, silently asking me to explore her body even though neither of us is corporeal.

I sigh and keep my gaze locked on hers, trying to see to her soul. A new darkness clings to her, shadowing the brilliant light that I've grown used to. It's as if her very being protects her. No, not her being. The babies she carries. It's strange to think about it, knowing that Raven now will bear life unlike anything the universe has ever seen. I'm excited and worried. What if it was a part of me that I gave to her. What if that part of me ends up being her destruction? I couldn't deal with that.

"Just give me a couple of minutes longer, little hellion. I need to ensure that Lucian's souls didn't harm you more than they already have." I lean in and close the distance to her face, filling up her vision with just me.

Raven shifts closer until she sits between my legs with her thighs squeezing my sides. She hangs her arms over my shoulders, and she brushes her mouth to mine, trying to get me to wake her up to return to my kingdom. But I'm not ready yet. Even if she was okay, I need this time with her more than

I realized. It's been what feels like forever since I've had the opportunity to visit her dreams. This is the one place that is mine and hers alone. At least, unless I let Elias in. Because he shares Raven's soul. I would consider it if I could trust him right now. Unfortunately, he's not himself on many levels.

I ease away from her, darting my gaze to her lips as she pouts. She leans in again, trying to capture my mouth. It takes everything in me to resist her and lean back out of reach.

"Please, little hellion. Just open up for thirty seconds. That's all it will take for me to infuse you with my power and to scare away any lingering residue that doesn't belong to you for the babies. If you don't let me, you might experience bouts of fear or nightmares or some other bullshit that you shouldn't have to deal with. Let me take care of that beautiful soul." I narrow my eyes on hers, silently threatening her to comply before I have to demand her to let me do what's best. That's not me. I don't like trying to control her, but I know that the other devils depend on me. I need to prove to them that I can handle Raven even when she puts up a fight and resists.

She groans and scrubs the heels of her hands into her eyes. "Fucking fuck. Fine. I know that if I continue resisting, you might bring in another devil for help. I don't want them to question you."

It's as if she can read my mind. Her comment brings a smile to my face, and I can't help showing her what she does to me in this moment.

"You love this way too much," she adds, trying to tighten her mouth to stop herself from smiling back at me.

"Only a little. It's nice that I don't have to demand things from you like the others do sometimes. I knew you'd see reason," I say, summoning a bit of hellfire and putting space between us. It warms my hands and jumps from me to Raven, startling her but not scaring her.

She finally gives in to her desire to smile and beams her happiness as she gathers the power, letting it crawl up her arms until it reaches her heart, tethering her to me. Her mouth falls agape, and her eyes widen at the sensation of our beings merging together. I reach out and plant my palm above the growing circle over her heart, taking a minute to touch her soul completely.

A cloud of darkness bursts free, and I growl at the intruding soul, trying to hide within the darkness surrounding her. Raven screeches in surprise and clutches her chest, jerking away from me. She lands on her back and arches, and I watch in fury as another soul pours out of her and disappears.

Shit. I can't believe that those bastards manage to bind to her, probably siphoning her light. It's no wonder the chains seemed darker, and she wasn't smiling as usual or feeling content as she usually does when I visit her dreams.

Rushing forward, I crawl to her and hover over her, watching tears leak from her eyes in glittering trails. Raven heaves a couple of deep breaths and snatches my hand, tightening her fingers around me. I scoop her up and bury my face into her throat, inhaling the scent of her body. Raven releases a small whimper, sounding so fucking fragile that all I want to do is fill her with my strength. I want her to know that she is not weak. She is the strongest soul I know. She is the strongest being in the entire universe. Stronger than even the devils.

"I'm so sorry, little hellion. They are gone now. That was all that was left." I kiss her clavicle and work my way up to her throat. "I can wake you up now."

"No, wait." Raven squeezes me tighter until I can only feel her soul and nothing more around us. Being so close to her makes it feel as if I've disconnected from Hell even though I know I haven't. But my attention is no longer split. It's just me and her in the sanctuary she's invited me in to.

"We can stay as long as you want. I know what you experienced was awful." I comb my fingers through her hair, working my way down to stroke her spine. "But we will ensure that never happens again. I swear to you."

"Thank fucking Hell. I don't know why it keeps happening. It's like I'm a magnet or something. It's not that they are trying to hurt me, but they share with me all of the horrors that they have done in their lives." Raven shivers as if she really lives through being in the middle of Lucian's souls again.

"They sense that you are different. I don't know if it's because they know you will one day rule Purgatory or if it's because you carry a spawn of light and another of dark in the most perfect balance between Heaven and Hell, or what. But I know it's something to do with that. I just wish we could've known and prepared you better. We only wanted you safe." I recount the plan that I helped Lucian create, wishing that we had decided against giving her a ring with a tether to Hell. But on the other hand, it saved her. I just hate that we have to pick our battles and deal with whatever consequences that come up from our decisions.

Raven doesn't respond to me, falling silent with my words. I wish I could hear her thoughts to know what is going on through her mind. I want to say something, but I don't know what to say. Micah is better at that kind of thing. All I can do is just be here.

"Andre, can I ask you something? I need you to be honest with me." Raven shifts and eases back, meeting my gaze. "Are you afraid?"

"Afraid? I'm not sure I understand where you're going with this." I say, pursing my lips together in thought.

She laughs with her nerves and motions toward her abdomen. "You know, the angelic and devilish twins."

I don't respond to her immediately. I haven't had much time to process the knowledge—none of us have, really—and I'm not sure what to say. She stares at the side of my face anxiously, and I drag my attention away from her stomach and back to her eyes.

"I am nervous, but not about you bearing children." I cringe at the way that comes out. "I'm concerned about what it will do to you…I mean, because of the miraculous gift given to you by…" I let my voice trail off. I don't have faith in this being the Higher Power's doing. Maybe fate? I wish I could articulate how I feel to Raven without it sounding like me rambling on.

She smirks and pats my cheek. "I can't explain it either," she says, resting her forehead to mine. "Thanks for being honest. It makes me feel better. I know Kase and Dante are weirdly excited. Elias is…lost in his light, and Micah has his hands full. Lucian isn't exactly a coddler. I don't even know what's going on with Zade. Is he—"

I chuckle and cut her off with a kiss, trying to slow down her whirling mind. "Take a breath and relax. I can feel your soul getting worked up, little hellion. Why don't I wake you up and you can see everyone for yourself? We're all here."

She licks her lips, bobbing her head. "Okay, yeah. I think I'm ready…but if you start an orgy between us—"

Tipping my head back, I howl a laugh. "No promises."

Raven giggles and pats my chest, her being no longer drenched in darkness as she lights up her angel-kissed soul, now filling with happiness and love. It's the same as it was when I first laid my eyes on her. A part of me worried that I wouldn't see her the same as she was before, but she's still my little hellion...and the woman I love.

"I mean it, Andre. I love getting the Hell fucked into me, but—I don't know. I don't want triplets. It was probably you who knocked me up." She twirls her finger at my groin. "That thing doesn't let go."

I snatch her up and pull her into my arms, cradling her in all her dazzling light. "You have other holes," I tease, grinning at her reaction. She denies everyone but Kase the luxury of finding pleasure from her ass.

"My ass is claimed. That was the agreement." Raven sticks out her tongue with her words.

"Until they hear your concerns." I chuckle again, savoring her light-hearted laughter.

She glares at me. "Fuck me. I'm doomed."

I hug her, guiding her soul with me from the dream world. "Open your eyes, Raven. You'll see that's not true."

The world shimmers around me as I awaken from my trance, hearing commotion coming from the other devils surrounding us. I peer down, staring at my empty arms in shock. Where did Raven go?

"Grab him!" Micah shouts. "He intercepted her soul."

"Elias, stop!" Raven's pleas ring through the air.

I whip my attention in the direction of Raven's voice. Elias expands his translucent wings and flies with Raven toward the balcony. The two of them disappear.

19

Binding

DANTE

THAT SON OF a fucker, soon-to-be cocksucker, twat, asshole. I'm going to choke the Hell out of him for trying to kidnap my pretty soul. I can't even believe he managed to intercept her while in Andre's control. This little bastard is way too powerful as an angel. I'm nearly certain that he could beat Cassius in a battle of who is the biggest righteous dick. And it sucks because I liked the guy. I know Raven loves him, but his greed will ruin everything. It's not even that he just wants Raven all to himself. He's greedy in thinking that he knows all and his decisions are right. He wants everything to go as he envisioned. I'm sure he never expected Raven to join our legion as our perfect soul in this cycle when he gave her his light. I know he remembers his past life with her, and I think combining that with his transformation into an angel again has really fucked him up. Being in Hell doesn't help. I know that the darkness gets to all pure entities. It's far more torturous for an angel than it is for even a mortal to enter our kingdoms.

"Andre, I want you to chase him, and I will cut them off. Raven still wears the Hell ring, and he won't be able to get far with her." I expand my wings and flex my muscles. "All you wingless bastards take to the ground. Send those souls after him and only him."

Without waiting for anyone to respond, I dash toward the balcony and after Elias. The heat of Andre closing in on my back warms my skin even more than the surrounding flames, and I use him to propel me forward. I need to get out first.

"I've called upon the winds," Andre says, launching off the balcony at the same time as me.

Howls and screams rip through the air, and I watch as Andre's collection of souls fly from their massive orgy on the ground. Thank the smart bastard. I spot the light of Elias and Raven amid the chaos of sex and lust. There's no fucking way that Elias is going to manage to get out of the sex storm. I bet the pheromones coursing through the kingdom are already getting to him. If only he would just land, because I'm afraid that he might do something stupid with Raven. Maybe drop her. Maybe accidentally let her go among the souls. I know she hates that shit.

"Elias, stop! You can't take her! If you take her from Hell, the guardians will capture her. They will separate the two of you. They know how important it is for you guys to be together," I shout, using Hell power to send my voice booming through the world.

A bright flash of light explodes through the air, and I watch as Elias opens a fucking portal right in the middle of the sky and flies into it. Unholy fucking Hell. How did he just do that? I can't even fucking do that.

"Head to Lucian's kingdom." Andre expands his black wings, far cooler than mine, and jets ahead of me.

I follow behind him, growling and gnashing my teeth through the sex tornado trying to stop me from getting out of this wind orgy. Usually, I would enjoy such a challenge, but I can't stop thinking about Raven and how scared she must be. How confused she must be, considering that Elias is her soulmate. She trusts him with her soul, even if she doesn't like what he's doing right now. She will never hurt him. If anything, she will try to persuade him to see reason. Unfortunately, Elias will not be able to see reason in this moment. Not with Hell surrounding him. It will take him leaving to get his shit together. By then, it could be too late. I know that the bastard angelic army is waiting. They will try everything to get Raven. I can't let that happen. She's carrying our babies. I never in my wildest fantasies imagined having a fucking spawn, but I'm so excited about it, especially after seeing that little blip of darkness. It was so enchanting next to the little ball of light.

I shake the thought of Raven's ultrasound from my mind and nosedive toward the ground and out of the wind completely. I navigate close to the terrain, managing to keep six inches of space between me and the ground. Andre uses his power and just pushes all the souls out of the way, but it takes him longer, and they beat him into Kase's kingdom.

The world blurs as I chase them at a speed far faster than anything I've ever tried. Fire courses over my wings with my Hell power, and I spit venom at every soul that tries to get in my way, sending them back to their homes in Hell.

The world shifts as I move from kingdom to kingdom until I reach Lucian's glorious palace in Hell. The fire pits are one of my favorite things, seeing the souls hung up and screaming, regretting all of their terrible life decisions.

I spot a brilliant light flying above one of the lava pits. Clenching my fingers into fists, I propel myself forward toward Elias.

That fucker. He's pulling Cassius from the souls. What a traitor. Cassius was supposed to stay in the damn fire pit for a bit longer. He would've eventually gotten out, but it would've been a torturously long time.

"You fucking bastard! I'm going to rip those wings off!" I shout, heading in Elias's direction.

I don't even get a chance to get within a dozen feet of them before Elias opens another portal and drags Cassius through.

I holler in rage and swipe my hand across the brilliant light, trying to grab onto them. My skin burns and sizzles at the touch of angelic power, and I have no choice but to jerk my hand back.

"Damn it! Raven, fight! Come back to me!" I land on the ground with a thud and lace my fingers to the back of my head, spinning around and staring up at the fiery world around me.

"Dante?" Raven's voice trickles to me, and I see a strange gray haze in the spot that Elias and Cassius disappeared through a portal. "Dante, where are you? I can't see you. I'm scared."

"Hold on, pretty soul. I think you're in between planes. Elias must not have been able to take you from Hell." I spit venom into the air, hoping to shatter the plane.

The world quivers, and bright light fissures through until Raven falls out of the hole with a scream. Launching toward her, I catch her before she falls into the pit of screaming souls. She gasps with a screech and clings onto me, burying her face into the crook in my neck.

"Thank you," Raven whispers, her voice shaking. "Elias is

fucking possessed with Heaven. It's like he can't control it."

"I know, pretty soul. I'm just glad he couldn't take you. We will figure this all out. We just need to ensure that you don't get lost between planes. Right now, you are bound to Lucian's kingdom, but we need to take more drastic steps. I hope you're okay with getting a couple of tattoos. We want to bind you to us." I stare at the sight of Raven's face, trying to decipher her reaction. It wasn't something we wanted to do, permanently marking her with our Hell power, but we don't know what else to do. We need to be able to reach her no matter what. "It will ensure that your soul and our beings are bound for eternity."

She bobs her head in agreement. "Why haven't you guys suggested this already? I'm assuming it's because it is something I probably won't like, huh?"

She's right about that. "We have been putting it off because what happens is that you will never be able to cycle again. Once you have been tagged, you will belong to all of us. The problem is that if you die, there is no trying again if we fail to bring the kingdoms together." I remain expressionless with my words. I know how important creating Purgatory is to her and everything we have been fighting for.

"That's not so bad. I've already decided that I want to be in this life forever. I don't want to go again even if we fail." Raven turns her beautiful eyes to me and stretches her neck to kiss me softly.

"You haven't told her the worst of it, Dante," Andre says, landing behind me.

This bastard. Of course, I wasn't going to mention the worst of it. It's nothing Raven needs to worry about. We have it handled.

"There's more?" Raven turns her neck and looks at Andre.

I press my lips together in silence. I'm not telling her. Andre can be the one to explain the shitty circumstances and what happens.

"Another reason why we haven't considered this yet is because while you will be bound to us, your soul is pure. It means that if you die, Heaven can very well intervene. It is not the same as having a contract with a devil. It means that Hell has a claim on you, but because you don't get anything in return, Heaven can and will try to save you." Andre expands and closes his wings, hiding them on his back. Fire lights his eyes, and his jaw twitches with the thought.

"Oh." Raven falls silent and loses herself in her thoughts.

"I wasn't going to tell you because we would never let that happen." I readjust her in my arms so she can hug me with her body instead of me cradling her.

"Dante...you can't be sure. Look how Elias tried to remove me from Hell. Think about the crazy abilities carrying a spawn of Heaven and Hell has given me. What if that changes things? What if I accidentally move on to Heaven or some shit?"

I growl deep in my throat and flare my nostrils. "I should punish that bubble butt of yours for questioning my ability to protect you."

"Her concerns are valid, Dante," Andre says, strolling even closer until he can look at Raven from over my shoulder. He doesn't realize that he's so attentive to her that his damn boner is poking me right in my ass crack.

I reach behind me and whack his dick. It only makes it worse, because the fucking massive pole jerks down only to swing back up between my legs, snapping against my damn balls through my pants.

I fly a foot in the air, knocking him back with my wings. My emotions get the best of me, and I flash my fangs and spit venom, nearly getting him right in the face.

"Dante, calm down. We have enough to deal with right now. He's only trying to relate with me." Raven's soft voice snaps me out of my anger. I almost tell her that it's not because he agrees with her, but then I decide to drop it. The sting in my balls subsides enough to focus again, or maybe it's because Andre hits me with a wave of hormones and turns the pain into fucking pleasure, and now I want to jerk off. I should've been the fucking king of the Lust Kingdom. I'm jealous that he can do that.

I puff out my chest and release my breath, relaxing my shoulders. "Sorry, pretty soul. I didn't mean to react like that. I know that your concerns are valid, but I also know that binding us together is more beneficial and worth the risk. You have to trust us."

"Of course, I trust you, Dante. That's why I agree. It is worth the risk. I know that we will get through this. Cassius is coming around. I know it. I felt it. We will only have to worry about getting Elias back for his throne. I just don't know how. He's tried. What happens if this ascension is permanent? Is there anything we can do?" Raven rubs her lips together, thinking about her own comment.

I wish I had the answer for that. I have never known an angel to give up their light only to get it back. Usually, they just fall into Hell and become part of our kingdom. From there, they either suffer for eternity, or they join our ranks. They usually give in eventually. They were once mortal, after all.

"I have a few things that we can try once we find him again. But first, we need to take care of you. We need to make sure that our little spawns are safe. Okay?" I turn to Andre and nod my head at him. "Do you want to go grab the others? Fly them here to speed things up. We'll do the binding ceremony here. Lucian's kingdom is best for that kind of transfer of power. It contains all the sins of Hell."

Without a word, but with a quick kiss to Raven's head, Andre launches into the air and leaves. I turn my head back and watch him go, his expansive black wings a bit larger than mine. I can't help appreciating his body. Andre has always been good-looking, but as a devil, damn. Raven is one lucky woman. Especially knowing what he can do to her. It's the one thing that keeps me from becoming super envious of him. He is perfect for our pretty soul.

Raven presses her lips to my throat, drawing my attention from Andre. I tip my head and graze my lips to hers, kissing her softly and sensually just the way she silently asks for.

"Damn, Dante. I am so fucking horny, but I am also so confused and nervous." Raven grins with her words, reaching her hand between us until she rubs it along the length of my aching cock. "It's worse here, isn't it? How are you not already trying to fuck me?"

I tighten my jaw, stopping myself from smiling at her. "What are you talking about? We've already fucked twice. You even squirted on me. It was hot."

Her brows furrow in confusion, and this time, I do break out into a smile.

"You fucker. I thought I missed it. It's not the same if it's only in your fantasy. Now do something. We have a couple of minutes, right?" Raven snags my bottom lip with her teeth, and she stretches my lip. I growl and extend my fangs, managing to poke her and make her bleed a tiny bit. The taste of her sets me off, and I kiss her deeper, adjusting her lower until I can rub her over my dick.

"It's not enough time, but no one will stop us when they get here. They'll probably join. You could use this type of distraction anyways. Get you high on our lust. It all makes the whole process of tattooing you easier. It won't be as painful." I slide my tongue into her mouth, tasting the sweetness of her lips.

"Fuck," she murmurs with a groan. "You better give me venom or something. Because now that you've mentioned it, I'm fucking scared. I don't like needles."

"Is that why you've been avoiding the pussy ring Kase gave you?" I ask, easing back to raise my eyebrows.

She crinkles her nose, scrunching her face at the thought of a needle getting anywhere near the soft, sensual lips between her legs. "Maybe."

"Come on, pretty soul. That pussy of yours can take one helluva pounding. That ring will only increase your pleasure. We've assured it. Why don't we do that now while we bind you? It'll be fun." The face she gives me is a cross between consideration and denial. She loves the thought of more pleasure, but her human rationale and fears want to ruin the fun. "I promise that the pain will be fleeting compared to what it will bring."

"I'll do it if you get a cock ring too." Raven smirks at me.

I shrug my shoulders. "I'll take one for the team. I've never really needed anything fancy, because you've seen my cock. It's glorious. But if piercing my dick means that you wear that pretty little soul stone on your pussy, then I'll do it. Kase will owe me."

"Fuck, I should've known." Raven grimaces, smacking her hands to my shoulders. "I want all of you to get something then. It doesn't have to be a piercing. It can be a tattoo. We'll do it together as a team."

I laugh and shake my head. "Whatever you want, pretty soul. I will make sure it happens."

A loud thud sounds through the air, drawing my attention away from Raven as Andre drops Zade and Kase to the ground a dozen feet away. I inwardly groan at the sight of them, because I wasted too much time making a deal with Raven instead of just fucking her brains out, and I'm horny as hell. Even more so now.

"Perfect timing," I call, finally setting Raven on her feet because she keeps squirming against my cock. I don't let her get far and lace my fingers through hers. "Raven and I have just made a deal. She is going to get her pussy pierced as long as we get either a tattoo or a piercing as well during the binding ceremony."

Kase claps his hands with a smile. "Fuck yeah, angel-girl. Finally. What do you want me getting done? I'll even let you do it for me. Not sure you can fit any more jewelry on my cock though."

Raven palms her forehead and ignores him, probably regretting the deal she made with me. "I don't know. Maybe I'll have someone tattoo Andre's fucking cock on your back as a tramp stamp."

I bellow a laugh at her suggestion, wondering if she would actually go through with it in making Kase do that. She's going to be surprised when she realizes that he won't give a fuck.

"I guess if that's what you want to represent our love and promise of eternity," Kase says, flicking his attention to me before smiling.

Raven groans. "Fuck, I give up."

Rushing toward us, Kase lunges and snatches Raven away from me, scooping her into his arms to kiss her. And hell, do they look hot right now. It does nothing for my damn desire watching their tongues glide together as Kase squeezes Raven's ass.

"What do you give up on, Ray?" Lucian asks, his boots shaking the ground as he lands beside her and Kase.

Andre lands with Micah next to Zade, and they all look at Raven as if she is the center of our universe, which she is.

Raven wiggles out of Kase's arms and sighs, throwing her arms out. "I give up on resisting giving you whatever the hell you guys fucking want. Now let's do this. I'm ready to be yours forever."

An ethereal light glows around her, followed by a darkness

that winds around all of us, connecting us together.

Raven laughs and touches her hands to her stomach, and I realize where the light and darkness come from. "I think these little spawns are ready too."

"I think we all are, angel-girl," Kase says.

He's right about that.

Raven will officially be ours forever.

20

Devil Bound

RAVEN

"WHAT DO YOU think, pretty soul?" Dante asks, swinging his cock back and forth. His new ring sparkles in the glowing fire around us, the metal catching the light just right. My devils created a protective fire circle, ensuring that no one gets in to ruin this for us.

I'm not even sure how to feel or what to think as I watch a demon go after Micah next, piercing his nipples like Elias had as a human. I'm not going to lie. I can't wait to play with them. My devils are already so much fun as it is, but just seeing something sparkly on their bodies tempts me even more.

"I think it's fucking sexy," I say, strolling closer and dropping slowly to my knees. I tease Dante by grabbing the base of his shaft and holding his cock still, feeling it harden in my hand. I toss my hair over my shoulder, giving him a view of my cleavage from his position. I lean in, staring at the silver ring with an onyx stone bead. "It's too bad that we can't see if it makes a difference with a blow job."

"What the hell are you talking about? Do you want to suck it? Go on, suck it. Let's see if it gets stuck on your tonsils or something. I don't need healing time, pretty soul. Neither will you." Dante grins at me from his position and grabs my hair, twisting it around his fist. He guides me closer, and I tease him by just flicking my tongue over his tip, feeling the strangely cool sensation of the metal.

"It's going to be hard to deny myself this pleasure," I say, glancing up at him with my lips pouting in disappointment. "You know, once we get started, it's incredibly hard to stop. I want to bind our souls first. Celebrate after."

Dante play-growls and pretends to hump my face, sliding his cock past my ear. I can't stop the laughter bubbling from my throat. This horny bastard. I bet if I even open my mouth a little bit, he'd see if I would let him stick it in. And I probably would. I could use a little high from his cum. The devils make it all look so easy, how they don't even flinch as the tall, lanky demon with two horns that curl like mountain goats' jabs them with needles that come from out of nowhere.

"You plan on celebrating with all of us?" Kase asks, sauntering in our direction. Another demon chases behind him and drops down to finish the tattoo on his back. It's not Andre's cock, but it is a Raven in honor of me. The expansive wings go all the way from his shoulders and down his lower back, almost how Dante's wings look when they're folded. He says that the tattoo is for me, but I'm nearly fucking certain that it's a little bit for Dante too.

"You are just so obsessed with everyone stuffing their cocks into me, aren't you?" I use Dante's hips to pull myself to my feet. I purposely do it close to him, so he has to drag his cock from my chest to my torso, because I don't leave any space between us. "I mean, I love that you're cool with sharing, but you guys are a little wild."

"You like it, angel-girl." Kase offers me a wicked smile and uses his tail to draw up my leg as he tries to tease me.

I shut him out by squeezing my legs tight.

"She not only likes it, but she will beg for it once we're through with everything." Lucian stomps over to us, a new tattoo glowing on his pec. The twisted design makes up what looks like a flame burning through my name. I still can't believe he did that. I've never been one for wanting my name tattooed on someone, but Lucian assured me that I would change my mind once I saw it.

And then I realize that it's more than the flames in my name.

There's a line above it that says, "property of". I can't believe he got a tattoo on his chest that says Property of Raven. This crazy bastard.

I shuffle closer, squinting my eyes and narrowing my gaze on his chest. I don't say a word, just studying the lava-like lines that flow and move with his power. Lucian shifts on his feet under my scrutiny. I know he's waiting for me to say something, and I purposely refrain from doing so. I just love how intense he gets waiting on me. I will never stop pushing his buttons. He's done it to me for so long that it's become a game, and it's all I can think about doing for the rest of eternity. It's not often that a soul can say that they fuck around with Satan and get away with it.

"Well, since you are now my property, does that mean I can do whatever I want with you? Are you my bitch? If I demand that you get on your knees, will you?" I grin with my words, watching the fire light his eyes. I think he likes the sound of that.

"Damn, Raven. I think I'm going to get the words Raven's Bitch tattooed on me just so you demand that I remain on my knees for the rest of eternity, licking that sweet pussy of yours for the rest of time. What do you think?" Dante asks, hooking his fingers around my waist and standing close, pressing his cock right between my legs, lifting me up slightly to do so.

"I think that I want that on all of you now." Turning slightly,

I peek at him over my shoulder. "I think you deserve a reward for a great idea."

"I don't fucking think so, angel-girl. You're going to have to command everybody to pin me down before you try to make me your bitch. I am your pleasure provider and protector. Lucian can still be your bitch though." Kase laughs with his words.

I shake my head in amusement and manage to slip away from them to stroll toward where Zade stands in silence with his arms crossed over his chest. He hasn't said much since he's arrived, and I wish I could know what he was thinking. He hadn't transformed that long ago, and I can already see that his wings are gone. A part of me grieves for their beauty, but a more dominant part of me is relieved that he has adjusted so quickly. The fire in his eyes makes the blue depths look like sunsets, and I already feel myself getting lost in them.

I hold out my hands to Zade, taking a minute to give him my sole attention. The other devils are far too great at keeping me occupied and entertained that I have to put in an effort to show him that I am here. I am thankful that he chose me and chose Hell over everything else.

"Are you okay?" I ask, strolling into his now open arms as he quietly asks for a hug. "I'm sorry I haven't had a chance to be alone with you yet. I hope that this isn't too much too soon. You don't have to get a piercing or a tattoo on my behalf. It was just a deal I had made with Dante trying to get out of him wanting to pierce me." I shift and watch as Andre goes next, getting a Jacob's ladder on the top of his shaft, encouraged to do so by Kase. "But I guess you can see how that turned out."

"Of course, I plan to get something in your honor, Raven. I've been wearing your mark for what feels like forever, and I would prefer to have it be of our choosing and not because of a deal you had previously made with Lucian." Zade brings his hand to his cheek and rubs his fingers over the symbol.

"What do you plan to get?" I ask, peering into his eyes again.

Zade offers me a smile but doesn't answer. Instead, he bows down and presses his lips to mine, caressing my mouth. In a way that awakens desire inside me. My skin buzzes, and a shockwave courses through me, traveling from my heart into my clit, turning me on. I know it has to do with Andre's sudden closeness as he approaches us, but it also has to do with Zade.

"Last up, Zade," Andre says. "While you get your mark, Raven can get her pussy ring done."

My heart pounds at his comment, the idea nerve-wracking and thrilling at the same time. I never in my life thought I would ever go through with this. Just the thought of sticking a needle somewhere near my vagina freaks me out just a bit. But my devils just got all bejeweled and bedazzled in my honor. I know what the ring means to Kase and Dante. It's more than just a way to add pleasure. It's them giving me a piece of power, through a soul stone that adorns the ring.

"I swear that if it hurts, I'm kicking you all in the balls," I say, shifting on my feet, meeting each of their gazes. I know that they all plan to watch. I don't know how I feel having to spread eagle for what feels like a damn audience. But I know that they love the idea and will enjoy the show.

"You will forget it as quickly as it happens, pretty soul. Don't worry. I'll give you a little bite to help out, but honestly, you're tough. You've been through way worse. You're in good hands. Lucky for you, Kase likes owning tattoo shops. The soul was one of the top piercers in all of Angel Canyon back in the 90s."

I squeeze my eyes shut and sigh. "That was a long time ago, Dante. He better not be rusty."

He chuckles. "He's not. He's only visiting this kingdom. He's hanging out in the Mortal Realm and watching over a couple of our businesses. Isn't that right, Bobby D?"

The demon turns to me and smiles, flashing a mouth full of sharp fangs. "Yes, sir. I've pierced thousands upon thousands of people. So many that I can't even count anymore."

I try to smile back at the guy, but Dante grabs me by my waist, scoops me up and carries me toward a bed, and plops down with me on it.

"I still can't believe this," I mutter under my breath to Dante. "You know he has to look at my vagina, right?" I will sit on his lap, hoping to drive him crazy.

"I've probably seen more pussies and dicks than a damn obstetrician or gynecologist or dick doctor, whatever the fuck you call those guys." Bobby D strolls closer and summons a tray, setting it on the bed beside us.

Kase grins and sets the small jewelry box containing the ring with the soul he wants me to wear onto the tray.

"Still not helping." I crinkle my nose, crossing my legs at my ankles. "You might just have to tie me up and strip me naked, Dante. I don't think my body is going to comply."

"It'll be my pleasure, pretty soul." Dante snaps his fingers, summoning a restraint. "And you should know that Bobby D is a professional and he can't see you like we see you. He mostly sees light."

Great. What if he misses and I end up with a fucking needle in my thigh?

But looking at the other devils with their piercings helps ease the anxiety coursing through me.

"Trust us, Raven. You're going to be perfect. Just wait and see how good it's going to feel. Just take a breath, and I'll give you a little venom now." Dante brushes his fingers through my hair, moving it off my neck. He slowly and seductively traces his hands down my body while kissing my throat. "Once it's all done, we will all feel a lot better."

With his words, he sinks his fangs into my neck, injecting

me with his venom. I moan and arch my back, enjoying the feeling of his lips sucking my throat. He enjoys tasting my blood, getting the same high as I do. Silence falls through the air, and I close my eyes and just listen to the sounds of my devils breathing and watching me with all their intensity, bottling it up inside me to ease my nerves. I feel like the sexiest woman alive as Kase removes my pants and exposes my body to all of them. Lucian and Andre each take a spot by my side and touch my body with their hot hands, drawing my attention elsewhere.

"Get ready, pretty soul. It'll be fast," Dante says, releasing my throat only to move up to suck on my earlobe.

"And as soon as it's done, I will kiss you better." Kase's breath turns husky, and I can sense the heat of his desire even though he doesn't touch me and hovers behind the piercer. It should be more awkward than this, but it's not. It's as if the demon isn't even here. I don't know how my mind manages to just avoid thinking of him, but it does. Micah and Zade come closer, and I savor the touch of each of their hands on my knees.

"You're so incredibly sexy, heathen," Micah says, his voice swirling through my mind. "And so tough. You didn't even flinch."

A second after he says the words, extreme pleasure zings through me at the sensation of Kase's tongue gliding over my body as he uses Hell power to heal me and also bring great ecstasy to the experience.

The world rumbles as the demon vanishes, and I finally open my eyes to see myself surrounded by my sexy devils, all hot and ready to claim me.

Kase doesn't stop until my whole body clenches, and I swear I can feel his power in every fiber of my being, giving me even more strength.

I moan and gasp, panting as I try to catch my breath. I want him to continue. I want all my devils to continue and to join me in one helluva good time. But Kase eases away with a wicked smile.

"Not yet, angel-girl. I know that you want more, but we're not finished with our binding ceremony yet." Kase kneels in front of me, biting his lip, his eyes glowing with his red power. "It's now time to pick the spot you want our marks. Mine will go first along with Dante's as we had you first."

I inhale and exhale a couple of breaths, trying to think about where their marks should go on my body. I consider allowing them to pick spots, but I can tell that it's supposed to be me. It is my decision and mine alone.

Staring at Kase, I imagine where he would like to see his mark on me. "I think yours and Dante's should go on my hips. One on each side."

Kase and Dante grin at the same time, and Dante says, "Perfect. That way I can always see it unless I'm fucking you from behind, of course." He chuckles with his words, his whole face lighting up.

"Damn, can I have two?" Kase licks his lips with his desire. He's utterly and completely serious.

I laugh. "If that's what you want, but it has to be tiny."

Kase snatches my leg by my ankle and stretches my body up to show off my ass. He spanks my cheek. "Right here will be the second one."

Lucian comes closer and grabs my other leg, curling me up at my middle. "I want the fucking tramp stamp."

I narrow my eyes and shake my head. "Actually, I've already decided that Andre gets that spot. I want yours to be on my boob near my heart."

Lucian tips his head to the side in thought. His face softens as our eyes meet, and he smirks. "You want me close to your heart? Why?"

I rub my lips together. "Because you need the reminder of the most important part of me you have earned."

"Damn, Ray. You're getting to my balls right now. I knew you had a fucking soft spot for me. You love me, don't you?" Lucian studies my face, waiting for my response.

I shrug my shoulders and grin teasingly. "Don't make a big deal about it. You're already a cocky bastard as it is."

Andre howls a laugh and smacks Lucian between his shoulder blades. "Feels good, being loved, doesn't it?"

"Only by Raven. Don't you start with that bullshit, you softy devil. Save the love for your new boyfriend. Or old boyfriend? Sub? I don't know what the fuck to call Zade these days." Lucian whips his attention to Zade. "What the fuck are you to him anyways?"

I sit up and grab Lucian's hand, bringing his attention back to me. "Zade is one of my devils. He's one of your brethren, and he's Andre's companion. Don't try to twist things in a way that makes him uncomfortable."

Lucian snaps his mouth shut, deciding to drop it. Zade flashes me a brilliant smile, his whole face lighting up. He loves that I stood up for him.

"Protective is incredibly amazing on you," Zade says, his voice remaining soft. "And so you know, Lucian, I belong to Raven and to Hell. All of my eternity revolves around those two things now. Hell includes you."

"Fucking sap," Lucian says the words teasingly, but I know he practically devoured the idea of being included by Zade.

"Not a sap. He's thoughtful and understands things around him. This is why his mark will be on my wrist because he can keep me grounded. He can also bind me to all of you." I turn my attention to Zade, watching his face light up. His beautiful purple power glows in his eyes, mixing with the firelight in his blue depths in the most brilliant color I have ever seen.

He reaches out and takes my hand, smoothing his thumb over my wrist. "It would be my honor to have such a spot that you will see all the time."

I didn't think Zade could get any cuter, but I really love seeing how happy my choice made him.

"And mine?" Micah asks, speaking up for the first time. The tether to Hell glows brightly in his chest, radiating with a pure power of all the kingdoms.

I shift and stare at him for a moment, considering everything that he has done for me and who he is to me. He is my strength and was the very first one to abandon Heaven on my behalf in this life cycle. "Your mark will be over my spine on the back of my neck, which will be above where I plan to have Elias's mark across my upper back and shoulders."

Micah nods his head in agreement, his face softening despite the sharp shadows from the hellfire.

"Everyone agree on the spots Raven chose?" Kase asks, interrupting the staring contest I hold with Micah, just savoring the pure emotions radiating from him.

"Doesn't matter if they agree or not. It's Raven's body." Dante ruffles his fingers through my hair and kisses my neck again. "Let's just do this and make things permanent and official. I can't wait."

"I think it's because you just want to fuck my brains out after," I say, bonking my head on his chest.

"Fuck yeah." Dante wraps his arms around me and hugs me close as the others remain in a semi-circle.

Lucian summons a bowl, and I watch as all of the devils blend their power together. The ever-silent tattoo artist demon comes from his spot just outside of the room where he has been waiting his turn to add the marks, and once again, I close my eyes and focus on my guys' presence around me, ignoring the stranger.

Dante pricks me again with his fangs, adding another dose of venom to my system. It's enough to take the edge off things and relaxes my body, but it doesn't turn me as high as a kite as the first time he bit me to leave his unofficial mark after he was jealous of the feather branding Micah had left on my skin.

A part of me is over the moon with excitement, but there's another part of me that is a bit nervous and sad. I want all of their marks, and I want to be bound to them forever. I just wish that those who are intended to rule Hell with us were all here. I wish Elias could give me his mark at the same time as Micah's. And funny enough, I'd like to have Cassius's mark as well. I have the perfect spot for his, because I plan to make his ass always be at my feet, so his mark will be on my ankle. That's what he gets for letting his pride consume him and not allow him to do what needs to be done.

Dante whispers in my ear about how beautiful and strong I am as the tattoo artist inks my skin with hellfire. The sensation doesn't hurt, but it does make it a bit hard to ignore as the spots heat up.

I unintentionally drift off to sleep, feeling my body and mind disconnect. Andre appears before me in my dream state, and I can't help smiling at him. I love the fact that I am never alone, even in my dreams. This is how eternity will be. I'm closer to my devils more than ever.

"You're almost done. Just one more mark for Zade." Andre opens his arms and invites me into them, and I inhale a breath of his delectable scent of coconut.

"I can't wait to see them," I say.

Smiling, Andre kisses the top of my forehead. "Then wake up and open your eyes, little hellion. You are now bound to all of us in body and soul."

The world crumbles around me as light and darkness blend and merge together, pulling me from a dream state. I open my eyes with a smile, my whole body buzzing and tingling, the marks tender yet exhilarating as I feel them blaze across my skin. I feel closer than ever to my devils.

"Raven, I'm so sorry. I fucked everything up." Elias's voice snaps me out of my haze of love and a bit of intoxication from Dante's bite. "I tried everything possible to be there for you. Hell got to me. I felt as if I was dying over and over again while I was there. I wanted to abandon Heaven for you. I wanted to take my throne. But I couldn't."

My eyes widen at the sight of Elias standing before me, his wings expanding on his back, the translucent color sending beaming rainbow light scattering across the strange world. I feel as if I'm still dreaming. I can sense the devils around me as Elias tries to take me from Hell. It's bizarre and almost like he has absorbed Andre's power to dream walk.

"Not dream walk. I'm manifesting myself through our souls." Elias steps closer, and I can't help taking an automatic step back. I'm afraid if he touches me, he will drag my soul away from my devils.

Hurt crosses his face, and he frowns and drops his hands at his sides. It's now that I realize he's not in the body I last saw him in. He is in his form that I know and love, his gray eyes sparkling. He even still has his nipple piercings and the tattoo over his chest.

It takes everything in me not to jump in his arms because something about him in this moment triggers fear inside me.

"Darlin', I'm sorry. You don't have to be afraid of me. I have a clear mind again, and I want to meet and see if we can come up with a plan to get through this. I'm lost, and I'm confused. It's as if the world is against us."

Tears burn in my eyes at how sullen he sounds in this moment. I can feel him on a deep-seated level as his emotions crash over me. He feels regret and he's mourning the life we had when he was still mortal. He feels utterly and completely defeated that he can't figure out how to fix things or if things can even be fixed.

"I don't think that is a good idea," I say softly, tears now streaming down my cheeks. I hate rejecting him, but it's too dangerous. I have more than myself to look after now.

"Please, Raven. I need you. I'm so sorry about how things turned out. I'll do anything. Please." Elias drops to his knees and clasps his hands together.

The world around us quakes, and Elias flashes in and out of existence. Andre whispers my name, prodding at my very being, trying to get me to wake up.

"I'm sorry. I have to go. I feel myself being pulled away from you." I can barely see through my teary eyes. My whole being aches in a way that it had when I lost Elias the first time. When he died in my arms, saving me. "I will talk to my devils, okay? I won't abandon you. But I can't risk being near you. Heaven wants me too badly."

"Raven, wait. Give me just a minute longer to be with you." Elias crawls forward on his knees and grabs my hands, setting my body aglow with his light.

Darkness erupts from me, shooting him backward. He can't touch me in this dream world. My marks won't allow him to. They won't allow me to stay either.

"I'm sorry. I can't. But I will reach you again. I promise." I ease my hands from his and cover my face, my whole body aching as my soul feels as if it shatters and falls to pieces.

The world vanishes with Elias.

My devils call my name.

I don't respond. I don't move. I just fall into the pain of knowing that Elias needs me, and I can't be there for him. I'm not sure I'll ever be able to again.

21

Haunted

RAVEN

TWO WEEKS FEELS like a year in Hell. Usually, the time flies by so quickly. Now? Not so much. But this is right for me and the devils, keeping me hidden within each of their kingdoms, but I can't stop thinking about Elias. He hasn't returned to my dreams since I abandoned him.

"Little hellion, why don't we go for a walk. You need to work on your skills. The stronger and more powerful you become, the quicker we can re-join the Mortal Realm. Isn't that something you want?" Andre hovers in the arched doorway of the room we share in his palace. "If it is not, we should still practice."

I close my eyes and shut out the world for a moment longer. I don't mean to ignore him and not respond to him right away, but there are so many emotions coursing through me, twisting my stomach, and it doesn't help that I feel nauseated. I shouldn't be sick from this pregnancy. I haven't gotten sick in a while. But I guess it was bound to happen. My babies might be spawns of Heaven and Hell, but I'm only mortal.

"I will if you can convince the other devils to be my victims. I want to learn how to fight against someone more powerful than me. I'm not in a good state of mind to punish souls." I rub my temples and comb my hair from my face, finally forcing myself to sit up. "I'll give you extra cuddles and a blow job if you manage to convince Lucian to dress more like Cassius. I know they don't look alike, but they feel so similar. I kind of want to just beat the hell out of that bastard angel."

Andre chuckles with his smile, and he spreads his arms wide and wiggles his fingers, coaxing me to slide off the bed. "I think I can manage that. Zade has also been looking forward to showing off his kingdom to you. Maybe we can start there?"

"How long has he been done?" I purse my lips together, feeling bad that I had no idea Zade had completed building his kingdom. I should've been there to watch him and to support him through everything, but I've been struggling to even go wherever the devils lead me through the day. They've been caring for me and coddling me. I can't even remember if I even walked on my two feet the last two weeks.

I know I'm a bit of a disappointment right now too. They have been yearning for my attention, to have fun and to consummate our new bonded souls, but I still feel as if I'm broken. They respect that and give me whatever I need even if I don't ask. What I could really use though is to have things return to normal.

"Not long. Promise. Zade isn't exactly motivated to punish souls. You know how he is." Andre smiles with his words, referring to the fact that Zade is the embodiment of Sloth, and he tends to stand and just watch without doing much.

"Let's go there first, then. The training can wait. I'm far too curious to see what kind of twisted punishment he has created." And truly, I am. It is so fascinating to see the kinds of punishments my devils create for the Hell-bound and damned.

Andre scoops me into his arms and positions me to where I hug him with my body. The world blurs with his movements, and I screech as he launches from the balcony and right into the middle of his tornado orgy. The scent of musk and desperation assaults my nose, and I hide my face in the crook of his neck, sniffing his coconut scent. I try to suppress my lust the best I can because when I'm out here and not in the safety of his palace, his power affects me in a way that I can hardly ignore.

"You better hurry, or you're going to be banging me along the way," I mutter, kissing his throat and exploring his broad back around his wings with my fingers.

"Then I guess I need to slow down. I've missed you." Andre's voice deepens with his lust, and he slides his hand between my legs with enough pressure to make me squeeze him tighter.

And fuck. It sets me off. I crash my mouth to his and glide my tongue between his lips, showering him with my desperation. It's as if his touch alone awakens my body, and I am tired of ignoring it. I feel so good in his arms. I want a moment with him. I know he's been yearning to be with me. I've also been unintentionally starving him.

"Little hellion, I want to give you what you desire," Andre mumbles against my mouth.

"Do it. I need you, Andre. Let me have your power. Fuck me how you want."

Hot air rips around us and fire blazes through the air, burning my clothes and his clothes right off. I gasp at the heat of our naked bodies pressing together, and Andre holds me out far enough for me to adjust my legs and align my body to his. I'm already worked up from his pheromones, my body ready for him despite the lack of foreplay. Actually, this is foreplay for Andre. This is just him getting started.

"You're so wet," Andre says, teasing me with his tip slowly without giving me what I want as fast and as hard as I want. "You feel so incredible."

I hold his gaze with mine and bite my lip at the pressure of his massive cock sliding into me, stretching me in a way that makes me feel every inch of him. My eyes roll back in my head with pleasure, and he manages to hold me with just one hand while using his other to flick over my clit, playing with my ring in ways that make me nearly throw myself out of his arms because I can't control my movements from the pleasure.

I can feel him swelling with his need for me, making it impossible for him to detach himself until he has had enough of my pleasure. The sensation will never grow old. At first, I was nervous and a bit afraid of how his body reacted to mine. But now, my pleasure escalates by the second. It makes him more feral and sexy. I enjoy keeping him to me as if it's my body that doesn't let him go and not the other way around.

"I can never get enough of you, Raven." Andre thrusts as much as he can. Every time he pulls out some, the pressure intensifies, zinging ecstasy through me.

"You never have to get enough. I'm yours." I crash my lips to his and kiss him deeply, exploring his mouth with my tongue and tasting his coconut flavor. I explore his muscles with my fingers, moaning as he thrusts in and out of me, managing to fly straight at the same time as he massages my clit, getting me to orgasm again.

I know I'll be weak by the time he's through, but I'm happy to do what he needs. His power comes from lust, and he can have every bit of mine.

Andre flies faster, the hot air swirling around us, and he manages to position my leg on his shoulder, stretching my body even more as he pushes in deeper. Impossibly deep. I know he uses Hell power to fucking rearrange my insides to accommodate him. It doesn't feel wrong, but it does feel a bit strange, as if he's fucking me in my soul.

Descending lower, Andre makes me screech and moan at the same time as my body goes haywire. A part of me wants to look as we head towards the ground, but another part of me can barely keep my eyes open. I just want to lose myself to the pleasure and ignore the world around us. Being in Hell has really messed with me on a physical level. It doesn't help that I am experiencing symptoms of my pregnancy. At least I was until Andre decided to make me leave his kingdom. Could his passion and love be the cure to my ailments? Possibly. Or maybe he's just fucking me so hard that I can't even process anything outside of how he feels inside me.

Andre lands on the ground and runs a dozen feet, slowing his pace but only long enough to swing me around and press my back into the hot wall of what I think might be Zade's palace. I haven't seen it yet, but all of the devils' palaces are made of the same black onyx material. They all resonate with heat that warms me to the core but doesn't burn me.

"Don't just stand there. Invite us in." Andre's rumbly voice cuts over my moan, and I break away from his mouth to peer behind him. He must have a special sense for Zade, because he doesn't even look in the devil's direction. He stands about ten feet away with his arms crossed and purple light flickering in his eyes with his Hell power.

"You never need an invite, Andre," Zade says, his voice deepening with his words. I lock my gaze to his blue eyes and smile through another wave of pleasure.

From his heavy, lustful gaze, I can tell that Andre's presence already affects him. Zade shifts on his feet and loosens his arms until he has to adjust his cock in his pants, the hard-on obvious as it tests the durability of the fabric.

"Come and join us. Raven could use even more pleasure, and I know she craves you. I can sense it as she watches you watch us." Andre digs his fingers into my ass cheeks and carries me as if he can walk blindly and never have to stop. Well actually, he can. This is his talent, and I will never get used to it, but I will always enjoy it.

"Is that okay, Raven?" Zade asks, his toasted marshmallow scent wafting to my nose. I'm so glad it hasn't changed, because his scent is my favorite, and he makes my mouth water just being within his reach.

I moan my agreement, bobbing my head. Reaching out my hand, I silently beg him to come closer until he stands behind Andre. He touches my cheek, guiding me to stretch a bit closer until he kisses me sensually, slowly, and in such a way that I want more. I need more.

I don't know how we manage, but Zade doesn't stop kissing me until Andre sets me on the edge of a gigantic bed big enough for every single one of my devils and me. I thought that Andre's bed was huge, but it's nothing compared to this. It's as if Zade wanted to be prepared for anything and everything. He truly is all in with me and my devils and our bond. He was hesitant before, his sloth making him unable to truly enjoy and do things with me, but it was also that same sloth that brought him here because he couldn't do what Heaven wanted him to do either.

"I can't pull out of her yet," Andre murmurs, repositioning himself onto his knees and spreading my legs wide, holding me by my ankles. He purposely puts me in this position to expose my clit to Zade.

Zade moves beside us, and he traces his fingers over my nipples first and works his way down my stomach until he reaches my clit and strokes his finger over it as if he wants to warm me up even though I'm plenty ready.

Bending forward, he licks his tongue across my exposed body, not even minding that Andre is still thrusting and moaning with both of our pleasures. He kisses the ring on my hood, getting it to vibrate with his power. And unholy Hell.

I reach out and blindly grab Zade's pants and manage to use

my strength to rip the button and zipper until I can pull his cock out.

"I want to suck you," I say, getting him to shift until he practically straddles my face, his girthy, hard cock long enough to meet my mouth as he continues to pleasure me with his tongue. I bob my head, craning my neck, and taste the sweet flavor of his pre-cum flooding my mouth. We all moan in unison, really getting off on each other's pleasure as our emotions tangle and Andre's pheromones turn us wild. Feral with lust and love and everything good that comes with physical intimacy.

"My two favorite people," Andre says, drawing my attention away from Zade as he admires the two of us in the sixty-nine position. I can't help wondering if Andre wants more from Zade. I also can't help wanting to see it if he does. I love how Kase always likes to mess around with Dante when the three of us are together, and I didn't realize how much I want that from Zade and Andre. I don't know if it's strange to ask or if it's too far out there, but I'm not ashamed to voice what I want. I know that Andre likes that.

"I want to see you guys kiss," I say, breaking from Zade's cock. "I love how much you guys care for each other and for me. I mean if it's something you want."

Warmth builds in my chest and blooms in my face as the two of them silently converse with just their eyes. I can see them from around Zade's hip as I continue to stroke my fingers over his cock, still wanting to get them off.

"I think I'd like that, little hellion. Zade is a handsome man, and the desire coursing through you over seeing us together is so fucking delectable." Andre hums under his breath, slowing down just a bit so that Zade can arch upward. "What do you say, Zade? Will you do that for Raven?"

"I'd enjoy doing that for her. You mean a lot to me and I want to be here for both of you in any way you please. I know how this feeds your very power. You're my best companion, Andre." Zade stretches up and slides off me, giving me a better view of the two of them.

Bringing his thumb back to my clit, Zade pleasures me as he leans in toward Andre but keeps his gaze on mine.

A burst of electricity crackles from his fingers, the thrilling vibration ricocheting through my whole body. Andre surprises me by snatching Zade by the throat and dragging him closer, meeting their lips together in the sexiest kiss I've seen.

My muscles tense with my orgasm, the sensation of Zade using his power on my clit as Andre fucks me stupid setting me off. The combination of the hot emotions running between them as they kiss like they've been waiting an eternity for this moment keeps my orgasm going until Andre grunts and his cock releases me.

"Claim her now. She needs more," Andre says, lacing his

fingers around Zade's cock and positioning him to my body. And holy fuck. I love how dominating Andre is, controlling the two of us only because he knows me and Zade and our darkest desires.

"Fuck yeah, she does. I can sense her desire from the fucking Mortal World. Her soul summoned me here by my cock." Kase's voice sounds over my moans, and I tilt my head, catching sight of him and Dante standing together in the doorway.

Happiness and love crash through me, and I stretch out my arms in silence, inviting them closer. I had no idea how much I needed them here until they showed up. I know the last two weeks have been hard on all of us.

The room quakes and fire explodes from the floor a few feet away. "Fucking damn it. What is—" Lucian snaps his mouth shut at the sight of Zade rocking his hips, sliding in and out of me while Dante and Kase flop on the bed and into my arms, each of them taking a side.

The cute, devilish bastards don't miss a beat and suck my nipples into their mouths.

"This is a fucking awesome side effect of the damn mark," Lucian says, stripping out of his shirt and dropping his pants before I even ask him to join us. And I love it. I enjoy how easy my devils make it without complaining about being summoned in the middle of...what might turn into a real kink fest.

"Micah, stop being a creep and get your ass in here. Raven

only likes it when she knows you're watching," Dante calls, his voice humming over my nipple. "Let her see you jerking off."

"I didn't want to intrude," Micah says, his deep voice turning raspy as he inhales a breath of Andre's pheromones permeating through the air, growing more intense by the second. "I wasn't sure if Raven summoned me by accident."

"Like it fucking matters," Lucian snaps, reaching for my hand. He guides my fingers along his shaft until I stroke him on my own, my body and mind separating in six different directions but still managing to remain tethered to me. "She's a bit occupied. If she didn't want you here, you wouldn't be here."

I moan and squirm, the sensation of all their hands touching me making me feel as if I'll explode again. "I want you all here. I've missed you. Let me show you."

"Careful what you say, angel-girl. There are six of us." Kase strokes my cheek and bows in, kissing my lips. "Seven if you count my tail."

"She can handle it. Look at Zade go. Damn." Lucian caresses his fingers along my thigh until he touches my clit, stealing my breath as he sets off the ring again. It's like a devil's touch triggers it.

"Whoa, fuck. More." I bite my lip with a smile and look at each of my devils. My heavy panting nearly makes it impossible to speak. "I trust you. Let me be your perfect soul. I don't care if you all share me. I just want your closeness." The heaviness of their lust permeates through the air even more, and my whole body buzzes with desire and need. Is it weird that I want them to use me how they please? That I get off by the idea of being their sex doll? Who fucking cares? All that matters is that we enjoy ourselves, we respect each other, and we are together forever. I'm not a whore of the devils like the angelic army likes to think I am. I'm their queen, and they are my kings.

"I love you, pretty soul. I love you so much that I will take one for you. Well, I'll take Kase's tail, because it's your favorite, which makes it my favorite too." Dante winks at me with a smile and snatches Kase's tail, rubbing his hand up and down the length of it, making Kase grunt.

"And I will fuck those pouty lips of yours, Ray. There's just something about your mouth that I love. I want to see you on your hands and knees while you do so. Get ready, Zade. I'm flipping her." Lucian snatches me up and flips me onto my stomach so quickly that I can't orient myself before Zade thrusts into me, hitting his hips to my ass.

Lucian spanks my ass, reaching around to spread my cheeks wider. I clench from the force, bracing myself for more. The sting only hurts a little, but his actions turn me on more than anything.

"Her ass is mine," Kase says, grabbing a bottle of lube from Dante's hand. I swear he's always prepared.

"I plan to get my fill just watching, touching, tasting every-thing that they do to you, little hellion," Andre says, his voice so deep that it vibrates through the whole room.

Damn.

"I think we can manage giving him an incredible show." I curl and uncurl my fingers, encouraging Micah to join us. "Isn't that right, my gluttonous devil?"

Micah moves closer to me, watching as Zade finishes, send-ing me into a state of euphoria. My entire body trembles with my moan, and my devils don't give me long before switching places.

"I think it'll be more than incredible. Just open your soul to all of us and drown in the pleasure you deserve," Micah says, shifting me onto him as I still remain on my hands and knees but crouch down a bit.

He aligns his body to mine and slides inside me. Lucian joins us, practically kneeling on Micah's shoulders, yanking my head up by my hair, and getting me to open my mouth to suck him in. His thick girth stretches my jaw and he takes over, gliding in and out of my mouth. I relax and drag my tongue over Lucian's shaft, my muffled moans coming in bursts as Micah fucks me as if he can't or won't ever get enough.

"Zade, hold her up. Let her relax and enjoy without having to concentrate on anything but her ecstasy." Andre shifts clos-er and rubs his big hand across my shoulder blades and down my back, reaching the spot of his mark above my ass. His touch zings through me, our beings connecting on a deep-seated level, and I roll my eyes to the back of my head, experiencing what he does.

Zade lifts me up and puts me in place, allowing Kase to position himself behind me, kneeling between Micah's legs. The cool lube pouring onto my ass makes me shiver, and Dante manages to slide his hand between mine and Micah's body to touch my clit. I yell with an intense orgasm set off by my devils as Kase slides into my ass, slowly spreading me wider. I don't experience pain, despite the amount of pressure created by him and Micah together. It's like pleasure is the only thing allowed in this room. And maybe it is.

Zade holds me, my hands now free, and I reach out and grab onto Dante's cock and stroke it. He moans as Kase uses his tail on him, and I shift my gaze enough to watch for a moment.

The room fills with the scents of our passion, lust, and desire. Andre is the only one to speak, telling me how amazing I am and how perfect all of us are together. I can feel his power zapping through me, and I accept it into my very being.

This is how eternity is going to be. I never want to leave this room. I just want to spend the rest of my existence in a state of achingly good bliss without the worry of the outside world.

Time doesn't seem to exist, and I lose myself to the darkness coursing through me from my devils as they lose themselves in my light. One by one, they finish, and each of them takes a moment to kiss and thank me and tell me how much they love me.

"I want this forever," I say, shifting with them into a cuddle pile while I lay on Micah with Dante and Kase on one side, and Zade and Andre on the other with Lucian playing with my hair as he sits above Micah at the head of the bed.

"This will be our forever. We swear to it." Lucian kisses my forehead. "Cassius will come to us soon. He will bring Elias with him. And then, Hell will rise. I'm sure that the guardians will fall."

I sigh and nod my head. "I know. I just worry it will take too long."

"It won't, angel-girl. It'll happen sooner than you think." Kase reaches over Dante and touches my chin. "Can you feel him?"

I frown. "What?"

"Someone is watching us." Dante rests on his elbow and leans in, bringing his lips to my ear. "Cassius is back. Elias might've taken them from Hell, but it seems he can't get himself to actually stay away."

I sit upright and peer around. Angelic pervs, I swear. "Should we get them?"

"Why don't you? We'll be right here and ready if he tries anything stupid. I don't think he will though." Andre looks into my eyes. "Not with the tattoos. Not in our kingdom. Things have changed and he knows it."

"Go on, heathen. See what the dejected angel wants." Micah helps me sit up, summoning a shirt for me to wear.

Damn it. I don't want to, but I know I should. He is part of our plan, after all.

"All right. Fine. But if you're wrong, you'll all get a little punishment from me," I say. My devils help me from the bed, ensuring that my legs still work. I stride toward the bedroom door that suddenly leads out of the palace as if Zade changes the very foundation of his kingdom.

I catch sight of Cassius standing under a tree made of bones.

Something comes over me, my world darkening. Thrusting my hands out, I blast him with hellfire. I just want him to pay.

22

Guardian's Path

RAVEN

CASSIUS FLIES TOWARD me, sending a gust of wind strong enough to throw the fire out of his path. He crashes into me and flips me around, taking the brunt of the fall onto his back. This fucker.

He knows how to capture me in a way that I struggle to fight. My devils are probably either thinking about punishing me for not fighting harder or dodging or some shit, or they are thinking about ways to help me without showing themselves. Except maybe Andre. He might be trying to get Cassius to give into desire. Because I swear that he is turned on already. I lay on top of him, straddling his waist, but my head rests on his shoulder and he restrains me by tightening his arms across my back.

"I am not here to fight or take you from Hell, Raven. You must believe me. I'm here with good intentions." Cassius has the nerve to stroke his fingers along my spine as if the gesture will settle me down.

Damn. It might be working, and I hate it. I want to punch him and just stay on top of him like this because the gesture feels amazing.

"Then why are you here? You still have your wings and your heavenly light. I don't understand what you're waiting for. You should just turn your back on Heaven already. I will get to you," I mumble against his tight chest, my mouth automatically inhaling a breath of his scent.

"Do you always sniff everyone?" he asks instead of answering my question.

I glower and wiggle, trying to break free of him. "If they smell good, yes. It's not that I want to fucking smell you, but we are so close, and you won't let me go. Be careful, because I might start kissing you too. Actually, I will start kissing you. I know that you'll be uncomfortable about it and let me go." I stretch my neck and prove my point by brushing my lips to his jaw. "Just another two inches, and I'm about to go to war with my tongue against yours."

"If it will get you to settle down and stop trying to fight

me, then okay. You may kiss me." Cassius drags me those two inches and kisses me first, slipping his tongue into my mouth and deepening the kiss quicker than I even have a chance to react.

The fucking bastard. He's always so hot and cold, and I should not be out here making out with him on the ground. I know the devils watch me. I only was supposed to come out here to find out what he wanted. Surely, it wasn't me...I think.

I jerk back and scowl at him. "What the actual fuck?"

He raises an eyebrow, his lips twisting to the side as he studies my face. "You threatened to kiss me, so I took you up on that threat. Was something wrong? Didn't you want that? I'm trying to be reasonable and open toward you. It's the only way for you to actually calm your tits and listen to me."

"You did not just tell me to calm my fucking tits." I narrow my eyes at him, trying with everything in me not to react to his words. Angels should not be telling me to calm my tits. He shouldn't even be saying tits. I swear his strange similarity to Lucian gets to me in a good way. It's like I have a thing for jerks, or maybe it's because I have my sweet psychos too, and I just like a variety.

Damn. I push the thought from my mind. I'm already distracted enough as it is, and Cassius's kiss only left me in a state of confusion.

"Of course, I told you to calm your fucking tits. You need to calm everything. I came here to talk to you. It's important, and I know if you start fighting as hard as you can, you're going to blast me right out of Hell. It hurts enough to stay here as it is." Cassius rolls over and plants his elbows at the sides of my head. Leaning in, he captures my gaze, his mesmerizing amethyst eyes so beautiful in this moment that I could stare at them forever. "Now, let me kiss you again until you finally realize that I'm on your side despite you being bound to the devils, which was a terrible decision on your part. By the way."

Fuck. I wish he didn't pin my arms over my head, making me excited and vulnerable at our current position. I'm not even sure he realizes how hot and bothered I am in this moment, still high from the passion I experienced with my devils. It doesn't help that I'm only wearing a shirt, and Cassius's body spreads my legs wider. I don't even think he realizes how close he is to me.

"You might as well fuck me too while your positioned like that. Just don't fucking cum. I don't need you to zap me to Heaven." I lick my lips with my words, watching his expression morph from soft to sharp as he realizes how easy it could be to fuck me right here. I know he's thinking about it. His body gives him away.

"Raven..." His voice trails off and he heaves a sigh and gets off me, taking a seat on the ground beside me.

"It's okay to like the sound of that. There's nothing wrong

with wanting me." I will keep pushing his buttons, making him question everything if I can't make him uncomfortable. Because he obviously is already adapted to my technique of trying to seduce him and just automatically gives in. Except, well maybe the sex. I think he's a bit afraid. And he should be.

He groans and scrubs his hands over his face. "You are not going to make me turn my back on Heaven by offering me the chance to just stick my cock in your pussy. I can do it without a problem. But right now, as much as I want to experience what it's like, I need help."

Help? He needs fucking help? I laugh in exasperation, tipping my head back with the gesture. And I can't stop. It's preposterous for him to come here and tell me that he needs help. He was not there for me when I needed it. He ignored me when I begged him. He can't just come here asking for my help.

"No. Go fuck yourself. You could use it. Maybe it'll knock some sense back into you, because how dare you come here, acting like you are some nice guy and that you have good intentions and want to just talk to me, and then you throw bullshit about needing help. I'm not helping you. You can just go to Heaven." I scoot away from him and try to get to my feet.

Cassius snatches the back of my shirt and drags me back to him. "You would be helping Elias too. I can't intervene. It is against everything I stand for to turn my back on the angelic army, but what they're doing...I need help."

Fuck me. He just had to go and bring Elias into this.

"If Elias needs help, he can come here and ask me for help. But the last time he was here, he said it was basically killing him." I rub my lips together, thinking about the last time I saw him. My heart aches, thinking about him intercepting my dream with Andre.

"He can't ask for help. He has no access to the Mortal Realm or to Hell. The angelic army has decided to imprison him until you have been taken care of." Cassius's words deepen with his comment.

I grab my chest, my heart feeling as if it'll explode. The angelic army has him. They took him to Heaven. If that's the case, what if he can never join us? I knew that could happen, but I just was hoping...I don't even fucking know.

"You have to get him. He can't be locked up there." I squeeze my eyes shut, suppressing my tears.

"I can't, Raven," Cassius says, stroking his fingers along my cheeks, wiping my tears away. I hate that I'm crying. I hate that he's trying to stop me.

Right now, I just want to return to my devils.

"But you can help me. You are tethered to him by your soul. We can do so together. I just can't do it alone. For one, they suspect that I might turn toward Hell despite the fact that I won't. They've gone too far off their path, and I don't understand what happens now. The Higher Power only stands by in silence as if this is a test, and we are all about to fail it. Whatever has changed with Elias...I think he can't help. He has started to change already." Cassius continues to caress his fingers over my cheek, his gentle touch doing more to settle my nerves than I want. He shouldn't be able to comfort me like this. I should be repulsed by his touch. I should be repulsed by him even suggesting that I help him. He knows what the guardians want. They will do anything to get me away from my devils. I'm trying to connect to Elias while they have him captive. That's not going to go over well.

"What do you get out of it? Shouldn't you be on their side? You say that they've gone off the path, but what does that even mean?" I finally lift my head and meet his sheening eyes. "What aren't you telling me? You are the leader of the goddamn saviors. You should be in charge of the army, yet you've been letting them walk all over you."

"It's complicated, Raven." Cassius sighs with his words. "Because Micah, Andre, and Zade have all left me. I'm all alone and it takes more than just one savior to keep things in order. The power that my brethren abandoned moved into the guardians. They have ascended into another level of power."

Of fucking course, they have. It's like Heaven has levels just like we're trying to do in Hell. "So, what does that mean? Are you just a useless little featherhead now? Is that why you keep coming around here, because they have taken everything from you?"

"They haven't taken anything. You have." Cassius tightens his jaw with his words, his nostrils flaring as anger rises in his features.

"Me? You're blaming me? Are you fucking kidding me? This is your fault. This is Micah's fault. This is Andre and Zade's. They all made their own decisions. You cannot blame me that they have descended. They saw something that you still can't seem to grasp." The tone of my voice sharpens with my annoyance and fire bursts from my fingers. I want to pummel Cassius for his righteous attitude even as he sits beside me in Hell. I can't believe him. Actually, yes I can. He's fucking Pride, after all.

"You were right. I'm sorry. I just...I'm lost but I also don't like the path set before me any longer. I still feel the need to take you away from Hell. I still need to protect that light and that darkness. But from who? I don't have the answers to that any longer, and it scares me. I thought perhaps that Elias would be able to decipher everything for me." Cassius reaches out and grabs my hand, bringing it to his chest to rest my palm over his heart. "Don't you think he might know? Especially now that he's been taken to Heaven. The Higher Power has blessed him, and only you can get those answers from him. So please help me."

I'm pretty sure that if I was standing, he'd be on his knees in front of me, clasping my hands and begging me with every fiber of his being. And I want to help Elias, but Cassius isn't the only one afraid. I don't even know how to help.

"I want you to plead with my devils. It is not my decision to make alone, and if you can convince them, then I will agree." I remain expressionless, though the satisfaction of seeing his frown over even thinking about pleading with my devils for help brings me far more joy than it should. I really am fucking twisted. I want to see him grovel. I want to see him admit that he was wrong and that we are right.

"Why can't you just ask them? I'm sure they are listening. I know they are nearby." Cassius releases my hand and crosses his arms over his chest.

"Because that's what I want you to do. I don't want to ask them. I will not speak on your behalf. If you want my help, you have to ask for theirs too. You need to get over your fucking pride and show us what kind of bastard you truly are." I push to my feet and dust my legs off even though none of the strange black dirt leaves any residue behind.

He growls in frustration, flexing his muscles as he sits quietly, thinking about what I have demanded he do in exchange for help from me. What he doesn't know is that I would go to the devils anyway. We need to think of a plan to bring Elias back. It's no longer as simple as waiting for him to return to me if he can't. But Cassius doesn't have to know that. Or maybe I should let him know that and still demand he ask my devils. He's put me through an immense amount of pain and anguish that he would deserve it. He must earn my forgiveness and the forgiveness of my devils.

Baring his teeth, he says, "Fucking fine. But if Lucifer even says one damn—"

"You're going to apologize to all of them as well," I add, cutting him off.

"If I didn't know any better, I'd mistake you as a demon, Raven." Cassius unfurls his wings and spreads them wide.

I smile at his words. "I'm not a demon, asshole. I'm the devils' queen."

He groans. "I should've known that you love to torture people."

My smile beams brighter. "You're just realizing it? And so you know, I don't like torturing only people. I like to torture those who have done wrong and need punishment. But that's not it. I want to teach them to be better. I want to lead everyone, including you, on a path of change."

"Bow down at my feet and beg me for forgiveness," Lucian

says, crossing his arms over his chest the second I stroll into the room with Cassius behind me. His naked body ripples with his muscles, and he transforms into his devil form. If Cassius were to kneel in front of him, Lucian could totally smack him in the face with his cock. And I have a real good feeling that he might try. A part of me really wants to see it. Another part of me...still wants to see it. I bet the sound of dick flesh hitting cheek bone would be like music to my sadistic, naughty ears.

Micah chuckles, hearing my thoughts. I can't stop the grin from crossing my face as our eyes meet. We both laugh, drawing everyone's attention to us. Crossing the room, Micah envelops me in his arms and hugs me close.

"What a sight that would be, heathen." Micah kisses my forehead. Straightening his back, he looks at Lucian and Cassius. "You should thank Hell that Lucian can't hear Raven's thoughts."

"Oh, now you better fucking tell me. I like how whatever crosses her mind makes her practically shoot beams of light and happiness from her soul." Lucian places his hands on his hips and narrows his eyes at me. "Please tell me that it has something to do with torturing this asshole."

"I'm nearly certain this is torturous enough as it is," Cassius says, his handsome face sharpening with his scowl. I know it bugs the hell out of him that I'm making him do this, but this is his lesson. Like when Lucian got a taste of his own fire chain,

Cassius will get a taste of what it's like to need help and have to beg for it. He's lucky that I already plan to see what we can do. If our roles were reversed, he'd probably deny me. He has denied me before. Every damn angel seems to have until they decide to turn their backs on Heaven.

"Far from it, Cass-hole." Micah grumbles under his breath with his words. "Be thankful that we are even humoring this. You belong in the pits."

"We could make him beg from there." Kase scratches his fingers over his cheeks. "What do you say angel-girl? Should we make him suffer?"

Dante bumps him with his shoulder." You know our soul has a thing for little rejects like this guy. But you know what would be better?" Wagging his eyebrows, Dante flicks his attention to me and then to Cassius.

Micah tips his head back and laughs, managing to hear whatever crosses Dante's mind. I'm a bit jealous that when the devils are open, he can listen into everyone's thoughts. I wish I had that ability. Or maybe not. I'm not so sure I want to know what's on Cassius's mind right now. Or Lucian's for that matter, with the way his cock hardens.

"Strip naked," Andre says, speaking up as if he can read Dante's mind too.

Heat flushes over my face. The devils aren't trying to humiliate Cassius. They're trying to give me a show, probably as a thank you for bringing him here and making him beg.

"What? You can't be serious. There is no benefit of me baring my body while begging for mercy." Cassius ruffles his feathers. He's nervous. I'm nearly certain of it. But I don't think it's because of the devils. I think he's nervous because of me.

"You guys, that's not necessary. I have plenty of eye candy right now as it is." I twirl my fingers at all of them. Because it's true. Lucian's not the only one naked. It's as if they just decided to go with the flow of things and this is our eternity now. I think Micah would be the only one to ever summon me clothing without me having to ask.

Cassius blows out of breath. "Thank you."

Lucian jerks his hand out, grabs the front of Cassius's shirt, and rips it off using his power. Heat flushes over my face at how fucking gorgeous Cassius is, showing off his muscular body.

"Just because Raven doesn't think it's necessary doesn't mean that we agree." This comes from Zade, who has been standing in silence beside Andre. "I think it's time for you to bare all to her and to us as you ask us for forgiveness, for mercy, and for help. Consider this being us letting you off easy."

Damn. I didn't think Zade had it in him. He's usually just going with the flow and allows the others to take control. I don't know if it's because he doesn't want to or if it's because he is completely incapable of taking charge. He is the devil of sloth, after all.

"Fucking out." Cassius clenches his fingers into fists, his whole body twitching with his annoyance.

I shake my head and hide my smile. This whole situation is far more amusing than I had imagined it to be. I had intended it to be pure torture for the bastard angel, but it's turned into one hilarious moment for me.

"Cassius," I say, breaking away from Micah to stroll the space to him. "You don't have to do that. It wasn't in our deal. But, they're not going to give it up. So it's up to you to decide how much time you want to spend here arguing about this. I know how angels think, and I know that nudity isn't a big deal. Unless you are completely different and happened to have adapted to mortal social norms."

"He's afraid to show us his tiny dick," Dante says, pinching his index finger and thumb together, creating an inch of space. It's far from true from what I have felt of Cassius, but it still bothers him. I can tell by the flash of heavenly light in his eyes. "I know it's embarrassing when you have all this glorious, gigantic devil cock around here. Even Zade is hung like a damn horse."

I cover my mouth, hiding my smile. "I'm going to leave the decision up to you. While I'm here in Hell, I have a very long time to wait. But if I start getting bored, I will turn to my devils for entertainment."

"I bet he'll just want to watch some more." Kase whips his tail out and manages to lash Cassius on his ass. "Isn't that right, you perv. You're just like every other damn angel. You love watching us defile this pretty soul in every way she desires, don't you?"

Cassius heaves a breath, unbuttons his pants, and kicks out of them, showing off the fact that he goes commando. It's rather surprising. "Fuck, everyone just shut the hell up. If this is what you want, then you get it. Are you happy now? Does this make you guys feel like the big bad devils you all think you are?"

Uh-oh. Lucian swings his arm and punches Cassius in the face, sending him flailing backwards. He struck a nerve in all of my devils, and I'm not so sure that there will be anything I can do to stop them from dragging him to the pits to throw him under with all of the damned souls.

"Stay down and apologize. You think you are some powerful almighty being like the Higher Power, but you're not. You're not even close. What do you do in this eternity besides watch as humanity destroys itself? What are you doing besides trying to keep us from doing our job at getting souls where they belong?" Lucian shifts into his devil form and towers over Cassius, his horns jetting from his head and his hands glowing with the fires of his Hell power. "You do nothing. You stand by and watch your army fall. You do nothing except whine and complain about me. The one you should be complaining about is yourself. Because you do not stand up to your full potential, and that is why you are here, ready to bow at our feet and beg for help."

Lucian is sexy as all get out in this moment. What he says is completely true. And I can tell from the look crossing Cassius's face that he might believe that about himself as well. I can see him questioning his entire existence, and it pains him. It pains him because he might finally see that he's been wrong this entire time, resisting turning his back and joining us as the sinners of Hell by not only his brother's side, but by his companion's. And by me.

He realizes just how alone he is, because even though the guardians are around, he is still alone. He is not like them. Far from it, actually. He is more like a devil than he knows.

"Is that what you want me to say? You want me to tell you that I am weak and pathetic? I'll say anything as long as you allow me to use Raven to get to Elias. I will gladly bow down and ask in the name of the Higher Power." Cassius drops on his hands and knees and does a deep bow in front of Lucian. "You can't see what I do, Lucifer. If you did, you wouldn't be such an asshole. It is more than about our past and what you want to do with the power of Hell. This is about Heaven and the changes that are happening because it no longer has the power of the saviors guarding and protecting it."

Lucian clenches his jaw, remaining silent as he stares at Cassius. A strange heaviness settles through the room, and I shift on my feet, wondering what everyone is thinking about. I wonder if maybe this is more serious than I had expected. It's not often that the devils would hear an angel out like this.

"If what you say is true, then Heaven will take care of itself." Lucian shifts back into his human façade and glances around at the other devils. "I don't want to put Raven at risk."

"Our rise can wait." Dante glances at me, his face remaining expressionless. "Elias isn't in any danger, pretty soul. It is merely inconvenient for us. We will be able to get to him once you are no longer carrying our babies."

"I'm going to have to disagree," Zade says, stepping closer and challenging Dante and Lucian with his intense stare, crackling with purple power. "Elias might not be in danger, but Raven needs him more than ever. He is your soulmate, and his being helps her to thrive."

"I have to agree with Zade." Andre flexes his muscles, opening and closing his wings. "But I think there has to be another way besides using Raven. I can reach his soul through her. Perhaps we can use that to our advantage."

"Hell yeah." Kase strolls toward Andre and whacks him on the back. "That sounds fucking better than trusting our girl with that asshole. Because I'm with Dante and say no. But I trust you."

Cassius throws his hands out while spreading his wings. "That's not going to work. I can't even get to him."

"You doubt my power?" Andre says, his eyes lighting with fire.

Cassius gets to his feet and squares his shoulders. "No, but you underestimate the guardians. Something has changed. It is enough to make me feel as if the end is coming."

I frown. "What? The end? As in the apocalypse?"

"Don't let him scare you. It's not what you think, little hellion. There aren't four Horsemen or demonic legions rising to Earth to fight against angels. If that were the case, we'd already be in the apocalypse." Andre shifts on his feet and stares at Cassius, but Cassius refuses to look at him. He doesn't look at anyone except for the ground before him.

"Which means I want to know what the fuck he's talking about," Kase says, his eyes lighting red.

Cassius finally lifts his gaze from the ground to look at the devils. And then, he whips his attention to me. "I can show you."

No one has a chance to respond or react as Cassius gathers light in his palms and shoots it at me. I scream in shock, my body zinging as I absorb his heavenly light. The world changes around us.

Cassius uses me to shift to a strange plane I've never been in. My devils remain by my side. I twist on my feet, unable to see anything through the strange light. But I guess my devils see it. Because they fall silent. Lucian swears.

And then the world around us shatters.

Beaten Path

CASSIUS

I GASP IN pain, the fires of Hell feeling as if they consume my very being as I use Raven to take us from my vision and back into Zade's kingdom.

My eyes well with painful tears. Pushing to my feet, I protect myself by summoning heavenly light. I use it to banish the residue of Hell clinging to my soul by connecting with the devils. I expect them to come after me and beat me into submission for using Raven as I had, but it was the easiest way considering she is bound to all of them by Hell power.

It still pains me to see the tattoos on her body. She shouldn't have had to resort to this. I know what the devils intended by doing so, but it doesn't make it any less agonizing as her light constantly siphons to them while their darkness leashes her all the same. It is far worse than a deal. She got nothing out of this. With deals, it's understandable. Mortals can't help themselves if they want something. But Raven? She did this by her own free will. It'll make things worse with the angelic army once they find out. I don't think they will standby and plan to just take her away any longer. I have a feeling that they will just deem her and the new beings that she carries complete abominations and try to remove them all from existence.

I can't let that happen. Not after I felt them within Raven's soul. The balance between the light and the dark was unlike anything I've ever experienced. It was so powerful even at such a stage of their souls' growth, that I know that with proper care and guidance, they could really solidify the balance between Heaven and Hell. They could be the perfect anchor for the whole Mortal Realm.

"That was only a vision. You know damn well that it could change. Look what happened with the vision we had that created Hell in the first place. You were supposed to be by my side, Cassius. Look what happened. You changed everything." Lucian's deep voice reverberates through the room.

If I didn't know any better, I would think he was hurt by remembering the day that I decided not to jump from Heaven. I couldn't. He made it look so easy standing from the highest point in all of the realms to create the deepest level of Hell, but as I stood on the edge and stared into the black abyss, I knew it was something that he would have to do alone. But then Kase and Dante followed behind him. I still regret not moving fast enough to intervene. They were two of the most powerful angels with a bond unlike anything. Seeing them lose their light hurt me even worse than watching Lucian give up his. With him, I always knew that he would one day decide to do things his way.

At first, after he showed me his vision, I thought that maybe he was right. Seven levels of Hell for souls to work through alongside the pits where there is no returning from, and Purgatory being the one place souls could be sent back into a cycle to make their way to Heaven.

It was an amazing vision, but then I realized that perhaps it shouldn't be that way. Souls cycle for a reason. It is their universe to live in. It's their duty to figure it out for themselves. And it worked for a while. But the mistakes started adding up and humanity was destroying itself. If that had happened, the souls would have nowhere to go except for Heaven. And allowing bad souls into Heaven? Unthinkable. So I stood back and watched Lucian fall to ensure that it could never happen. I couldn't trust that his vision would be correct and the souls would actually change once they have made it out of Hell. The darkness should stay.

Except now I'm starting to think otherwise, seeing what the light and dark accomplish together. I just can't turn my back yet. Heaven is my home. And if the guardians, the purest souls of humanity that have joined the angelic ranks, continue with their mission, everything could be lost. It is not in their nature to do anything except fight, guard humanity from Hell, and stop the devils from taking over the Mortal Realm. They could ultimately be our downfall. I don't have the power to sway them otherwise. Before, with my brethren, I had it. We could control Lucian, Kase, and Dante. We ensured that things remained balanced. But they now see that the balance has shifted, and I am weak. My vision could very well mean that there will be no guidance. No guardians. Only war. The cycles will return if they have their way, and humanity will be lost.

We are flying blind, and it doesn't help that Elias is being held captive. His soul, granted to him from his fall from grace, allowed such a thing to happen. Devils aren't the only ones able to manipulate souls. Angels are just as good.

"He's not the only one who changed everything. Andre, Micah, and Zade also didn't follow through with the plan." Raven's voice rips me from my thoughts, and I catch sight of her in the arms of Kase. I don't remember him moving to pick her up, and I feel as if I might have lost time. It would be very possible. Hell does things to me. The power tries to call to my mark, the same one as Lucian. I need to leave. And soon.

"It is more complicated than that," Micah says, speaking up. "I suggest that the two of you set your bad blood aside for now and let's proceed with reaching out to Elias. If we stand here and fight over things which cannot be changed, we will never move forward. We must focus on what we can do in this moment."

Micah might be a devil, but he still carries the wisdom from being an angel. And he is absolutely right. I cannot hold this anger against Lucian. Our differences have already severed our bond. I know that I will never have him by my side as my companion again, but I can try to summon forgiveness for his abandonment.

"Fucking fine. I will set this bullshit aside for now. Only because of Raven. I can see it on her face that she wants me to give Cassius a break for the sake of her soulmate." Lucian balls his hands and glowers at me. "Do not forget it. This is not for you. This is not for Heaven. This isn't even for Elias. This is for Raven."

I never thought I would ever hear Lucian do something for someone else. Raven has really opened up a soft spot in that devilish being of his. It is eerily familiar to what I remember him being like long ago. He wasn't always such a dick. He cared enough about humanity to proceed to jump even when I wouldn't follow. If only he didn't change things along the way. And the way that he, Dante, and Kase created demons and armies ruined everything. If they would've just remained on their thrones and taken care of the souls, things might've been different.

It's hard to say. So many things have happened over existence. I haven't thought much about it until now, until I had to.

A burst of fire slams into my chest, sizzling across my skin. I holler in pain and jump back, shielding myself as another orb flies in my direction.

"Is Hell getting to your head? You keep turning into a fucking light show. Knock it off. If you want our help, you have to stop trying to hurt us." Lucian gathers more Hell power in his hands, but he doesn't throw it at me.

"Maybe I can help," Raven says softly, surprising me by leaving Kase's arms and holding out her hand to me. Bright light illuminates from her fingers, and it's as if she manages to tap into Heaven. I still can't believe she's able to. That light inside her draws from the pure goodness of grace.

Fire burns around me as the devils watch Raven take my hand. If they had the opportunity, they would probably try to cut it off me for not resisting touching her. They are quite possessive. I don't even know how they manage to work together.

"Only a little. If I catch you trying to bathe yourself in her light as if she's a fucking well of Heaven, I will cut your balls off. I know how good it feels, and she is our soul. You have no claim on her." Dante moves nearby, crossing his arms over his chest and looming close enough that he could truly go after me, considering I still stand here naked. I hadn't realized that I was until he pointed it out.

And fucking hell. I hate this place. This damn body refuses to calm down. I swear that something is up inside me because I can't get my damn cock to go flaccid. It wants to just point out the fact that I have the same amount of the lust coursing through me as any of the devils. It's humiliating.

I grab myself and try to push it down. I immediately regret the gesture, because Raven whips her attention to my hand, her eyes lighting with the fire of a thousand levels of Hell, the intensity of her gaze making it worse. Why is she so fascinated? I have no idea.

"It looks like we need to hurry before Raven gets distracted more than she is already. We need her thoughts clear for me to tap into her soul and summon Elias." Andre steps forward and reaches out, surprising me by tapping my junk and zapping me with energy hard enough to make me cum.

I gasp in shock, the exhilaration of an orgasm shooting right to my toes. Raven's jaw slackens as she opens her mouth, and she laughs. So do the rest of the devils. Heat burns in my face, and it takes everything in me not to blast Andre away.

I grind my teeth. "What the actual—"

"Cassius, it's okay. You don't have to be ashamed. Andre

was only helping. We can tell that you were uncomfortable. It happens to the best of us." Raven clears her throat, trying to stop herself from laughing more.

Kase winds his tail around her body and dips up between her legs, stealing my complete attention. I can't help myself. I know that she is naked under her shirt. And suddenly, I want to see more of her. I want to kiss her again. Andre's lust consumes me.

"It especially happens to our soul. You liked that, didn't you? You were so fucking wet." Kase sinks his tail in and out of her, the gesture turning my body hard again. I watch as he pulls his tail out completely, the appendage now glistening in the light of fire.

Raven releases a soft sigh and whacks him on the shoulder. "Andre, Cassius. Come with me. We're going to another room to do this. If we stay here any longer, I am going to need some relief."

"Not fair, pretty soul. Do you know how much I want to watch? I need to see what you do to Cassius." Dante flicks his forked tongue, a hiss escaping his mouth.

Raven wags her finger. "Maybe some other time. This is hard enough as it is. Cassius is obviously not ready. I'm not going to do anything with him until he jumps from Heaven."

I press my lips and tighten my jaw, the idea of not being able to kiss her or give her anything she wants bugging the crap out of me. She has to be full of shit. I know that she enjoyed our physical intimacy.

Lucian howls a laugh and points at me. "Maybe lust will be his downfall after all. I swear, Ray. If you don't stay good on your word, your ass is mine. Do you understand?"

Anger rushes over me as I watch Lucian grab Raven by the back of her hair and yank her to him, manhandling her as if she is his to do as he pleases with. She gasps and kisses him, letting him glide his tongue into her mouth, and I can't stop stepping forward.

My hand jerks out before my mind has a moment to process, and I grab Raven by the back of her shirt and haul her away from him. My heavenly light blasts out, keeping him back, and he morphs into his devil form. So do the other devils.

"Everyone, calm down. It's fine. Come on, Andre, let's go." Raven's voice sharpens with her words. "Cassius, quit it with that light before I extinguish it. If you can't keep yourself in control, we aren't doing this and you will have to go."

"I'm sorry. I don't know what happened. I won't do it again. Please, let's just get Elias and move on. Once I do, I will not return here. I won't bother you again." I stiffen with my words, the thought paining me more than I imagined it would.

Raven remains expressionless, and she detaches herself from me and walks to Andre. The fires of Hell course around us as the other devils watch us leave. I'm surprised that they let

Raven control them as she does. I can tell they are unhappy that she has requested privacy with me and Andre, yet they don't argue. It's strange. A bit unsettling. But then again, Raven happens to be the most mesmerizing woman in the universe. And it has taken me far too long to realize that. I see it now though. If only we were on the same side. If only we had the same path.

Time will tell if we will eventually come together as one.

"I need you to lay on the bed on the other side of Raven. She will open her soul to you, but I swear to Hell if you try anything, I will destroy you. You do not have to participate with us, but I know that Raven thinks that you can help." Andre points to the bed. "You will guide us once we get connection."

I nod. "Yes. I know where he is. I won't let you down."

Raven shifts on her elbows, sitting up. She pats the spot beside her, and I carefully ease onto the bed, managing to keep space between us. I wish I could steal the blanket to cover myself, or that Andre will give me a minute to put some pants on, but he nestles beside Raven and pulls her close. The weight of their bodies together forces me over and I end up flush against Raven's body.

"Raven, close your eyes. We're going to go into a meditative state, okay?" Andre softens his voice with his words, stroking his fingers over her forehead and down her eyelids until she relaxes beneath his touch.

I tense as I watch him caress her in ways that I wish I could. He is far more gentle than Lucian and Kase were. It helps ease the anxiety rolling through me. I don't know if I can handle watching her be manhandled again. She deserves to be cared for like the pure soul she is.

"Go on, Cassius. Open yourself to both of us." Andre remains even-toned, though I know he doesn't want to open himself to me. He doesn't want to feel the sting of my light or be reminded of Heaven and everything that he gave up taking a throne in Hell.

I inhale a deep breath, filling my lungs to the brim until I can't suck in anymore, and then I slowly release it and feel my body lightening and my anxiety easing as Raven's warmth, light and darkness, and soul seep into me as if I'm a sieve and she wants to merge our bodies and beings together.

A moan escapes my lips, and a wave of desire burns over me. It doesn't hurt me like it should. Raven's light is enough to extinguish the fire of Andre's power coursing through me. I clench at the sensation of his lust smacking me right in the balls. I was more concerned about opening myself up to Raven again when I should've been concerned about Andre. It feels as if I was sucked into the vortex of desire and I will die if I can't find pleasure.

"Damn, Andre. What are you doing to us?" Raven's voice sounds everywhere as if she speaks in my mind and out loud.

"That's Cassius. If it's too much, I can see what I can do again." Amid the darkness, a bright flash of fire grows until Andre materializes before me with Raven by his side.

I clutch my cock at his words. "Please don't."

"Then learn how to control yourself." Andre flashes me his devil form with his threat. "Everyone must be grounded and tethered or else this isn't going to work."

I suck in another deep breath and force away the strange, intoxicating desire deep inside me. Raven catches my hand and offers me a smile. As if the beauty of her face can distract me from the feeling of our emotions intertwining, I manage to suppress my urge to kiss her and finally see the beautiful world around us as it is. I thought that Andre would create some sort of nightmare world, but this is identical to his sanctuary in Heaven. He always had a thing for beautiful landscapes, and instead of the quiet isolation of the pure white buildings, he always chose to be amid sprawling greens and flowers. Blue skies and bright sun. It showed his connection and appreciation of the Mortal Realm and how he brought it into Heaven.

"I think we are good now." Raven squeezes my hand again, studying my face for a moment.

Andre steps forward and grabs me by the chin, dragging my attention from Raven. "I need you to tap into Heaven. Use Raven's soul very carefully."

I lick my lips and bob my head, reaching out and pressing my fingers to Raven's chest, feeling the light within her very being as it strikes me to my core in a way that leaves me yearning for more.

Haze drifts over the world as bright light rains down like mesmerizing stars showering from the sky. Raven intakes a sharp breath and nearly cuts off the circulation in my fingers with how tightly she holds my hand. She uses her Hell strength to do so as if she might fall into the strange abyss surrounding us as the dreamworld vanishes and leads us in what I can only describe is another realm of Hell. One not connected to the Mortal Realm, nor to Heaven. I nearly lose my nerve and release Raven and Andre, because I realize how fucking crazy this is. This world is Elias's prison. I know it is. I can feel the angelic power creating this horrendous place, tapping into the darkness that Raven carries. They use his connection to Raven to torture him as if they are the devils.

Fury rolls through me and I glower and spread my wings, my whole body tensing at the sight before me. A shadowy figure sits on the ground with his knees pulled to his chest. Only a small glow of his heavenly light shines through the strange darkness of this place.

"What in godforsaken Hell is this?" Andre uses his free hand to rub his hand over his hair. "I don't understand."

"Are we still in Hell?" Raven asks, her eyes darting around and squinting as she tries to figure out where we are. "It feels wrong."

How am I going to tell her that the angelic army not only captured Elias and is keeping them apart, but they are torturing him by imprisoning him in this place? It makes me question everything. I am on Heaven's side. There's no doubt about that. But them? Who are they fighting for? Because this isn't for humanity or the Higher Power.

"This is Heaven," I say, keeping my voice even. It pains me to even say the words, and I considered lying about it, but Raven isn't stupid. She would've known immediately, the second she saw Elias.

"You're shitting me?" Raven asks as she gets to her feet and pulls Andre up with her, forcing me to stand at the same time. My whole body trembles and fear tightens my chest. Heaven help me. Your Almighty Grace, what do I do? How do I handle this? I know this wasn't in your plan.

"Hello?" Elias's voice sounds through the air, drawing everyone's attention to his shadowy figure. "Is someone there? Let me the fuck out of here. I don't belong here. This is some fucked up bullshit, and if you don't, I will figure out how to escape and you will be in fucking trouble."

"Elias? Holy fuck. Shit." Raven tries to yank from us, but both Andre and I tighten our fingers around her petite hands. "What have they done? What are you even doing here?"

"The angelic army doesn't trust me. They have taken it upon

themselves to practice judge and jury and punish me for giving you my angelic light in the first place. They have ruined everything. Mikail and Meri are psychotic."

Raven growls under her breath. "Don't worry. We're going to get you out of here."

"No, Darlin'. It's not safe for you and the babies. Just leave me here. I will figure this out. You need to stay in hiding." Elias's voice cracks with his words. I can feel it in his very being that he doesn't want to say them, but he's afraid for Raven.

Dragging us closer, Raven says, "I won't—"

"Andre, take her back to Hell," Elias commands.

Raven explodes with bright light. "No! No one is touching me! I'm getting you out."

Before Andre can react, Raven rips her hand free of his, and he vanishes into the shadows. I'm too quick for her and tighten my arms around her. I won't let her go. I don't want to leave Elias here as much as she wants to save him.

Screw everything. This bullshit ends here.

24

Imprisoned

ELIAS

EVEN THOUGH I prayed for mercy, I didn't want Raven finding me here. I don't want her getting any-where near me or the wrath of the righteous bastards who deemed me an abomination despite my angelic light and soul. I wish with everything in me that I had stayed in Hell. It was just too painful. Even with the help of Micah constantly trying to keep me calm, it was too much for my very essence. I wasn't meant to be there. But I'm not meant to be here either, because it's just as bad. Actually, it's way fucking worse. I don't even know how much time has passed. It feels like it's been decades, maybe even a century, though I know that's impossible. Raven looks exactly like she had when I was forced to abandon her and save Cassius from the pits because he didn't belong in Hell either.

"Raven, please. Don't come any closer. I don't want them to know you're here. If they do, they will come, and they will get you. They're using me to tap into you and your Hell power." I clench and unclench my fingers, the rage that they use my soulmate to torture me bringing me such agony that I want to destroy the entire angelic army. They don't deserve the title of warriors of Heaven. They are no better than the damned souls of Hell.

"What? How is that even possible?" The softness of her voice stabs me through the heart, and it takes everything in me not to crawl toward her. If I move, she might rush toward me. And if she passes into the angel trap binding me, then everything will turn to Heaven. We will probably end up amid the army, and it will all be over.

"Careful, Raven. You can't touch him. We are on a spiritual plane, and if we connect, I can't stop what happens. You connect yourself to Hell, but he is connecting you to Heaven right now. Andre was your anchor, and without him...please just don't touch him." Cassius holds Raven tighter, pulling her close enough to wrap his arm around her, ensuring she doesn't fight and try anyways. It wouldn't be unlike her to put him to the test. And usually, I would love to see that powerful woman really prove to the angelic army that they are nothing in comparison to her, but I have a strong need to protect her. I need to protect our future. I need to protect the babies she's carrying.

"Then you do something, fucker." Raven yanks at her black hair and tips her head back, staring up into the void of nothingness. "You said that you could use me to help him. So do it. Get him out of here now and take us back to Hell."

Cassius squeezes his eye shut and rubs the back of his neck. He can't help me. Not in this state. The only way he could truly help me is if he managed to break through the ward keeping him away from me. He's an angel, but they have purposely created this world to keep him out. They don't trust him as much as they don't trust me. And they shouldn't. Because the second I am free from here, I will take them to Hell myself. I will cut their damn wings off and throw them in the pits. I will feed them to Micah's hellhounds.

"I am not strong enough to straddle the worlds. I don't have Andre's gift, and I don't trust myself to get you through this," Cassius says after a moment of quiet thought. "But perhaps you can do something, Raven. I know that you have enough light and darkness to battle this world. You've been able to create portals through different planes. You might be able to do so here. If you can manage to do it quick enough, we can grab him and go."

Shock zaps through me, my eyes widening at his words. What the actual fuck is he saying? He should want to take her away and not help me. It's far too dangerous. The devils would never allow such a thing. Cassius has nothing to lose. Not like I do or Raven.

"No. I am not going. Don't even fucking try it." I get to my feet and spread my wings out, feeling the sting of the air penetrating me to my very being. It hurts to move. It hurts to suck in air. This whole world was created to cause me agony for the rest of eternity.

"Don't be fucking stubborn, Elias. You don't deserve this fate. The Higher Power has guided me along this path to get to you. It is my duty to do what I can so we can re-join our power and get things back in order. If it wasn't supposed to be, I wouldn't have been able to keep Raven grounded to me." Cassius stands tall and matches my stance by opening his wings, his heavenly light glowing bright enough to see through the haze.

"He's right. I don't know how I know, but I do know deep in my heart and in my soul that we were supposed to come here. You don't belong here as much as we don't." Raven shuffles closer with her fingers twined through Cassius's. A part of me hates seeing them together. I don't know why, but I feel as if he hasn't earned the right to hold her so dear in this moment. He hasn't earned the right to make this kind of decision. He doesn't have the same ideals as the devils, and he cannot see the reason why this is a terrible idea. He has too much faith in his ability.

I hold my hands up and shake my head. "I mean it. Don't come any closer. I will not risk your very existence at the chance of leaving without a guarantee."

"How can you not even let me try? You know I'm powerful. You know I can handle anything. And if the fucking angelic army shows up, they will regret it. I will destroy them. They have no idea what I'm capable of." With Raven's words, light emits from her, cutting through the darkness. It's as if her essence cools the heat of the air around me, bringing me sweet relief. For a moment, I believe her. If only my fear didn't argue with me. She might be able to handle it, but there's always a possibility that something could go wrong. I couldn't live with myself if something happened to her or the babies. I would rather suffer here until someone comes up with a better plan.

"Because I love you. I know you're capable, darling. You are the strongest being I know. But it doesn't mean that I want you to jeopardize everything for me. You've already been through enough because of me. Let me handle this. I don't want you to do anything rash. Please. I'm begging you." I clasp my hands together toward the black abyss above me, sending a prayer to the Higher Power to please guide me and help me figure out what to do next.

"Elias." Raven holds her palms up, light seeping from her fingers and crawling up her arms, her strange new power exhilarating and shocking in the best way possible. I can feel the purity of her soul and the power she carries. It's enough to crack the realm, allowing her and Cassius into my prison.

"You did it, Raven. We have to hurry. Go to him first, but don't let go of my hand." Cassius says, motioning toward the crystal clear space within the hazy clouds.

"No. No. Please fucking no." I stare at the crack in the veil and pray for it to close. I pray for the Higher Power to intervene. I pray for something, anything to help us.

Raven gasps, her whole body stiffening as she touches the portal between the veil separating us.

And then she vanishes, a peculiar darkness swallowing her and stealing her away from me.

My prayers have been answered, but it wasn't divine intervention. It was something more. It was dark enough to even devour Cassius. It takes the darkness and the haze with it, shattering the strange realm completely until I'm standing in pure white light.

Holy fuck.

I feel the serenity of returning home to Heaven. I expect the angelic army to tackle me. I expect them to drag me back to my prison. Even though I feel at peace and I feel the tranquility of connecting to the greater good, something feels utterly wrong.

But the world is empty around me. There is nothing here. I don't understand what's going on. There should be thousands of angels around. This isn't the Heaven I remember. Have they all gone to the Mortal Realm? I can't see that happening. It is usually only the saviors or the guardians to do so. Someone usually would stay here to tend to the pure souls that keep Heaven powerful. I know Heaven hasn't lost that power because I can feel it deep inside me. Something else is up. This is not normal. Shit.

Where the fuck did everyone go?

A freaky growl sounds from behind me, and I flip around and stare at the demon standing before me. How in the fuck is this guy here?

"You escaped your cell, traitor." The demon strides forward, showing his sharp teeth. How in the fuck is he here? I don't understand. I thought I was in Heaven, but demons aren't allowed here. There is no way for them to even get in.

My heart sinks into my stomach, and I search around the empty world, expecting to see an entire legion of demons. I don't think that the devils would have arrived so soon. I didn't even think that it would be possible for them to do so. Maybe they used Raven. But this guy? He called me a traitor. He is not part of any of Hell's army.

I summon angelic light and prepare to fight him. I need to get him out of here. The urge is all-consuming, and my body lights aglow with my heavenly power. I gather power between my palms and hoist it over my head, preparing to thrust it. I want to knock this asshole back to Hell. He is going to mess up the balance. This place is intended for only the pure of soul.

Something rams into my back, stealing my breath. I don't get a chance to fight before a blade sinks into my body and pain shadows the edges of my vision. I stumble forward, trying to put space between me and my attacker.

I see Hell for a split second. It confuses the fuck out of me. I don't understand how. How is this even possible?

Wait. I'm mistaken. If it was Hell, I would sense Raven nearby. It's not Hell. What I see are the Mortal Realm and the angelic army. But something's different. Something's changed.

"Well, look who it is. What a precious gift. I wasn't sure I'd ever see your soul again. It's just as intoxicating as the first time, Elias." The familiar voice is like a punch to the balls, whipping my attention to the sinewy, gangly demon.

"You fucking bastard," I say, staring at Vincent as he summons Hell power in his fingers. "You're going to regret this."

"Actually, the devils are going to regret this. They should've paid more attention. They've lost sight of what we're trying to accomplish in the Mortal Realm. They are too focused on that damn one soul. But things will change." Vincent whistles lowly and motions for the demon to go to his side. "You see, this here is dedication. This angel, who chose to sacrifice himself to get into Hell, is what it's all about."

No fucking way. An angel wouldn't do this. The angelic army would never team up with demons.

Except anything is possible. I have always said it.

And it's worse than I thought. It's not just Heaven against me now. It's Hell, too. It's the entire universe.

I need to figure out how to warn Raven and the devils. There must be something I can do.

I can't just stand idly by and do nothing as this bullshit goes down. I'm not afraid of Vincent anymore. I'm not afraid of the fucking angelic army either. I will do whatever it takes to ensure that Raven is safe. That my future child and its twin are safe.

Tensing my body, I summon a sword made of heavenly light. It has been a while since I've been able to really tap into my powers. But I won't back down. I know that I can handle this. Vincent deserves to end up back in Hell and chained to the bottom of one of the fucking pits. He doesn't deserve to be strolling around as if he owns the mortal world. He will see. I will ensure that he regrets ever messing with me in the first place. Because of him, things got fucked up. He knew and he used it against me because I didn't know that I was an angel before I had fallen and given Raven my light.

"Now, now. That's not necessary, Elias. You know we're all on the same team. I'm sure you would prefer to have that soul all to yourself anyway. Why don't you be a good little angel as the Higher Power intended and get out of my way." Vincent summons his own Hell power, his body morphing from his skeleton-like façade into his disgusting demon form.

It triggers my angelic nature, and I grind my teeth as I attack, swinging my sword, hoping to slice the fucker in half.

Bright light shines from my right, and the world spins around as my breath escapes me. Someone just hit me with angelic light, knocking me off course.

I flap my wings, trying to brace myself for impact. I smash into the hard pure white ground and manage to flip over and swing my sword again. I stab through the chest of an unfamiliar angel, a new one that is probably only a decade old. I don't know how I know, but it's as if I have a sense for it.

"Stand down. I am your superior." I use my wings to launch myself back to my feet and hold my sword out, keeping space between us. "Do not fight against me. I will take your wings. You are undeserving of the light you have been gifted with."

The man stands there and shocks the Hell out of me by summoning his own sword, grabbing his wing from over his shoulder, and slashing the heavenly blade through it, sending it burning to the ground.

Oh fuck.

It's not just one angel who has sacrificed himself to connect to Hell.

I can't believe this is happening. I never in a million years expected for angels to turn to Hell only to go against it. They are not about saving humanity. They are about keeping the power.

"Elias, stand down immediately. This is Heaven's war, and if you do not bow down and prove your loyalty, we will imprison you again. You will not be free to make your poor choices any longer." I spin around and look at Mikail as he stands before me with white wings, not unlike the saviors. He has managed to gain more power, no longer carrying the gold ones associated with the angelic army. He's no longer a guardian. He is a savior like me.

"Fuck off, you asshole." I spread my legs apart and re-position my body to fight him.

But I don't get the chance.

A dozen figures materialize around me, and I don't have the chance to do anything except tense my muscles as the angelic army blasts me with heavenly light. They chain me to the weird world again. I can't escape. I can't help Raven.

Once again, I have failed her.

I've failed humanity. I have failed Heaven and Hell.

God, help me.

25

Angelic Demons

KASE

I SPEW RUBY power at Cassius the second he materializes with Raven. I nearly ripped Andre's wings off for returning without the love of my fucking eternity. I was about to destroy his entire kingdom for losing her like he had. I had trusted him, and he failed by not binding himself more tightly to Raven.

"Give her to me!" I holler, launching through the air in my devil form. Cassius doesn't even have a chance to release Raven before I sink my teeth into her shirt and drag her away from him.

She screams at the sudden movement, and Zade catches

her in his arms. He summons his purple power into a shield, stopping Cassius from trying to rush him to get to Raven once more.

"Take me back!" Raven screams, her voice stinging my ears. I haven't heard her sound so desperate ever. Whatever she saw has left huge, gaping scars across her soul, inked in black far darker than anything found here.

"What the fuck?" Dante shouts, spreading his wings to separate Zade and Cassius. I consider launching over him and plowing into Cassius to growl in his face. My wrath controls me, stealing away any sense. All I want to do is punish him. He should have returned immediately with Raven even though Andre lost the tether. Instead, he fucking stayed on the other plane with Raven for what felt like years.

"Everyone, calm the fuck down." Lucian's deep, raspy voice reverberates through my bones, and he stomps his feet and shakes the world around us hard enough to send us all toppling to the ground. He taps into Hell, using the tether he currently shares with Micah. I don't know when he took it, but he obviously needed the extra power to get through to us.

"I said take me back! Zade, let me go! I need to go to Cassius. Now! They are torturing him." Raven smacks her hands against his chest, fighting for him to release her.

"Don't let her go," Andre says. He strides toward Raven, but Zade shuts him out by turning his back. Even though they are companions, this affected Zade as much as it affected me.

I know it wasn't Andre's intention, but even if it were an accident, it still happened. Things could've been worse. What if Cassius didn't return here? I'm nearly fucking certain it was our little devil spawn to bring her back. I see a dark chain tethering me to her stomach.

"Raven, you need to take a breath. There is nothing in this world that I want more than to bring Elias back, but not at your expense. He wouldn't want that." Andre locks Raven in his gaze, towering over Zade and staring at her.

Her eyes water with tears, but she doesn't cry. She's not sad. She's pissed the fuck off, and I can feel the heat of her anger and fury from over here. Usually, I would think it was hot, but it burns over me, making me a bit uncomfortable.

"I need you to please forgive me. Please trust me. It is not safe for you, considering that they manage to use him to tap into your darkness. We need to keep you out of reach. No more shifting planes. No more going to the Mortal Realm for anyone." Andre expands his leathery wings and slowly spins around to meet my eyes. He stops and stares at me. "It's worse than we thought."

I clench my fingers and turn my gaze from his to Dante's and then Lucian's. We are the ones who lead our kingdoms. The other devils are still learning how to manage and navigate Hell. But we built this place from nothing.

"I need everyone to go to their kingdoms immediately." I stride towards Zade and Raven. Andre doesn't stop me as I dodge past him and open my arms to my angel-girl. "Raven, you're coming with me and Dante. We need to take you to a place between our kingdoms and away from any of the ruling palaces. If what Andre said is true, we need to get you somewhere that will cut you off from your soulmate completely."

"Let me help," Cassius says, speaking up for the first time. "Something is utterly and completely wrong. The angelic army is—"

The world quakes and a large fissure cracks through the floor, exposing hellfire. A blinding light explodes from the crack, and I have no choice but to shield my eyes from the holy light. Raven screeches in fear, and I snatch her from Zade and summon my Hell power. I don't wait before I shoot the ruby orb at the forsaken angel pulling himself from the pits that run throughout all of Hell. I've never seen anything like it. How did he break the chains? How did he get here in the first place?

"Give us the soul, and we won't take your kingdoms." The angel unfurls his burned wings, the golden feathers disintegrated with only bones now in place. "She is ours."

"The fuck she is," I say, blasting him back a dozen feet. He somehow manages to tap into Heaven.

Micah roars and grabs his chest, his mortal façade exploding into his Hell form. It seems almost uncontrollable for him, and he yells out. "Something is yanking on the tether. Someone is trying to break it."

"Impossible!" Lucian yells, summoning his fire whip and taking his devil form as well.

"Hell is no longer yours. It belongs to those who sacrifice their beings in the name of Heaven." The angel once again manages to summon heavenly light and prepares to blast it at Micah.

Lucian whips his fire chain around the angel and drags him to him. He uses his nails and slices across the angel's throat, severing his head from his body. It won't stop the angel for long, because Hell will just reset him to experience the torture over again, but it will slow him down enough.

"Get Raven out now!" Lucian says as another angel rips itself from the pits and tries to crawl through the crack in the floor.

I rush toward Dante, and he wraps his arms around me and Raven and drags us toward the arched doorway leading to the open air of Hell. Cassius follows behind us, and usually, I'd try to fight him, but he brandishes his heavenly sword and stabs a flying demon through the chest. I didn't even see the fucker coming. It seems as if those who have jumped from Heaven have decided to try to take over Hell instead of bowing to the kingdoms, and this demon isn't one we've created. It is a former angel.

Unholy fucking shit.

We would never give a fucking angel a ranking position among our army. Only the souls that come straight from their cycle to join us are offered such luxury. We don't trust angels. And if they fall, they fall as Elias had done. They wouldn't just come to Hell. They would join the mortal world and all that business.

"Fuck, they are releasing all of our captives." Dante soars high above Zade's kingdom, and I glanced down at the aisles of burning tombs containing the souls of sloth. I have no idea what's inside those tombs, but I don't really want to know. I'm sure the fucking bastard figured something twisted to punish those who have fallen to Hell in his kingdom.

"Cassius, if you were going to remain by our side, you need to fight. I need you to clear a fucking path." I swing my arm and shoot another wave of ruby power at a demon that launches from on top of one of the tombs. His wings are too far gone to carry him, but it doesn't mean that they won't grow back with his missing limb. It's as if someone cut the chain that kept him at the bottom of the pits.

"Your Almighty Grace, please give us the strength—" Cassius growls as I cut off his prayer with a burst of my power.

"That shit doesn't belong in Hell just as these fucking angelic bastards don't either. Did you know about this?" I ask, using my tail to whip at another mutated angel.

Cassius swings around and slices his heavenly sword through

the demon, cutting him in half. He quickly severs his wings as well, and the limbs fall back to the fiery ground.

"I would've never allowed such an act against Heaven." Cassius flies ahead and stabs his sword through the neck of another mutated flying angel. I struggle to think of them as demonic, despite them being so. They haven't earned the title.

"Why do they even try? You guys are far too powerful to be overthrown." Raven speaks up for the first time, her voice echoing as she shouts over the wind. "I don't understand."

"I will explain everything when I can concentrate, angel-girl," I say, kissing the nape of her neck and holding onto her tightly. I shift my tail to wrap around Dante's waist to tie us to him, allowing him to free his hands to fight properly.

There are at least ten more bastards launching from the ground. One of the assholes throws another, trying to knock us from the sky. Cassius rams into the traitor of Heaven and manages to hack him up so quickly that I nearly miss his scattered remains falling away.

"I don't know this place. Where are we going?" Cassius asks, shooting his heavenly light in a semi-circle, clearing another path. The demonic angels can't crawl from the pits fast enough to keep up with us. They are weak in their new states. They haven't been tied to any one kingdom, and it shows.

"Head toward that towering mountain over there. The one made from fire and bones. That is the border of my kingdom.

Once we cross it, we can use a portal. I don't want anyone to follow us, so hustle your fucking ass." Dante stays right on Cassius's back, using him to shield both me and Raven from any threats. I never thought I'd appreciate being in a half-angel, half-devil sandwich with Raven, but I worry that she could get hurt in the middle of this battle. We don't know how much she can handle, and I don't want her to be tested anyways.

"I swear if I lose my wings, I will be worse than my brother ever was." Cassius mutters under his breath, though he doesn't shift into a devil like he expects. He hasn't turned his back yet, and unfortunately for us, I'm not sure exactly how or when that will happen. Right now, we need heavenly power.

"If you were going to lose your fucking wings by helping us, you would already be in the fucking pits," I say, poking my finger against his wing and burning the skin.

He growls and swivels, glowering at me. "Things have changed. I don't even know what I'm doing anymore. All I know is I serve Heaven."

"Apparently, those fuckers think they do too." Raven tightens her fingers around my arms as if she's afraid that something will rip us apart.

We manage to make it from Zade's kingdom and into the mountain, and Dante shoots his Hell power at one of the crevices and opens a crack big enough for us to fit through at the very peak. Only someone with wings can manage to get this high, but I doubt anyone will find it now.

"Go first, and I'll follow," Cassius says, slowing down and shifting to stare behind us.

I nearly tell him to stop being such a cowardly angel and to just go through the portal, but Dante flies ahead and leads the way.

We enter into my kingdom, and he nosedives with Raven and me toward the forest of souls. It's the furthest place from the pits. I have protected my kingdom with power to keep it separate from Lucian's because he pissed me off a century ago by trying to take some of my souls while I was in the Mortal Realm.

Unlike in Zade's, my pathway is impenetrable. I can see my souls, but they can't escape unless I open the gate to the prison. And that only counts for the worst of the worst. The others are fighting an endless battle on the fields and some are trees in my forest. There are no angels here. That was all Lucian.

"Almost there, pretty soul," Dante says, his voice lowering to remain quiet.

Cassius swoops beside us, and Dante and him land with a thump. I jump from Dante's arms but keep Raven in mine and head toward the thickest part of the forest where the trees start to merge together and become one entity with the souls silently screaming as their bones protrude from the bark.

"It's just up ahead," I say, gathering my power in my hands.

We reach a gigantic tree with a trunk twenty feet across, and I blast my power against it until a portal opens up and darkness greets us.

"You can't expect me to go in there," Cassius says, tightening his jaw, increasing the vibrancy of his light to try to peer into the veiled world separating all the levels.

"Fucking fine. Stay out here. I don't give a fuck." I stroll ahead with Raven into the cavernous tree as it shifts to show the veil separating my kingdom from Dante's while still keeping it together. We created this place as our sanctuary before we decided to return to the Mortal Realm and leave Lucian to tether Hell as we figured out how to bring the others to their thrones. It was probably another reason why he was bitter, but the guy has always been a little bit of a dick. But not as bad as Cassius. It's one of the reasons why we chose to follow through with his plan instead of resisting and remaining in Heaven. That shit was too boring for us. The power was too good.

"Damn." Cassius begrudgingly follows behind us and I seal the portal and use hellfire to light the small space between realms aglow.

"Wow." Raven wiggles in my arms until I set her on her feet, but she doesn't look at my hand. "This place feels exactly like both of you. It's so strange and exciting. I can't comprehend what's going through me."

"Because it's made from a part of our beings. Our power

comes together and unites in this very location," Dante says, offering Raven a smile.

"It feels fucking awful to me." Cassius rubs his hand on the back of his neck and swivels on his feet, staring around at the now empty place. It used to have furniture, but it has since been cleared out. I can't even truly remember the last time I've been here.

"So, what now?" Raven asks, stepping closer to hug her arms around me. She extends her hand to Dante and beckons him closer until the two of us wrap her in our arms, squishing her between our muscular bodies.

I can't stop the smirk crossing my face as Cassius stares at us as if he's desperate to be invited into our sandwich. Raven doesn't even look at him though. I don't know if it's because she's wrapped up in the emotions that course through her from being in such a place or what, but I fucking love how she ignores him.

I love how it gets under his skin. He deserves it. He has far more to make up for than Lucian. If he wants even another moment of Raven's attention or to touch her soul ever again, he's going to have to earn it. He will have to jump from Heaven.

"We need to figure out how to get back to the Mortal Realm without the angelic army knowing." Cassius twirls his fingers until an orb of heavenly light breaks through the air to light the world around him. It doesn't last long, extinguishing as a wave of darkness steals it away and vanishes it from this place. He groans and shakes his head in annoyance.

"You can go back to the mortal world. We are staying here." Dante flashes his fangs at Cassius. "Don't even try to argue."

I growl and warn him with my gaze to keep his mouth shut. If Dante tells him not to argue, he better not fucking argue. I will enforce it. Hell, I will kick his ass out of our sanctuary and feed him to the hellhounds.

"That's a mistake. You're going to lose everything if you don't fight. Come with me. You can help me get Raven to Elias safely. Obviously, Hell isn't as protected as you guys thought it was. These angels are so clever. Who knows what they will do next?"

I really wish he wouldn't have said anything, because I swear to fucking-fuck that he just jinxed us.

Raven gasps and clutches her stomach, bowing forward with a cry. I watch as light seeps from her, trickling in every direction and shaking the world. The angelic army is using Elias again. I can tell. And it's hurting Raven.

"He's right, Kase. We can't stay here. Not if they keep using Elias to get to her. She is protected, but not from the pain that they can make them both suffer through their bond." Dante flashes his fangs and hisses, his green eyes shining brightly.

"Is there a way to fix it? I know that he's my soulmate, but can I break the bond? There has to be something we can do. I'm scared." Raven groans and heaves a couple of deep breaths, the pain bunching her muscles.

I feel helpless. I hate this goddamn feeling most in the world. We are stronger than this. We are stronger than the fucking angels, yet they have an advantage over us.

"It's dangerous. They'll be waiting." I ruffle my hand through my hair, my anger turning my vision red.

"And we will be ready. I will not stand for this. This behavior is against everything Heaven stands for." Cassius places his hands on his hips and glowers at Raven as if he can see the angels trying to mess with her very soul.

I grin. I can't believe I'm about to agree to this. I never imagined I'd be fighting alongside Cassius while he was still a goddamned featherhead.

What choice do I have?

"Dante, go and reach out to Micah. Tell him that they must keep everyone distracted even if it means leaving Hell for a bit." I flick my gaze to Cassius. "I swear if you do anything that hurts Raven or goes against us, you will be torn apart and scattered along every kingdom. You know that we can't go with you into Heaven, but we can fight against the angelic army. We can give you time."

Cassius proffers his hand to me. "You have my word. If I fail, I will turn my back on Heaven. There will be no point in fighting for something I cannot in good faith go along with any longer."

A part of me hopes he fails. But the more reasonable part of me needs him to succeed.

For Raven.

For humanity.

For Hell.

I clench my teeth for a moment. "You have a deal."

26

Power Struggle

RAVEN

AGONY CLENCHES MY stomach. It hurts to breathe. It hurts to move. It even hurts to just exist. I fear that whatever the angelic army is doing will hurt the precious beings growing inside me. I don't know what they are doing to Elias, but I fear the worst. It is hard when angels and demons can't be destroyed. That is how the devils ended up creating Hell. They moved to their own plane, but they don't have access to what they once did before. And now? The angels are seriously screwing shit up with the balance. Not only has their righteousness got to their heads, but I'm also nearly certain that they have lost themselves to who they were as mortals. It's funny in the worst way possible to think that these soldiers of Heaven were once the purest of souls. Too pure. They can't even see what is before them. They will be the ones to destroy the universe in the end.

Unless we can stop them.

How did my life turn into this? I was supposed to just make a couple of angels jump from Heaven to bring balance. Now, I am pregnant with twins. My soulmate is being held captive. One prideful angel swears that he will never join us. And then a legion of angels are now purposely falling from grace in an attempt to steal Hell from us.

It makes me want to fuck some shit up. If I weren't in so much pain, I would summon a fire chain and show them exactly what they are dealing with by trying to stand in my way from taking Purgatory. They will regret everything they have done. I will not stand for this much longer. I have more to lose. My devils have a lot to lose as well. But even so, we are stronger. We have more power. We have each other, and no one can ruin that for us.

"Take slow breaths, pretty soul. I know it hurts." Dante rubs his big hand between my shoulder blades as we stand in front of the Hell portal that will take us into the Mortal Realm. Beside it, brilliant light shines from an angelic portal that Cassius summons. It will be him and I going through that one while Kase and Dante take the other. We won't be ending up in the same location. But we will be nearby. It's the only way I will be able to escape from Hell without the angelic army getting to me. They will be too distracted by sensing the devils. They won't suspect them of having allowed Cassius to take me.

"They will be surrounding all of the demonic hotspots. We are going to go directly to the Demon's Den where Gia and Tamia are currently holed up. They said that some of the local demons have teamed up with the angelic army. That's how they are managing to navigate Hell." Kase rubs his hands together, shooting red sparks through the air. "I think that Vincent might be a part of it. He wouldn't come when summoned. Gia hasn't heard from him. He is the only one that might be able to stabilize at least one kingdom with his power, considering how old he is and how Lucian had given him part of his power to overlook the Mortal Realm when he was being a dickhead and trying to piss us off."

Just hearing Vincent's name stabs me in my heart, and I cry out in pain. This is worse than pain. This is torturous and all-consuming despair.

"This is his doing. I know it." I clutch my knees and try to push the pain away, but it feels as if my soul is being torn in half. I can feel the disgusting darkness of the demon now that I know he is a part of things. I wish that they had never allowed him to remain on Earth. But they had a lot more things to deal with because of the angelic army and Elias's sickness.

"And when we find him, he will pay. I will destroy him completely. There will be nothing left of his being to even scatter through Hell." Dante flicks out his forked tongue, the barbells of his piercings catching the firelight and glittering at me.

"We must hurry. They will start regrouping now that their surprise attack isn't going to get them anywhere." Cassius holds his hand out, his fingers glowing with his heavenly light and coaxing me to grab on to him.

My body refuses to do anything but remain bent over as tears sheen in my eyes. Instead of waiting for me to get my shit together, Cassius comes up behind me and slides his arm around my back and my knees, lifting me off my feet. I expect to cry out, but it's as if he manages to steal the pain. Whatever he is doing helps me breathe. I can think more clearly now.

"I got you, Raven. Just stay open to me, and I will continue to flood you with my light the best I can. It should help you get through this." Cassius adjusts me in his arms and meets my gaze. "I will try to hold onto your soul for as long as I can, but it does weaken me, and I don't want to risk you getting hurt because of my shortcomings."

I lick my lips and swallow, shivering at the thought of him releasing me back to the unbearable pain shredding at my be-ing. I need to be stronger than this. The angels can't win. "I need you to be able to kick fucking ass, even if it means that I have to suffer for you to do so."

"I'm good for now. You need me, and I am here for you." His voice softens with his words, and I can feel the truth to them. He has gone from being an asshole to someone who actually cares for me. I almost don't believe it. Of course, angels have decided to try to take Hell. That's basically the same as if it is freezing over.

"Thank you, Cassius. I know this is a weird way for us to come together, but I am glad that you are on my side right now. I don't know what I would do without you." I smile the best I can, though I'm not into it. I don't want to smile. I want to cry my eyes out because we shouldn't be in this position in the first place.

A hot hand touches my cheek, drawing my attention from Cassius and to Dante and Kase. "Be a pain in Heaven's fucking ass. You will be fine, okay? You are the strongest soul we have ever met in this entire existence, and we know that you can handle anything. If you can handle all of the devils and even that bastard angel, you can handle what the angelic army has in store. Prove to them that you cannot be messed with. We can't be messed with. And get Elias back. We will have a killer celebration, maybe even some dick cutting of these mutated angels. We'll take their wings too." Kase kisses me softly, his lips like a breath of air that I had no idea I needed.

"See you soon, pretty soul." Dante leans forward and presses his face to my belly. "Take care of Mama, our little spawns. She needs you. So does Elias."

My heart swells with his words, and he kisses my stomach before kissing me on the forehead and then on my lips.

Kase and Dante go through the Hell portal, and it closes behind them, leaving me with Cassius. He stares at the heavenly light portal for a moment and takes a couple of deep breaths. He's nervous, but he doesn't want to show it. He thinks he has to be the toughest badass in all of existence.

"We got this. You have me to destroy all these bastards. If there's something that you feel you can't do, I'll do it. I do things that I have to." I pat his cheek and surprise him with a kiss.

It's enough to get him to relax, and he softens his features. In this moment, he's so incredibly handsome that all of the disdain I've had for him melts away into just a faint memory. I know I shouldn't let my guard down so much. He made it clear that he will not join Hell. But a part of me knows that I will be his undoing, and he knows it. Until then, I know that I will probably suffer from his rejection and his inability to just give in to what is right.

"Brace yourself, Raven. This might hurt your darkness because the light will try to consume it." Cassius unfurls his wings and straightens his back, tightening his hold around me.

"Just get it over with. I don't need to brace myself. I'm used to feeling the pain that comes with Heaven." I blink a few times, trying to keep my voice even.

Cassius frowns, and I swear that his eyes sheen over with tears. "I wish that were never the case. I know you feel as if Heaven is against you, but it's not. It's against the evil in the world. It wants things to be balanced and right and good. It hurts because I've failed you. But I will make it right again. I will do it for you and the devils and for those precious beings growing inside you."

Cassius steps forward without another word and enters through the portal to Heaven. I gasp at the shock of an electrifying pain that quickly fades as my body absorbs it, and I begin to glow as my spirit tries to leave my body even though I know it's just my angelic spawn.

"That is the purity of your soul realizing that you are where you're intended to be. I know you don't think so, but you have an angel-kissed soul so it would recognize where it came into existence." Cassius adjusts me in his arms so that I hug him with my arms and legs, allowing him to free his hands. "At least, it is where you would have gone had the devils not found you."

"You don't know that. You can't predict that sort of thing, which is obvious because of where we are currently at now." I don't mean to snap at him, but he needs to realize that he can't just say whatever the fuck crosses his mind without me putting in my two cents. Because if I belonged in Heaven because of Elias, I think we would already be there. Instead, we chose another soul cycle together. There was a reason. I'm not sure exactly what it was because Elias hasn't had a chance to tell me. All I know is it had to be a good one.

He wanted me so far away from the angels and the angelic army that he even tried to make a deal with Lucian. It's why Lucian acted like such a dick, thinking that he could still claim me as his and no one else's. He was pissed off because Elias didn't see good to his word.

I won't lie. I'm glad for it. I can't imagine what my life would be like if I was never reborn as Raven Rose and remained Grace. I don't know what she was like, and I'm not sure I truly want to know. Just because it was my past life doesn't mean that it was me. It is a soul, and I am what my circumstances have molded me into, which would be far different from Grace.

"You're right. I'm sorry. I still can't get over how brilliant your soul is and how lucky the devils are that you chose them, all things considered. Not many people would." Cassius keeps his voice low as if he speaks any louder that I might snap again.

I close my eyes and suck in a breath, trying to settle my nerves to have a rational conversation with him even though I know we need to get our act together and find Elias as quickly as possible. "That's because the angelic army did an awesome job at scaring humanity. I was never truly a believer. I'm not sure why. Maybe it's because deep down, I knew that it was different."

"Perhaps." Cassius expands his wings and steps forward, ending our conversation. I'm glad for it. I'm not in the mood for any life and eternity pondering moments with him. I just need to find my soulmate. I need the pain that the angelic army puts him through to stop. He saved me once as Grace. He found me again as Raven. And now it's my turn to find him. It's my turn to save him. I won't let him down.

"Please let us make it through unnoticed. Please allow Raven's light to suppress her darkness." Cassius whispers the prayer so lowly that I nearly don't catch it. If I wasn't resting my chin on his shoulder, I would've missed it. And it's strange. I can feel the weight of his words as if they will work here. And maybe they will. He has his faith in the Higher Power and in Heaven, just as I have my faith in the devils and in what we want to accomplish.

I have so many questions. I want to know if he hears a response or if he just feels it. I want to know if he has ever seen God or the Higher Power that he works for. I want to know where the pure souls are. I want to see if the angels that don't go to Earth or become a part of the angelic army stay up here. Up here? I don't even know why I consider ourselves above the other planes. We are just on an alternate plane. I think we're all on the same level. Maybe except for Hell. I do feel myself fall when I go through a portal. But that's only because the devils created that new plane with their descent and the blast of power as they landed.

"This is so empty. Am I supposed to see something? There's just so much light." I press my lips to his earlobe, keeping my voice at a whisper. I'm far too nervous to break the heavy silence enveloping us along with the light.

"You can see things as you want. You just have to think about it. Heaven looks differently to everyone. Just like the kingdoms in Hell, we can create our own places." Cassius shifts me once more to his hip, and I cling to his side, feeling incredibly small and fragile against his muscular frame. I cross my legs and my ankles, ensuring that I won't fall away from him. The ground looks so strange as if I could just fall into nothingness. I had no idea that I was afraid of the idea. Pure, utter nothingness.

I shiver at the thought.

"Here, I will show you as I see it." Cassius touches his fingers to my temples, and the world shifts from light to shadows and then a beautiful, brightly colored world comes into view around us.

We stand amid a meadow, not unlike the one that Andre favors to build within my dream world. Fields of rainbow flowers pepper the ground, sprawling into a distant sunset made of pinks and purples and colors I can't even describe. Colors that

I am pretty sure I've never seen in my life before. They don't exist on the mortal plane or in Hell. Hell tends to carry only the warmth of reds and oranges and yellows in the darkness of blacks as fire consumes everything.

The indigo sky remains crisp and clear without any clouds, the bluish-purple hue stunning. I wonder if it ever turns dark here to show off glittering stars or if this world for Cassius is only painted in pure light and colors.

"It's so beautiful," I murmur, shifting in his arms, my sudden need to get on my feet to touch the grass consuming my thoughts.

But still, Cassius doesn't let me. I know that this is just how he views things, and in my reality, it is just made of light.

"But where is everyone? Are there new buildings here? Where do the mortal souls stay?" I never believed that I would be able to ask someone these types of questions. It's always been one of the things I knew I'd have to wait to find out until I died. Even then, I wasn't sure. I imagined that it could be completely mind-blowing or nothing at all. Either way, I guess I didn't really think much about it. I didn't care. What was important to me was living. I was never going to live like I was dying. But now, I'm living as if it will be forever. It's why I fight harder.

"I am shielding us from everything. We will not come into contact with any heavenly beings except for Elias." Cassius strides forward, his feet seemingly gliding over the field of flowers as he heads in a direction where I see nothing. There are no buildings here. There are no portals. It's confusing as all get out.

"Doesn't answer my questions." I press my lips together and peer around, squinting as if I can maybe see through the world he has built around us to discover the answers for myself.

"Those answers don't matter because this isn't where you are choosing to belong. All that matters is that we find your soulmate." Cassius remains expressionless with his words. "Unless you decide to change your mind and ask for me to help you unbind yourself from Hell to come here."

I grimace at his comment, my annoyance getting the best of me. Swinging my arm, I whack him in the chest. "Seriously? It's such a dick move. I'd answer your damn questions."

All he does is tighten his jaw and shrugs his shoulders. "Like I said, it's not important. Maybe some other time. It's not as if I can show you right now. We cannot disturb anything in the realm."

I decide to drop it and focus on the world around us. Cassius glides across the meadow and the world starts to shift and move as if it bends to his will. The meadow disappears and we find ourselves standing in what I can only describe as a long white hallway with portals on each side, glowing with different lights.

I try to peek into the portals, but I don't see anything. They must lead into the other levels of Heaven created by the beings who take over this realm.

"I need to tap into your soul. To do so, I will have to untangle mine from you, and you might feel the pain again." Cassius doesn't look at me with his words, but his lips tilt downward, and I can tell that they bother him. He doesn't want to release me to feel the burden of being Elias's soulmate as the angelic army tortures him. But what choice do we have? I knew that this would come. I knew that the pain would return, and I would have to suffer alongside my soulmate.

"I'm ready. There's no way for me to prepare, so just do it. The faster we get to him, the faster we can get him out of here, and the pain will stop." At least, I hope that's the case. It's strange how there's no one here. It seems too easy, but Cassius doesn't give anything away. If he's worried, he doesn't show it to me.

"Pain is fleeting. I promise that it won't last long." Cassius closes his eyes, and a heart-stopping pain stabs me in my chest. I bury my face into his shoulder, suppressing the sob trying to escape me. It feels worse than before. Much, much worse. I can hardly keep my eyes open. I just want to squeeze them shut and disappear. I want everything to end.

"Hold on, Raven. We are close. I can sense him." Cassius tenses, his muscles rippling. A gust of wind blows my hair, and I inhale a sweet fragrance permeating from his flapping wings. He smells so good that I concentrate on his scent to help distract me from the pain. It doesn't do much, but at least I can keep my mouth from sobbing.

A strange cooling sensation trickles down my back, seeping through me and easing the fire gripping at my soul. Cassius isn't the only one who can sense Elias. My heartbeat picks up pace, and my stomach flutters. That coolness continues to grow until the pain subsides and I can focus on the portal we now stand in front of."

"I need to set you on your feet. It is heavily protected, and I need to be able to defend you," Cassius says.

I squeeze him a little bit tighter, hoping that he changes his mind, but Cassius detaches me from him and sets me on my feet. He summons an angelic sword, and the blue glow of brilliant fire erupts. He is using the same power he uses against the devils and demons.

"Are you sure you're going to be able to handle this? I can see if I can summon a weapon. Or maybe you can give me yours. I know you don't want to fight against the guardians." I don't know why I offer because I know he will deny me. I just feel as if I should because I know how much it bothers him to have to fight against beings that should be by his side. Cassius feels more alone than ever, and I bet he can finally empathize with what Lucian had gone through when Cassius chose not to jump from grace.

"It is worse than I feared. The room that they're keeping him in is between planes still. It's a realm that is open to both angels and demons. And Elias isn't with the angels. He's being kept by a force far darker." Cassius straightens his back and spreads his wings, cutting me off from trying to figure how to get past him and into the portal.

Without having to see, I know that the angelic army gave Elias to the demons that they have teamed up with to get them through Hell to take control.

"It's Vincent. I know it." Just the thought of the disgusting demon laying his hands on Elias sends fire coursing through me, and my hands explode in flames.

I scream as agony steals my breath, the world around me reacting to the Hell I manage to summon. This place really isn't intended for Hell beings. It's not intended for me either.

I lose my footing and drop to my knees, bowing forward as I try to extinguish the flames. But they don't vanish. My body shudders and fights against me. I feel as if I'm being torn apart and I'm killing myself. My soul wants nothing more than to escape.

"Fuck. We have to go. The angelic army will sense you." Hooking his fingers under my arms, Cassius drags me to my feet and tugs me into the portal.

He releases me immediately, and I fall back to the floor,

smacking my chest and chin to the cold concrete ground. I barely have time to turn my head to look as Cassius swings his heavenly sword and cuts off the head of a demon. No, not a demon. It's an angel who seems to have failed to fall, yet still cut off his own wings in an attempt to do so. And he's guarding Elias as Vincent stands behind him with a fiery blade to his throat.

"Elias," I whisper, my voice rasping with my pain.

The whisper of my voice catches Elias's attention, and he jerks his gaze to mine, pulling his head up more instead of letting Vincent hold him by the hair.

"Raven, no." Elias frowns with his words, desperation and fear crossing his features. "You shouldn't be here. You have to go. Hurry."

"Come any closer, and I will take his head and hide it, where you can never find him. He's been deemed an abomination, and it's not welcome in Heaven nor in Hell. I will see to it myself that he and the devils never have control again." Vincent leers at me, flashing a mouth full of fangs. Fire lights his eyes, and I remember the moment he killed me. It sends an overwhelming wave of fury through my body, and I manage to push up on my hands and knees.

I want nothing more than to kill him. I don't want to send him to Hell. I just want him to never exist again. But I'm not capable of doing as much.

"Release my brother." Cassius doesn't wait and blasts heavenly light at Vincent, knocking him back.

I don't know if the demon expected us to freeze or to beg him to stop, but Cassius isn't dealing with demons. His rage is enough to match Kase's wrath, and he somehow gives me the strength to get to my feet.

This is it. This is the moment we've been planning for. The angelic army underestimated us. They thought they could keep Elias from us and torture him by giving them to Vincent, but they were wrong.

I will end them. I will end all of this.

Stumbling forward, I rush towards Elias and go behind him, catching sight of the fiery chains binding him.

"Raven, stop. Don't touch them." Elias tries to jerk away for me, but it's too late.

The second my hands touch the fiery bindings, the world shifts. I scream as my stomach drops, and I freefall in a strange world of light and dark. The binding wasn't only holding Elias to the chair. They were tethering him to the demented prison world.

Without that tether, we fall through the realms.

I can't see Elias anywhere. Cassius disappears as well. I'm alone, out of control, and unable to do anything.

"Raven!" Elias yells, his voice ringing through the air.

But I can't respond. Silence soon follows. I feel nothing.

Broken

RAVEN

"RAVEN, I GOT you. Hold on tight." Elias's voice rings in my ears, and the familiarity of his arms engulfs me, grabbing me from the strange world I free fall in. The nothingness unsettles me on a deep-seated level, and I feel hopelessly trapped. "I'm sorry. I'm so sorry for all of this."

I try to open my mouth to speak, but my words don't come. I feel as if I am everything and nothing at once. I also feel as if I am complete. It's bizarre yet comforting, and I think it has to do with Elias's soul entangling with mine. We don't have physical forms in this strange place. He's pure light as am I. But then, I feel a beautiful chain of darkness wrapping around us and slowing us down. The tether yanks us from the spiritual realm, and I cling on tight to Elias with my very being as the world shifts.

I jostle in his arms, my mind and body struggling to realize that I have reconnected. Cool air whips around me, and I catch the fragrance of burning charcoal and something more gourmand. Maybe vanilla? I'm not really sure.

"You need to back down. I have brought Raven, and we are here to turn ourselves into the Almighty Grace. Do not fight us." Elias's voice stabs me in my chest, and my eyes widen in shock. What the fuck did he just say?

"Are you certain that she will comply?" The feminine angelic voice hurts me even worse than Elias's comment. My vision refuses to clear, but I know it's Meri. Just her presence leaves me panicking. I hate the angel. I want nothing more than to destroy her. I want to destroy everything she stands for.

"Of course, she will comply. She is here, isn't she? She has my soul, and I have hers. You underestimated us and just assumed that we would be against you. She is no longer under the influence of Hell and is where she needs to be. But you need to step back because she's terrified that you're going to hurt her or our child that she carries." He doesn't mention the demonic spawn, and I don't know how much the angels know yet. I know that they consider me a threat. But how much now that I no longer have the devils by my side? Obviously not a lot. They don't bind me or anything. They don't attack Elias either.

"We are here to bow in your heavenly light. We ask that you banish her darkness completely, so we can finally have peace." Elias shifts his body, moving weight from foot to foot.

I have the urge to fight him. To punch him in the face for even saying such a thing. My whole body goes on guard, and instead of light exploding from me, darkness seeps from me, trying to swirl around in a protective haze.

Angelic light blasts through the air, stinging my skin. Pain radiates through me as the darkness recoils and buries itself inside me again, the power afraid and reluctant as the light tries to banish it.

I scratch my nails into Elias's shoulders. "Let me go now. I told you that I didn't want to be here."

"Darlin', this is the only way. I want to protect you." He whispers the words, and his voice shakes.

I can't tell if he's serious or not. I know that he has played both sides before, but this is different. If he could've taken us from that realm, he could've taken me anywhere besides here.

"Hell has a strong grip on her. It could take a while. It also might cause great pain to the both of you." Mikail steps closer, his angelic form coming into view. He steps close enough to set my body off, but another flash of light stops me from fighting him.

He touches his fingers to my chin and lifts my head up to

look into my eyes. I wince at the sensation of his skin brushing mine, and if I could find the strength to punch him, I would. But Elias restrains me. He keeps my hands smashed between his body and mine.

"We are ready. We know what kind of sacrifice we have to make for the greater good. All I ask is that you allow us to stay together. We will fight your fight. We will give you the knowledge you need to control all the planes. The devils won't stand a chance." Elias rumbles with his words, the gruff sound of his voice reverberating through me. "I have made mistakes in my existence, but I see this as a second chance. The Higher Power would not have graced me with its light once more if I wasn't intended to be part of Heaven. Grace understands. Once she sheds the weight of this body, tainted by Hell and the bad circumstances thrown at her in this life as punishment for my wrongdoings, she will fully cooperate. The light she creates will ensure that the balance will always stay toward Heaven."

My mind whirls with his words. I wish I had a moment alone. I wish I could lash out at him and scream at him. I wish I could tell him that he is out of his damn mind if he thinks that I will ever act like Grace. Grace isn't me. I am Raven. I am the queen of the devils. I am intended to rule Purgatory, and I will not let anyone stop me.

"Your obedience will ensure great things, Elias. Now, bring her to the portal. We must move fast. The devils are reigning in control of Hell, and we need to use her darkness against them. It will be them trapped in the pits for the rest of time for their treacherous ways." Meri steps beside Mikail, and I raise my eyes and glower at her.

I can't stand here and do nothing. It goes against my very nature to even humor them.

Jerking my hand free of the lies, I swing out my arm and smack the pretty angel across the face hard enough to send her head sideways.

Elias inhales a deep breath and steps back, spinning around to protect me from retaliation. He grunts and jumps from the sudden blast of heavenly light. That bitch. I will destroy her.

"Hand her to us immediately. You are obviously still protective of the soul, and it is imperative that we remove the darkness from her." Mikail's words steal my breath away.

He better not mean what I think he means.

"As I said, my stipulation is that we remain together. I am her strength, and she is mine. We come as one. You must allow me to help her through this torturous time." Elias straightens his back and spreads his wings. "Do you understand? Do not undermine my authority as a savior. We are equals here. As you can tell, I'm on your side. I'm on Heaven's side."

The words scratch deeply into my soul and open up a wound. It feels as if just his admission of which side he's on breaks me into a million pieces. Because if he's on their side, that means he's not on my side. He's not on our side. I don't know if he has lost sight or if he's doing this out of desperation because he feels as if we've lost, and there's nothing else we can do except comply. All I know is that I can't stand for this.

"Elias, if you do this, I will never forgive you. Do you understand? I can't stand by and let you try to take the most precious thing to me. You damn well know that my darkness and light go together. And if you're even insinuating what I think you are, you better fucking run now. I will ensure that you can never use that fucking dick of yours again." I sneer with my words, digging my fingers even deeper into his shoulders, making him wince in pain as fire sparks against my palms and battles with his heavenly light, burning him.

"Darlin', what have I told you time and time again? I need you to remember those words. Please." Elias relaxes his body, ignoring the pain the best he can.

Remember what words? That he loves me? That he'd do anything for me? It's hard for me to think in this moment with my panic driving me crazy in the presence of the angels. It feels as if I'm about to go into a murderous rage worse than any devil. I need him to let me go. I need to fight, even if it's by myself.

"It is time. Turn around." Elias squeezes me once more and shifts my body, pinning me to his chest. He breathes into my ear and whispers, "Trust me. Please trust me, Raven."

I squirm in his arms, watching as a dozen angels gather their heavenly light, blending it as one. It stings my eyes, the world around us so bright that I don't even know where we are.

The light is both intoxicating and nauseating, and my stomach flops, threatening to expel the nothingness from my body. I don't know if it's the babies reacting to the presence of an army wanting to hurt me or what, but the strange tranquility suddenly suppressing my panic helps me think clearly. These angels can try all they want, but they'll never be able to unchain me from the darkness of the devils. It's no longer their darkness. It's mine. All mine. I'm not only the soul of the devils, but I'm also a soul of Purgatory and humanity. There is no light in this world brighter than my own and no darkness as pitch-black as mine.

"This will be over quickly. Your soul might leave your body, but Elias will return it. We don't want anything to happen to Heaven's new savior." Mikail steps forward, his eyes narrowing on me.

He's out of his goddamn mind if he thinks that he can just blast Hell from me.

"Just let it all go, Raven. Release the darkness and let the light consume you. Let it consume us all." Elias kisses the nape of my neck, his words raising curiosity in me. My fear was too intense for me to realize that he was acting this way because he does want to protect me and him. Not only that, but he also knows that I can protect myself. I have two incredible beings growing inside me that won't allow anything to happen. We both see it. Not only can my angelic spawn send my devils to Hell, but I'm also sure that my little devil spawn can blast angels away.

"May a Higher Power have mercy on your soul and forgive you for your sins, Raven." Meri joins Mikail's side, and all of the angels raise their hands as if they are reaching toward the Heavens. Except instead of praying, they all shout out like warriors of God and throw their power in our direction.

"Hell, help me," I whisper, squeezing my eyes shut and expecting the most agonizing pain to basically kill me and knock my soul from my body long enough for the darkness to vanish.

Utter and complete silence fills the air, and nothing happens. There's no pain. There's no more screaming. No more praying. I find myself with Elias in the middle of shimmering white and dark blending to make the perfect shade of gray. The perfect balance between white and black, light and dark, good and evil.

"Fuck yeah," Elias mutters, his voice lightening with his excitement. "That's our little devil. Our angel baby too."

I blink through the mist, staring at the frozen angels, chained within the beautiful shadows protecting me. Their light continues to shine brightly as if they're trying to break through the veil, but they can't. My babies won't let them. This world is pure and balanced, almost like the perfect Purgatory, keeping them away.

But it doesn't stop me from reaching them.

A dozen emotions crash through me, and I force myself from Elias's arms and summon a fire chain and an orb of heavenly light. My body buzzes and zings, the power exhilarating and all-consuming. All I can think about is walking toward the angels and serving justice for everything they've done. For everything they put me and my devils through.

"Raven, stop. Please, we have to go." Elias grabs my hand, trying to yank me back.

Something shocks him, separating the two of us and sending him to his knees. I stare at the angels again and watch as a strange glowing light grows behind them. It's fire. It's Hell power. But not only that. It's also the same brilliant light summoned from a savior. Cassius is with them. He found the devils.

But it's the strangest thing. Neither the angels nor the devils can see each other. It's as if the new planes keep us all apart.

"Raven! Raven!" Kase yells, the deep tone of his anger muffling through the veil.

I spot him strolling through the angelic army as if they're not even there. Red power glows in his eyes, and he scowls and spins, shooting a burst of power at Cassius. But it goes right through him and explodes against a shimmering wall.

I was mistaken. Cassius isn't with them. He's with me.

"I can sense her. She's nearby." Dante appears beside Kase, and the two of them stand almost within the angel light.

"She's gone. They're both gone." Mikail's voice sounds through the air next, stealing my attention. Everyone seems to talk at once, trying to figure out what happened. He squints his eyes, trying to see the space in front of him where we once stood.

"Where is she?" Dante hisses with his words, his inky black wings spreading out and darkening the world around the angels.

"Where are they?" Meri asks at the same time, her words blending with Dante's.

Elias grabs my hand again, lacing our fingers together, keeping me from breaking through the veil. "Raven, if we leave now, the angels can't follow us. Please, we have to go."

I shake my head. I can't. I can't just run away from this. I can't stand by and watch as Heaven tries to take Hell from my devils. "Stop it. I won't leave them. You need to help me break through this fucking realm. They're worried."

"They'll get over it. They will understand why we have left. It doesn't have to be forever. We can find them." Elias steps into my personal space and touches my cheek, forcing my eyes away from my devils. "I know you want to fight but think about everything we have to lose. Please. We can't stay. If we stay, Heaven won't stop. The devils will fight until there's nothing left as well. We can end the war here and now."

"No. I won't leave them." Whipping my head back-and-forth, I send my hair sweeping around.

"Raven," Cassius says, his soft voice drawing my attention away from the anger building up inside me again at Elias. He's been so silent that I wasn't so sure he was in this realm. I thought he could've been in another one completely or with the angels. "Your soulmate is right. We must get you out of here. I can return to the devils and tell them."

I scowl at his words. "Of course, you want me to fucking go. You want nothing to do with Hell."

"It's not about Heaven or Hell. It's about you." Cassius shuffles closer, his looming presence igniting panic in me. I have a feeling that Elias and Cassius will team up and force me away. I can't let it happen. I need to get to the devils.

Jerking around, I shoot hellfire at Cassius and Elias. They both holler my name, but I rush away from them and toward my devils. I need to get to them. If I can get to them, they can help me get through. We can leave together. We can figure a better plan that can keep the angelic army away. I just know it.

"Raven, stop!" Elias rushes after me. He shoots heavenly light at the same time that I blast hellfire at the veil. The world rumbles with a massive earthquake, knocking me off my feet and onto my knees. The veil shatters, and I find myself looking up at Mikail and Meri. All of the angels intake a breath at once, and I expect them to blast me out of existence with angelic power.

"You are an abomination to this universe. Where is Elias?" Mikail asks, pointing his sword at me.

Anger bursts through me, and I summon a fire whip and swing my arm, lashing it at the angel. It sizzles across his chest, and Meri tries to tackle me, pinning me to the ground. My whole body shudders at her closeness, and I bring my fist up and sucker punch her in the nose. Angelic power whips through the air, and I arch my back, the sensation of it stealing my breath. My stomach twists as hellfire crackles from my body, shaking this world and breaking whatever protection ward is in place keeping the devils out.

Kase roars in his devil form, towering over the angels and sending them scattering. Meri presses her palm to my forehead, and her angelic light blinds me. The world turns to nothing, and I think I pass out for a split second. Burning pain drags me from my unconsciousness, and I manage to pull my shit together and fight back. I scratch my fingers into her cheeks, blistering her skin as hellfire burns in my palms. Jerking my knee up, I strike her in the stomach and manage to roll her off me. I scramble away, trying to get to my feet. The devils and the angels fight, sending fire and angelic light around the shaking world and making it nearly impossible for me to stay upright.

"This must end here. You cannot go on carrying the blessing

that has been gifted to you if you are going to waste every-thing." Meri opens her wings and flaps them hard enough to send me sprawling forward. I land on my hands and knees, my body aching at the force.

She kicks me in the side, stealing my breath away. I flip over and meet her angry face.

Summoning a sword, she aims it at me, preparing to smite me with her heavenly wrath. The devils can't get to me. Neither can Elias and Cassius as they remain frozen in the other world.

"May Heaven have mercy on your soul." Meri swings her sword, aiming for my throat. I squeeze my eyes shut and lift my hands up protectively. "It's time to go where you belong."

A chain materializes between my hands, stopping the blade from cutting into me. It clinks against the power, and Meri wails in agony. Fire crawls up her arm, forcing her to drop her heavenly sword.

I push through the pain and anguish coursing through me and get to my feet, straightening my back. I will not stand down. I will serve justice.

"You will burn in the pits for this." I unwind the fire chain and lash it at her, the power of Hell slowing her and dragging her to me. "I'm not an abomination. You are. You claim to fight for Heaven, but you fight for no one but yourself."

"You will not win. The Higher Power will not stand for this

behavior. It will see to it that you never get Purgatory. Things will return as they should." Meri's eyes flash with light a second before fire bellows from her body, stealing away everything angelic about her.

I punch my fist hard into her sternum, knocking her off her feet. She screams as the light and dark swirl from my body and tangle around her, locking her in place. She grabs at the ground, calling to the Almighty to save her.

But it's over.

She will never see Heaven again.

A blade materializes in my hand, and I stab it through her heart, penetrating the ground. The world rumbles as a Hell portal opens, and Meri falls into it and disappears into the fiery pits.

I gasp at the pain of sending an angel to Hell, and my energy zaps away from me, sending me to my knees.

Silence greets me. The fighting between the angels and devils stops. Turning my head, I stare at the angelic army as they gawk at me in horror.

Kase and Dante take advantage of their distraction and cut off the closest angel's wings.

"Fall back!" Mikail shouts, spinning and trying to fight the devils with his sword. But he's not trying to end them here. He's making room for himself to launch into the air.

I stare up at the strange cloudy sky as the angels circle above me.

"Raven!" Elias shouts, his voice booming through the air as he and Cassius's world merges with ours.

But it's too late. I can't move. I can't fight. The devils can't reach me either.

Mikail nosedives, blasting me with his heavenly light as he aims his sword at my being. The sharp point of the blade slices right through my chest. I can't even scream with the pain and torture. All I can do is stare up at the shadows of wings. At the light.

"Your life ends here. Your soul is mine. Heaven has won." Mikail rips his sword from my body, touches his hand to my chest, and steals the light from me.

My body gives out, and darkness claims me.

28

Dearly Departed

RAVEN

"I**T'S A MIRACLE.**" Cassius's voice hums in my ears. "This shouldn't be possible."

"Which is further proof that this is how it's supposed to be." A hot hand touches my chest with Lucian's words. Burning pain scorches me, but I can't open my eyes.

"Give her another bite, Dante. She's coming around." Kase's voice projects to me the same as the others, beckoning me to stay with him. Where exactly? I have no idea.

My sense of existence is thrown off. It's as if I'm nothing and everything at once. But there are no veils here. I don't feel the heat of Hell or the weird tranquility of Heaven. If I'm with my devils, that means that I'm not with the guardians. What the hell happened?

Open your damn eyes. Open them now. Hurry the fuck up. You can do it, Raven. Do it now.

My body jostles, and sensation returns to me. Dante's familiar scent permeates the air, and I feel his soft intake of breath against my shoulder as he sinks his fangs into my skin.

I moan, his intoxicating venom kicking my heartbeat into a rapid pace as tingles course through me.

"I need to hear more of that." Dante's whisper tickles the hair hanging over my ears. "That feels good, doesn't it, pretty soul?"

I arch my back and stretch, grimacing at the sharp pain in my chest. It's enough to jolt me upright, but Dante doesn't let me go. He holds me down against his chest and ends up wrapping his muscular legs around mine.

He restrains me, and I automatically fight him, trying to break free of his hold.

Cool fingers touch my cheek. "Raven, I know it hurts. I know you've been through a lot. But hold still. Your wiggling ass is going to get yourself hurt even more." Elias's familiar voice steals my breath away and returns it at the same time. "Look at me, darlin'. I need to see your eyes."

"I'll do it for you." Lucian's rough voice stirs something dark inside me a second before light burns my vision.

I groan and frown. "Knock that shit off, dickhead. It hurts to open my eyes."

"It's pointless to force her to do something like this. We all see it for ourselves. Give Raven some room so she can orient herself. This is going to be tough on her." Zade's voice hums in my ears, the softness opening up a deep ache inside me.

What does he mean? His words frighten me on a level that nothing should be able to penetrate. It's a part of me that has been hidden by my light and kept safe. It's as if the wall is broken, and I feel things that I haven't in a while. It hurts me deeply. I can't explain it, but it feels as if I lost something.

I open and close my mouth, licking my lips. "The babies?" Tears already fill my eyes at my comment. I know that I was stabbed by Mikail. I know that he stole something from me. What if he took the light of my angel baby? I never thought a thing was possible.

Fuck.

Muscular arms engulf me, sandwiching me to Dante. "They're perfect. It's okay. Nothing happened to them, so take a breath, little hellion." Andre squishes me in a way that doesn't hurt me but makes me feel as if he is keeping me together.

I gasp a breath of relief, the sudden fear vanishing but only to be replaced with confusion.

"Fuck. What the hell does that mean, then? What happened? What did Mikail do to me?" My words tumble out of my mouth as my voice finally manages to escape, though it cracks.

I'm greeted with silence. No one wants to answer my question. It must be bad.

I nudge Andre back and look down at my bare chest, the knife wound burned closed. It looks gross and hurts even worse than before, but I know that the devils did this to stop me from bleeding out.

"Whoever tells me first will be rewarded." I pant through the pain, wishing with everything in me that Dante would give me another bite of his venom. He's only giving me enough to take off the edge instead of numbing me completely and sending me on a high that could last for days.

Again, no one responds. It's unlike them not to fight over who gets the reward.

Annoyance rushes through me, and I gather my strength and dig my nails into Dante's legs hard enough to get him to let me go. The way everyone looks at me strikes me to my very soul. It opens me in a way that I can't stand. Elias and Cassius both back up, and I watch as fear crosses their gazes. I'm nearly certain Micah and Zade are afraid of me too.

"Tell me!" I scream, rage blooming from my annoyance. "What happened to me?"

"There are too many of us here. Our presence is affecting her.

I know you all want to be here, but Raven is my soulmate. I am begging you to give me five minutes. Let me break the news to her, and then you guys can give her what she needs." Elias tightens his jaw, his whole being radiating with heavenly grace. Something is different, though. I don't feel the same familiarity I had before. Actually, I'm not sure I feel anything at all. I know I love him. I know that I have missed him. But for some reason, I can't seem to feel anything except for this deep, dark anger roiling through me.

"Maybe you should let dickhead tell her. That way, if she wants to kill someone, it can be him. He's a tough guy." This comes from Lucian as he motions to Cassius. "This is kind of his fucking fault anyways. If he had just stuck to the plan—"

Elias twists and shoots heavenly power at Lucian, a deep bellow of frustration escaping his mouth. "I asked everyone to give me a minute! Go!"

I lie in shock as the devils and Cassius listen to him. Micah vanishes within the summoning circle without a word. Dante kisses my temple and shifts me off him and onto the rickety cot. It's not even a bed. I don't even know where the fuck we are. This place is bare bones with nothing much in it. If I didn't know any better, I'd think we were in a prison cell. Not an angelic one either. Human. Mortal. A place that is beneath my devils.

My breathing quickens in anticipation. If the devils leave

without complaint, it must be bad. It must be worse. But what? I can only think of two things that are world-ending to me in this moment. One, something happening to the twins. Or two? Something happening to my guys.

Elias sits beside me and drapes his arm over my shoulders, pulling me in close, adjusting my legs to sprawl across his lap. His iridescent wings fold around us, and I cringe. It's an automatic reaction and unlike me. Usually, I'm more fascinated by angel wings than this.

He must notice because he ruffles them, and they disappear, turning him into the handsome mortal I fell in love with. I had no idea how much I missed what he had looked like before he died as a human. I know his body was just a body, and this is his soul in a new form, but I don't know. I can't explain it.

"Take a couple of breaths, Raven. You're going to hyperventilate." Elias strokes his fingers across my spine, trying to smooth out the shivers trembling through me. "It hurts me deeply to see you like this."

"Stop avoiding telling me what the fuck is going on," I snap, my whole body stiffening. I don't mean to yell at him, and I can tell how hurt he is by my short temper. I just can't control it. All of these dark emotions run wild through me. I can't get thoughts of the angelic army out of my head and how they just got away with hurting me.

"I'm sorry, darlin'. I don't mean to. I just...this is tough. I wish I didn't have to tell you any of this." Elias hangs his head at the apartment floor, keeping his eyes trained on the threadbare carpet. "I am also sorry for failing you. I failed you so badly that I don't know what I can do to fix this or if I can. What Mikail has done was unexpected and unthinkable. He should've never been within reach. I should've fought harder."

"None of this is making sense. How are you a failure if it was me who went after him? It was me who broke the veil. Not you." The words come as if they have been waiting on my tongue, but a part of me feels nothing as I say them. I should feel for his pain and hurt. But still, the anger and annoyance won't release me.

"What I'm about to tell you is going to freak you out. I want you to know that no matter what, I will never leave you." Elias finally tips his head and looks at me. He reaches out and combs strands of my hair behind my ear. His drawing out this information he keeps from me drives me crazy. I must bite my tongue to stop from demanding he just spit it out already. "When Mikail stabbed you, he was trying to end your life and take your soul. But something happened. Our sweet babies saved their mama, and now it's them keeping your body alive. Because even though Mikail didn't kill you, he still managed to intervene and take your soul. The devils felt their binding snap. I felt the part of you that is part of me just rip away as if my heart got taken."

I gape at him, my eyebrows furrowing as I try to process the information. What he's saying? That Heaven took my soul, and my body still lives because of the beings growing inside me? What the actual fuck?

"Oh shit. Oh fucking shit. This can't be happening. What does that even mean? Am I just a corpse walking around? What's going to happen when I have the babies?" My chest tightens with my words, and I clench my fingers into fists. I try to summon power. I try to do anything that gets my body to tap into the devils' power. But nothing happens. I don't feel anything really except for the ever-present anger.

And then I realize why I can't feel anything right now toward Elias. If what he says is true, my soul, the one that tethers us together as soulmates, is gone. And if it's gone, then the part of me that he loved and that he gave me is no longer here. The part of me the devils fell in love with is gone as well. I'm just a shell. A host, even.

"Without your soul, once you deliver, you will die. Your soul is already in Heaven." Elias's words weigh so heavy on me that I just stare at the floor. I can't die and go to Heaven. If I die and go to Heaven, I can't take Purgatory. My eternity with the devils is over.

"No. No, this can't be happening. This couldn't have happened." I squeeze my eyes shut, trying to will myself to feel something, anything.

Turning toward Elias, I crash my mouth to his and kiss him with the same passion I have a dozen times. I expect to feel my body buzzing as our souls get close, but all that remains between us is just lust. Just my body awakening for his. Nothing more.

Elias groans and doesn't pull away, kissing me until I'm ready to release him, my mouth at war with his as I try to siphon his angelic light into myself again. Maybe that's the key. Maybe he can give me his light once more.

"You can fix us. I know you can. You've done it before. Give me your light again, and maybe my soul will come back. Or go to Heaven and grab it. Bring it back to me. You have to. You fucking have to do this." I gasp with my words, clutching onto him and staring into his face.

His bottom lip puffs out. "Raven I—"

"Don't you fucking do it. Don't you deny me. Don't tell me that it's impossible. Because me being here right now pregnant with an angelic and a devil spawn is impossible, Elias. We can do this. Anything is possible. You've told me that." I clench my teeth together, watching his face. He doesn't believe me. Doesn't believe his own damn words he's told me time and time again.

"I will do everything I can. I'm not giving up on you. I'm not giving up on Hell either. But right now? We need to take care of your body and those babies. We can't let anything happen."

Elias leans in closer, his pouty face begging me to kiss him again but not out of desperation. He wants me to kiss him with the love born from our bond as soulmates.

"They can't win. They can't keep my soul. I don't care what it takes, but we will get it back. You have wings now. You can access Heaven." I think of the words over and over again, and hell, it might be possible. We just need to take down the guardians and put them in their places.

"It has never been done. Souls don't move from Heaven or from Hell. That is why we were creating Purgatory." He sighs against my mouth.

"Then we create Purgatory. It can open access through all the realms." I press my lips into a thin line as I stare at him.

"But Hell? How can we do that? We need an angel-kissed soul, and we need the seven sinners. I've tried to jump from Heaven a dozen times." Elias scratches his hand to the back of his neck, his body slackening as he sulks.

I shake my head. "So, you're just going to give up? I'm not going to fucking allow it. You don't get to just think that this is the end. We've been through too much already."

He slowly nods his head. "I'm sorry. I struggle to have faith right now."

"Because you have faith in the wrong thing. I can tell that you keep turning toward the Higher Power for answers. You keep asking for guidance. But that's not how we get things done. We need to have faith in us. In the devils. You need to have faith that we can fucking do this." I clutch his cheeks, digging my fingers into his skin. I narrow my eyes on him and hold him hostage in my gaze. "Do you understand? This is what I am demanding of you. You will do as I say. We need to start with figuring out what happens next. Can you do that for me?"

"God, I love you. I can do that." Elias graces me with a smile, his being lighting up with my words.

I squint through the brightness. "Turn it down, angel boy. It hurts my eyes."

He chuckles and caresses my cheek. "I'm sorry. I'm just...you make me feel as if things are going to be okay even though all I feel is grief over the part of us missing. And the way you talk to me...it's fucking hot."

His words manage to calm the anger rolling inside me for the first time since I woke up, and my mouth curls up in a smile. I lean in and kiss him, wanting to feel the strange lightness radiating from him. It doesn't feel a part of me, but it feels as if it seeps inside of me to fill in the hole in my being.

"You naughty angel boy. You want me to corrupt you, don't you? Is that why you made all the devils leave? You wanted to get me alone, so I could push you around and use you to fill the space my stolen soul left behind?" I lick my lips with the words, the thought not necessarily a bad idea. Actually, it's exactly what I feel like I need in this moment. I just need to remember. I need to feel his light on my body.

He raises his eyebrows with my words. I can tell he's conflicted, but this deep-seated nature as one of the loves of my life persuades him to suppress his morals. He wants to be corrupted. And I really want to do it right now. I need this.

Elias kisses me again. "The devils are going to roast my ass if I—"

"You're tough. I'm sure you can handle it. Now give me what I want. Let me feel your being." I grab the front of his shirt and push him down, climbing on top of him and unfastening the button on his pants.

Elias play-growls at me, sounding more devilish than angelic, and he sits up and cups my face. He kisses me deeply, sliding his tongue into my mouth. His angelic light stings my skin, but I don't complain. I use it to help me feel. I use it to remind me that even though my soul is gone, I'm still here. I'm still alive. This isn't over. The angelic army hasn't won.

I use the knowledge to push me faster, not giving him a chance to do anything but allow me to take control and slide his cock from his pants. Bowing forward, I shimmy back and position myself between his legs, licking my tongue from his balls and up his shaft until I suck him into my mouth. He locks his fingers through my hair, guiding my movements at the same time he massages my shoulder with his fingers. His balls tighten as I cup them and rub my finger over them.

"God, Raven. It feels so good. So much more intense. I want more. Sit on my damn face now and suffocate me. Use that sexy body of yours to drag my ass from Heaven. I know you have it in you." Elias eases my chin up, blocking me from continuing. "Drench me. Treat me how you do a devil."

I bite my bottom lip, so turned on by his demands. "Prove to me that you can be a devil then, even with those wings, angel-boy."

He pushes me back and grabs my legs, restraining me with one hand while using the other to drag my pants off me. "Call me that one more time and see what happens."

I raise my eyebrows. "You know, angels tend to be all talk.. .angel-boy."

"Damn it." Elias snatches me by the waist and hoists me up while he throws himself back. I land on his face with a squeal, my knees hitting the flimsy mattress beneath us. If his look could set me ablaze, I'd be on fire. He rubs his thumb over my new piercing, setting it off.

I moan and throw myself forward, planting my palms above his head, and Elias hums and licks my clit, spanking my ass at the same time. He rocks my body for me, licking and kissing and sucking me in ways that steal my breath. My whole body trembles, the sensation zinging through me, igniting something deep-seated in my core. I feel whole again. I feel complete.

It feels as if I can somehow touch my soul in Heaven as I ride Elias's face. My body tenses with my orgasm, and I scream out in pleasure, gripping the sheet in my fingers. The sting of his angelic light vanishes for a second, and the overwhelming sense of reuniting with the missing part of me fills me to the brim with pure, blissful emotions.

Elias guides me back, re-positioning himself between my legs. Heavenly light shines in his eyes as he aligns his cock to my body and thrusts inside me, the pressure sending another wave of ecstasy through me. I'm sure the universe can hear our passion as my mouth refuses to shut up.

Elias stretches my legs, working my muscles, remaining on his knees to still manage to play with my hood piercing and clit, his thumb strumming over me until my toes curl, and I spray him with my orgasm, his hot body now glistening from our passion. Elias thrusts harder, putting my body to the test, and I clutch onto my thighs as the cot squeaks and bangs on the dingy wall. If my devils are around, I'm sure they're either listening or watching the show. But I don't give a fuck. I'm wrapped up in Elias and his light. I lose myself to his very being until he grunts and thrusts one final time.

The room shakes, and I gasp, my whole being screaming in relief as I touch Heaven with him. But just as quickly as Heaven fills me up, it vanishes.

I feel more empty than ever.

I blink my eyes, suppressing the dark emotions stealing away everything good from this moment and clutch onto Elias, not allowing him to see my face even though he tries. Instead, I bury my mouth to the crook of his neck and breathe in his scent until my heart stops pounding in overdrive, and I can pull myself together.

"Raven?" Elias asks, his voice softening as reality hits him at full force as well. "I love you."

I nod my head and force my voice to work. "I love you too."

I know I do. I remember what the feeling was like.

Yet, here I am, trying to convince myself of something that is no longer here.

"We're going to get through this," Elias adds, settling in next to me as he pulls me into his arms.

"Fuck yeah, we are," Dante says, his voice drawing my attention across the room to where he peeks in. "Especially if you let us in to take care of our sou...woman." His hesitation to refer to me as his soul doesn't go unnoticed.

I purse my lips. "Hurry up. I could use some cuddles. I feel like shit."

"That's the high of Heaven wearing off. I'll take care of that." Dante crosses the room, but none of the other devils follow behind him. "Make some room, Jizz Master."

I open my arms for Dante, meeting his glowing green eyes.

My heart sinks into my stomach. I expected to feel something, anything for my devil of envy.

But nothing rises inside me.

Without my soul, I lost a huge part of me.

I really am just a body.

A shell.

I'm empty and numb.

Heaven stole everything from the devils and me.

They will pay.

29

Salvation

RAVEN

"DO YOU HEAR that?" Cassius tips his head back and stares at the ceiling. "We're being summoned."

"What do you think we should do? I want to resist the call. There's no point." Elias rubs his scruffy face, turning to look at me. "There's only one reason I will go back, and it's not time."

"It's a call for help. It's not the angelic army or the guardians." Cassius rubs his hands together, his body rigid and aloof as he stares at nothing in particular.

"Maybe you fuckheads can just peek in. We know that the guardians are currently distracted. They are going to surely feel what happens next." Lucian stands next to Micah a couple of feet away. Kase and Dante stand by his sides while Zade and Andre complete the circle.

"Are you sure you should do this?" I ask, my voice cracking with my words. I don't even know why I voice my question. I know it must be done. It's the only way.

"Does this mean you are concerned? That's a good sign." Micah offers me a smile, his orange gaze glowing with the fires around him.

I wish I could tell him that I do feel the concern, but it's more of a curiosity. "It's out of habit. I honestly don't really care."

Micah grimaces at my words, and Elias pets my knee, knowing that I think and feel differently. Micah can no longer get into my head because the part of me that allowed him in has gone. I like to keep my whole self guarded. I'm ashamed. I don't want him to listen to me work through this bullshit of trying to find the part of me that I know, if it remains gone, means I could very well lose everything, including my devils' love.

"I'm not leaving Raven. Never again." Elias responds a little late, answering Lucian and ignoring the quiet moment between Micah and me.

"I will go. I need to see things for myself." Cassius turns toward me and touches my knee. "I'll be back in a bit."

He says it as if I care whether or not he returns. I don't.

"Whatever." I shrug my shoulders. I'm not going to try to

with him. It's hard enough that I have to push myself to act normal with the others.

Cassius nods and disappears in a circle of blinding light, shaking the world as it trembles against the Hell power emanating through the air.

Micah releases a deep breath and straightens his back, spreading his legs wide to brace himself. "Let's do this. I'm ready to release the power."

Elias grabs my hand and holds it tightly, bringing it to his chest, allowing me to feel his rapid heartbeats as we watch the devils.

This could very well be the end of things, but they have decided that until I get my soul and the angelic army is destroyed, they're giving up power. They are going to untether him from Hell and allow our enemies to claim it.

With the absence of Hell, my devils will weaken. It could lead to something awful.

But they've made their decision, and I stand by them. We are in this together.

"This is going to hurt like a fucking bitch," Lucian says, gathering his fire chain. "Brace yourself, Micah."

Heat radiates through the air and sweat drips from my hairline. Each of the devils gather their power and blast it at Micah. He yells in pain, but he doesn't fall to his knees. Instead, he grabs onto their power and lets them yank him out of the circle.

An earthquake shakes through the room, and things topple from the dresser. The floor cracks and dust swirls in the air along with the scent of Hell. Micah crashes to the floor outside of the circle and arches his back. The tether hooked to his heart, pumping Hell power through his veins, snaps and whips through the air, slashing burning lines across the wall until it recoils and disappears.

The summoning circle vanishes with only ashes remaining in its place.

Silence falls around us. I get to my feet across the room from Micah, staring down at him. He heaves a breath and clutches his chest, and I press my hands over his.

"Are you okay?" I ask.

"I'm better than okay, heathen. I get to be with you freely now." Micah reaches up and caresses my cheek.

"Don't get used to it, asshole. This isn't permanent." Kase offers his hand out and pulls Micah to his feet. Elias hovers behind me and doesn't react to his companion.

"I know. but I will enjoy it while it lasts." Micah holds his hand out to me. "Come here. It's been a while since I have touched you on the physical plane."

I stroll into his arms and bury my face against his chest. "You all should enjoy it while it lasts," I say, repeating what Micah had just said. "This could be it. At least in my final days, I'll have all of you by my side."

"Don't talk like that, pretty soul. This isn't the end. These aren't your final days." Dante sharpens his features at me. "If I hear you talk like that again, you're going to be in deep trouble."

I don't respond to him. I can't. I don't have it in me to tease him like he wants.

Because it's hard for me to believe in anything now. Heaven has my soul. When I die, I will be going to the supposed paradise.

People are usually happy about that. It's what they want. But me? No. My heart was set on Hell.

So was my eternity. Stupid, fucking salvation. It will be our ruin.

To be continued...

Other RH Books

OMEGAVERSE SERIES

Saint Vista Pack Regimes

Bonds of Steele Omegaverse

PARANORMAL

The Seven Sinners of Hell's Kingdon

The Pack Mates of Lunar Crest

The Wolfpacks of Shadow Moon Island

The Fated Mate of the Dragon Clans

The Divine Vampire Heirs

The Royale Vampire Heirs

The Academy of Vampire Heirs

La Vega Vampire Showstoppers

Rise from the Flames

About Ginna Moran

GINNA MORAN IS the *USA Today* Bestselling author of over seventy novels including the popular Knotty Lessons and The Seven Sinners of Hell's Kingdom novels.

She always carried a fascination for all things paranormal and wrote her first unpublished manuscript at age eighteen. Her love of the supernatural grew stronger through her adult life, and she now spends her days with different creatures of the night. Whether it's vampires, werewolves, dragons, fae, angels, demons, or mermaids, Ginna loves creating and living in worlds from her dreams.

Aside from Ginna's professional life, she enjoys binge-watching TV, crafting and design, playing pretend with her daughter, and cuddling with her dog. Some of her favorite things include chocolate, mermaids, anything that glitters, learning new things, cheesy jokes, and organizing her book-shelf.